SANITY & TALLULAH
SHORTCUTS

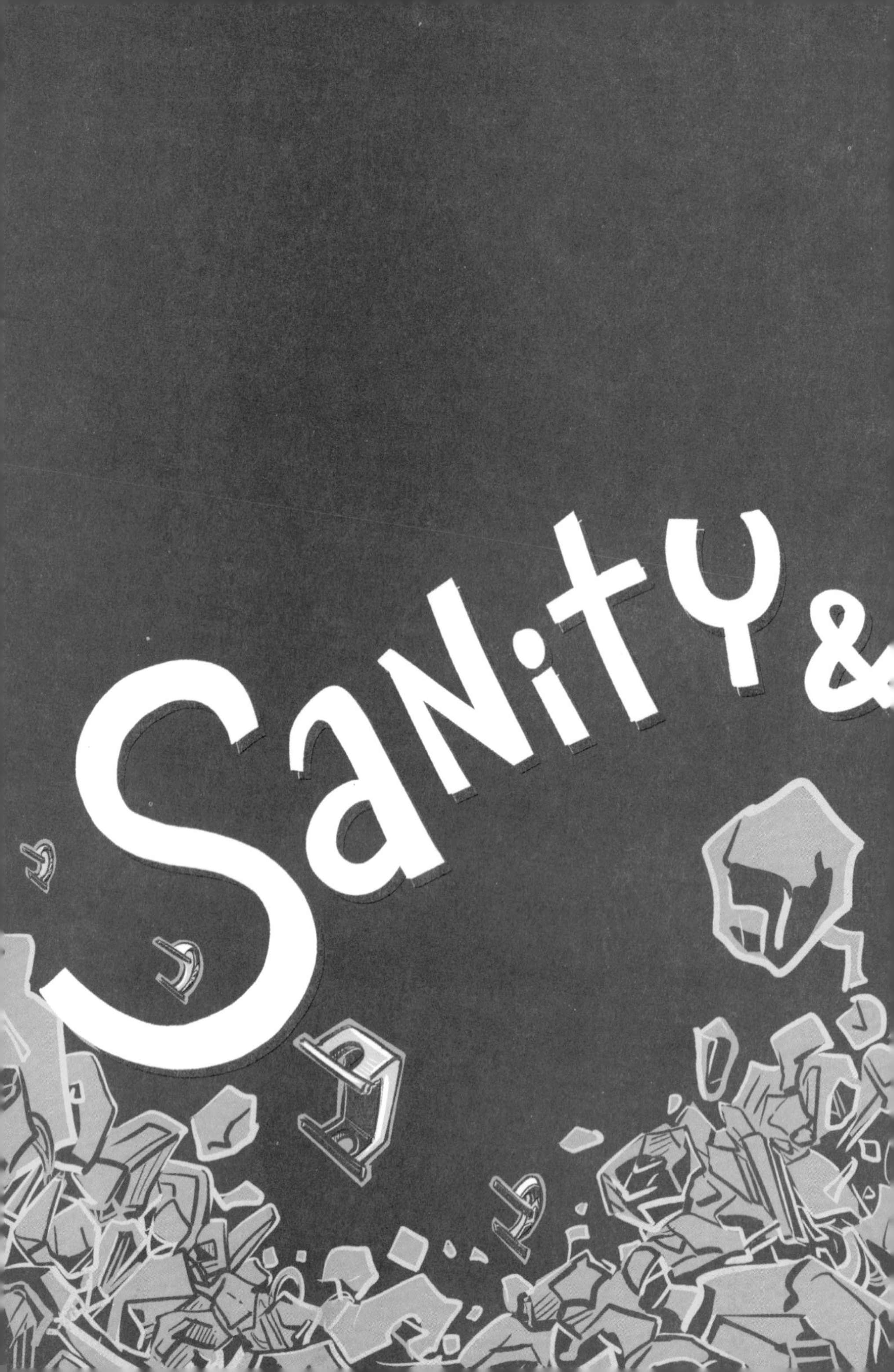
Sanity &

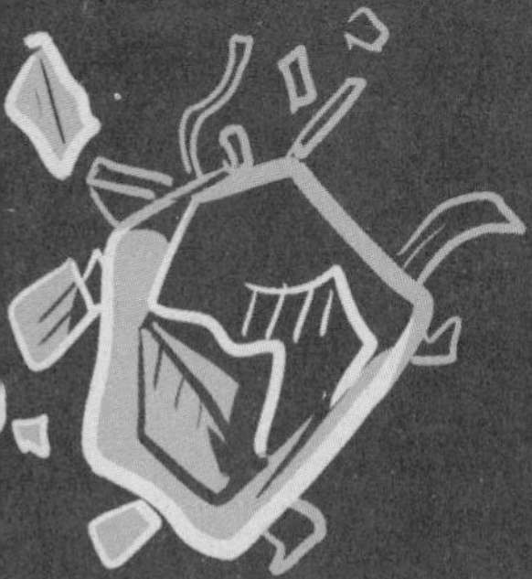

TALLULAH

SHORTCUTS

MOLLY BROOKS

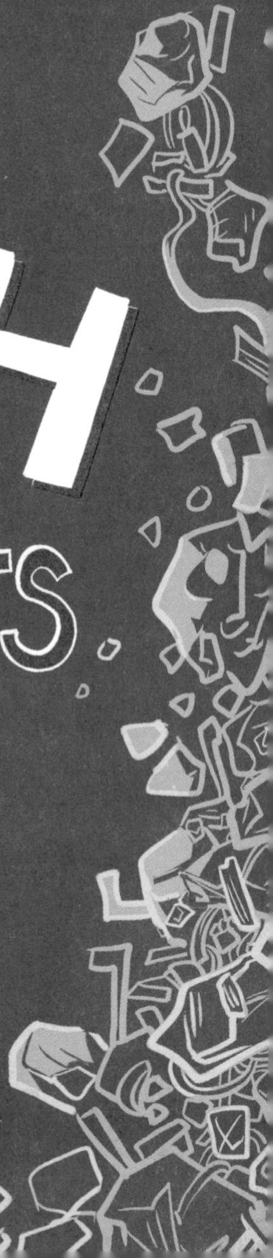

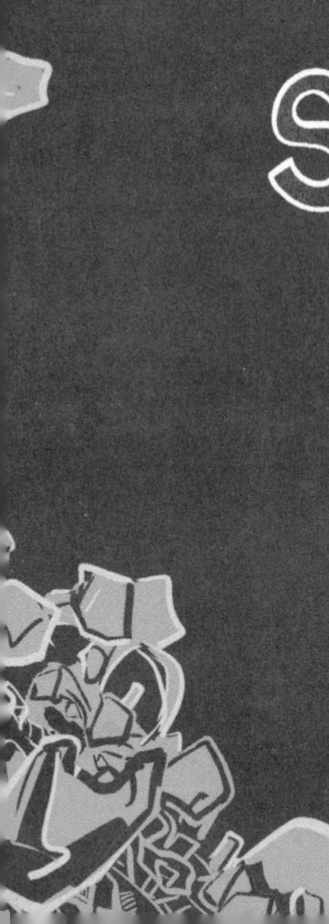

LB
Little, Brown and Company
NEW YORK BOSTON

About This Book

The illustrations for this book were drawn on 96 lb. recycled bristol with Deleter G-Pen nibs dipped in Koh-I-Noor Rapidograph ink. This book was edited in succession by Rotem Moscovitch, Tracey Keevan, and Andrea Colvin and designed by Ching N. Chan. The production was supervised by Bernadette Flinn, and the production editor was Jake Regier. The text was set in Gargle, and the display type is hand lettered.

Little, Brown and Company
Hachette Book Group
1290 Avenue of the Americas, New York, NY 10104
Visit us at LBYR.com

First Edition: April 2021

Little, Brown and Company is a division of Hachette Book Group, Inc. The Little, Brown name and logo are trademarks of Hachette Book Group, Inc.

The publisher is not responsible for websites (or their content) that are not owned by the publisher.

Library of Congress Cataloging-in-Publication Data

Names: Brooks, Molly (Molly Grayson), author, illustrator.

Title: Shortcuts / Molly Brooks

Description: First edition. | New York : Little, Brown and Company, 2021. | Series: Sanity & Tallulah | Audience: Ages 8–12. | Summary: When most of the adults on space station Wilnick come down with the flu, Sanity and Tallulah are tasked with delivering turbopumps to another station, but when they take a shortcut, they accidentally end up on the other side of the blockade.

Identifiers: LCCN 2020042076 | ISBN 9780759555532 (hardcover) | ISBN 9780759555525 (trade paperback) | ISBN 9780759555884 (ebook) | ISBN 9780316628488 (ebook other)

Subjects: LCSH: Graphic novels. | CYAC: Graphic novels. | Space stations—Fiction. | Science fiction.

Classification: LCC PZ7.7.B765 Sh 2021 | DDC 741.5/973—dc23

LC record available at https://lccn.loc.gov/2020042076

ISBNs: 978-0-7595-5553-2 (hardcover), 978-0-7595-5552-5 (pbk.), 978-0-7595-5588-4 (ebook), 978-0-316-59231-4 (ebook), 978-0-316-62849-5 (ebook)

Printed in the United States of America

LSC-C

Printing 1, 2021

For Amy,
the mother of my cat-children

Sanity & Tallulah
Short Cuts

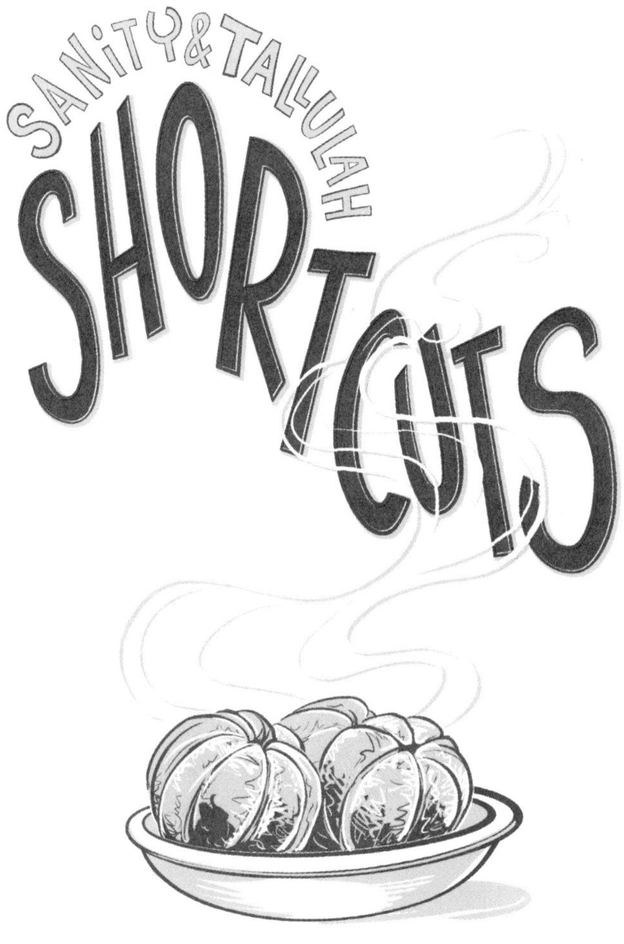

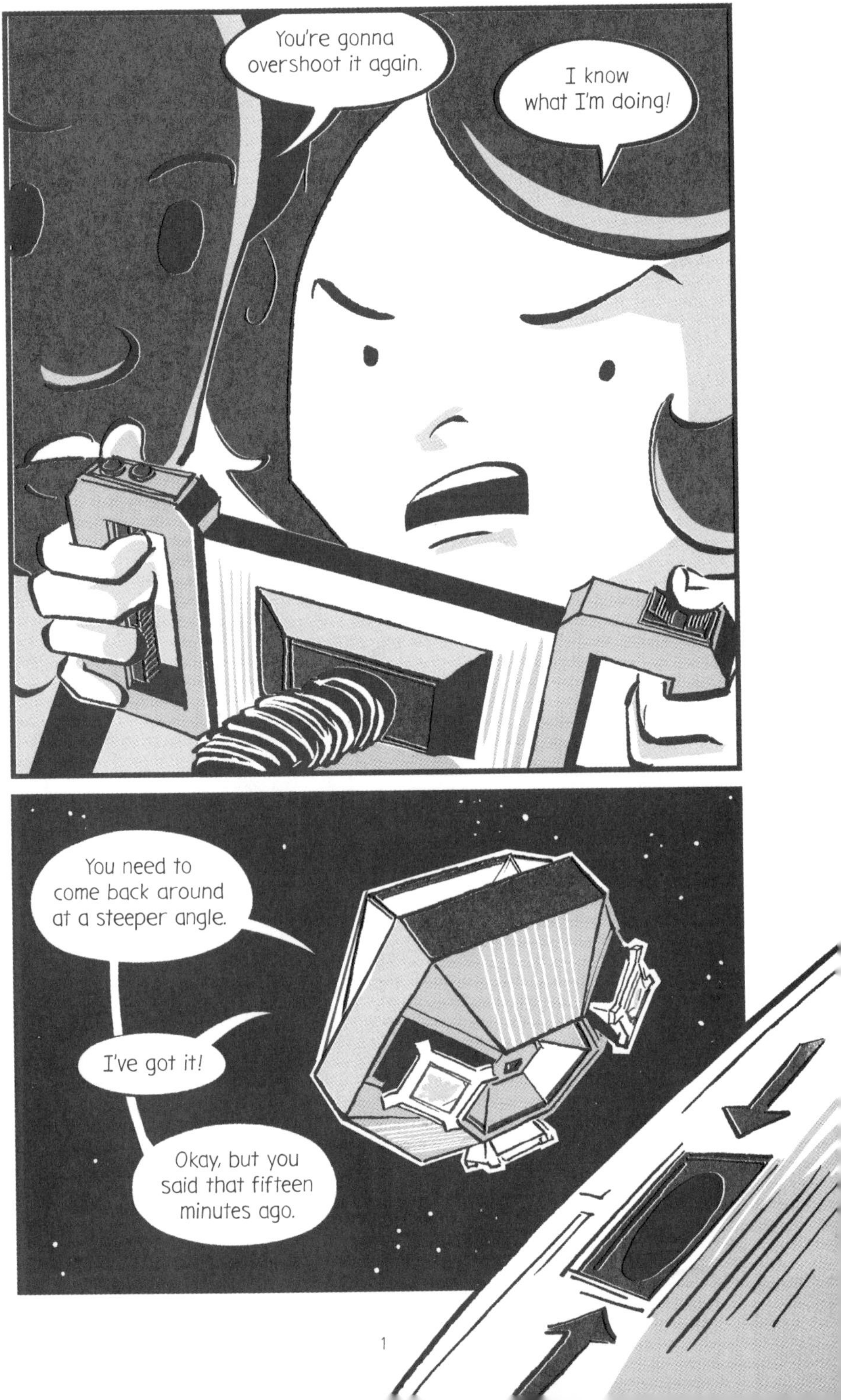
You're gonna overshoot it again.
I know what I'm doing!
You need to come back around at a steeper angle.
I've got it!
Okay, but you said that fifteen minutes ago.

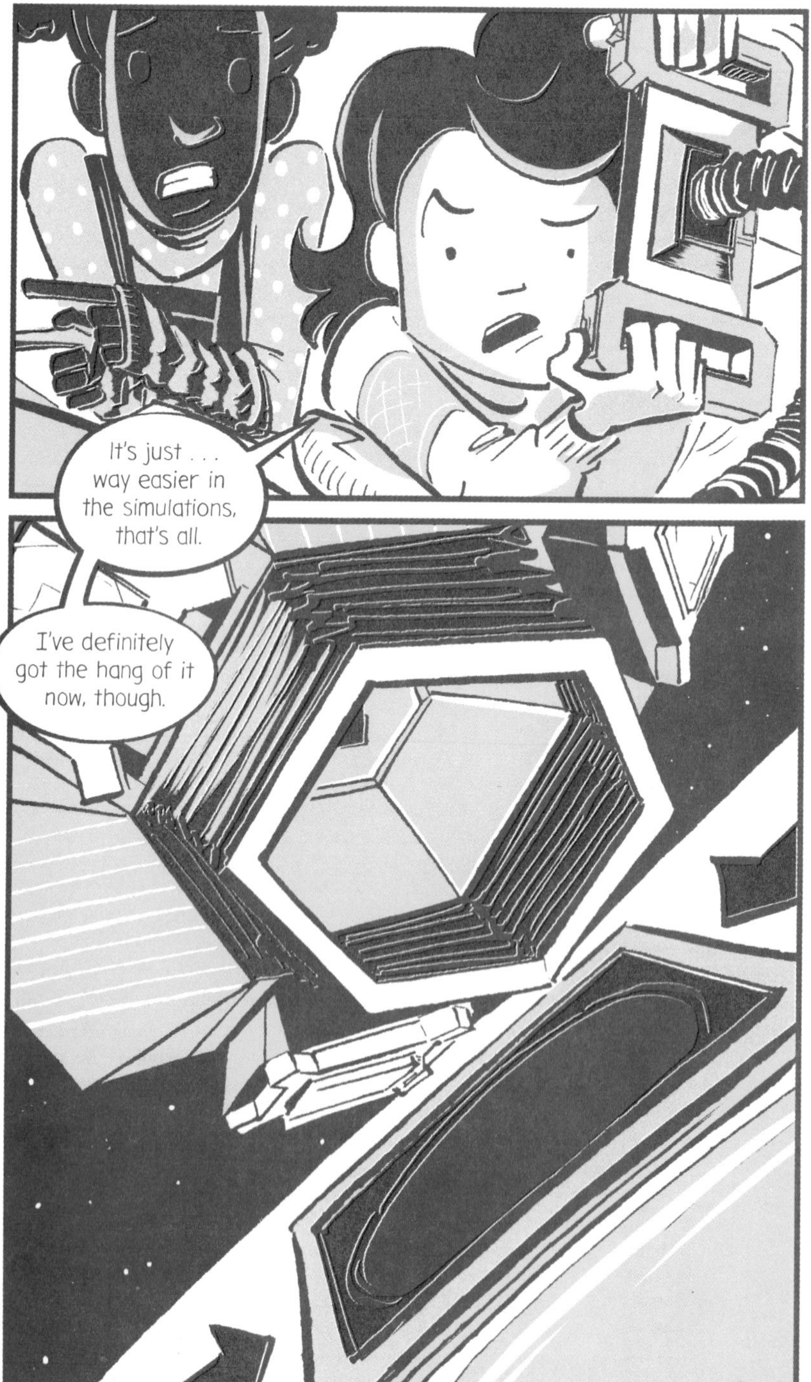
It's just . . . way easier in the simulations, that's all.
I've definitely got the hang of it now, though.

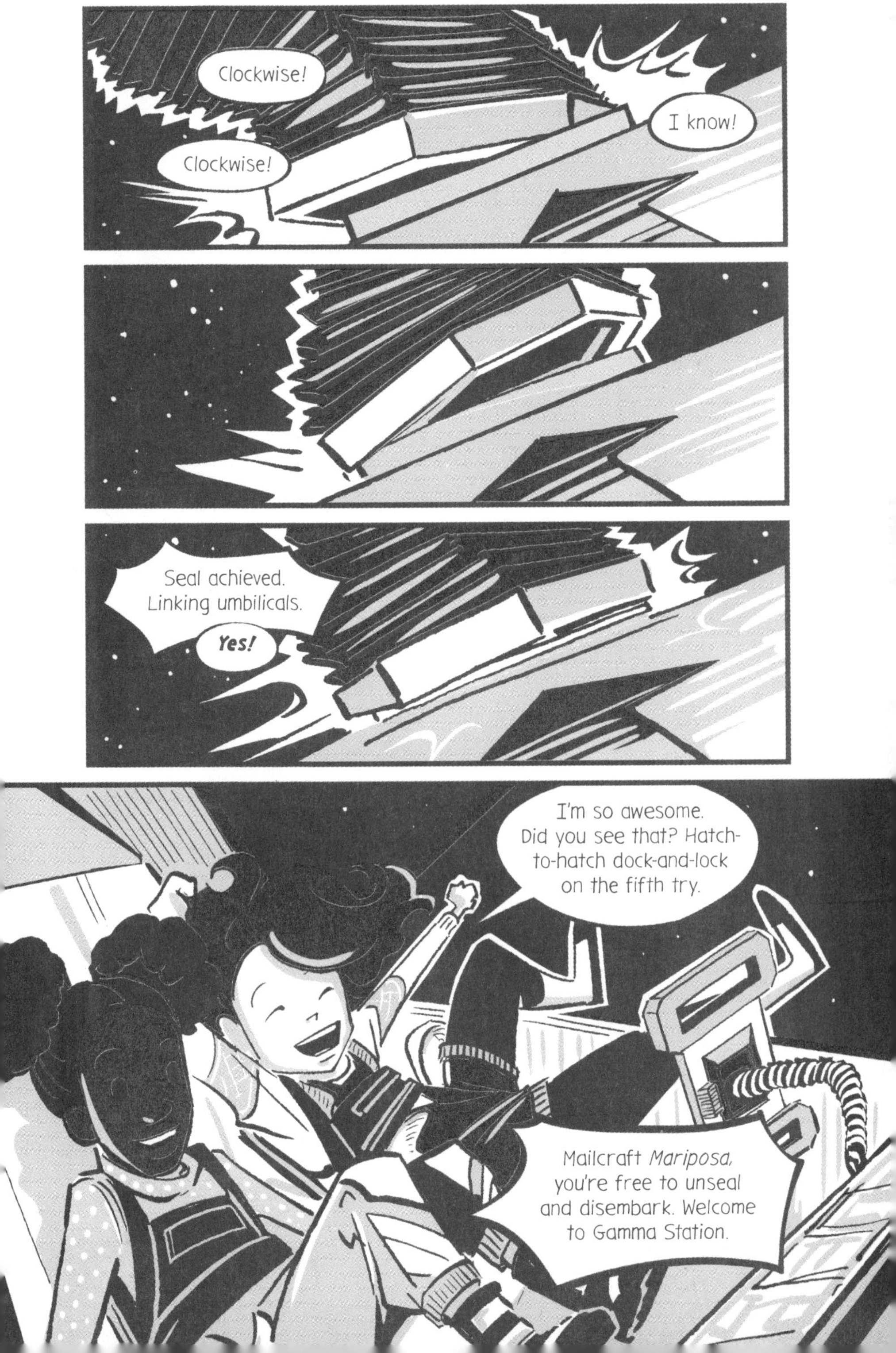
Clockwise!
Clockwise!
I know!
Seal achieved. Linking umbilicals.
Yes!
I'm so awesome. Did you see that? Hatch-to-hatch dock-and-lock on the fifth try.
Mailcraft *Mariposa,* you're free to unseal and disembark. Welcome to Gamma Station.

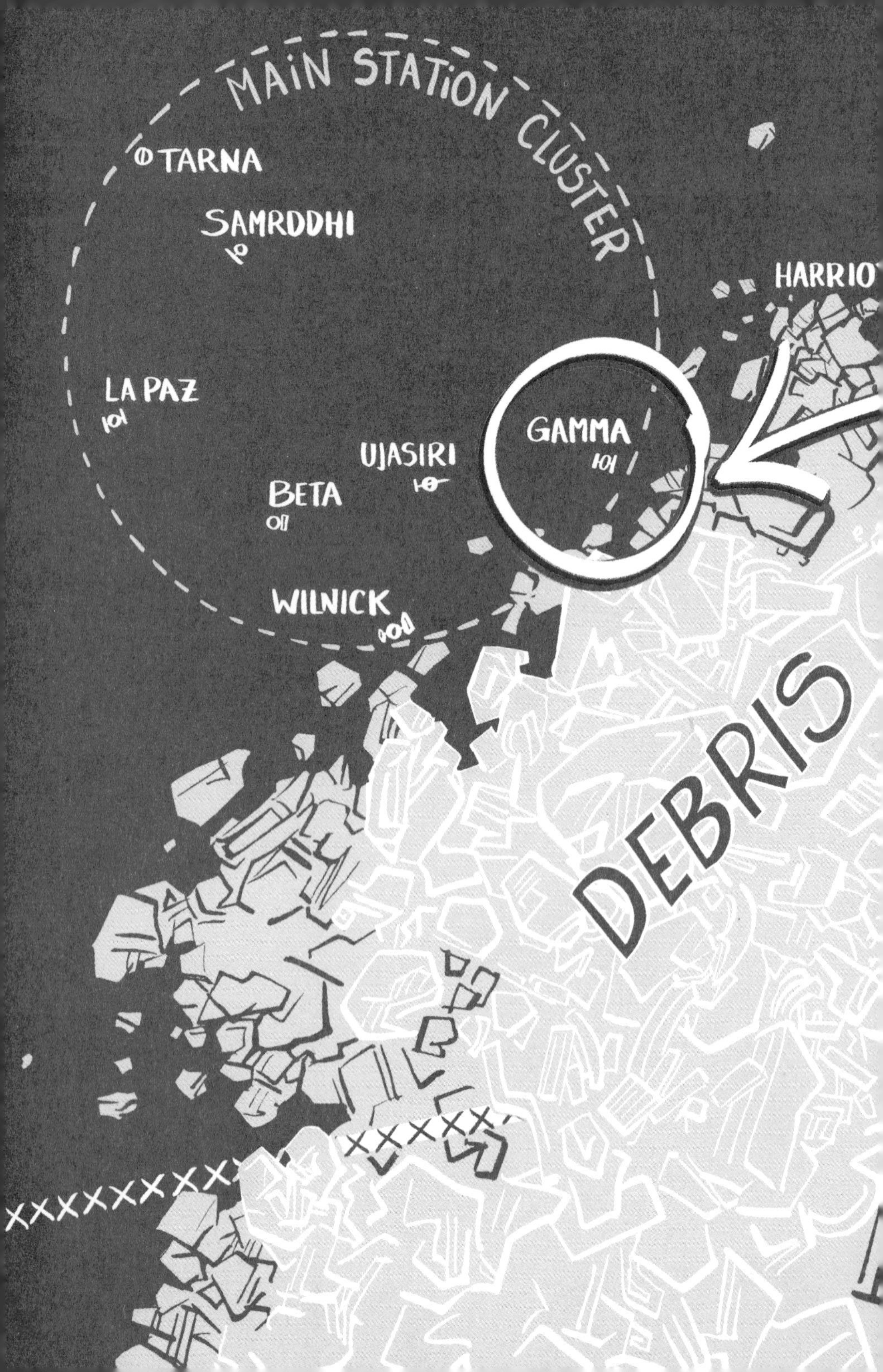
MAIN STATION CLUSTER
TARNA
SAMRDDHI
LA PAZ
GAMMA
UJASIRI
BETA
WILNICK
HARRIOT
DEBRIS

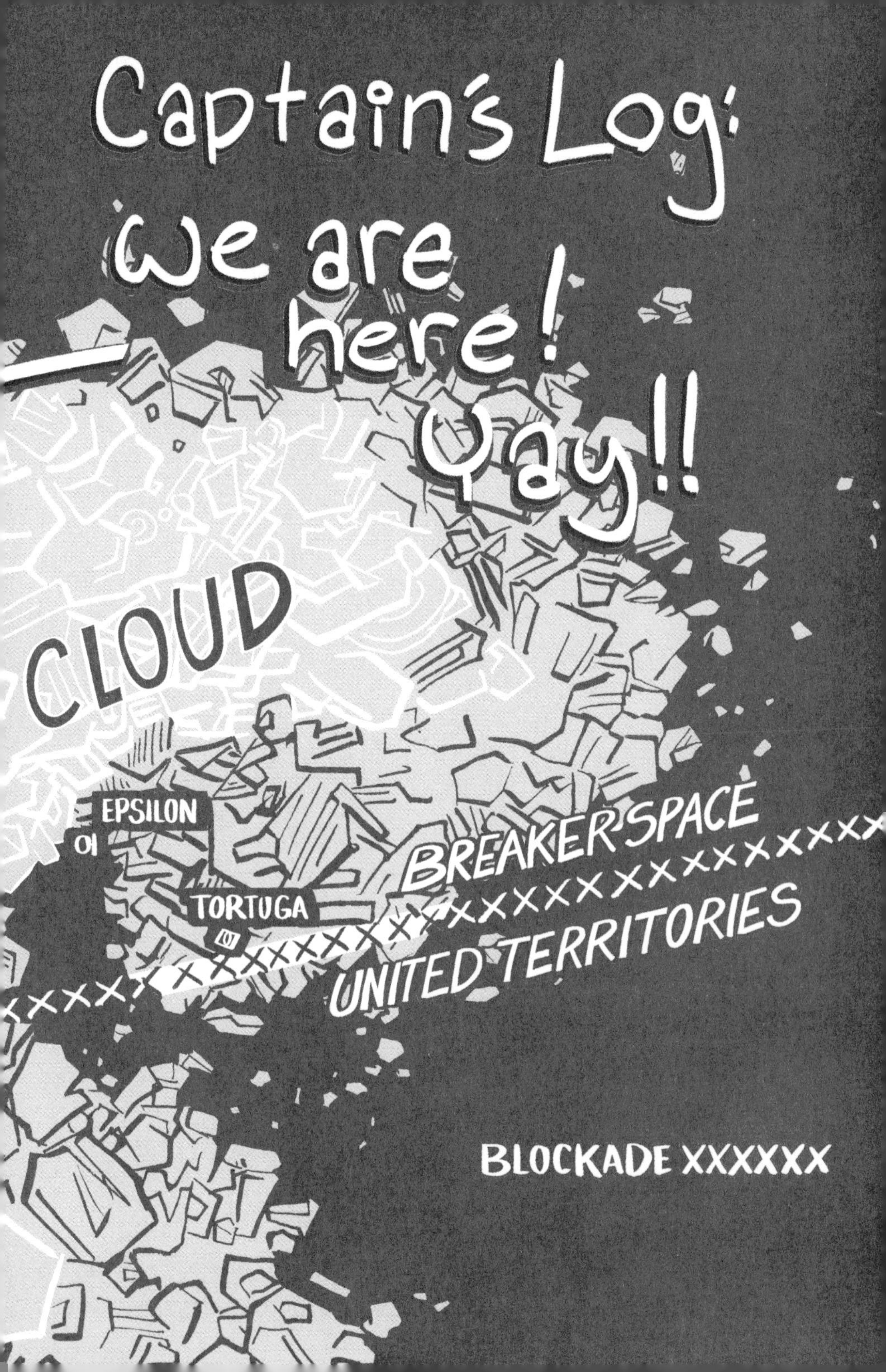
Captain's Log: we are here! yay!!
CLOUD
EPSILON 01
TORTUGA 01
BREAKER SPACE
UNITED TERRITORIES
BLOCKADE XXXXXX

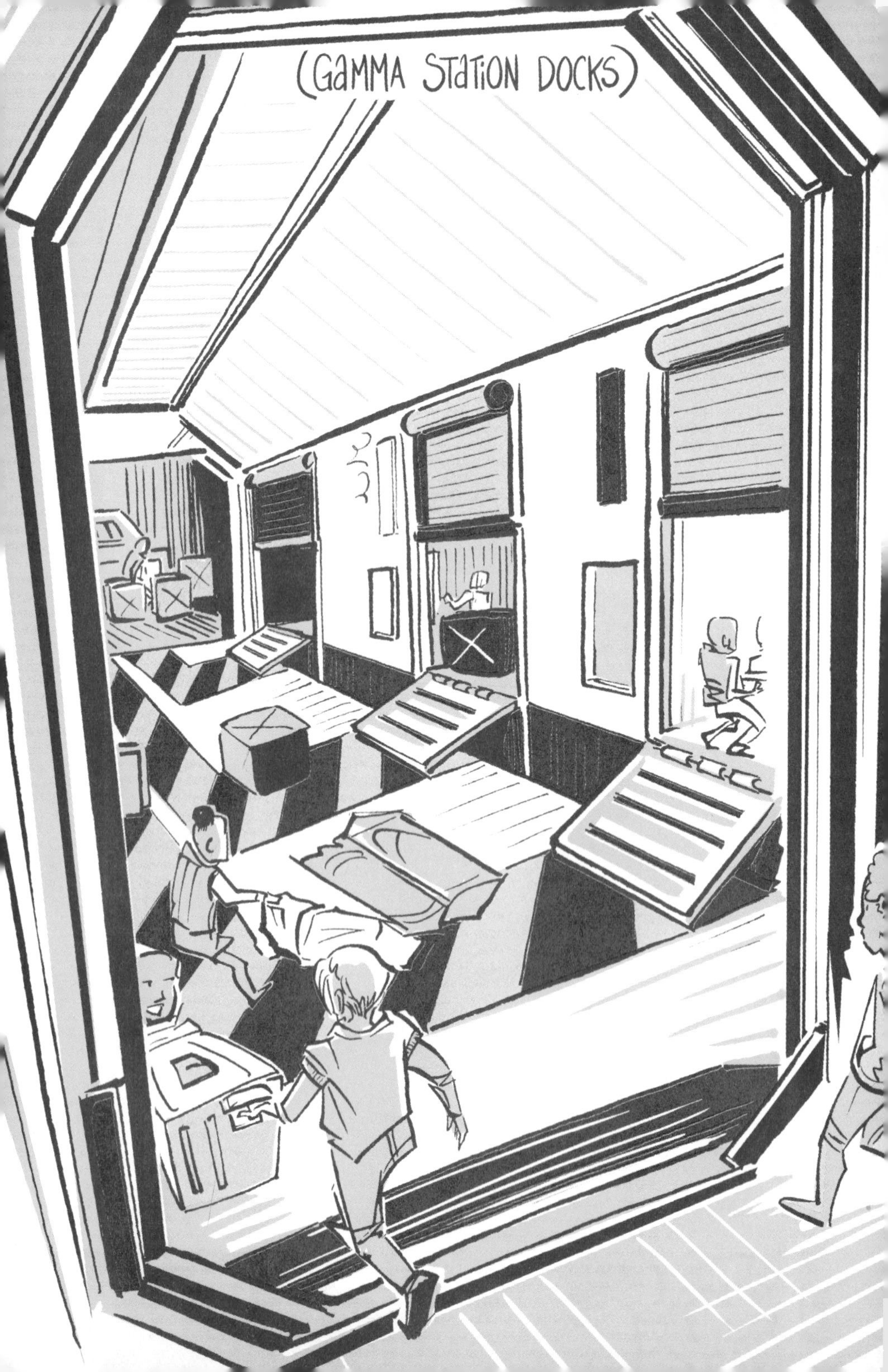
(GAMMA STATION DOCKS)

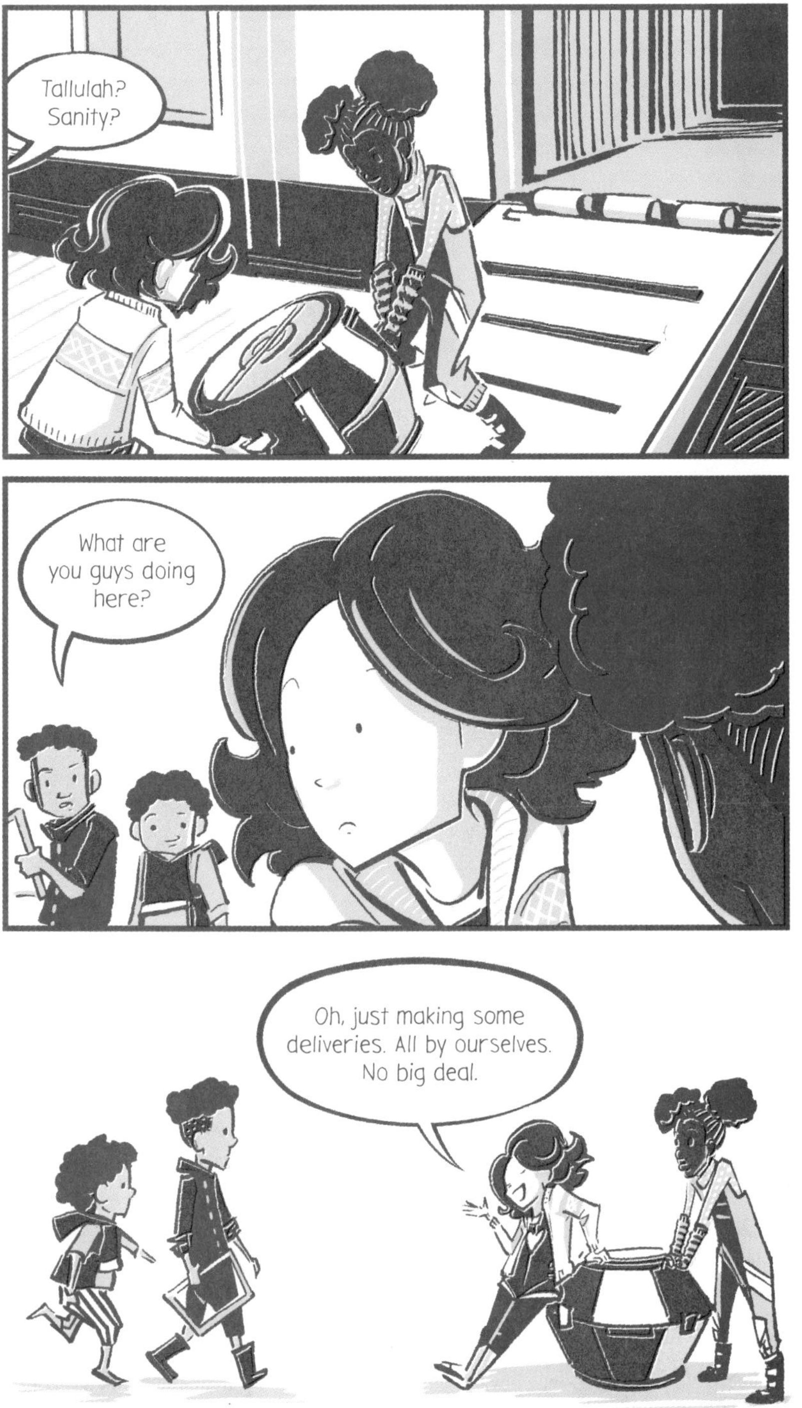
Tallulah? Sanity?
What are you guys doing here?
Oh, just making some deliveries. All by ourselves. No big deal.

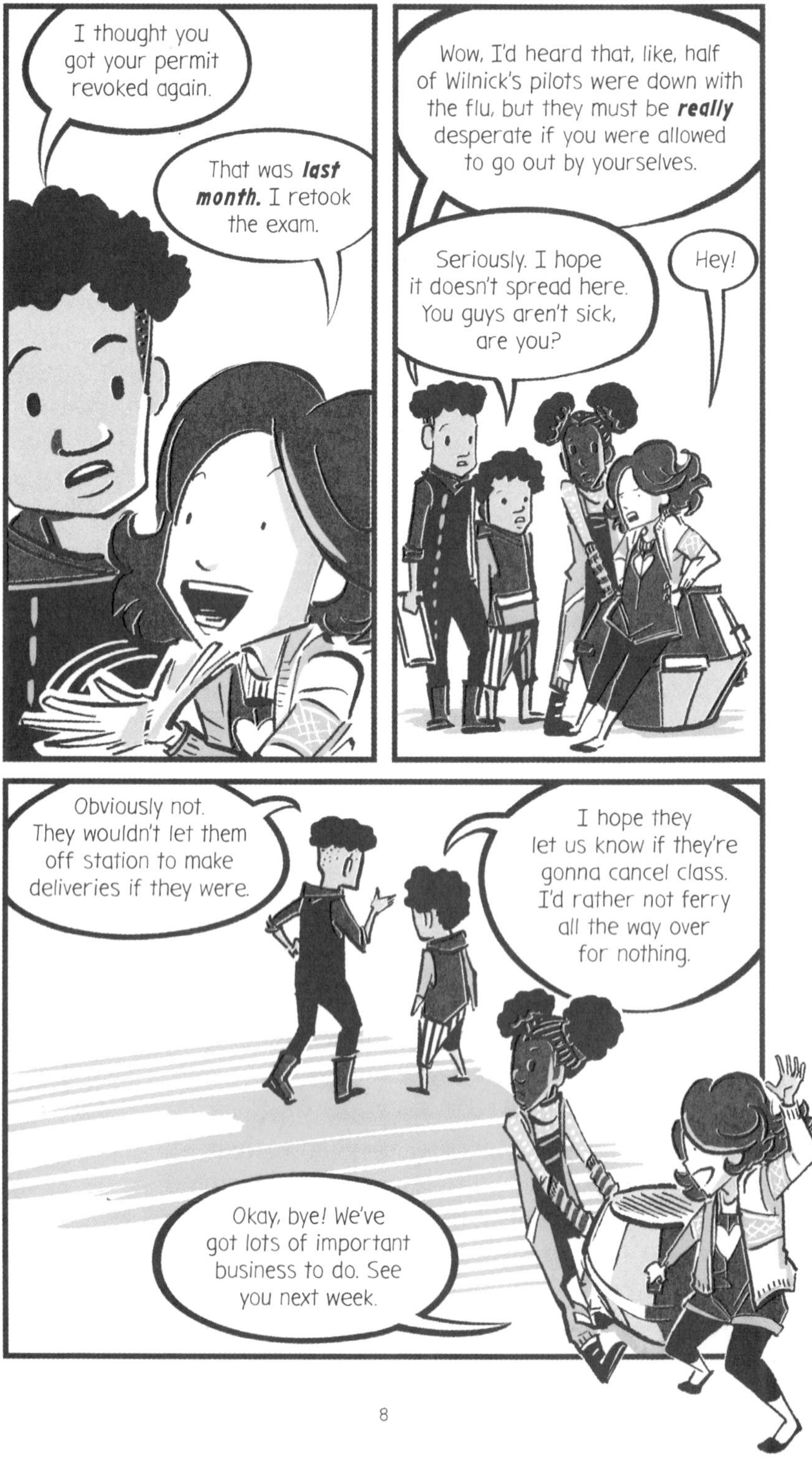

I thought you got your permit revoked again.
That was **last month.** I retook the exam.
Wow, I'd heard that, like, half of Wilnick's pilots were down with the flu, but they must be **really** desperate if you were allowed to go out by yourselves.
Seriously. I hope it doesn't spread here. You guys aren't sick, are you?
Hey!
Obviously not. They wouldn't let them off station to make deliveries if they were.
I hope they let us know if they're gonna cancel class. I'd rather not ferry all the way over for nothing.
Okay, bye! We've got lots of important business to do. See you next week.

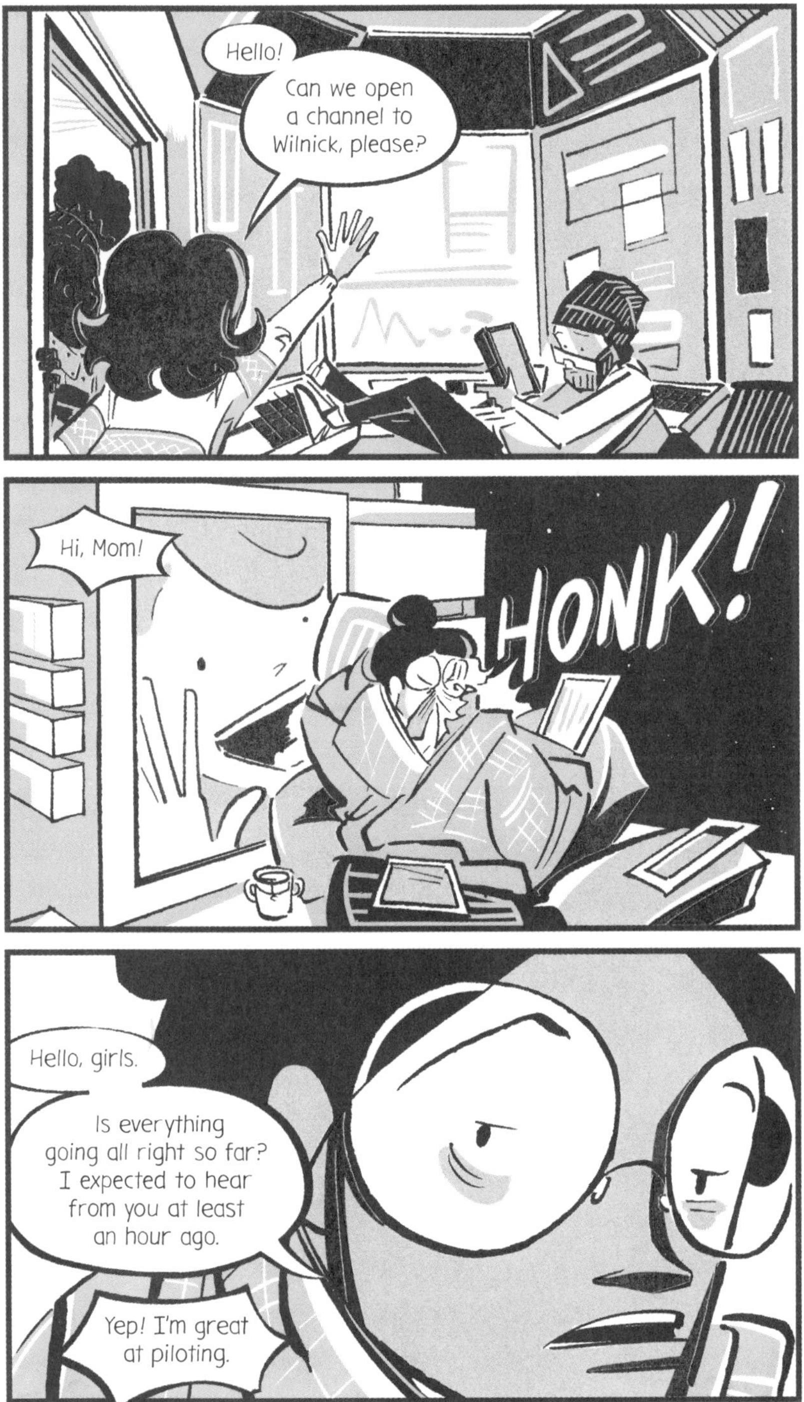
Hello!
Can we open a channel to Wilnick, please?
Hi, Mom!
HONK!
Hello, girls.
Is everything going all right so far? I expected to hear from you at least an hour ago.
Yep! I'm great at piloting.

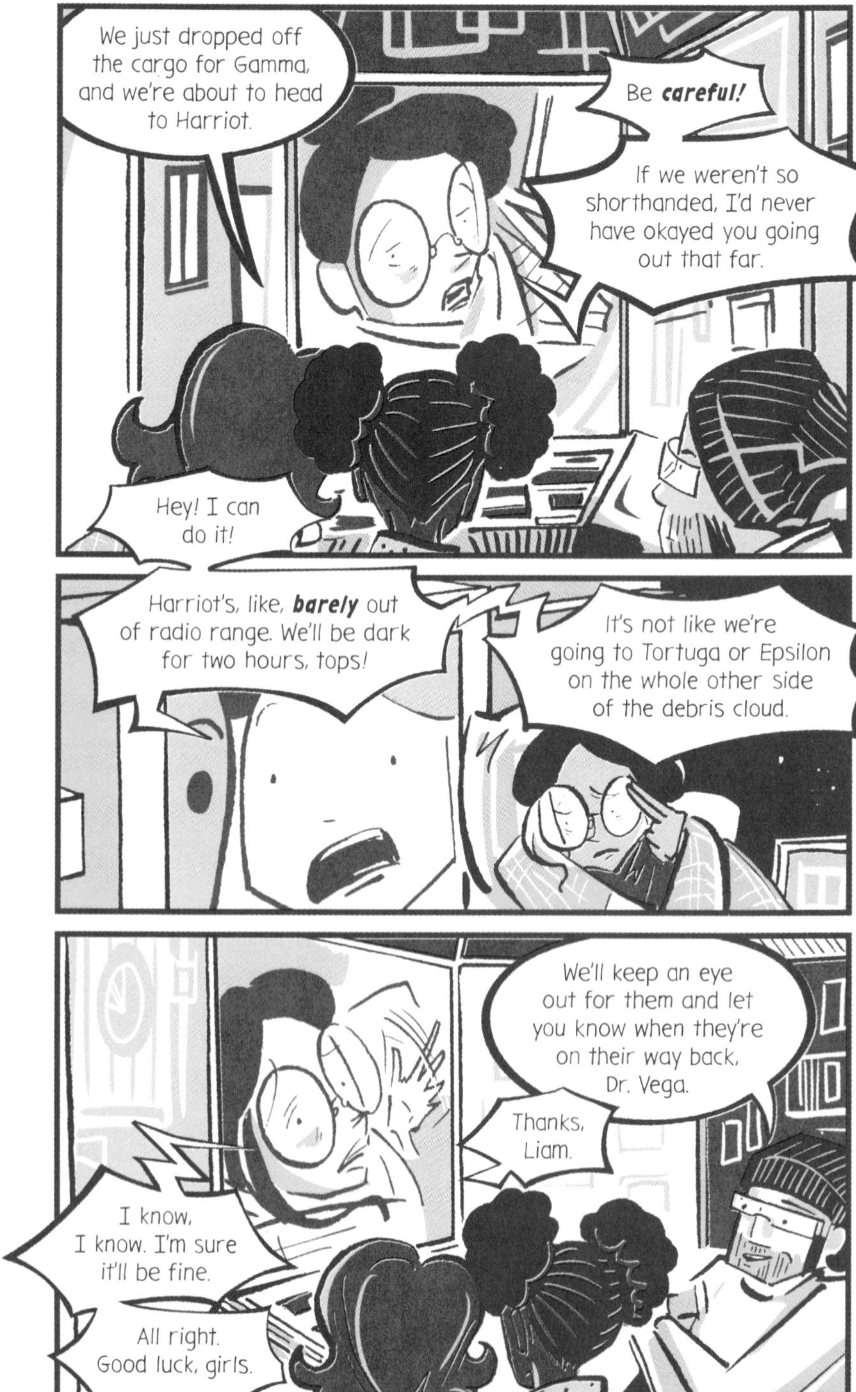
We just dropped off the cargo for Gamma, and we're about to head to Harriot.
Be **careful!**
If we weren't so shorthanded, I'd never have okayed you going out that far.
Hey! I can do it!
Harriot's, like, **barely** out of radio range. We'll be dark for two hours, tops!
It's not like we're going to Tortuga or Epsilon on the whole other side of the debris cloud.
We'll keep an eye out for them and let you know when they're on their way back, Dr. Vega.
Thanks, Liam.
I know, I know. I'm sure it'll be fine.
All right. Good luck, girls.

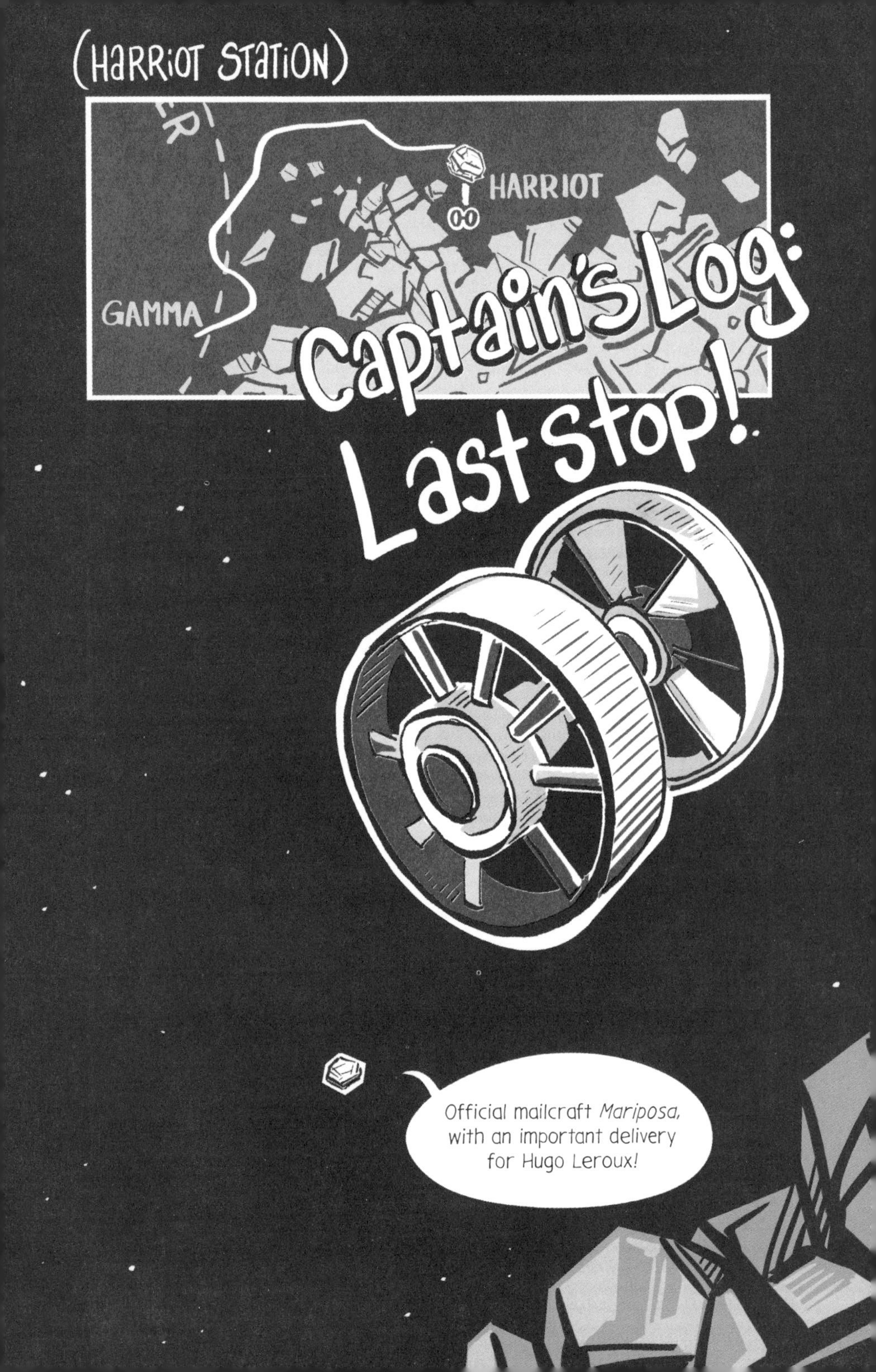
(HARRIOT STATION)
HARRIOT
GAMMA
Captain's Log:
Last Stop!
Official mailcraft *Mariposa*, with an important delivery for Hugo Leroux!

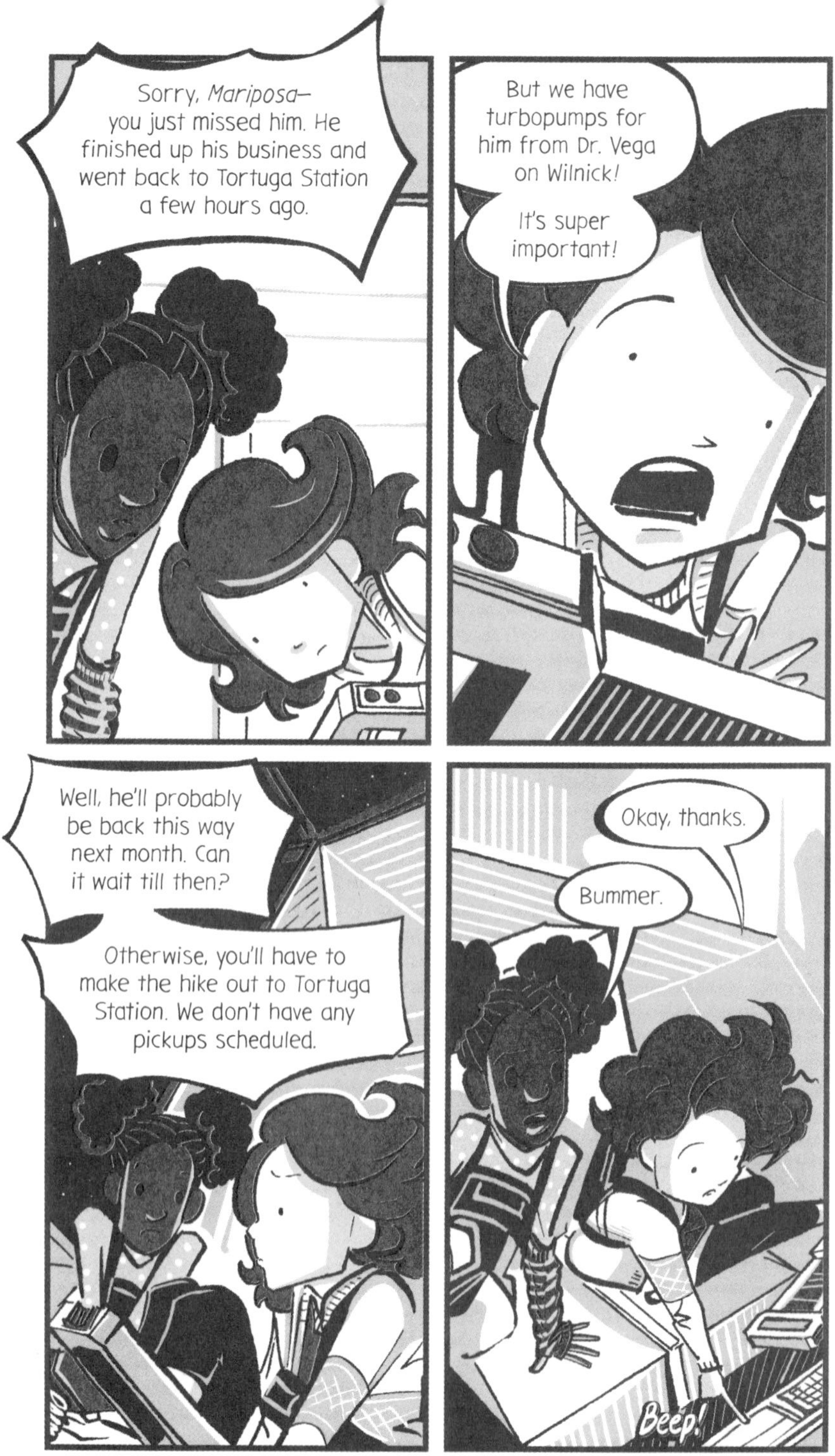
Sorry, *Mariposa*—you just missed him. He finished up his business and went back to Tortuga Station a few hours ago.
But we have turbopumps for him from Dr. Vega on Wilnick!
It's super important!
Well, he'll probably be back this way next month. Can it wait till then?
Otherwise, you'll have to make the hike out to Tortuga Station. We don't have any pickups scheduled.
Okay, thanks.
Bummer.
Beep!

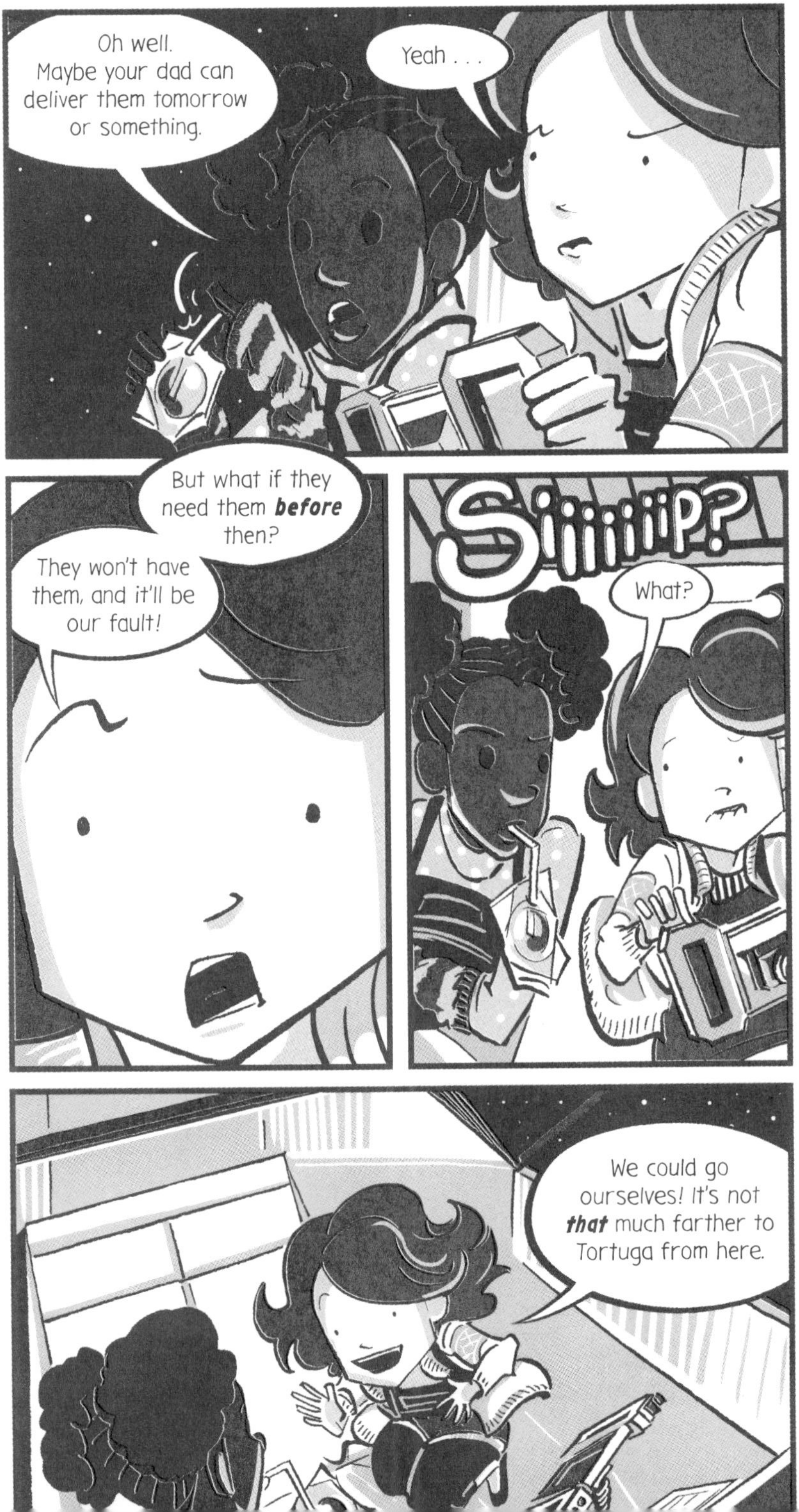
Oh well. Maybe your dad can deliver them tomorrow or something.
Yeah . . .
But what if they need them **before** then?
They won't have them, and it'll be our fault!
Siiiiiip?
What?
We could go ourselves! It's not **that** much farther to Tortuga from here.

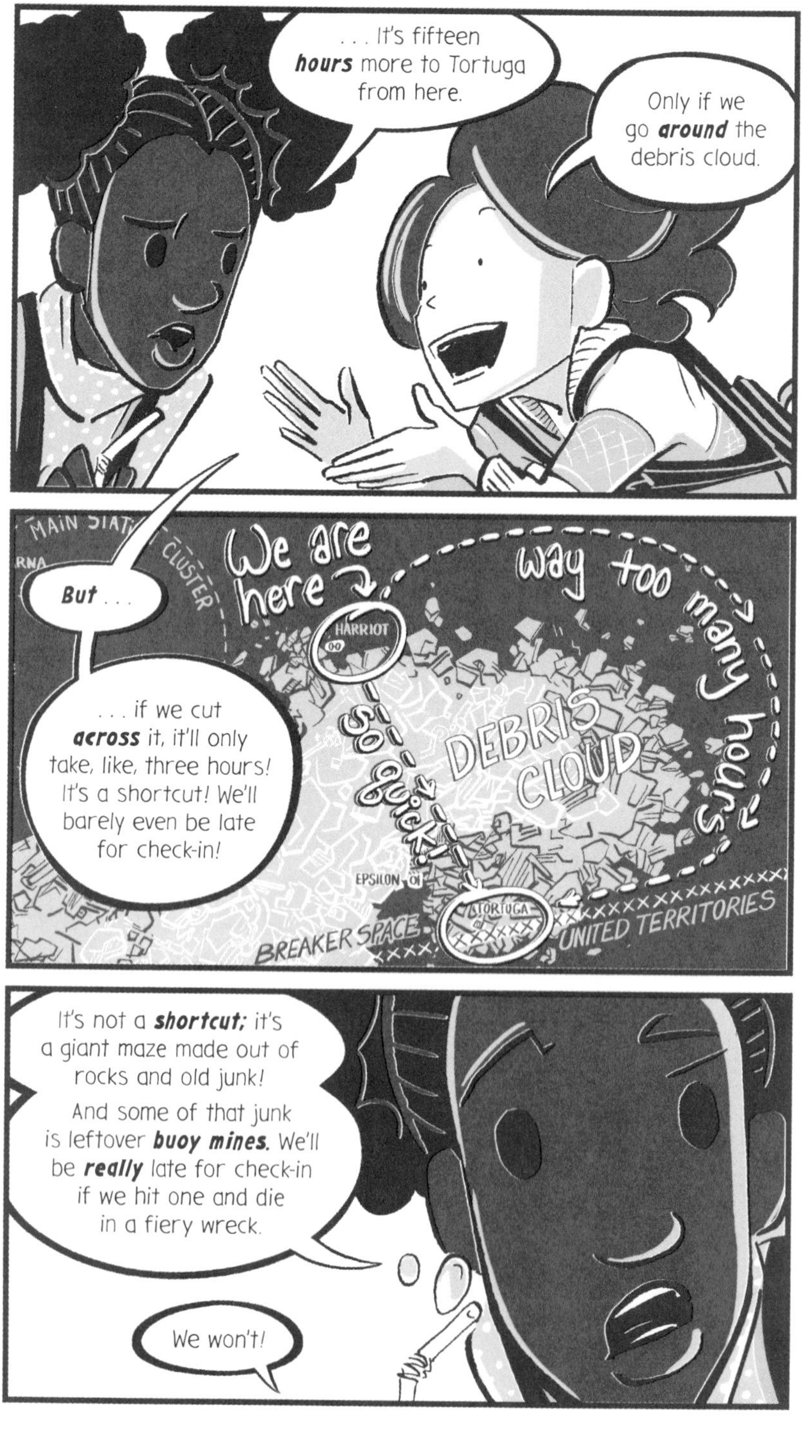

. . . It's fifteen **hours** more to Tortuga from here.
Only if we go **around** the debris cloud.
MAIN STATI
CLUSTER
RNA
But . . .
We are here
way too many hours
HARRIOT
so quick!
DEBRIS CLOUD
. . . if we cut **across** it, it'll only take, like, three hours! It's a shortcut! We'll barely even be late for check-in!
EPSILON 01
TORTUGA
BREAKER SPACE
UNITED TERRITORIES
It's not a **shortcut;** it's a giant maze made out of rocks and old junk!
And some of that junk is leftover **buoy mines.** We'll be **really** late for check-in if we hit one and die in a fiery wreck.
We won't!

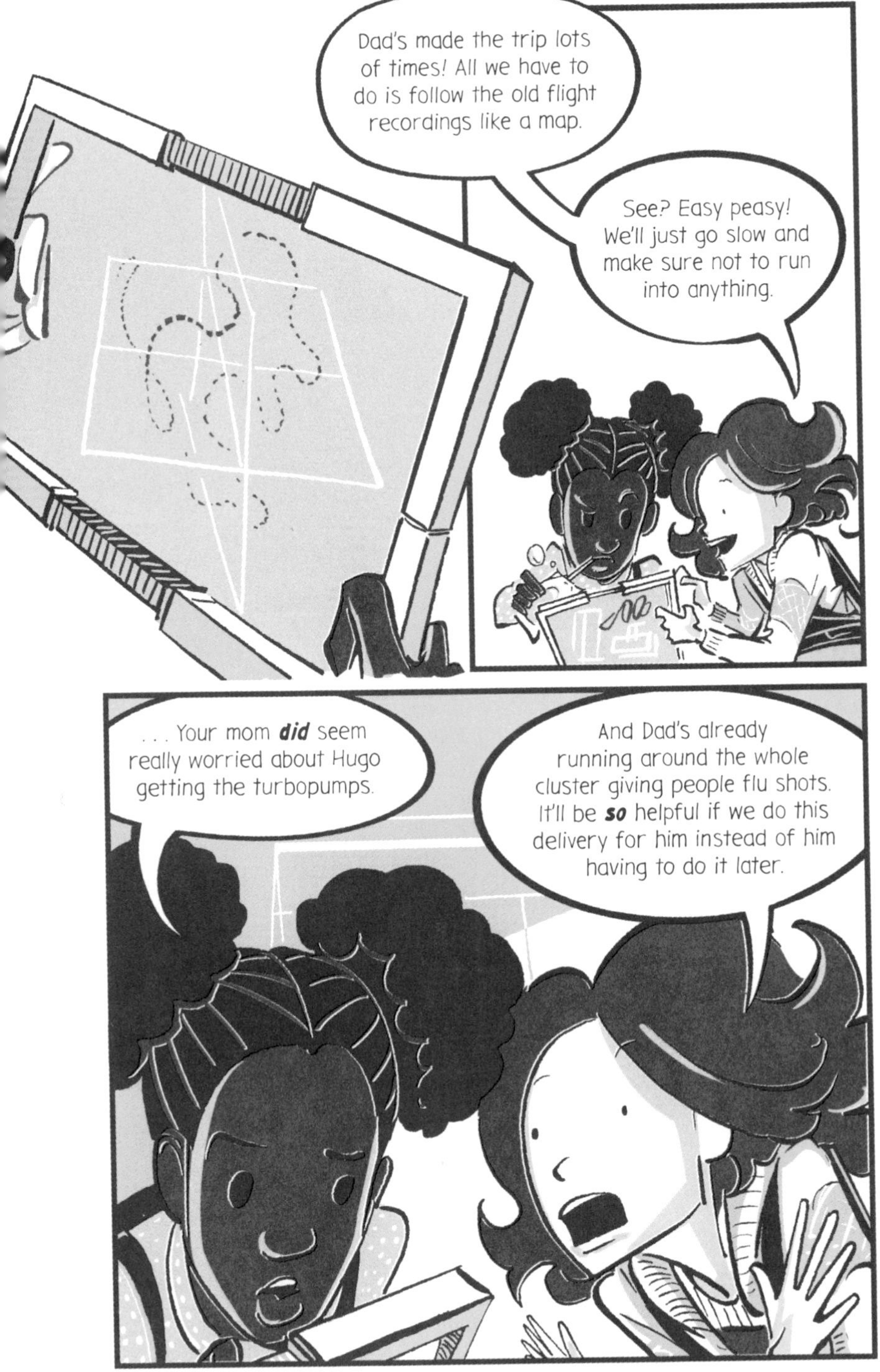
Dad's made the trip lots of times! All we have to do is follow the old flight recordings like a map.
See? Easy peasy! We'll just go slow and make sure not to run into anything.
. . . Your mom **did** seem really worried about Hugo getting the turbopumps.
And Dad's already running around the whole cluster giving people flu shots. It'll be **so** helpful if we do this delivery for him instead of him having to do it later.

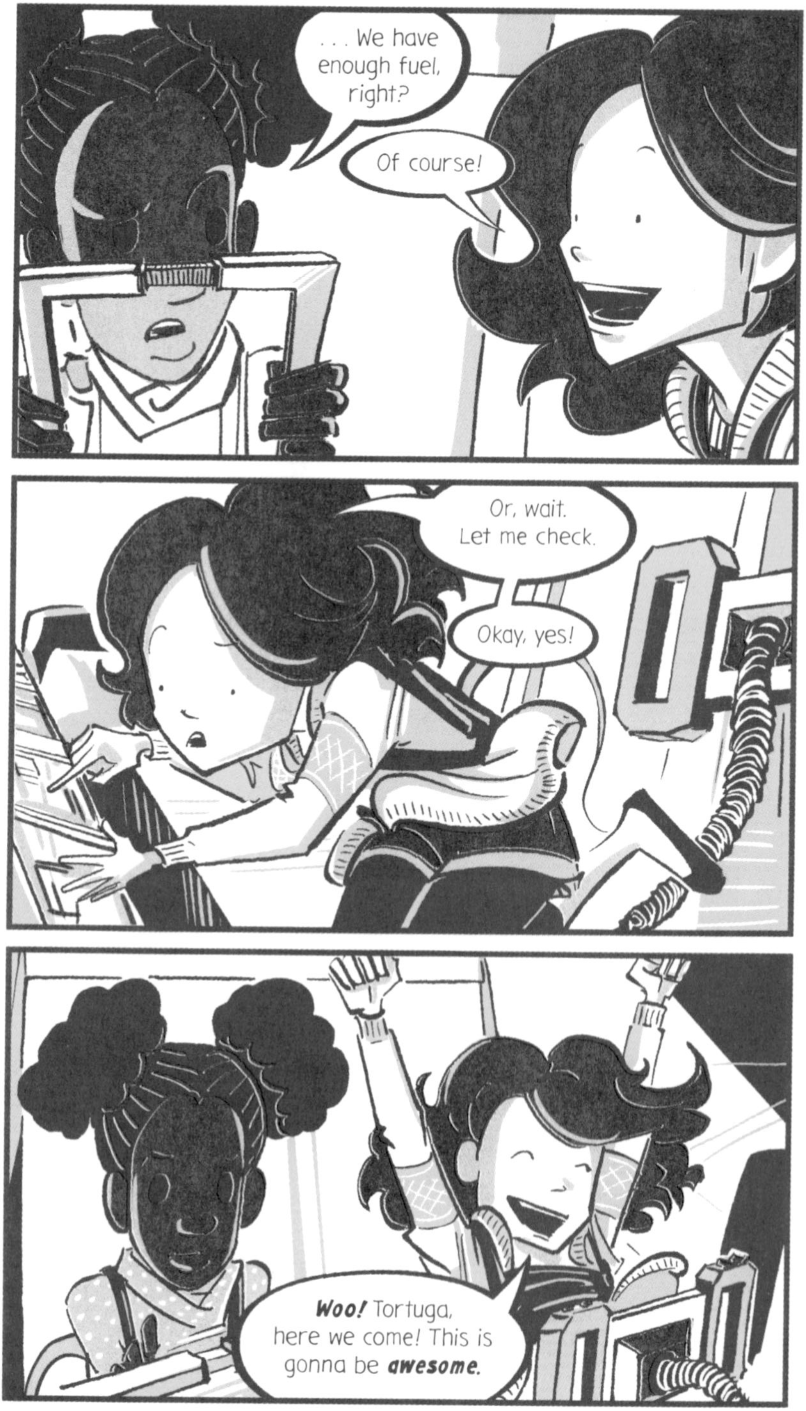
. . . We have enough fuel, right?
Of course!
Or, wait. Let me check.
Okay, yes!
Woo! Tortuga, here we come! This is gonna be ***awesome.***

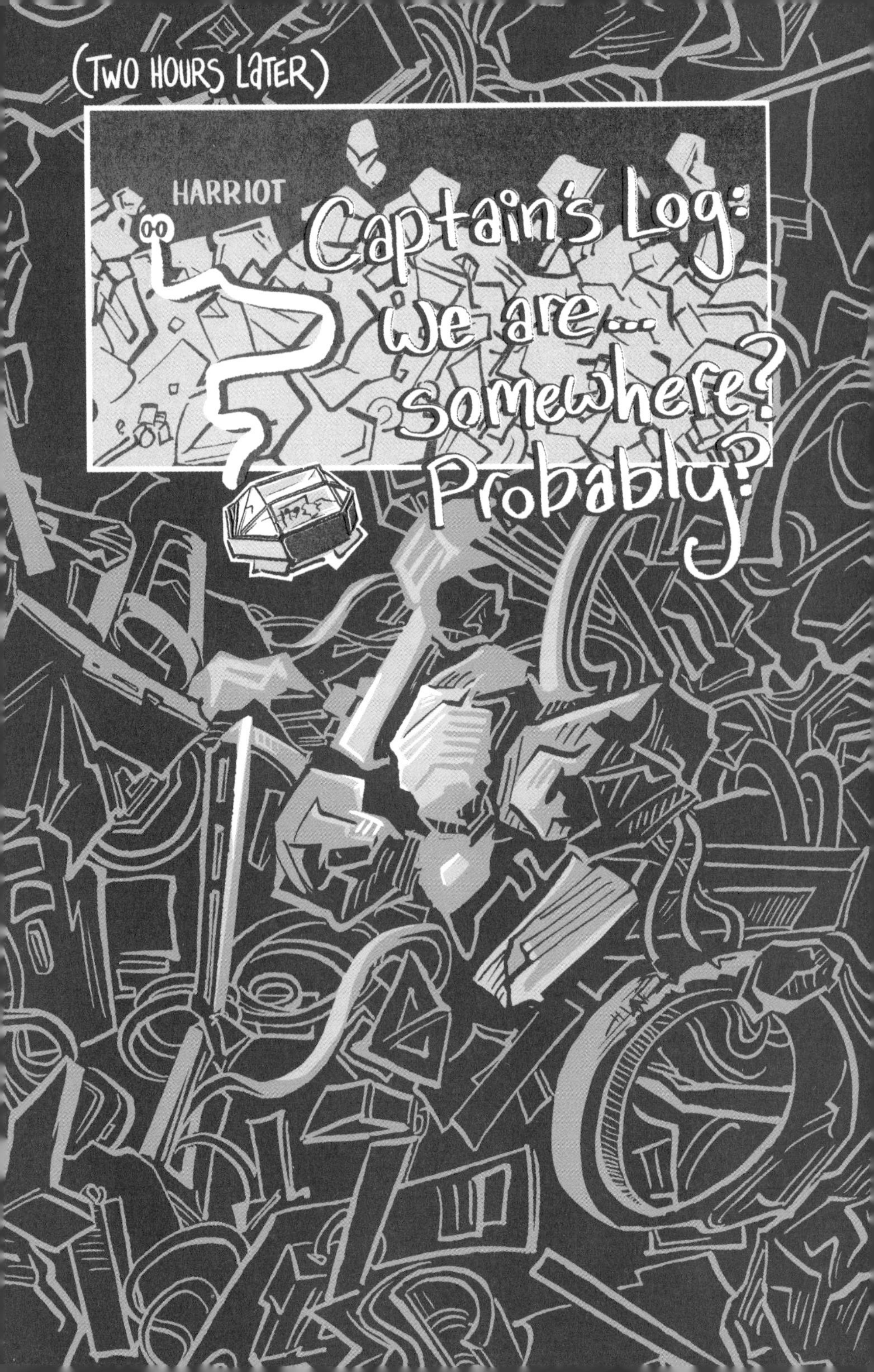
(TWO HOURS LATER)
HARRIOT
Captain's Log: we are... somewhere? Probably?

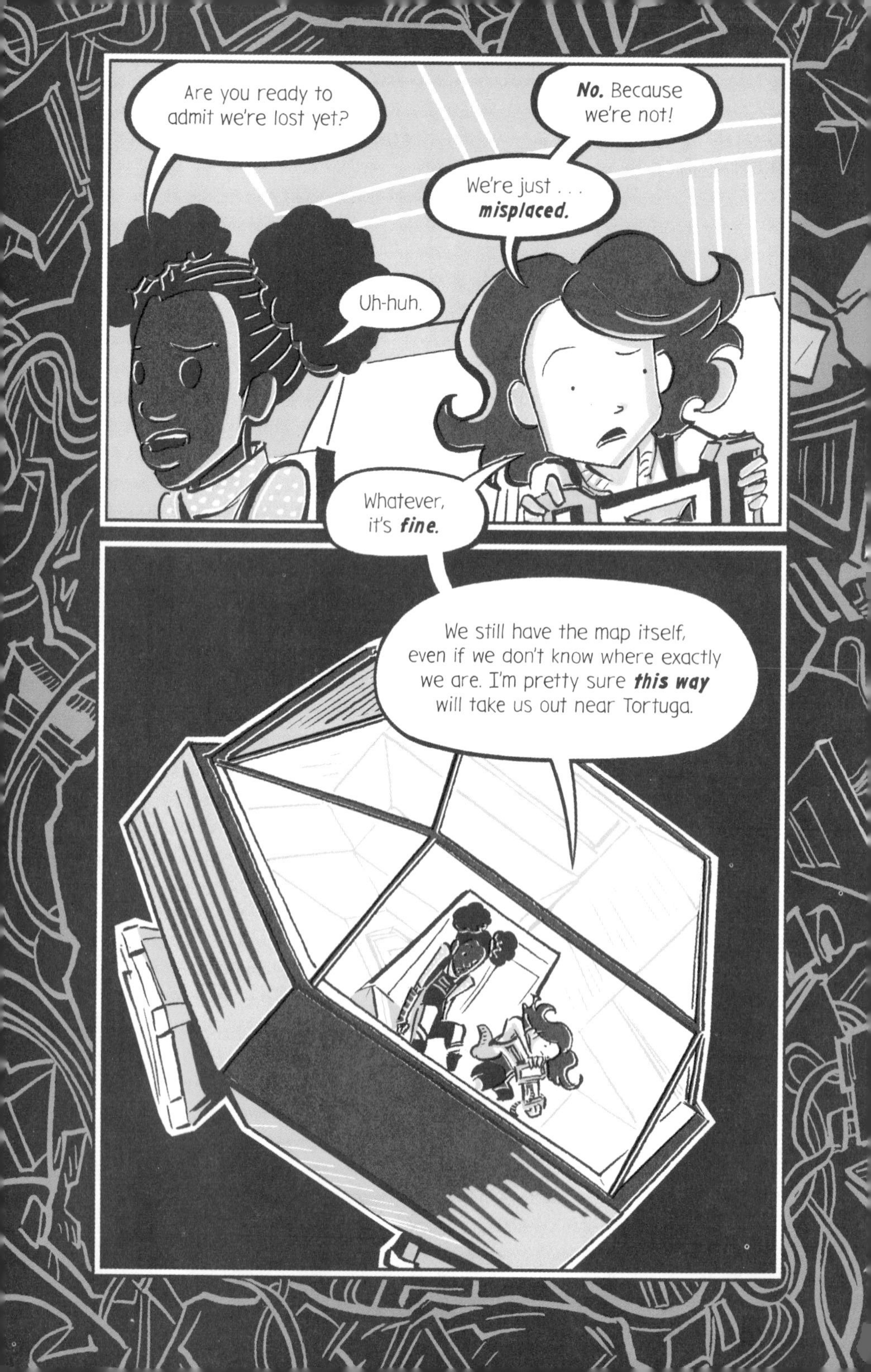

Are you ready to admit we're lost yet?
No. Because we're not!
We're just . . . **misplaced.**
Uh-huh.
Whatever, it's **fine.**
We still have the map itself, even if we don't know where exactly we are. I'm pretty sure **this way** will take us out near Tortuga.

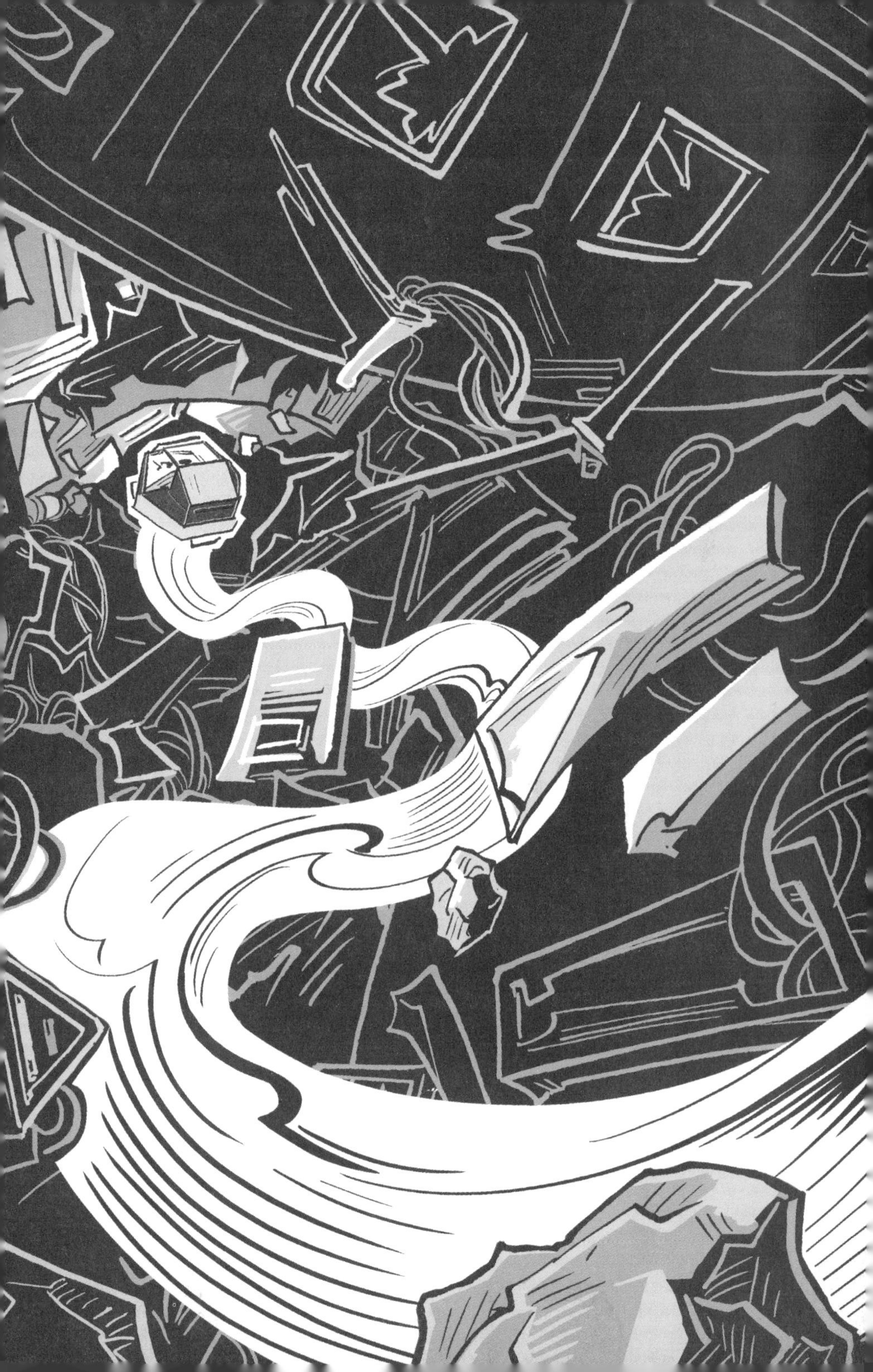

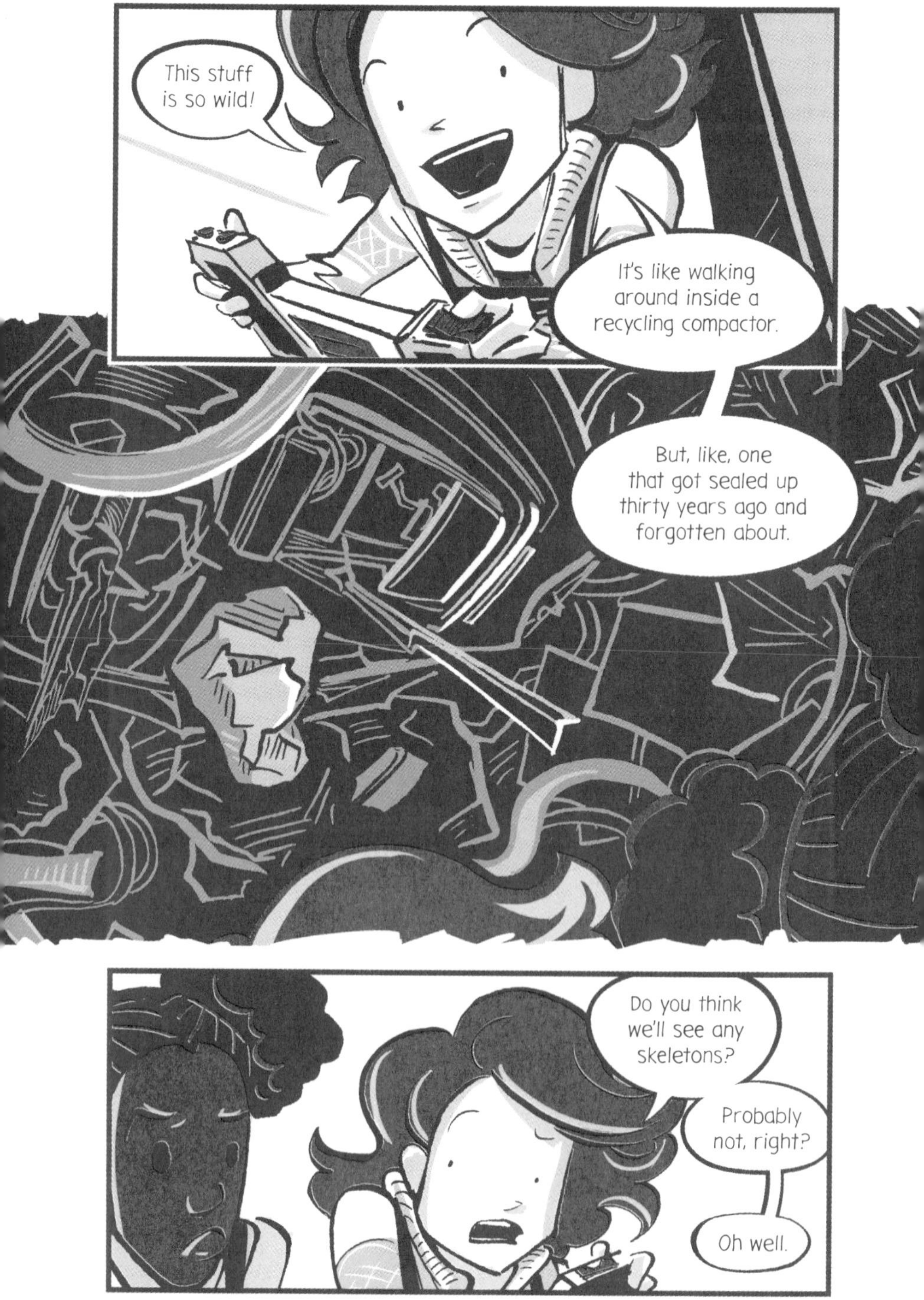
This stuff is so wild!
It's like walking around inside a recycling compactor.
But, like, one that got sealed up thirty years ago and forgotten about.
Do you think we'll see any skeletons?
Probably not, right?
Oh well.

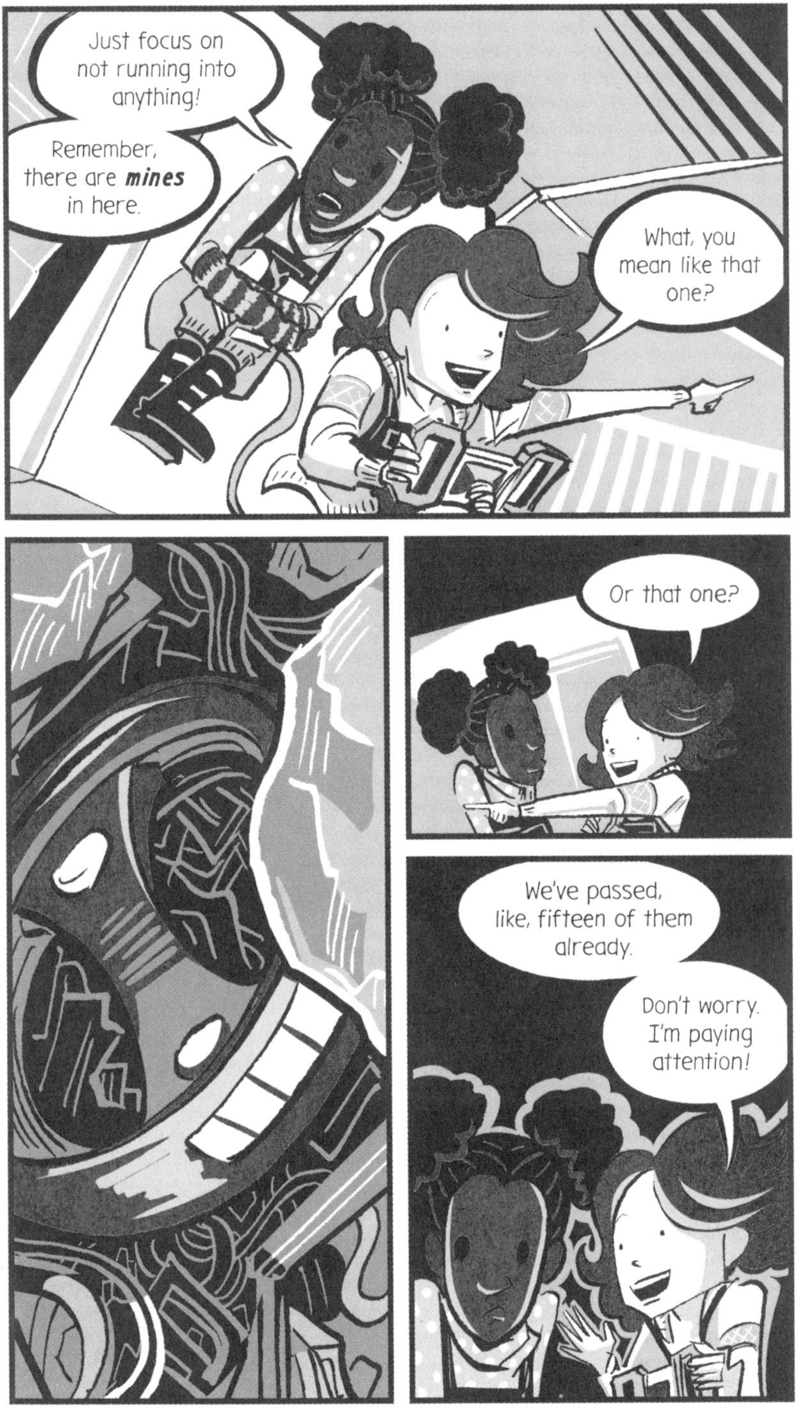
Just focus on not running into anything!
Remember, there are **mines** in here.
What, you mean like that one?
Or that one?
We've passed, like, fifteen of them already.
Don't worry. I'm paying attention!

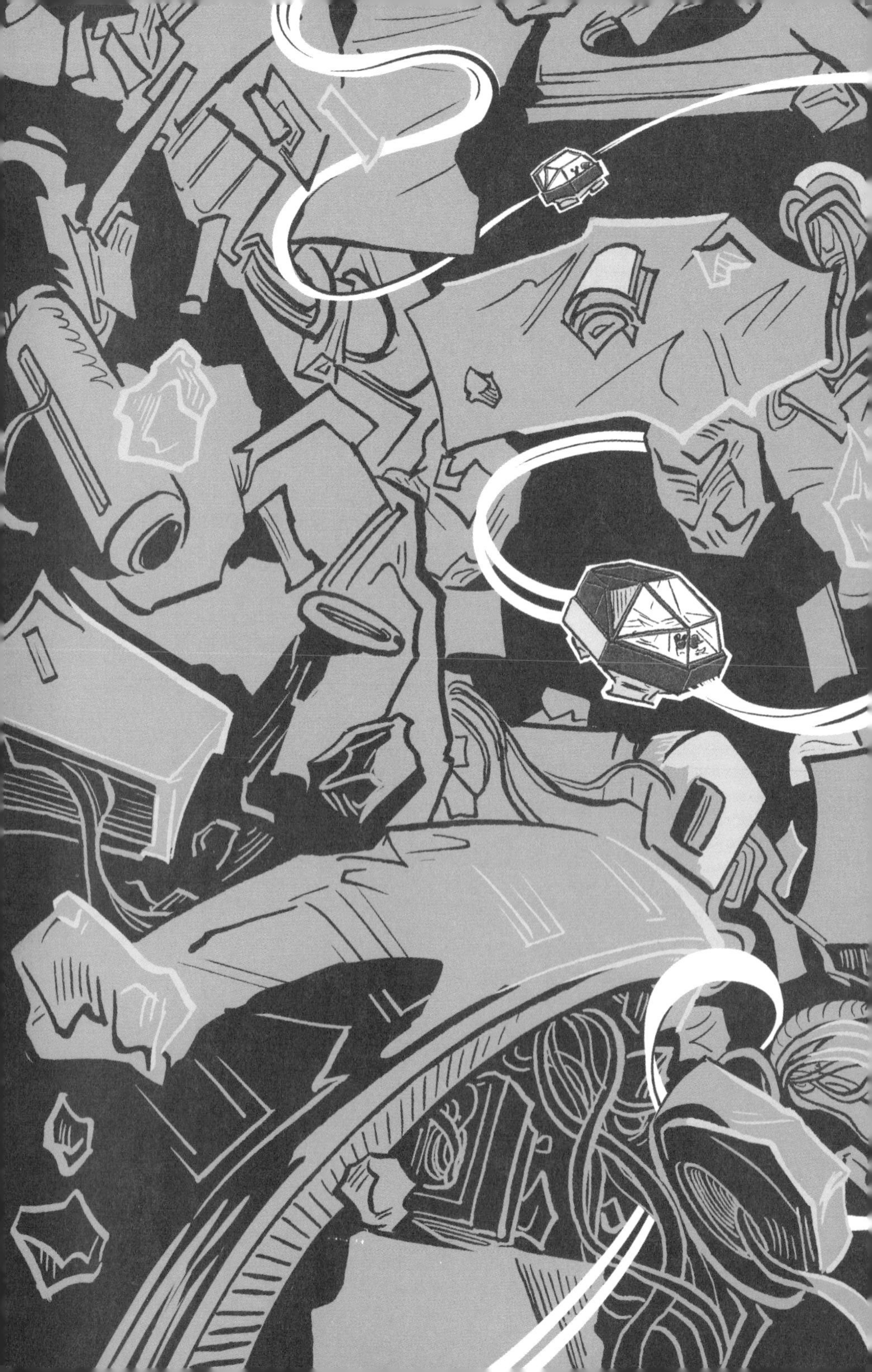

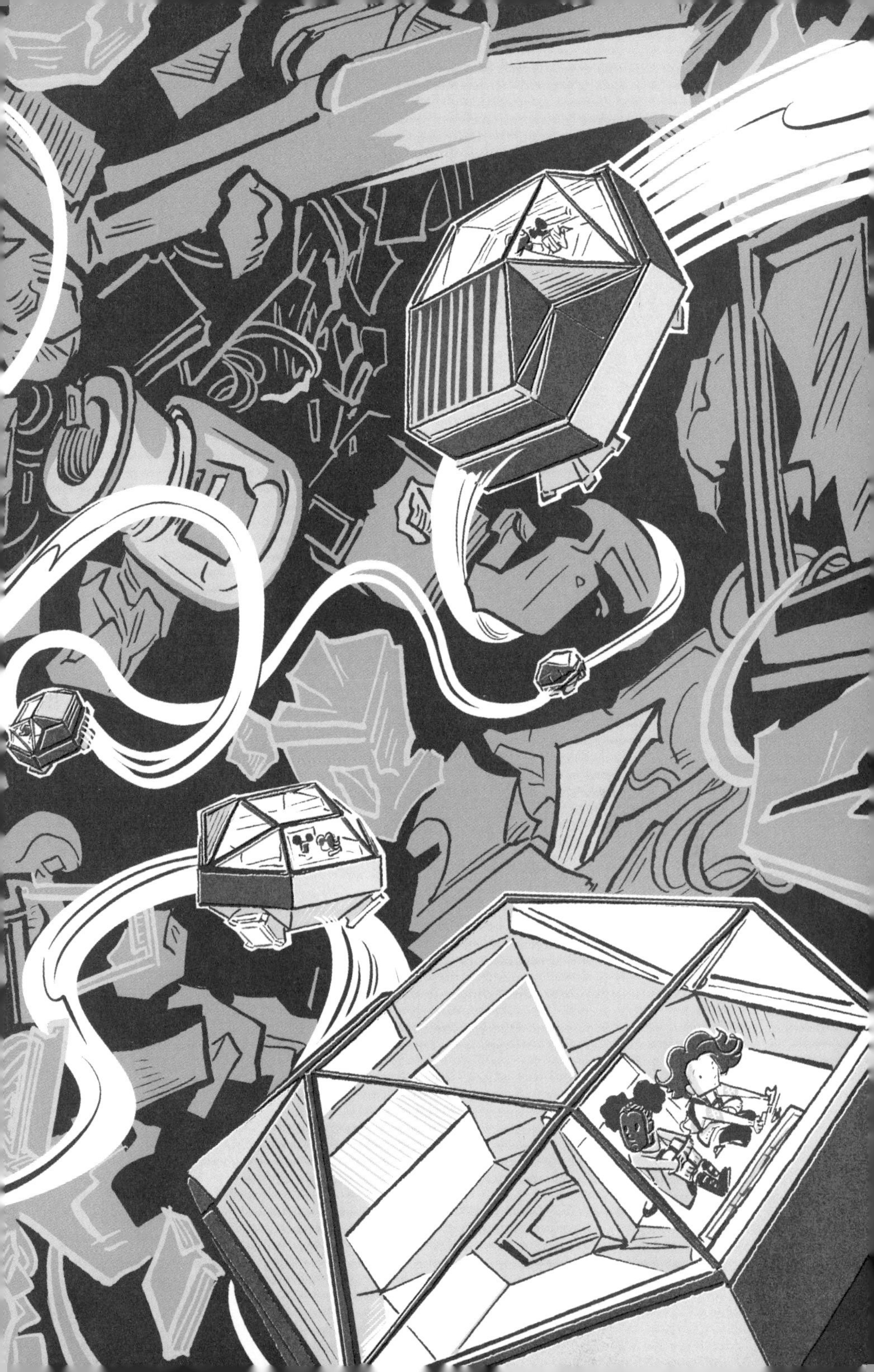

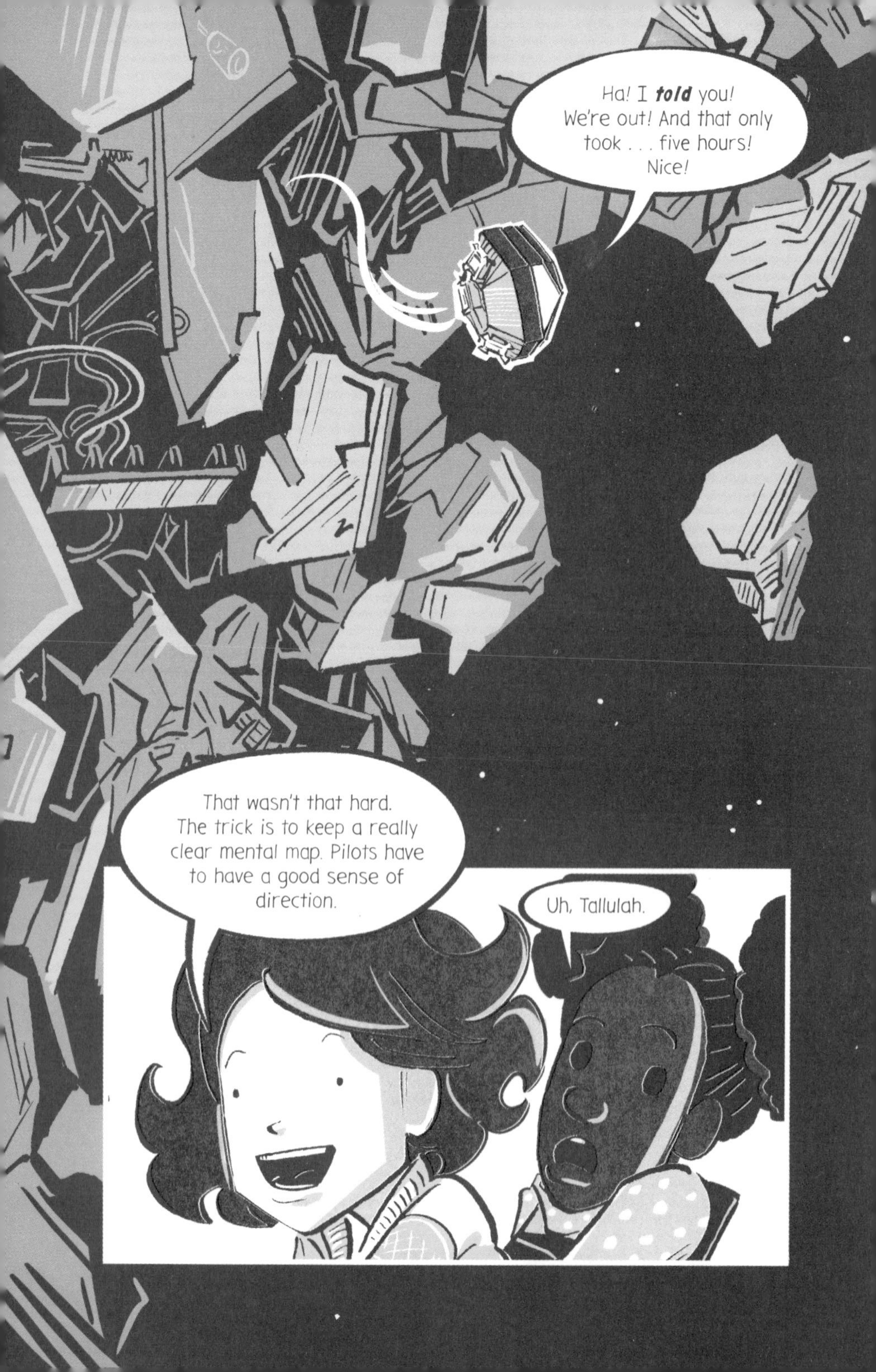

Ha! I **told** you! We're out! And that only took . . . five hours! Nice!
That wasn't that hard. The trick is to keep a really clear mental map. Pilots have to have a good sense of direction.
Uh, Tallulah.

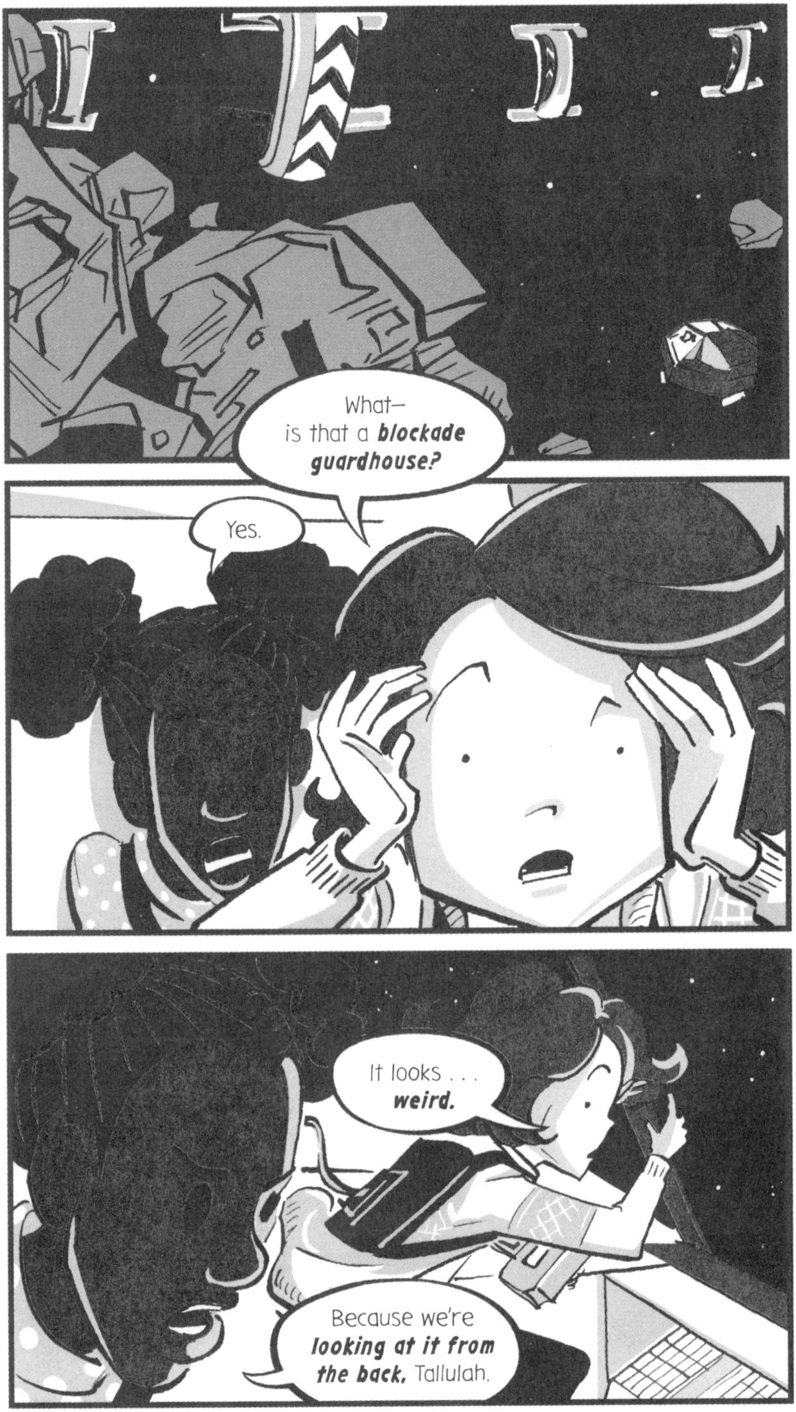
What—
is that a **blockade guardhouse?**
Yes.
It looks . . . **weird.**
Because we're **looking at it from the back,** Tallulah.

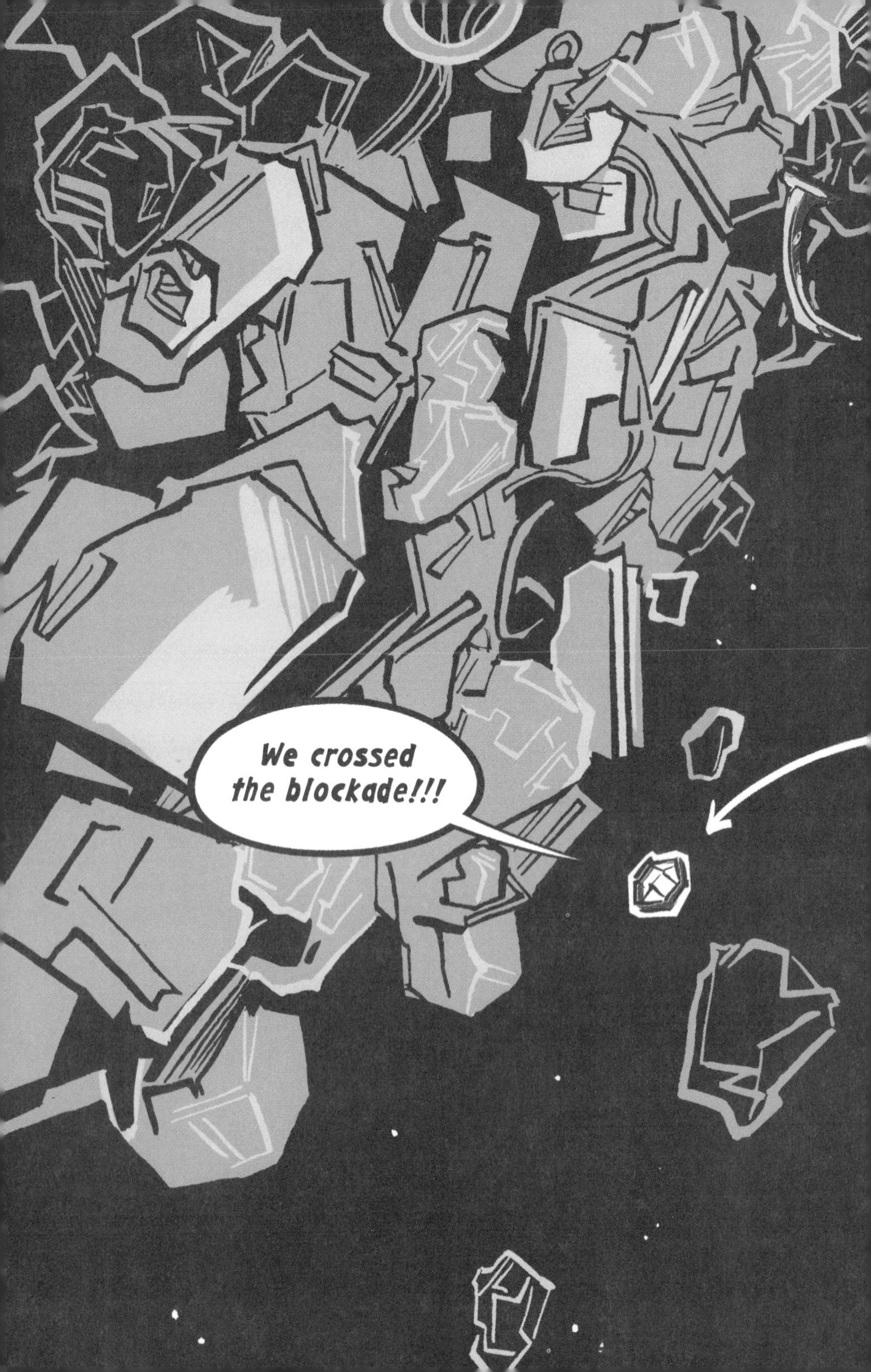
We crossed the blockade!!!

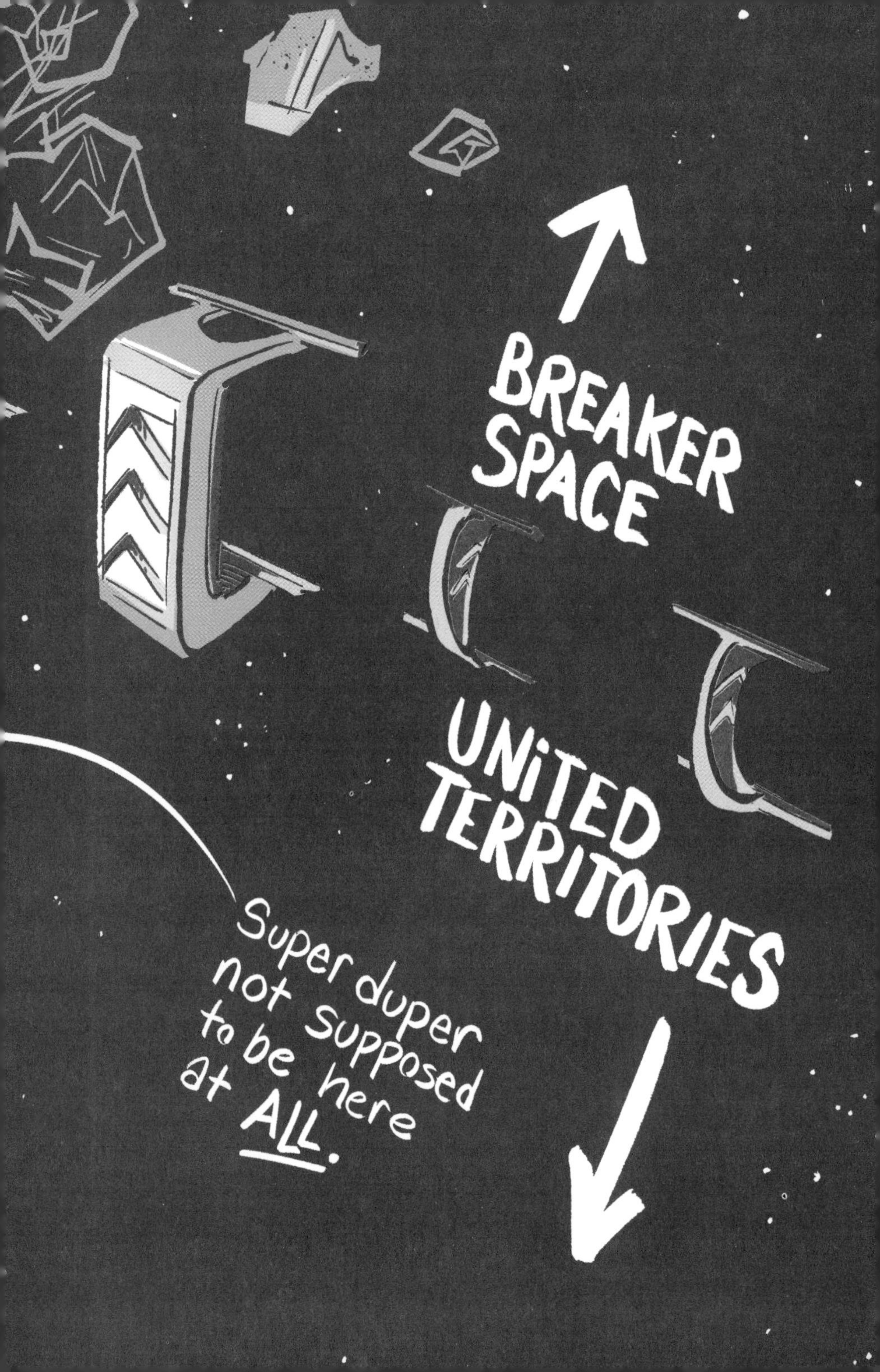
BREAKER SPACE
UNITED TERRITORIES
Super duper not supposed to be here at ALL.

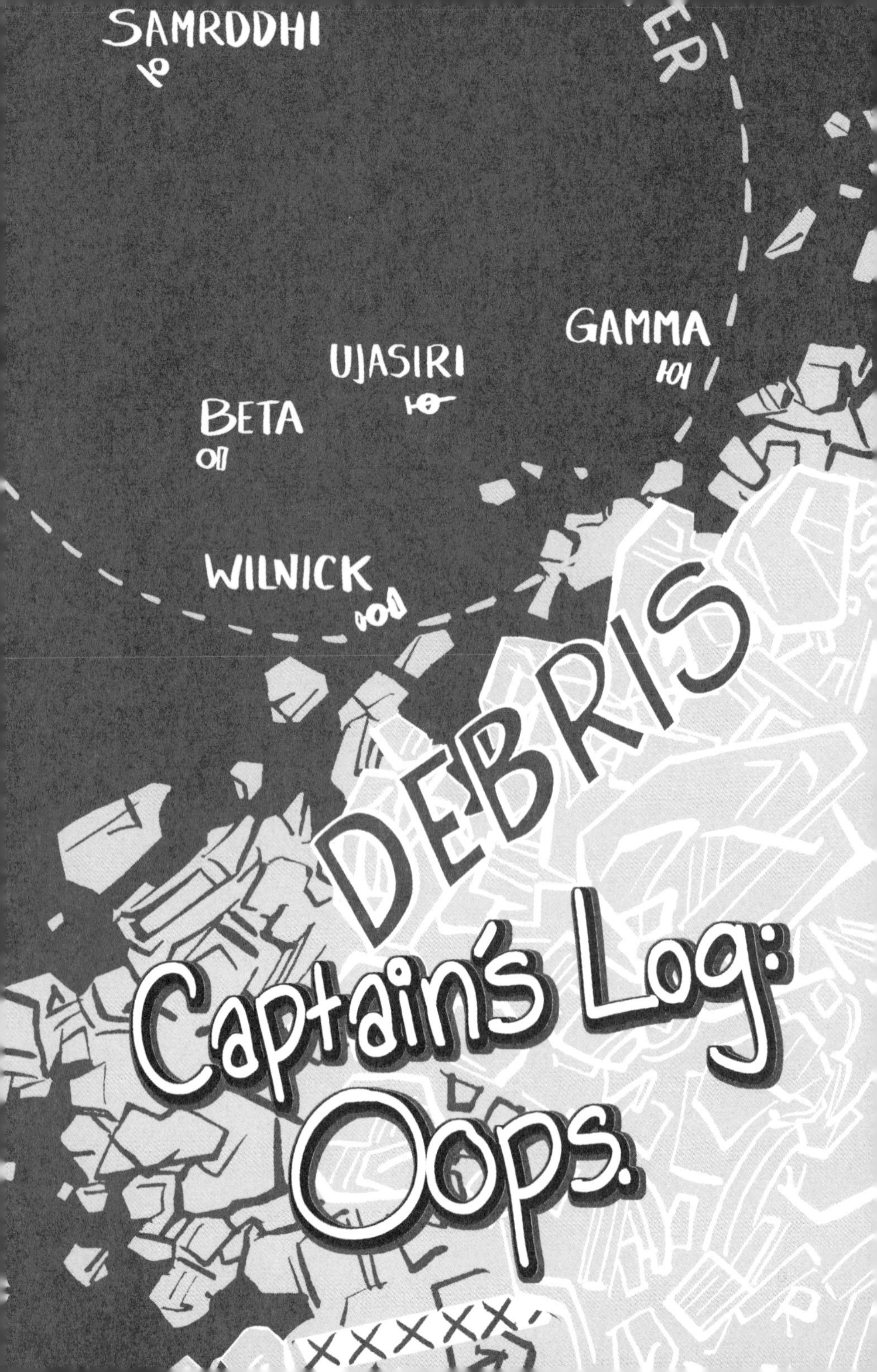
SAMRDDHI
GAMMA
UJASIRI
BETA
WILNICK
DEBRIS
Captain's Log:
Oops.

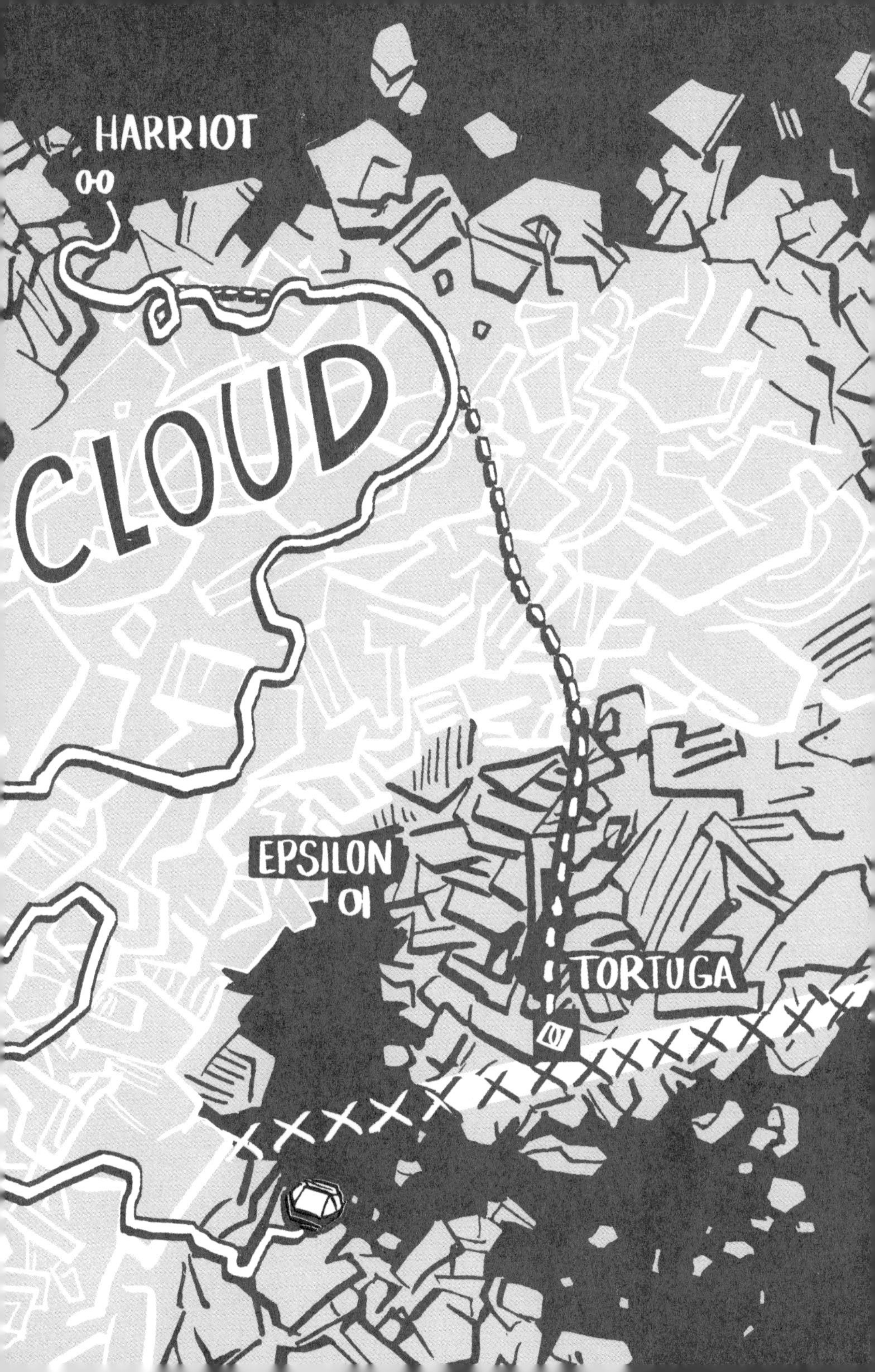
HARRIOT
00
CLOUD
EPSILON
01
TORTUGA
01

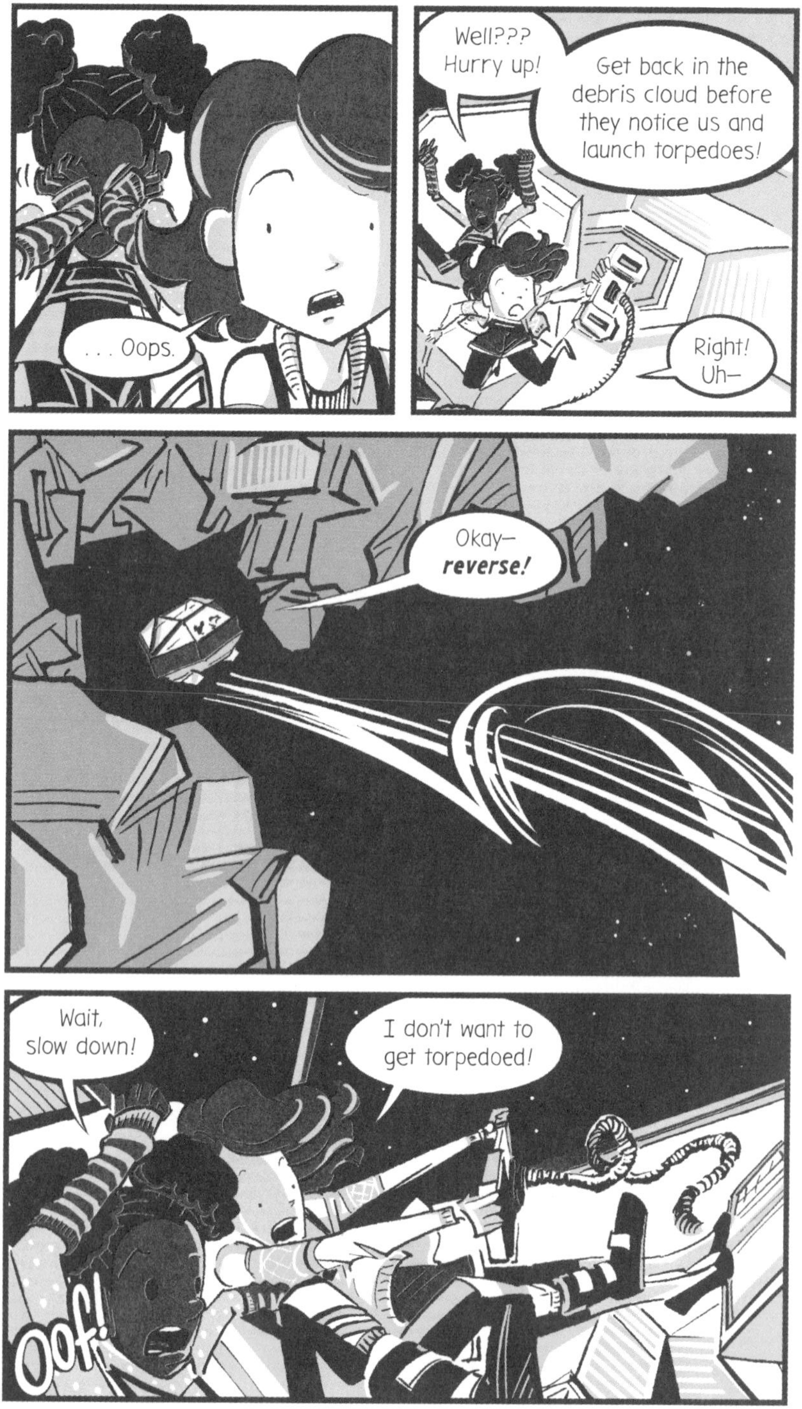
. . . Oops.
Well??? Hurry up!
Get back in the debris cloud before they notice us and launch torpedoes!
Right! Uh—
Okay— **reverse!**
Wait, slow down!
I don't want to get torpedoed!
OOF!

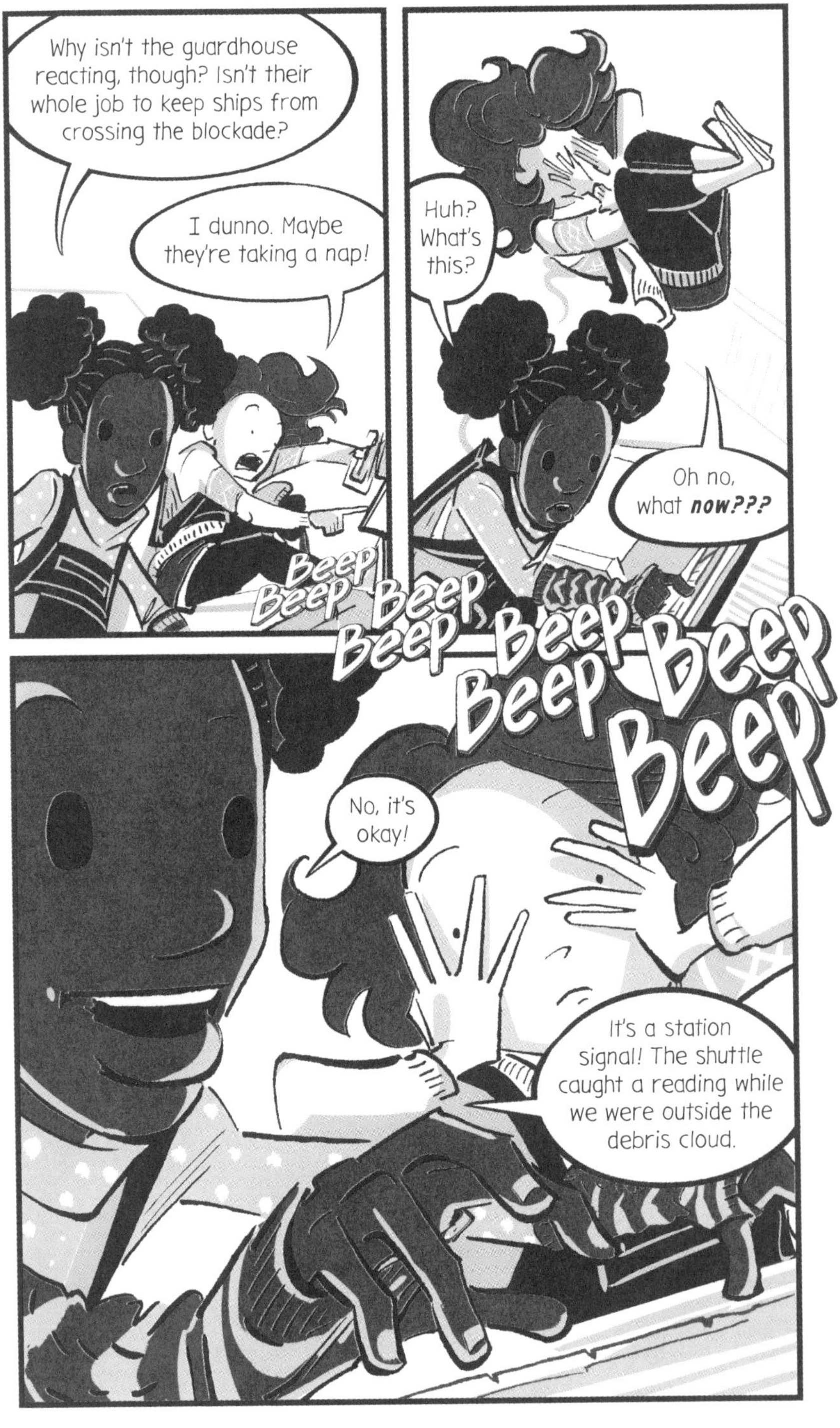

Why isn't the guardhouse reacting, though? Isn't their whole job to keep ships from crossing the blockade?
I dunno. Maybe they're taking a nap!
Beep Beep
Huh? What's this?
Oh no, what **now???**
Beep Beep Beep Beep Beep Beep Beep
No, it's okay!
It's a station signal! The shuttle caught a reading while we were outside the debris cloud.

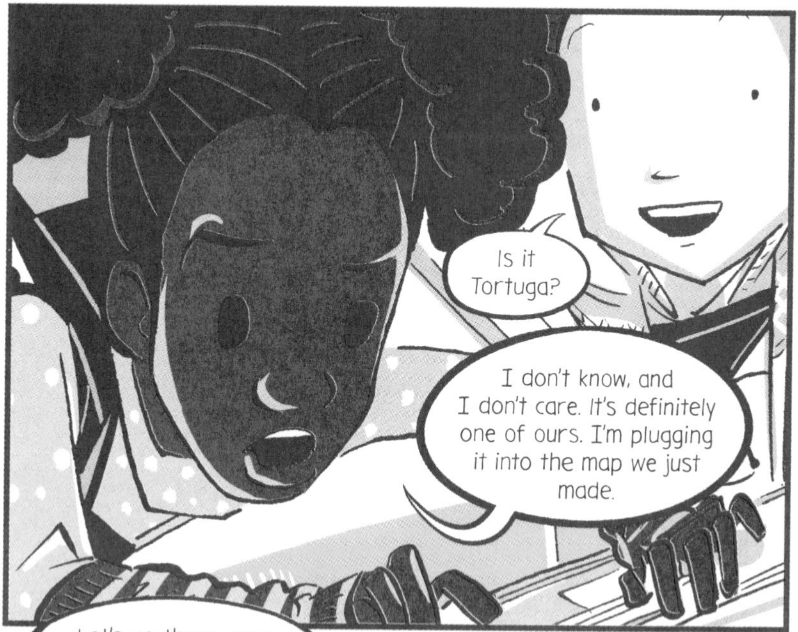
Is it Tortuga?
I don't know, and I don't care. It's definitely one of ours. I'm plugging it into the map we just made.

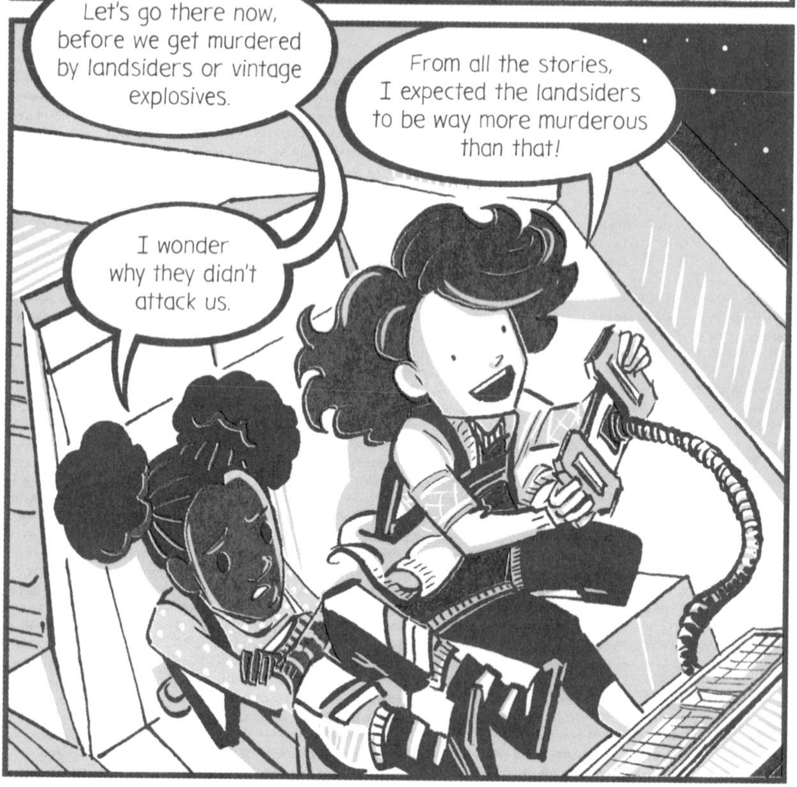
Let's go there now, before we get murdered by landsiders or vintage explosives.
From all the stories, I expected the landsiders to be way more murderous than that!
I wonder why they didn't attack us.

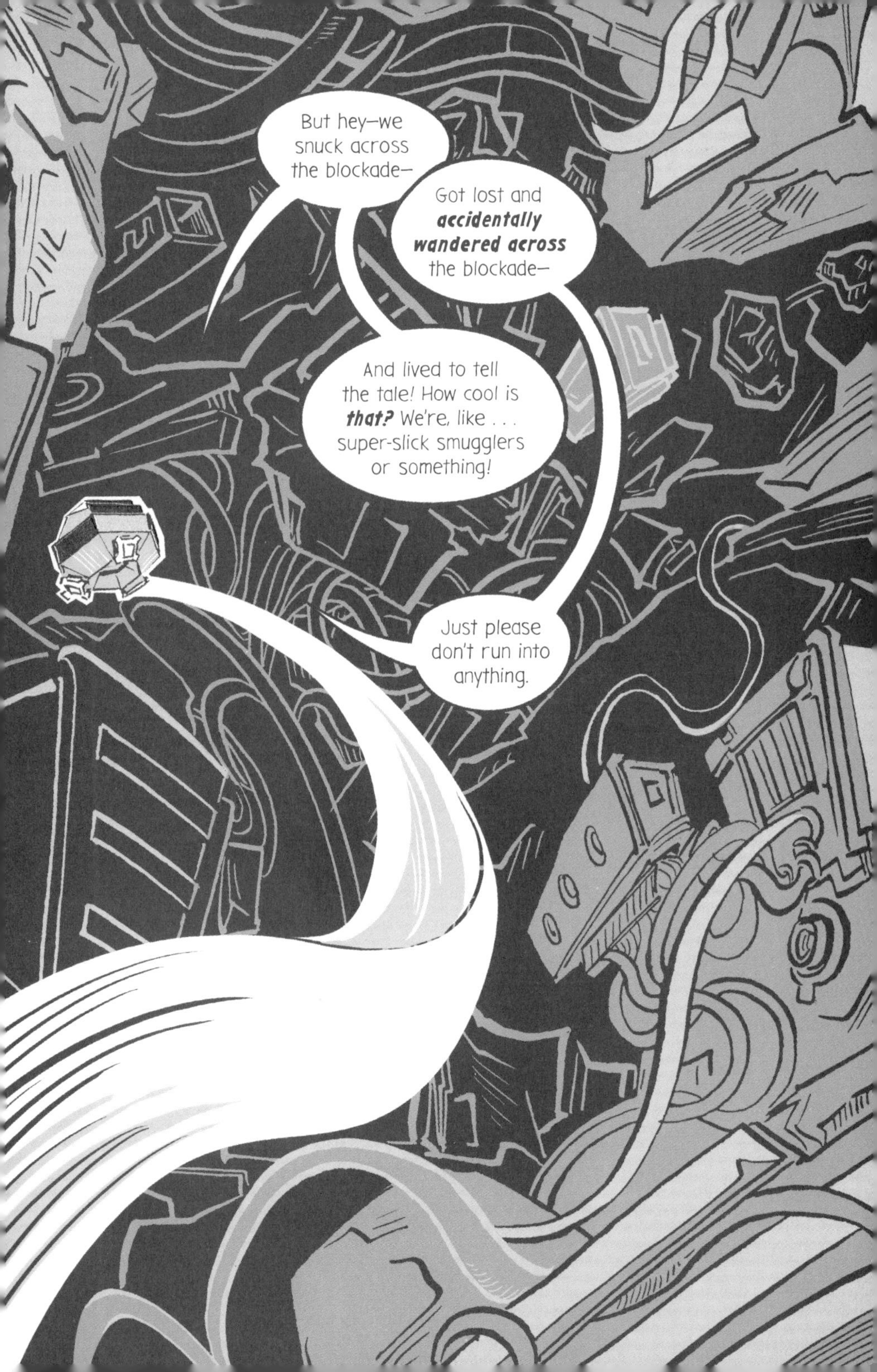

But hey—we snuck across the blockade—
Got lost and ***accidentally wandered across*** the blockade—
And lived to tell the tale! How cool is ***that?*** We're, like . . . super-slick smugglers or something!
Just please don't run into anything.

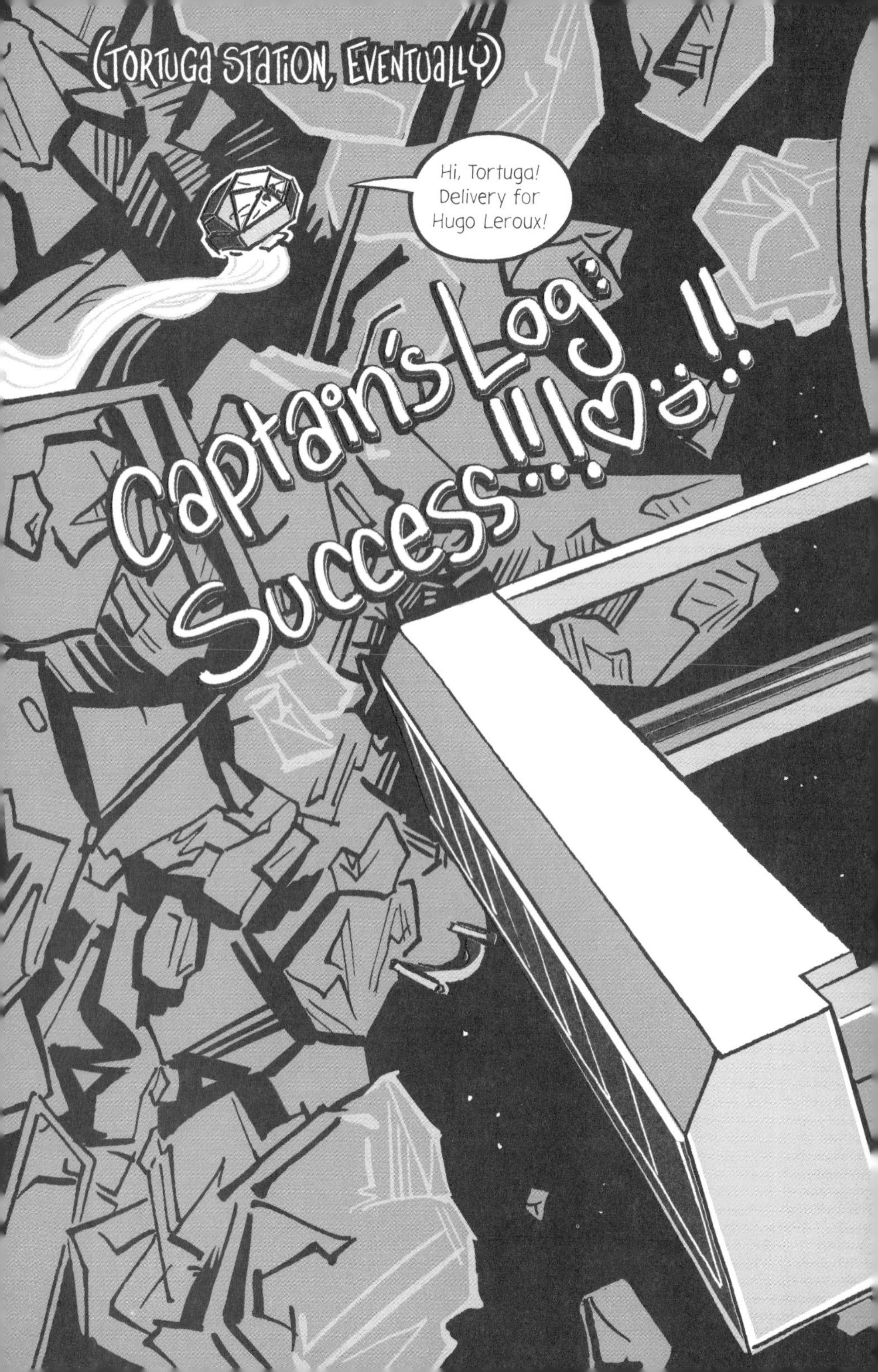
(Tortuga Station, Eventually)
Hi, Tortuga! Delivery for Hugo Leroux!
Captain's Log: Success!!!♥ :D !!

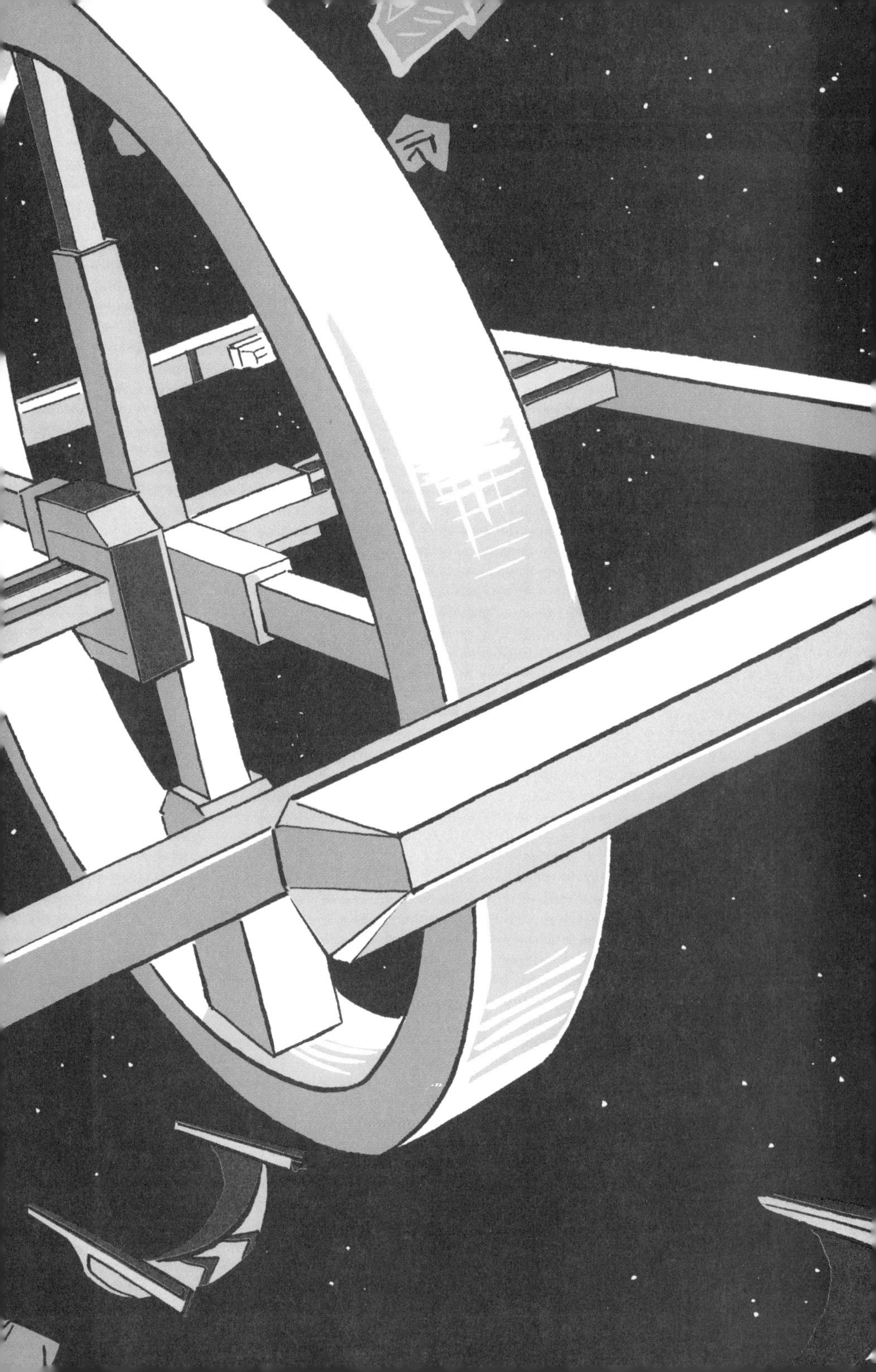

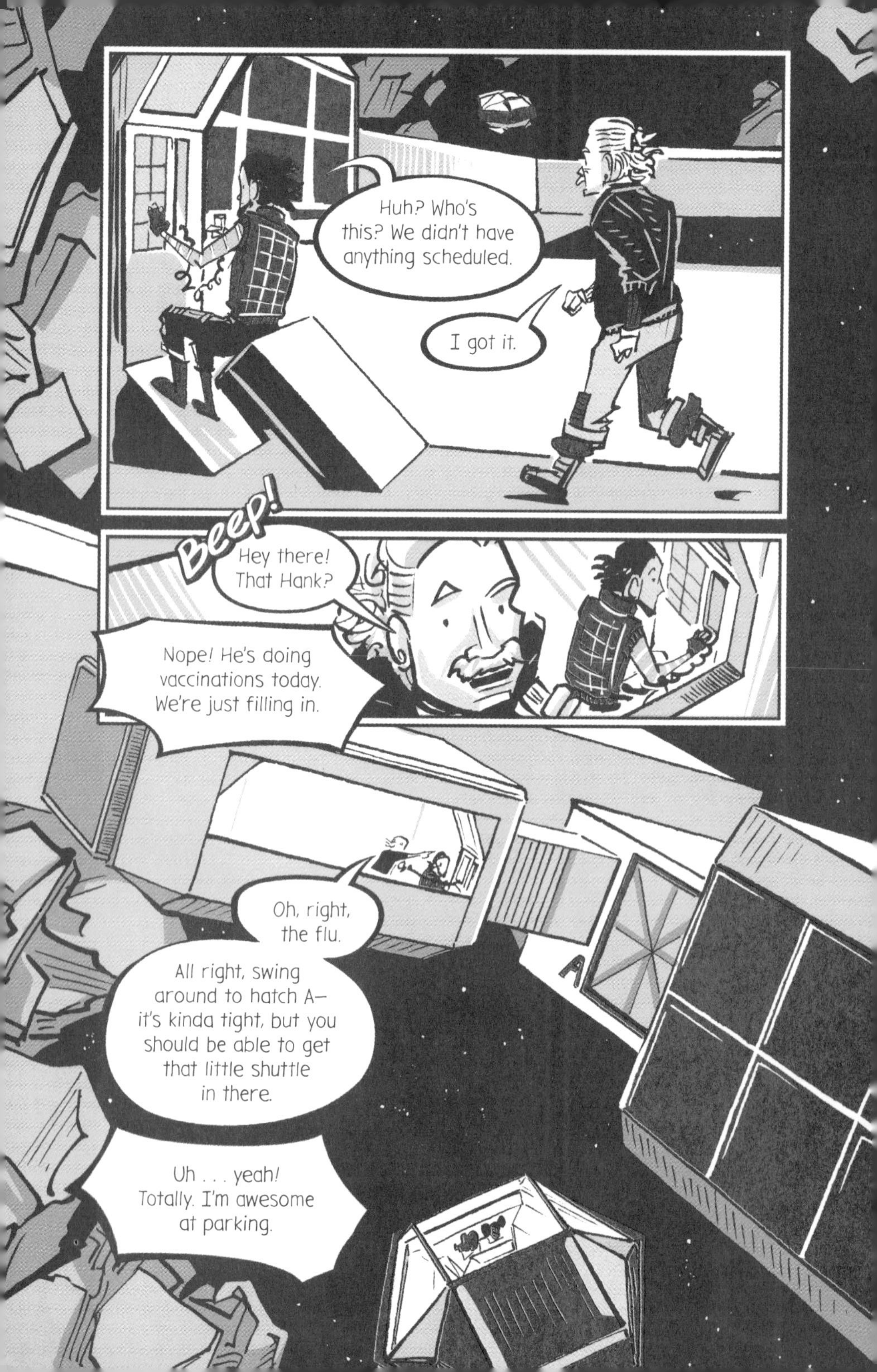
Huh? Who's this? We didn't have anything scheduled.
I got it.
Beep!
Hey there! That Hank?
Nope! He's doing vaccinations today. We're just filling in.
Oh, right, the flu.
All right, swing around to hatch A— it's kinda tight, but you should be able to get that little shuttle in there.
A
Uh . . . yeah! Totally. I'm awesome at parking.

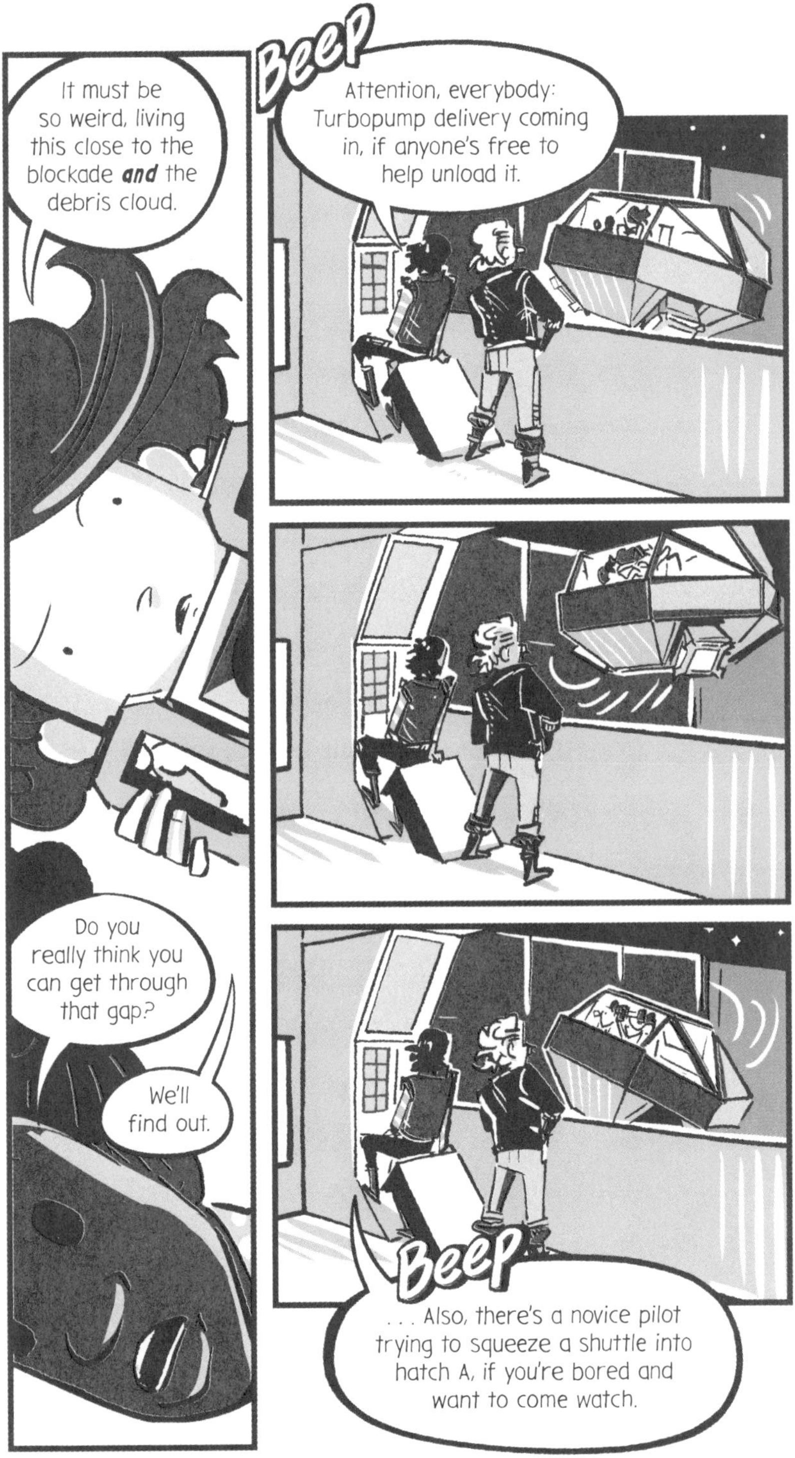

It must be so weird, living this close to the blockade **and** the debris cloud.
Beep
Attention, everybody: Turbopump delivery coming in, if anyone's free to help unload it.
Do you really think you can get through that gap?
We'll find out.
Beep
. . . Also, there's a novice pilot trying to squeeze a shuttle into hatch A, if you're bored and want to come watch.

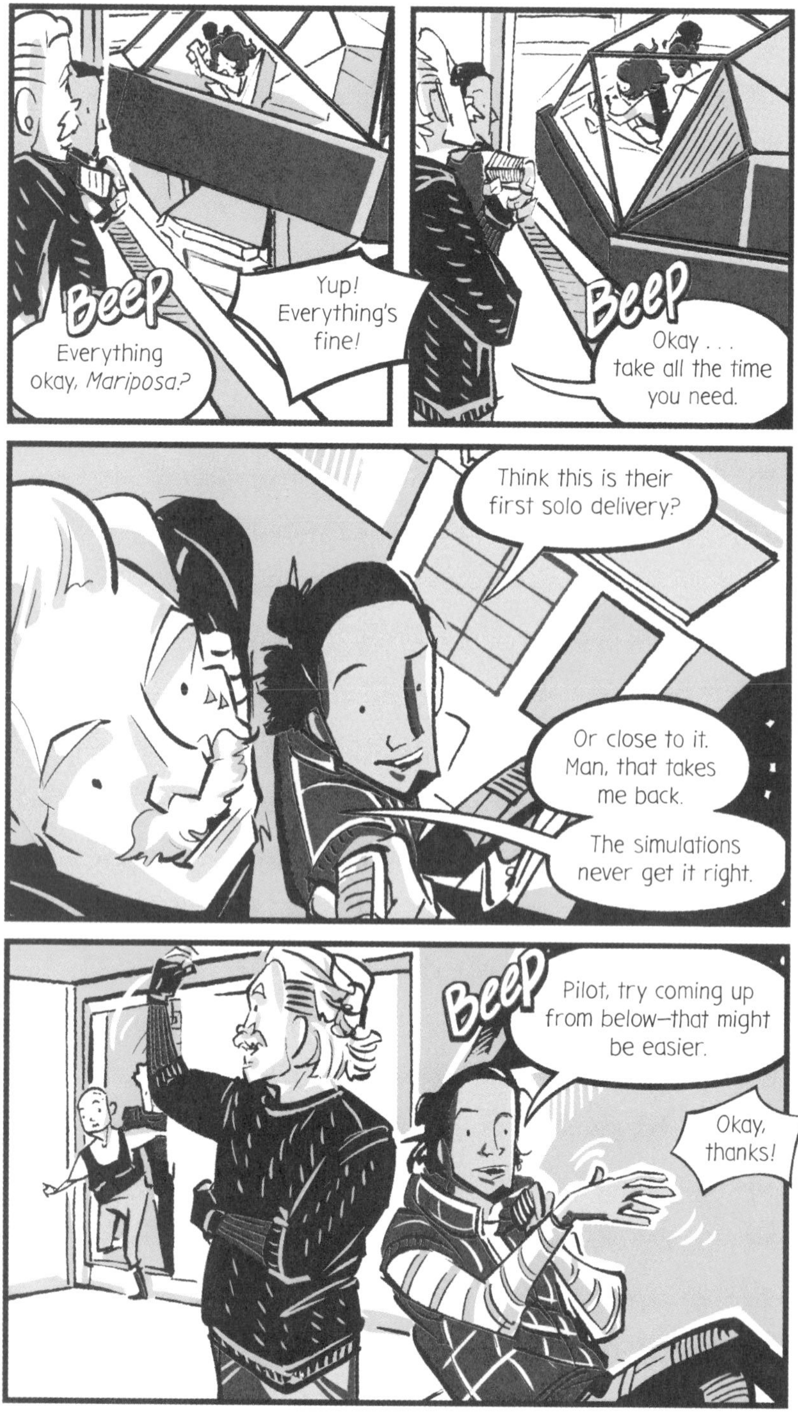
Beep
Everything okay, *Mariposa?*
Yup! Everything's fine!
Beep
Okay . . . take all the time you need.
Think this is their first solo delivery?
Or close to it. Man, that takes me back.
The simulations never get it right.
Beep
Pilot, try coming up from below—that might be easier.
Okay, thanks!

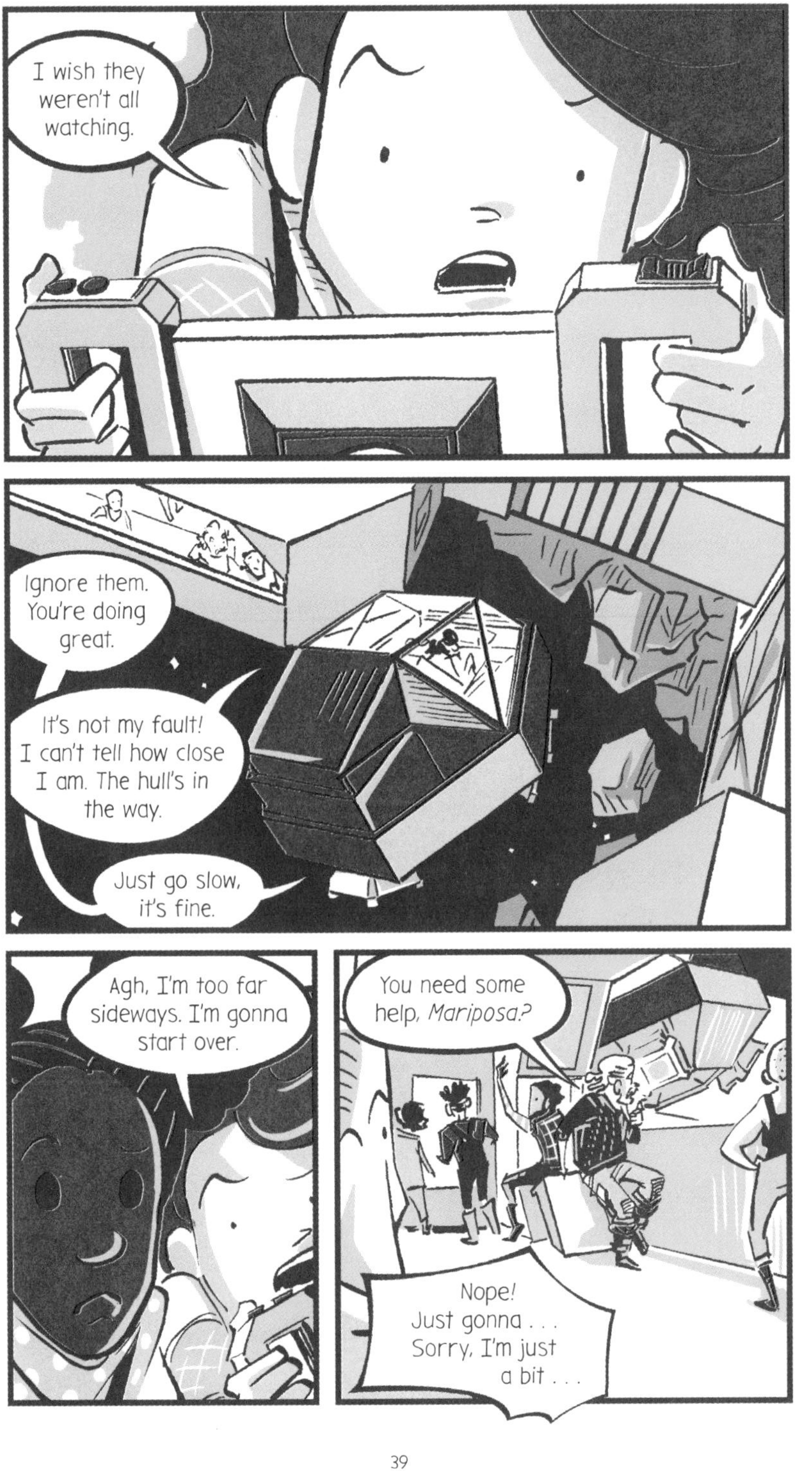
I wish they weren't all watching.
Ignore them. You're doing great.
It's not my fault! I can't tell how close I am. The hull's in the way.
Just go slow, it's fine.
Agh, I'm too far sideways. I'm gonna start over.
You need some help, *Mariposa?*
Nope! Just gonna . . . Sorry, I'm just a bit . . .

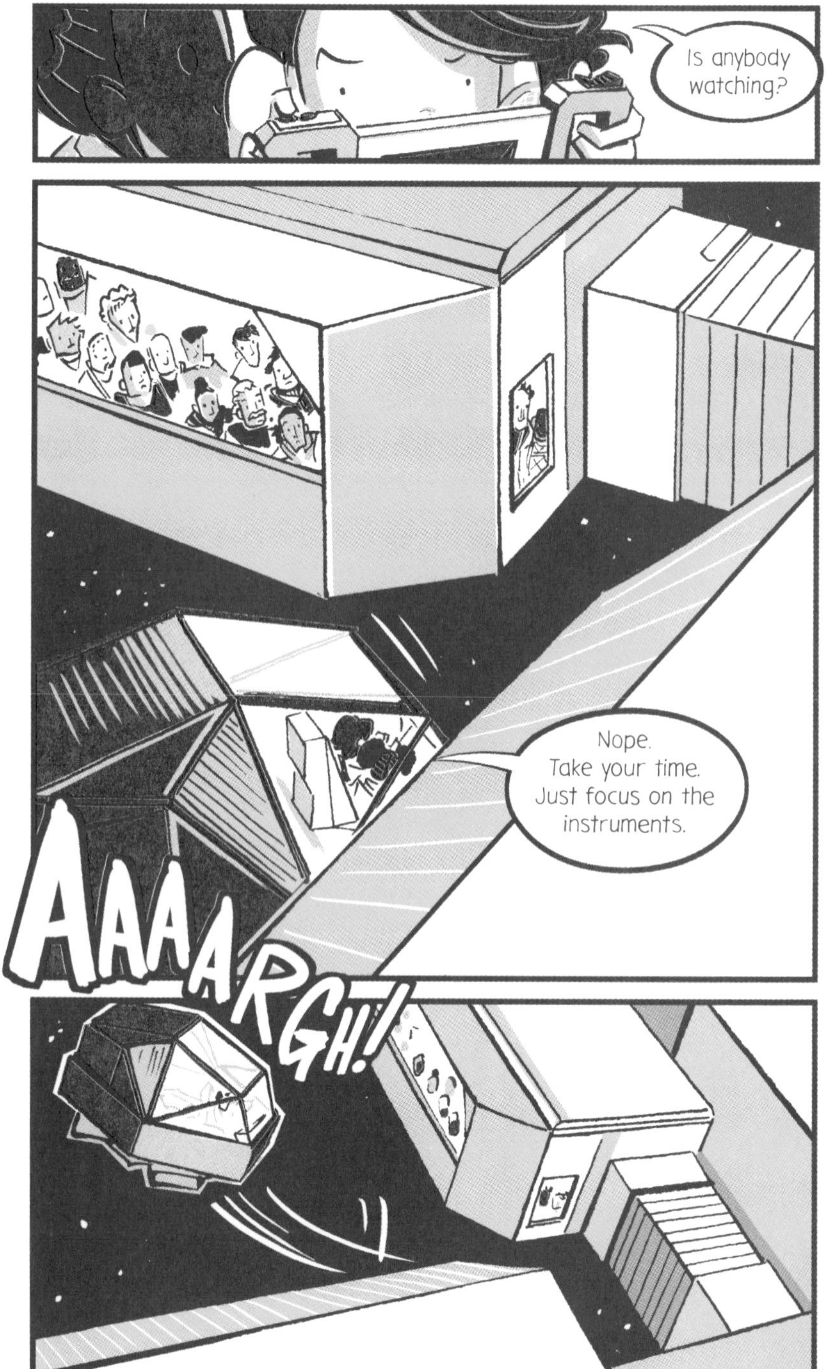
Is anybody watching?
Nope. Take your time. Just focus on the instruments.
AAAARGH!

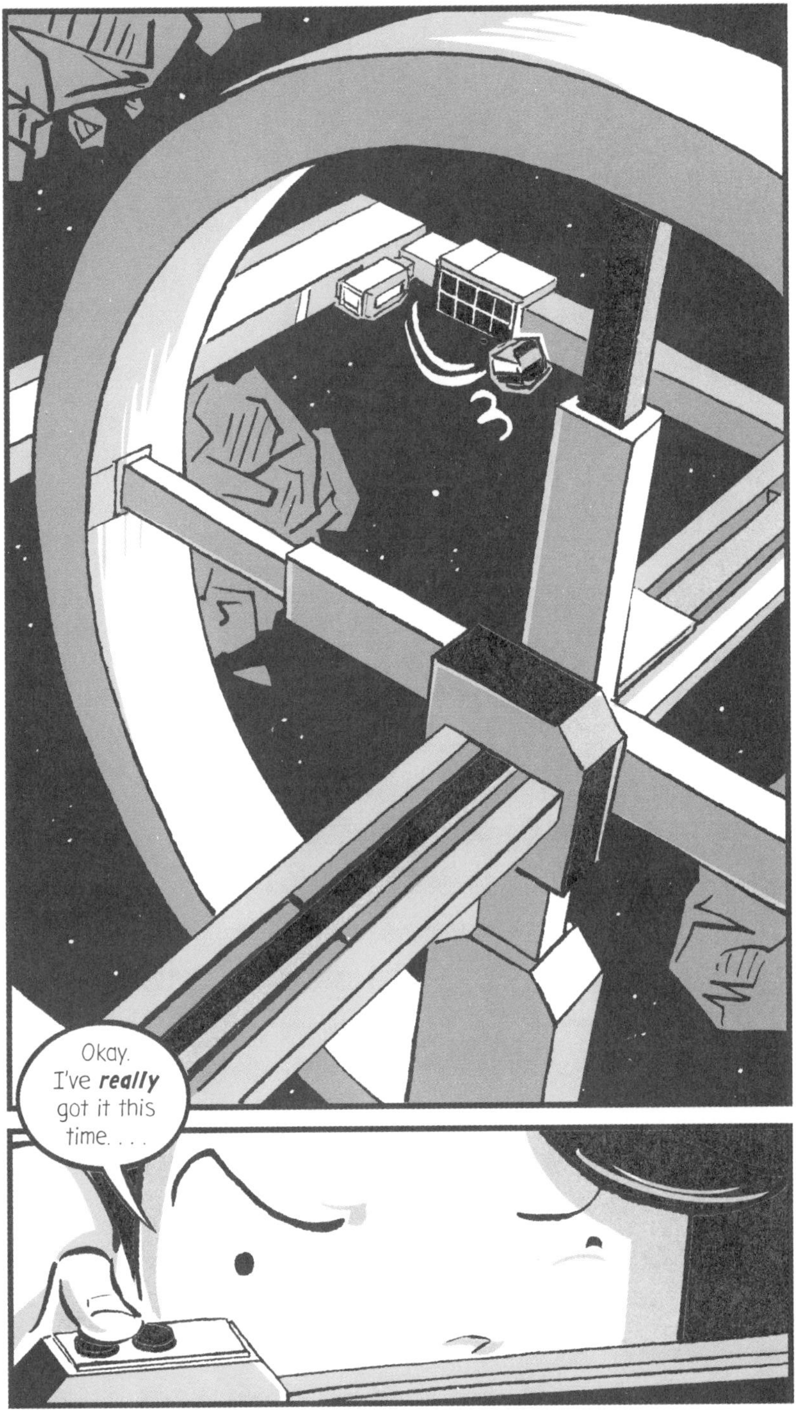
Okay. I've ***really*** got it this time. . . .

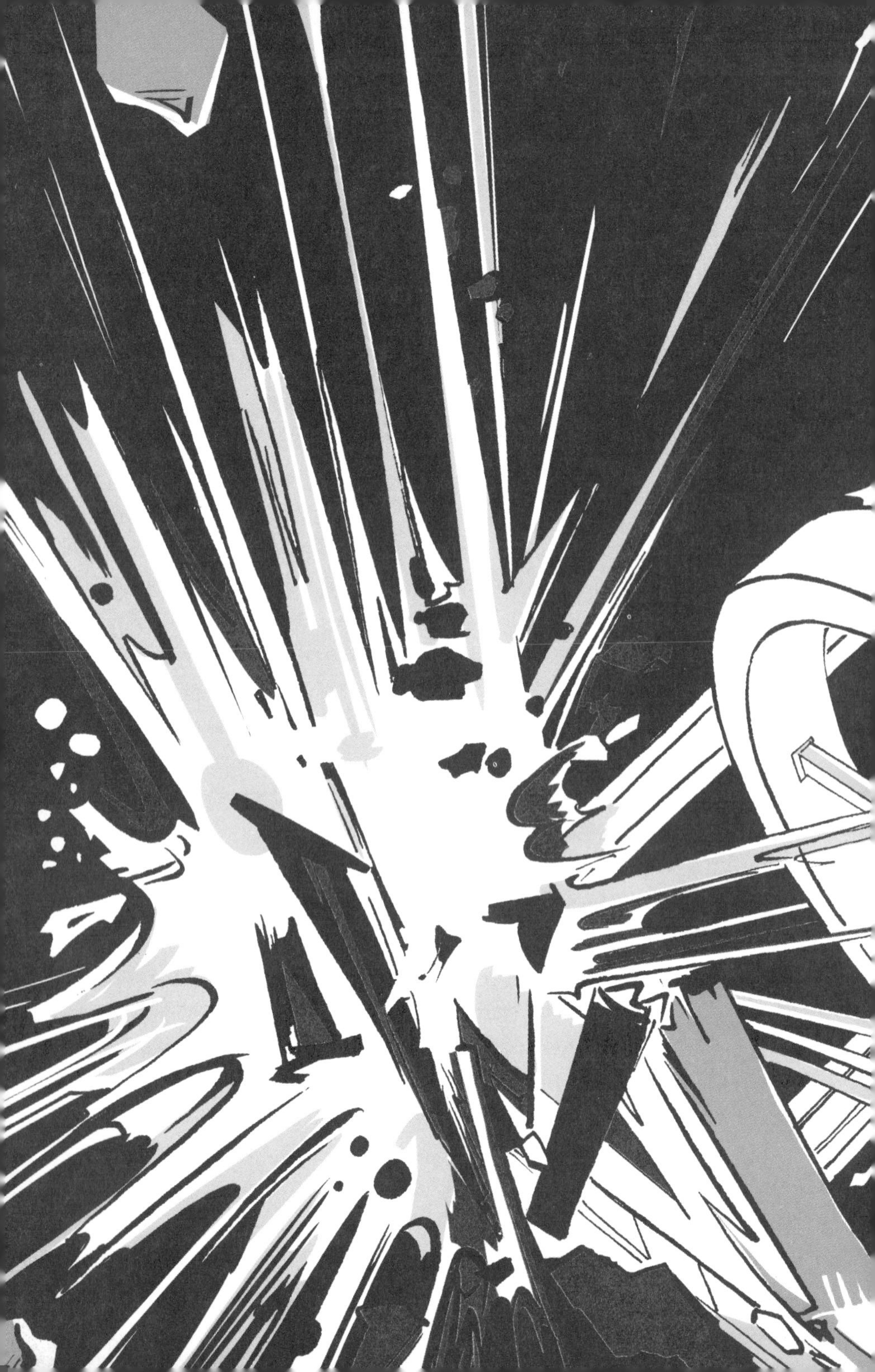

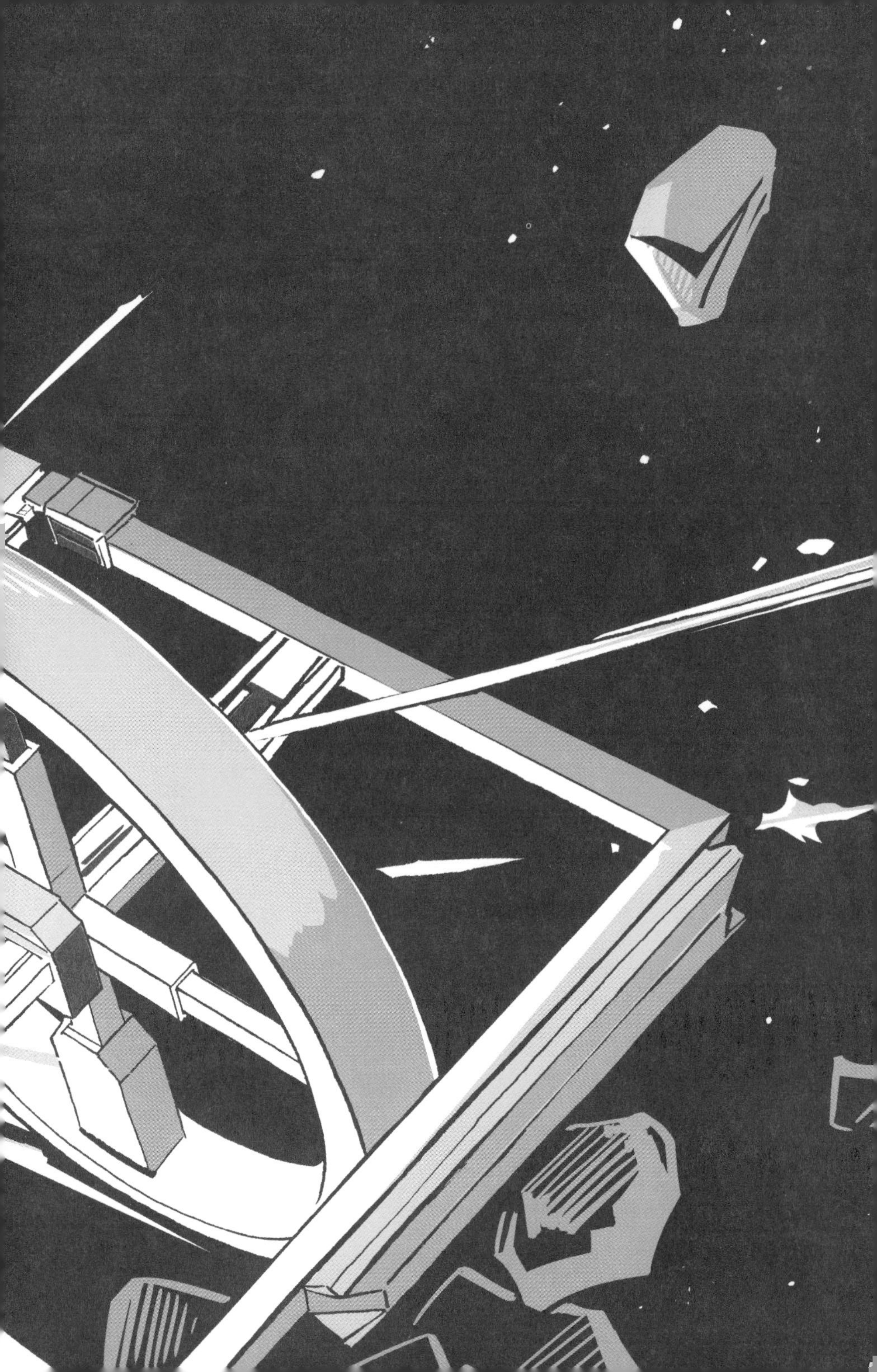

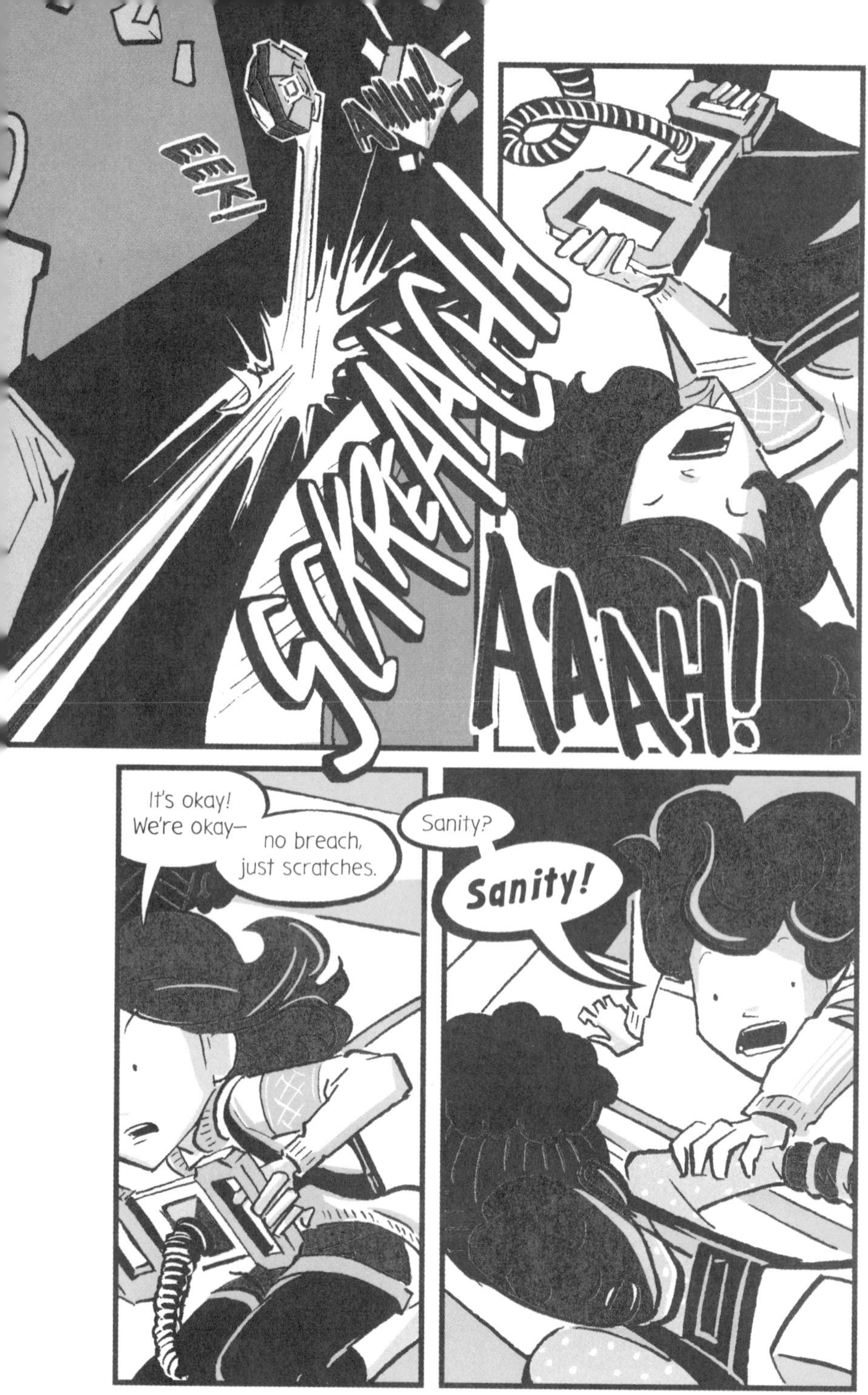
EEK!
AHHH!
SKREEACH!
AAAH!
It's okay! We're okay—
no breach, just scratches.
Sanity?
Sanity!

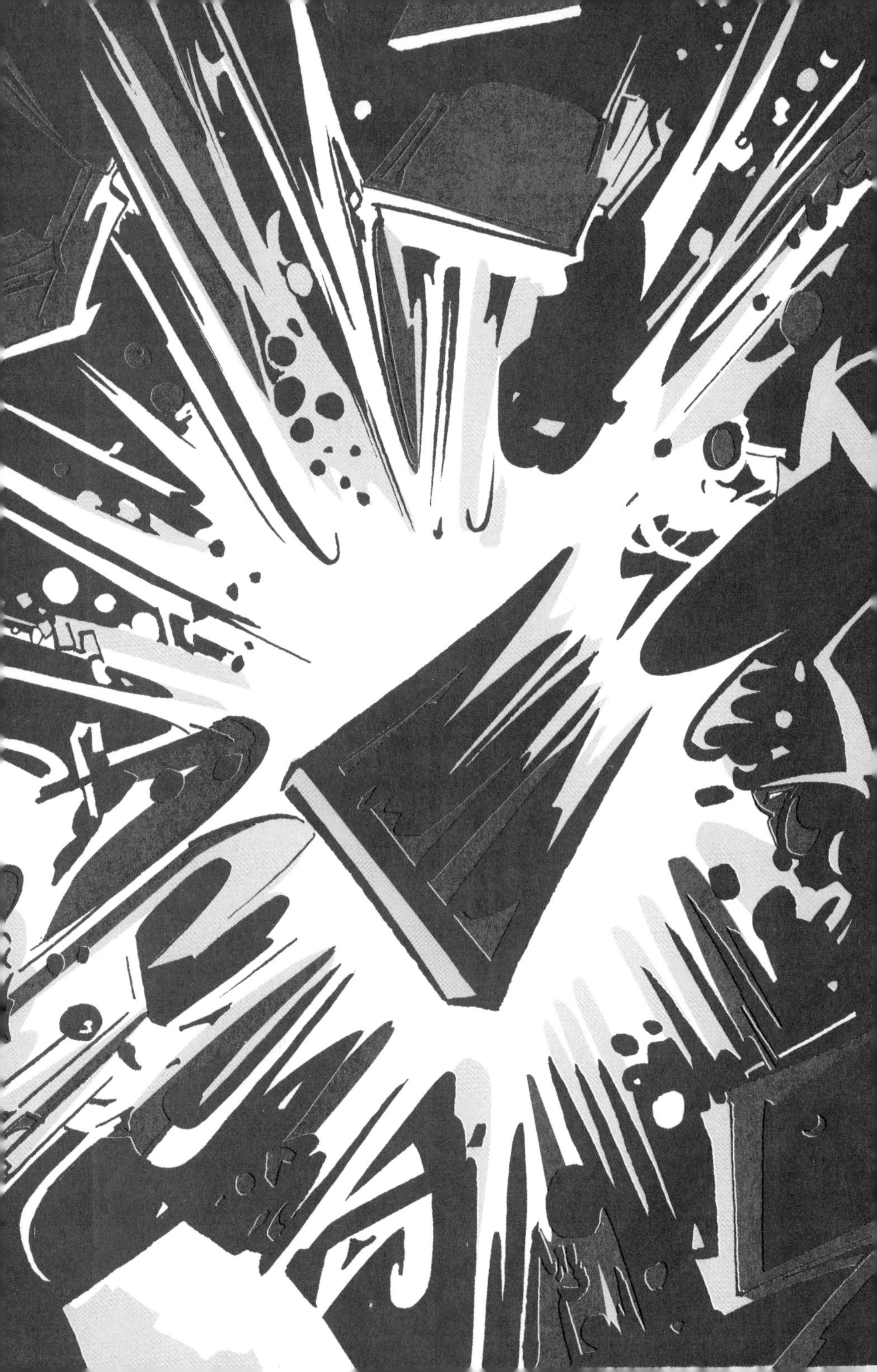

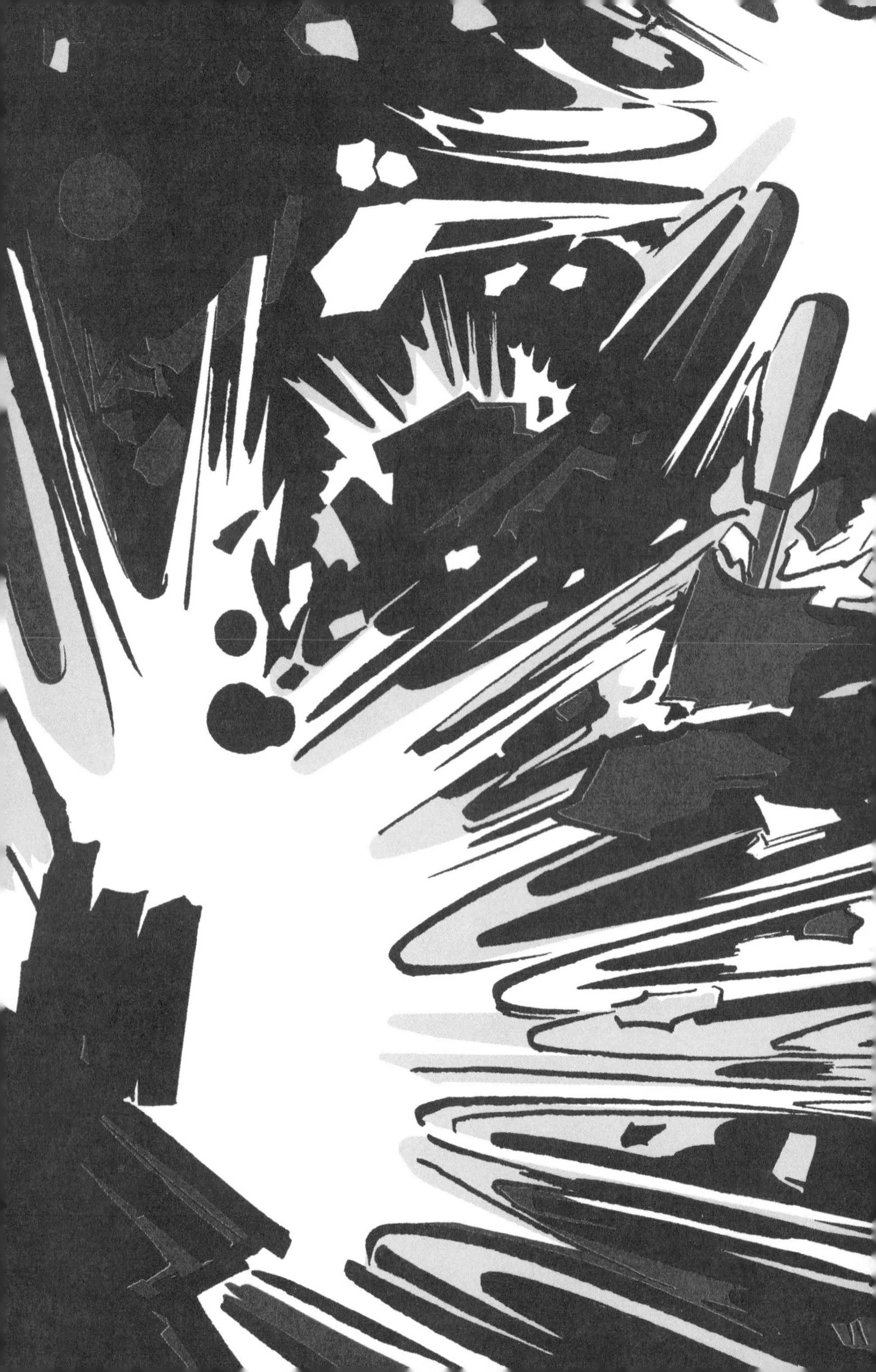

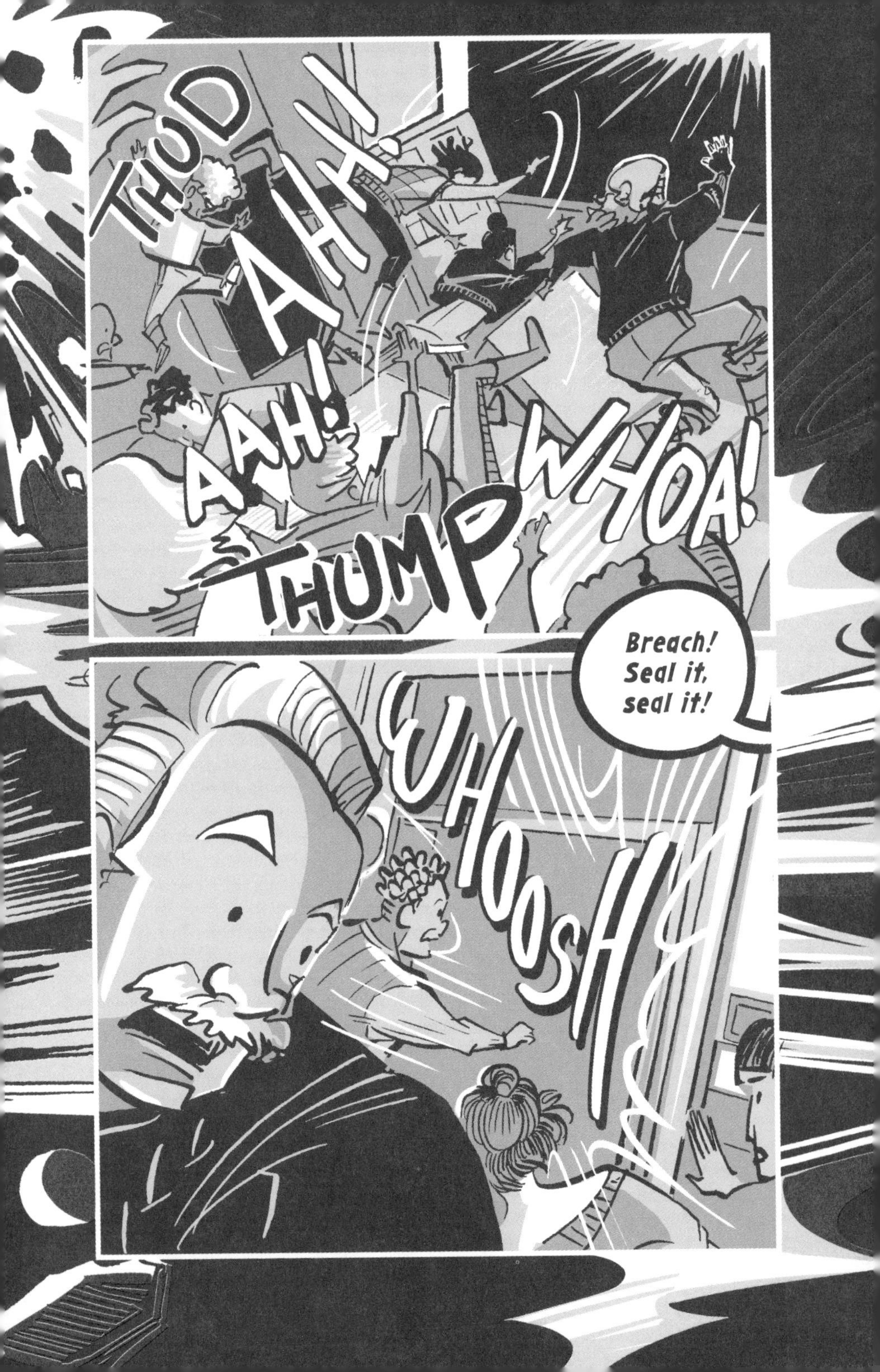
THUD
AAH!
AAH!
THUMP
WHOA!
Breach! Seal it, seal it!
WHOOOSH

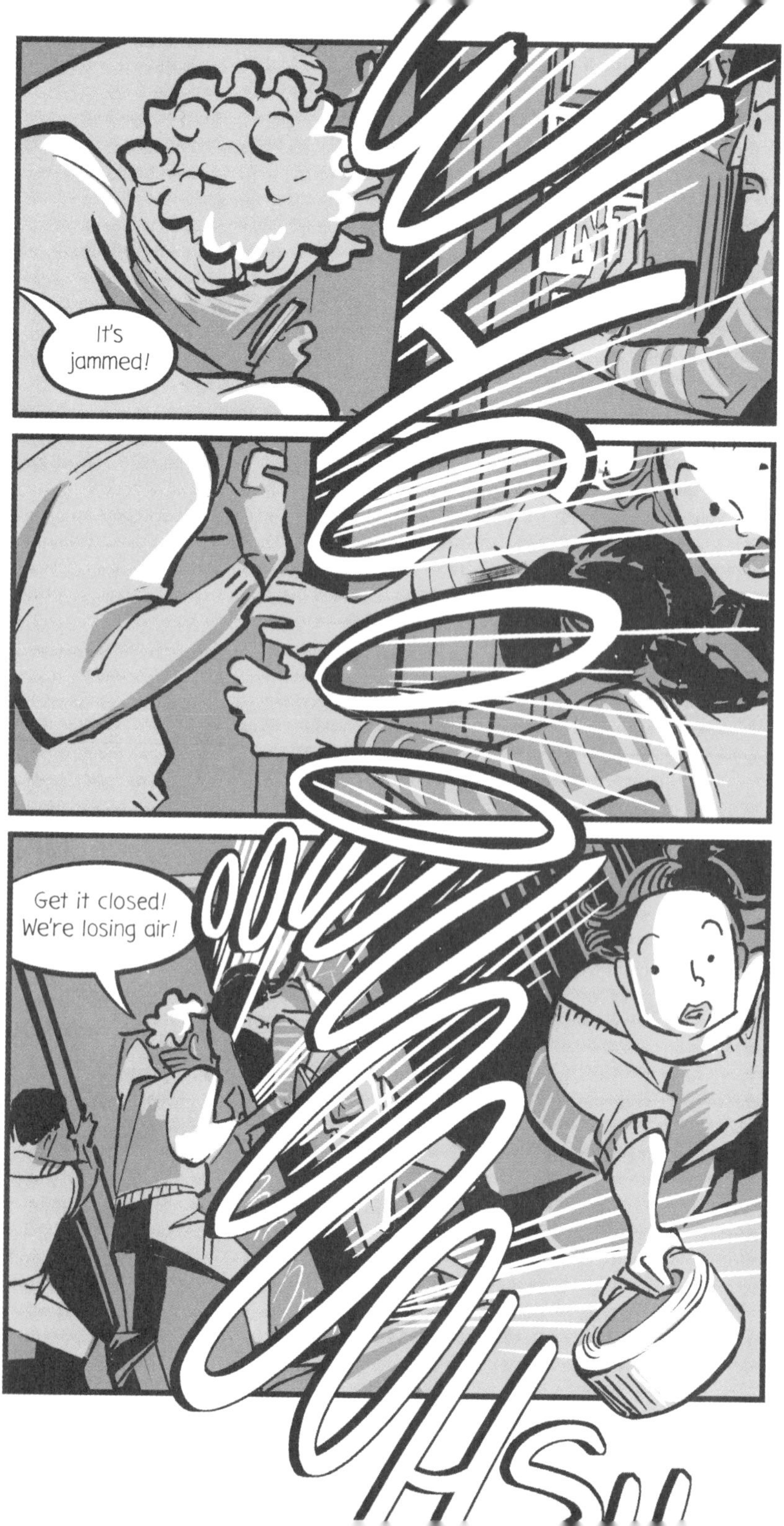
It's jammed!
Get it closed! We're losing air!

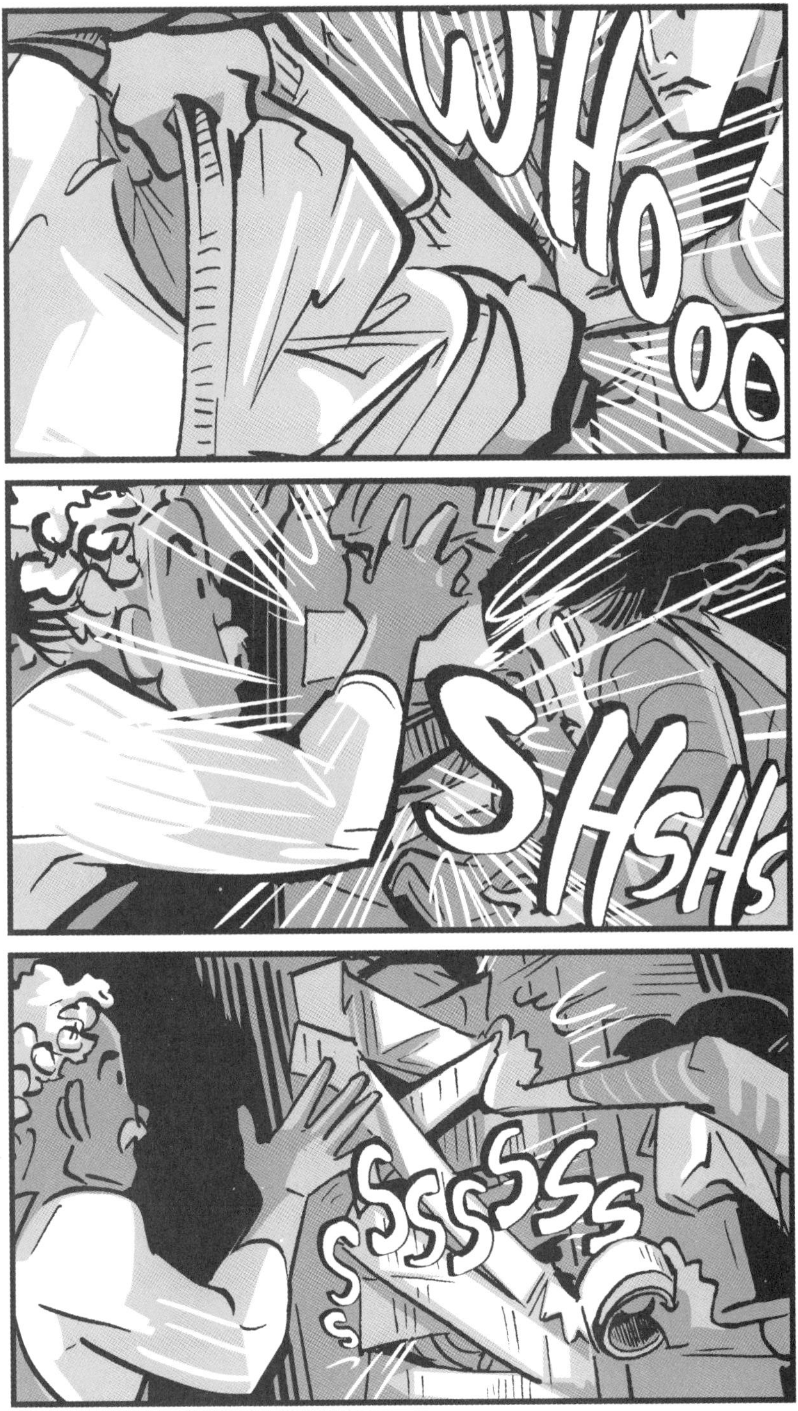
WHOOOO
SHSHS
SSSSSSSS

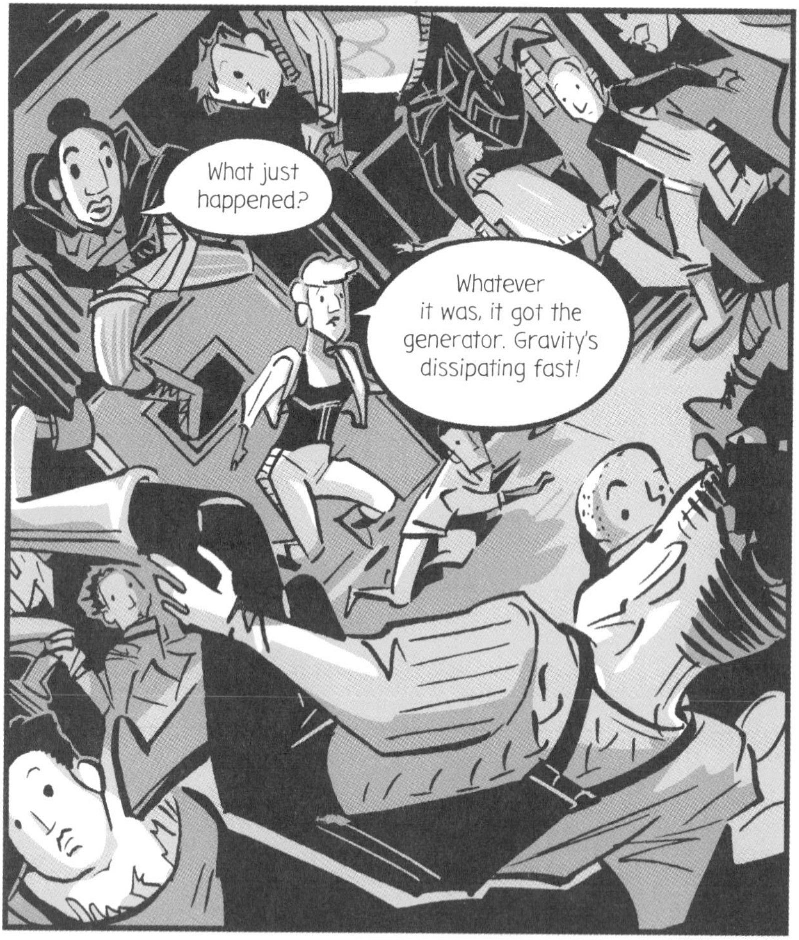
What just happened?
Whatever it was, it got the generator. Gravity's dissipating fast!

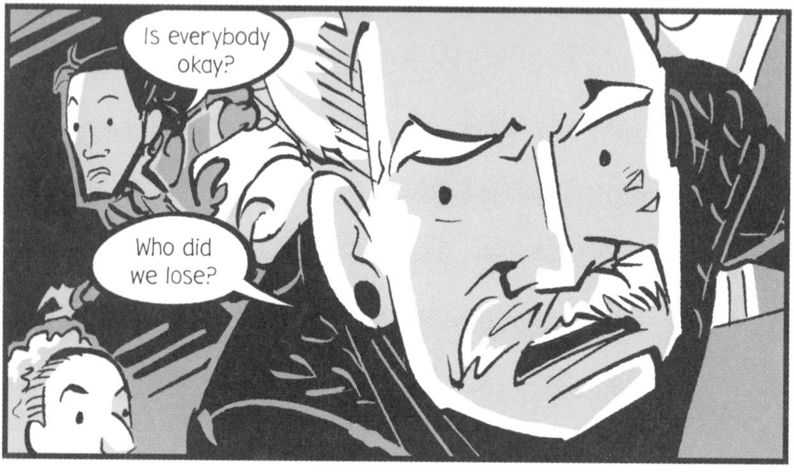
Is everybody okay?
Who did we lose?

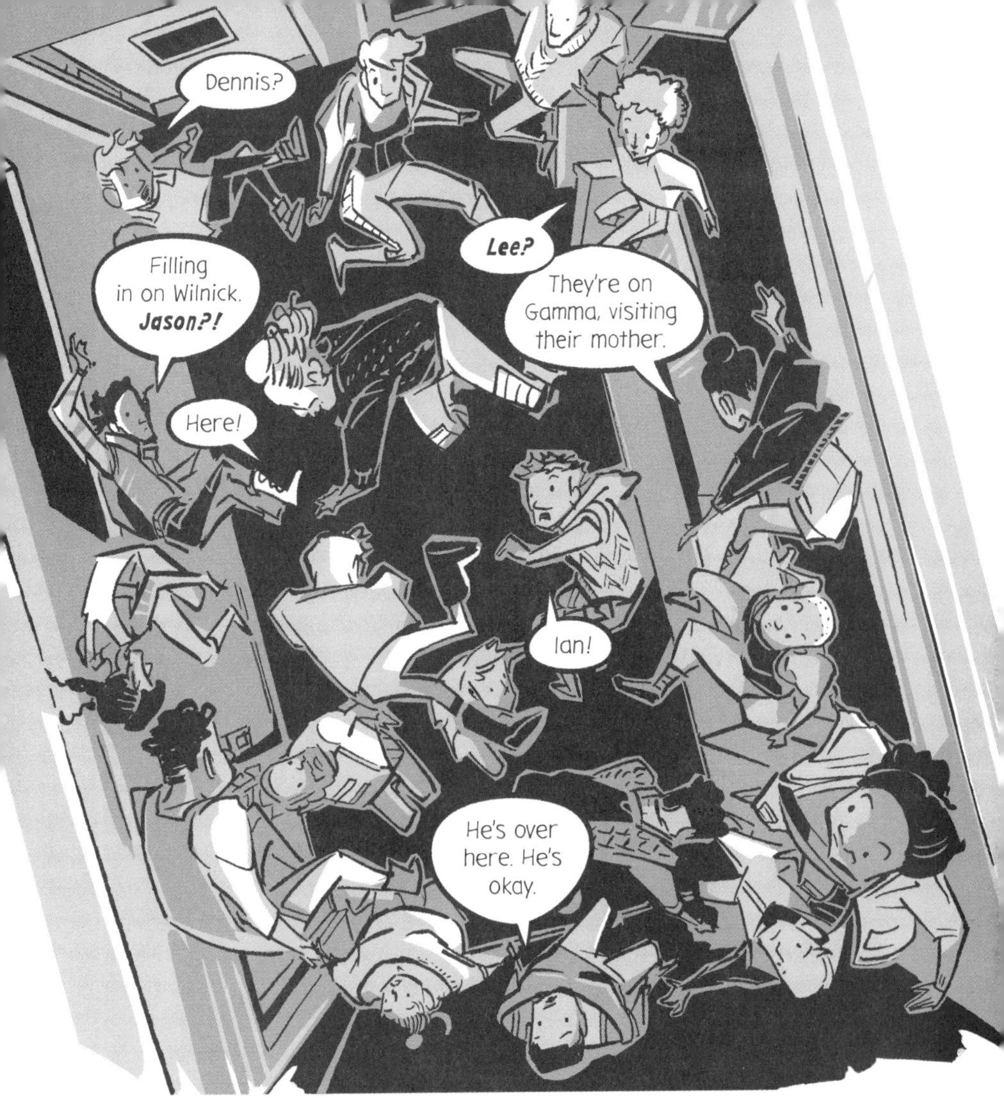
Dennis?
Lee?
Filling in on Wilnick. **Jason?!**
They're on Gamma, visiting their mother.
Here!
Ian!
He's over here. He's okay.

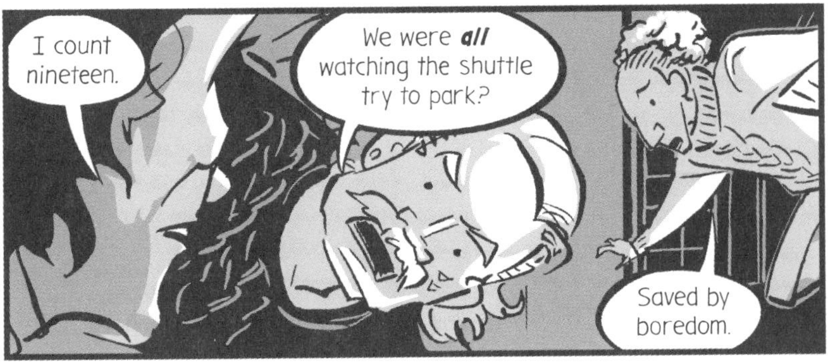
I count nineteen.
We were ***all*** watching the shuttle try to park?
Saved by boredom.

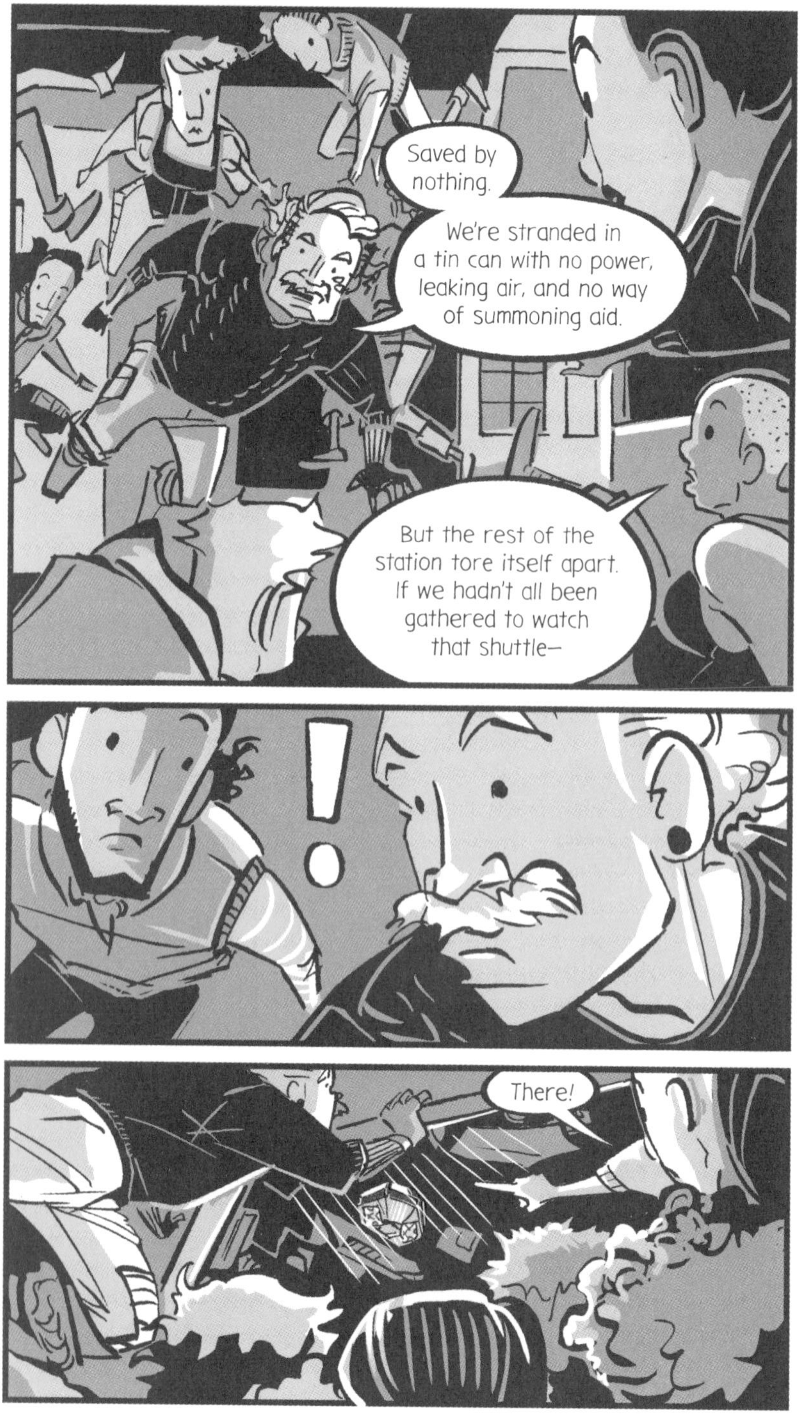
Saved by nothing.
We're stranded in a tin can with no power, leaking air, and no way of summoning aid.
But the rest of the station tore itself apart. If we hadn't all been gathered to watch that shuttle—
!
There!

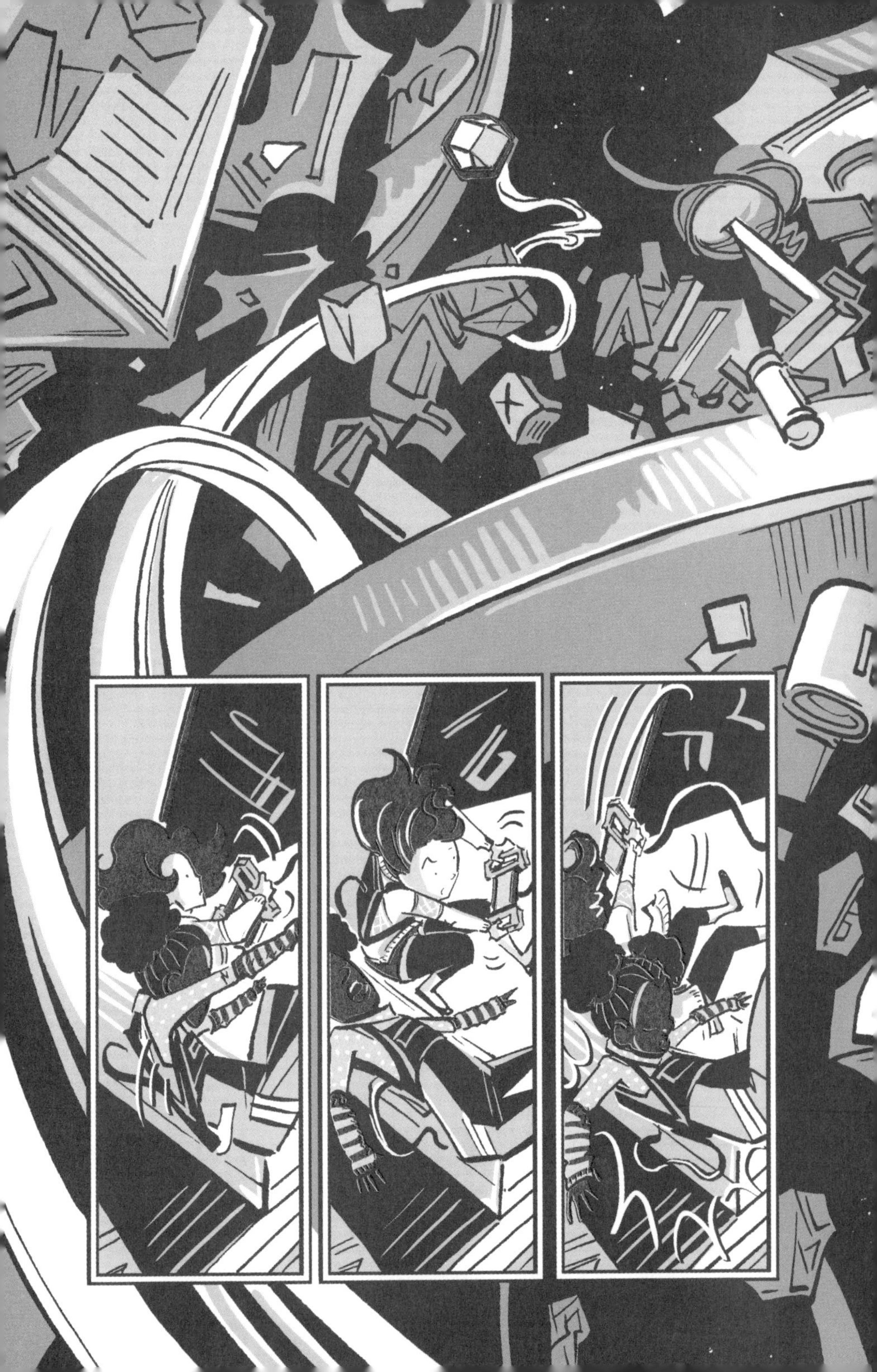

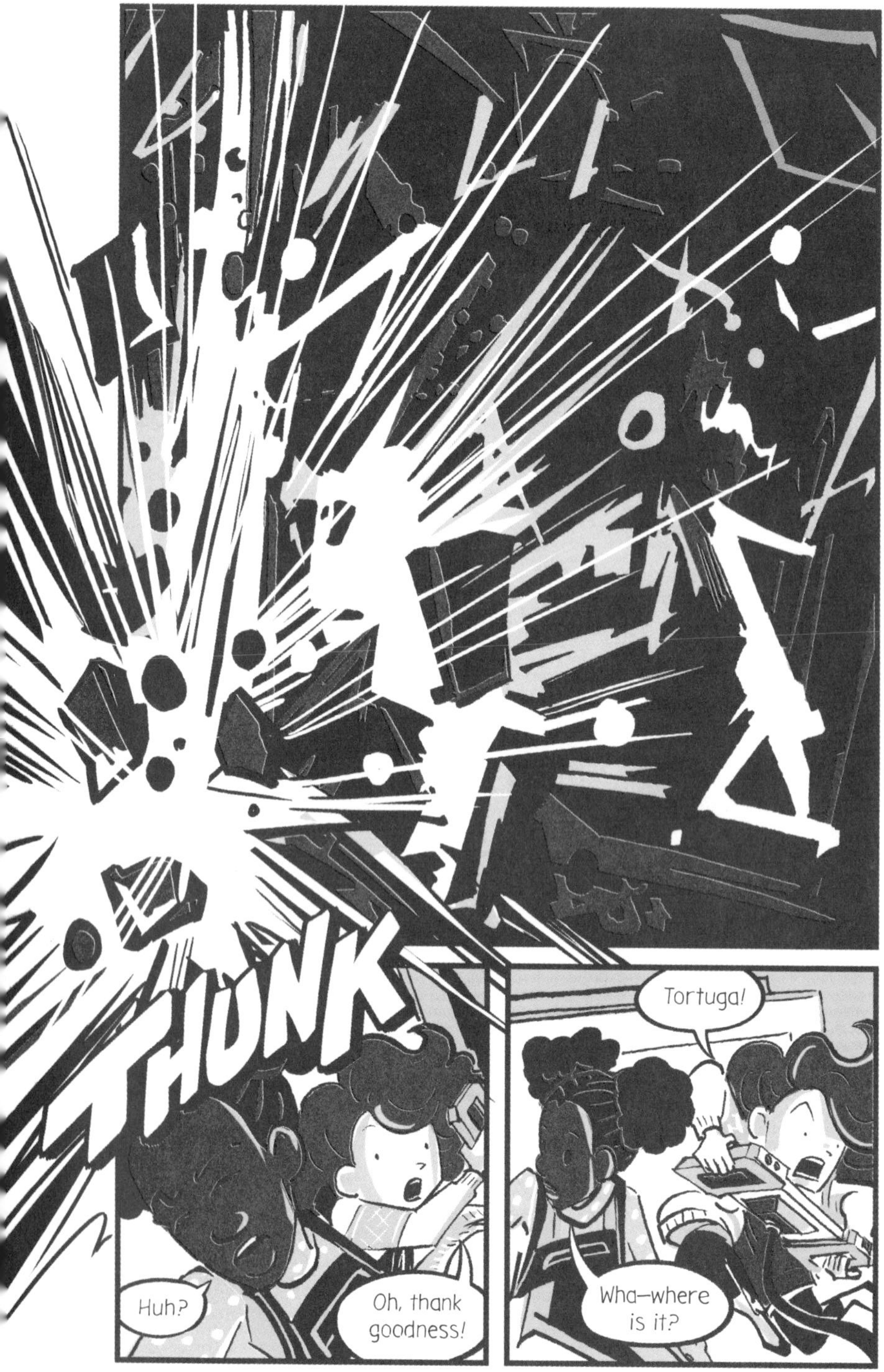
THUNK
Huh?
Oh, thank goodness!
Tortuga!
Wha—where is it?

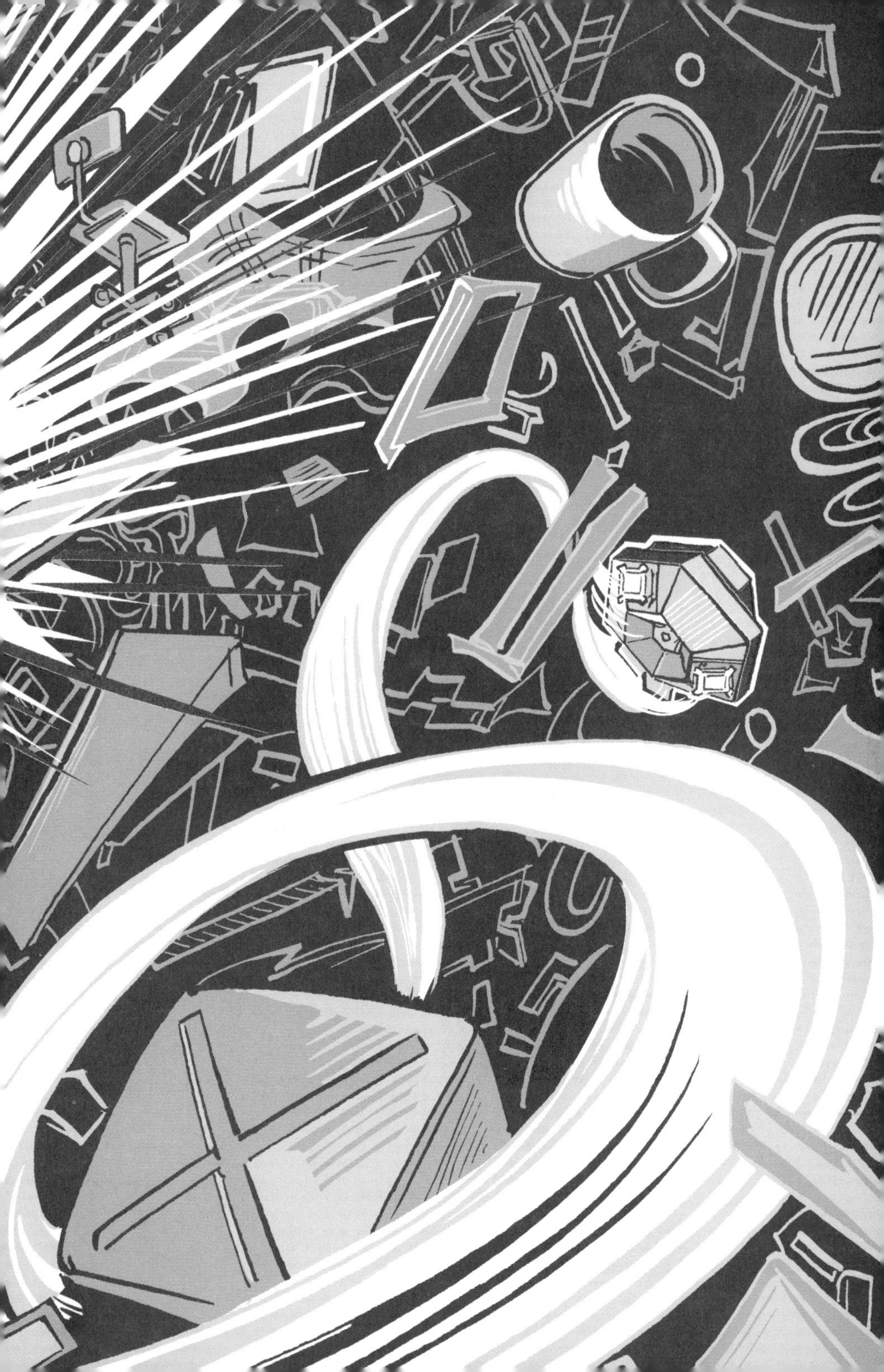

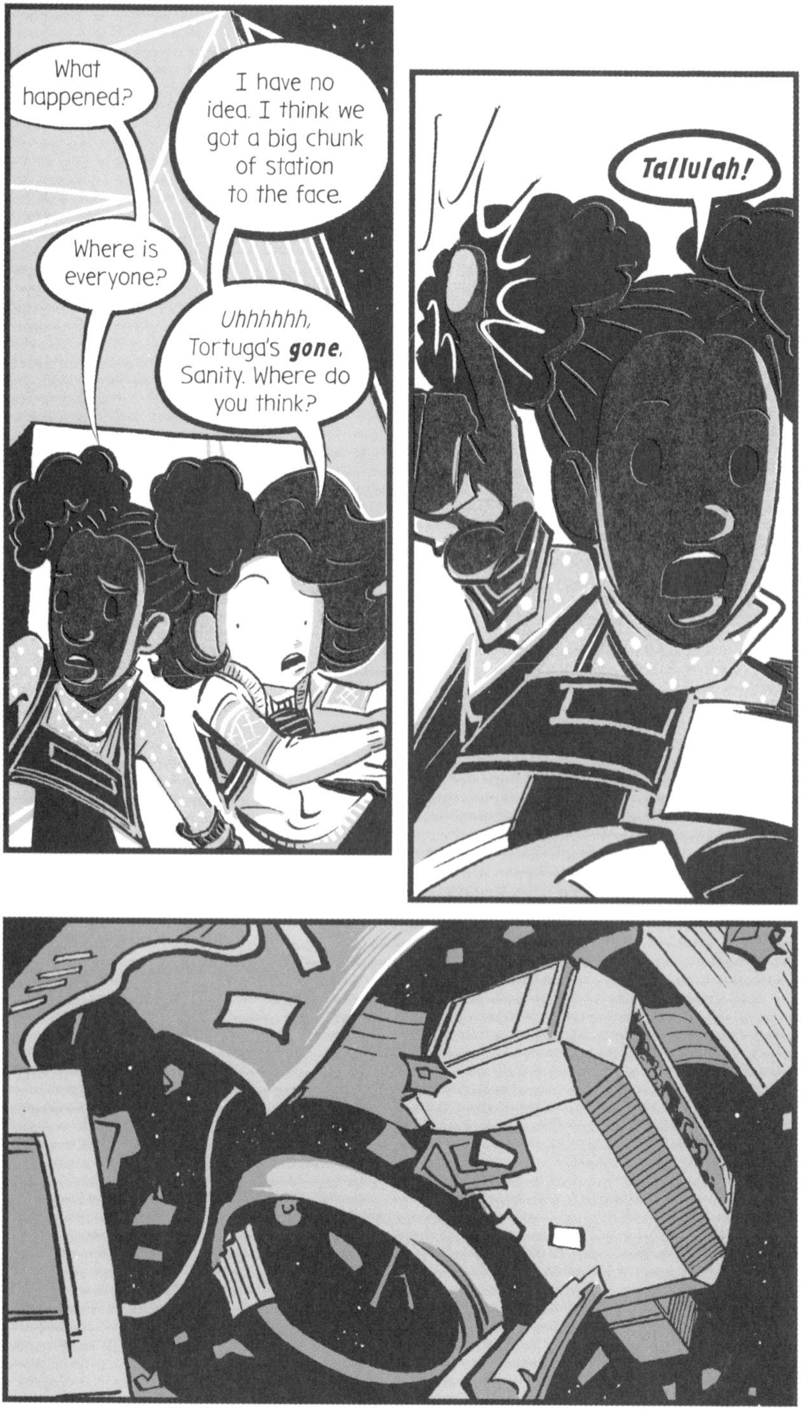
What happened?
I have no idea. I think we got a big chunk of station to the face.
Where is everyone?
Uhhhhhh, Tortuga's ***gone***, Sanity. Where do you think?
Tallulah!

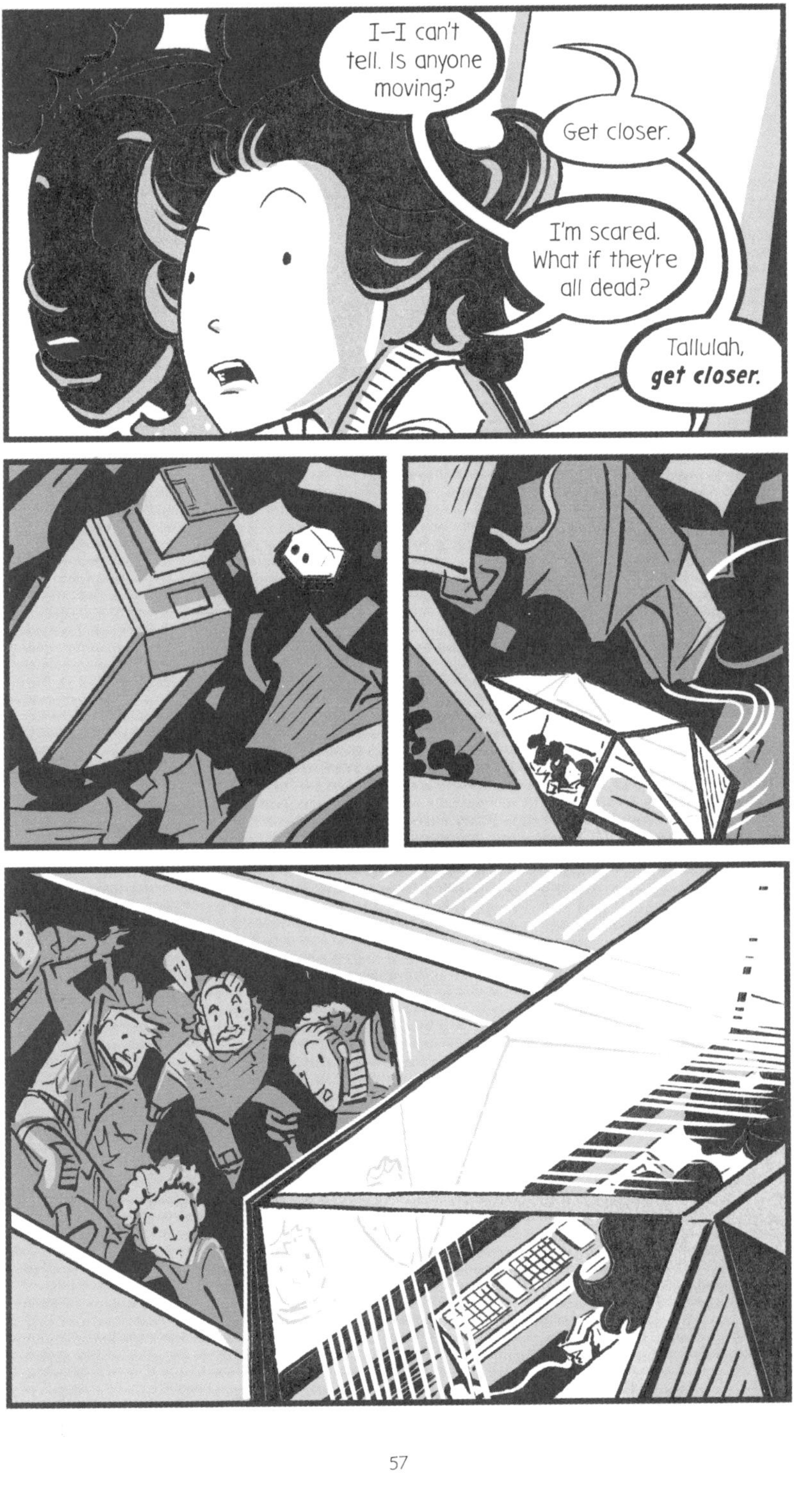
I–I can't tell. Is anyone moving?
Get closer.
I'm scared. What if they're all dead?
Tallulah, **get closer.**

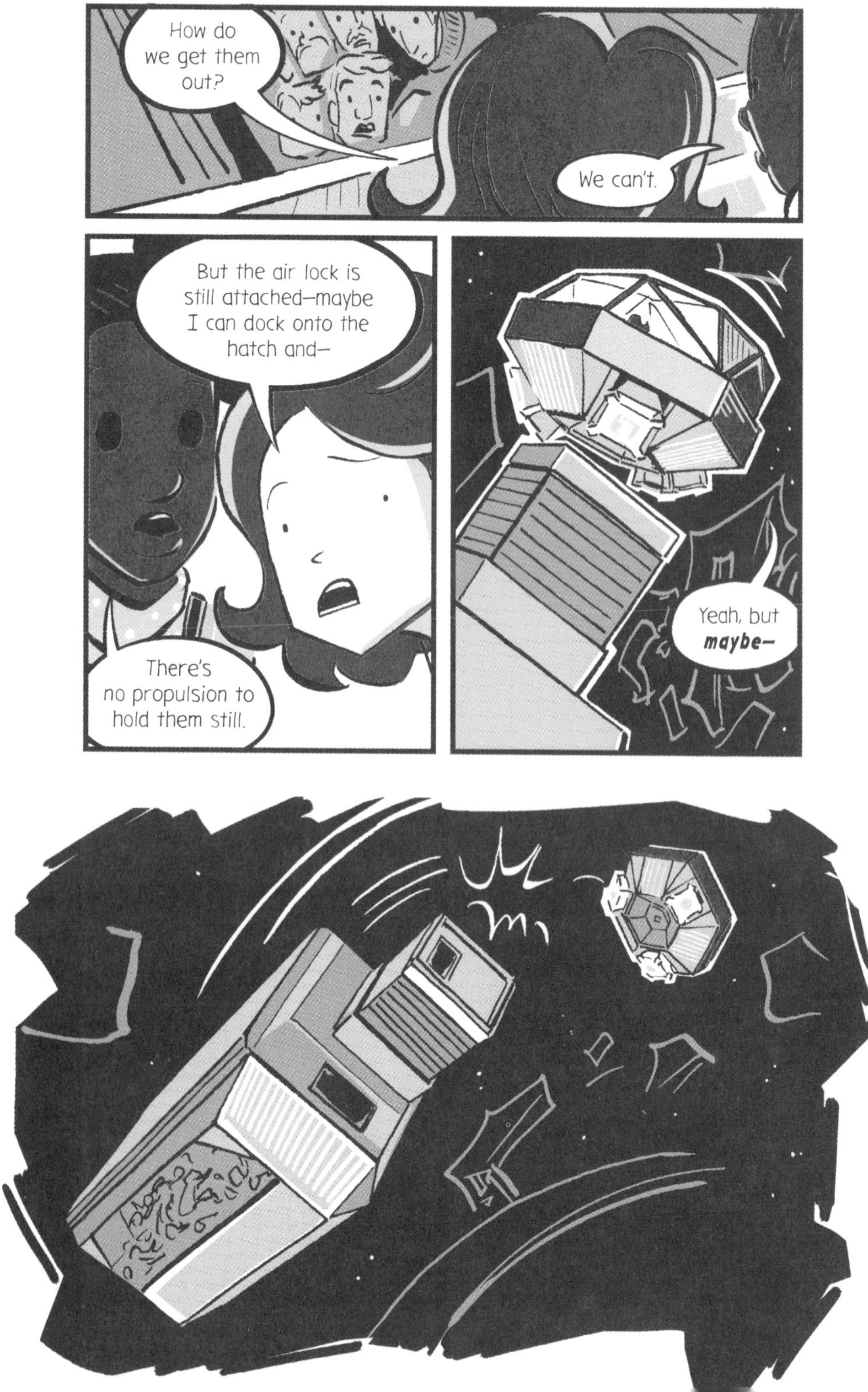
How do we get them out?
We can't.
But the air lock is still attached—maybe I can dock onto the hatch and—
There's no propulsion to hold them still.
Yeah, but ***maybe***—

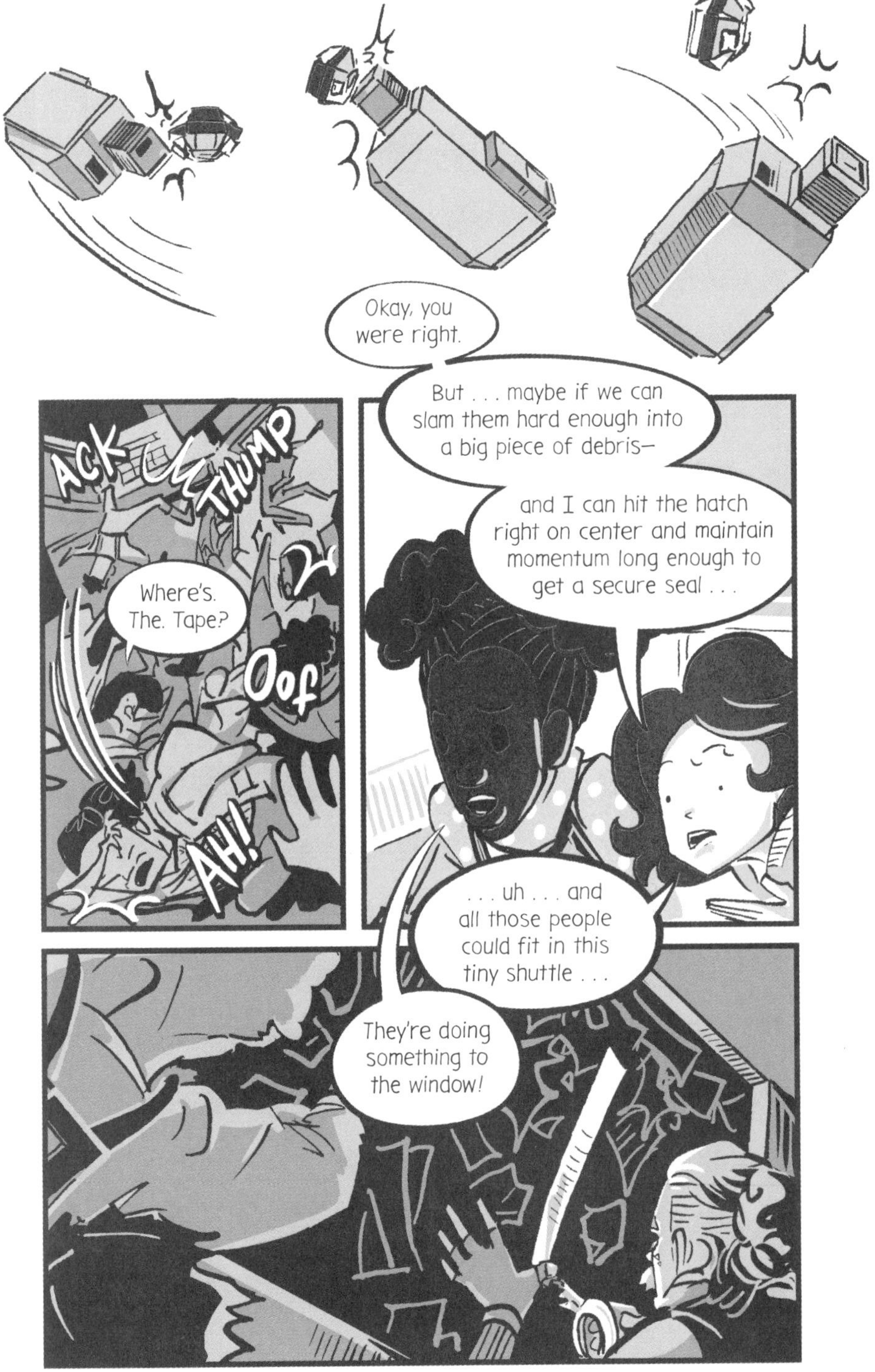
Okay, you were right.
But . . . maybe if we can slam them hard enough into a big piece of debris—
ACK
UM
THUMP
Where's. The. Tape?
Oof
AH!
and I can hit the hatch right on center and maintain momentum long enough to get a secure seal . . .
. . . uh . . . and all those people could fit in this tiny shuttle . . .
They're doing something to the window!

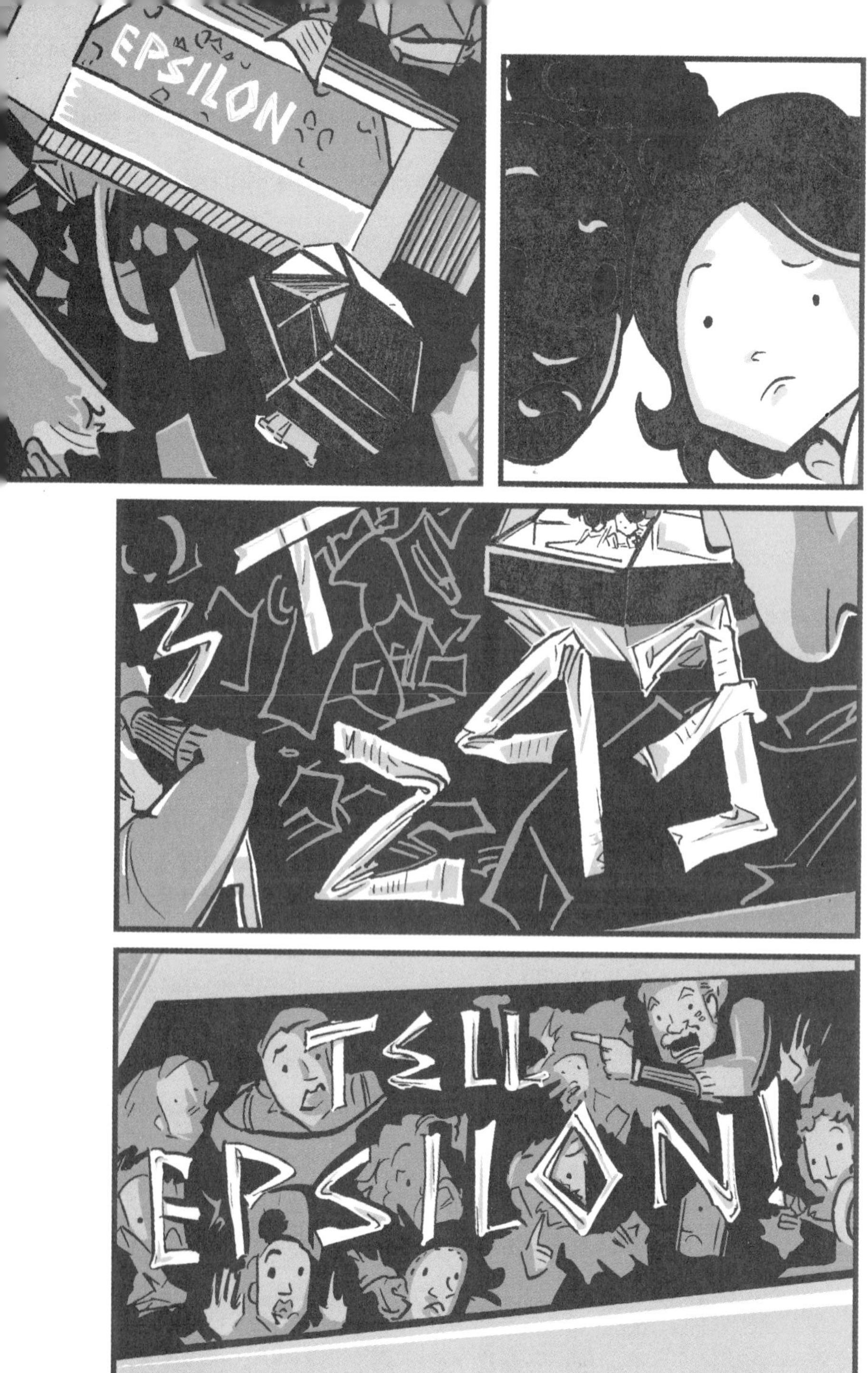
EPSILON
TELL EPSILON!

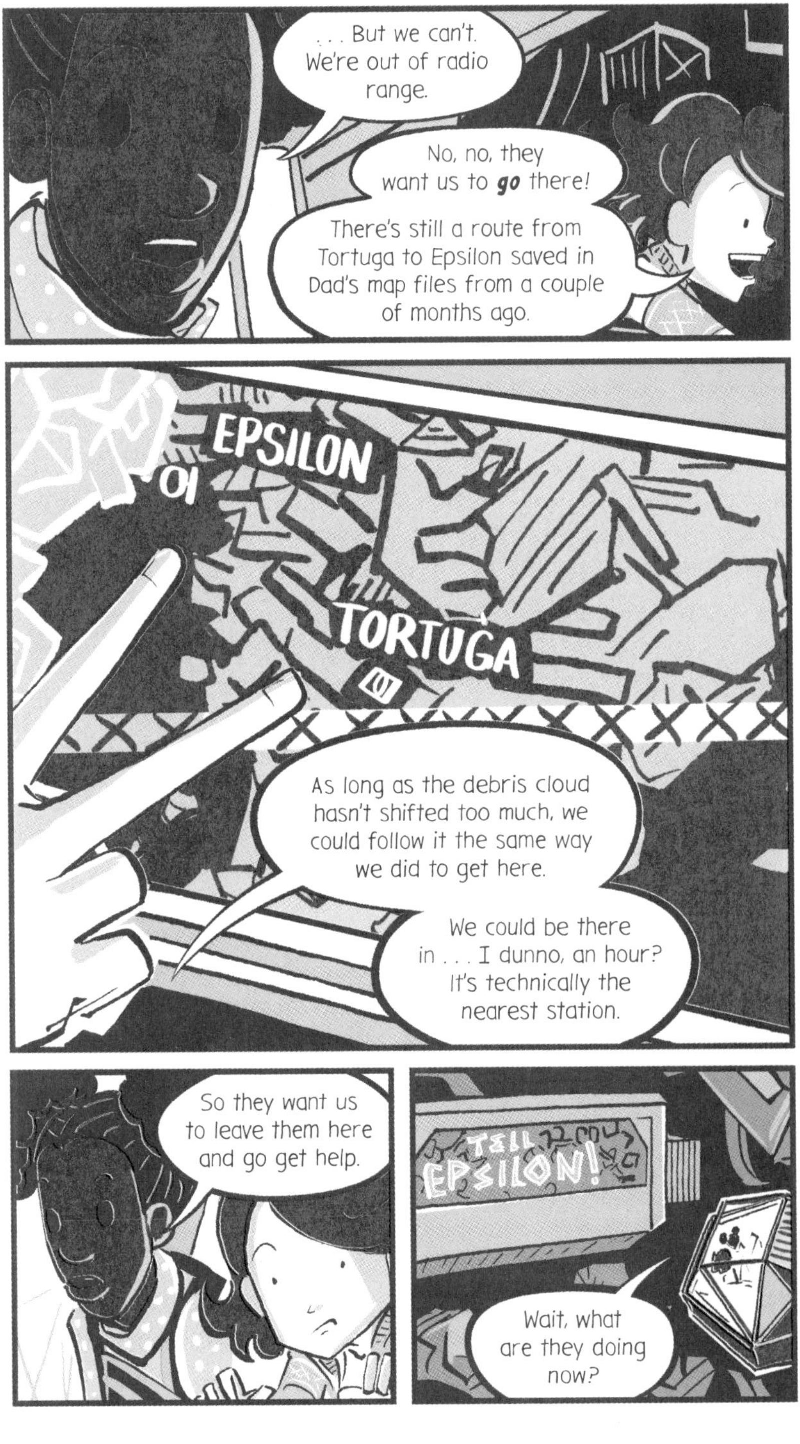
. . . But we can't. We're out of radio range.
No, no, they want us to **go** there!
There's still a route from Tortuga to Epsilon saved in Dad's map files from a couple of months ago.
EPSILON
01
TORTUGA
01
As long as the debris cloud hasn't shifted too much, we could follow it the same way we did to get here.
We could be there in . . . I dunno, an hour? It's technically the nearest station.
So they want us to leave them here and go get help.
TELL EPSILON!
Wait, what are they doing now?

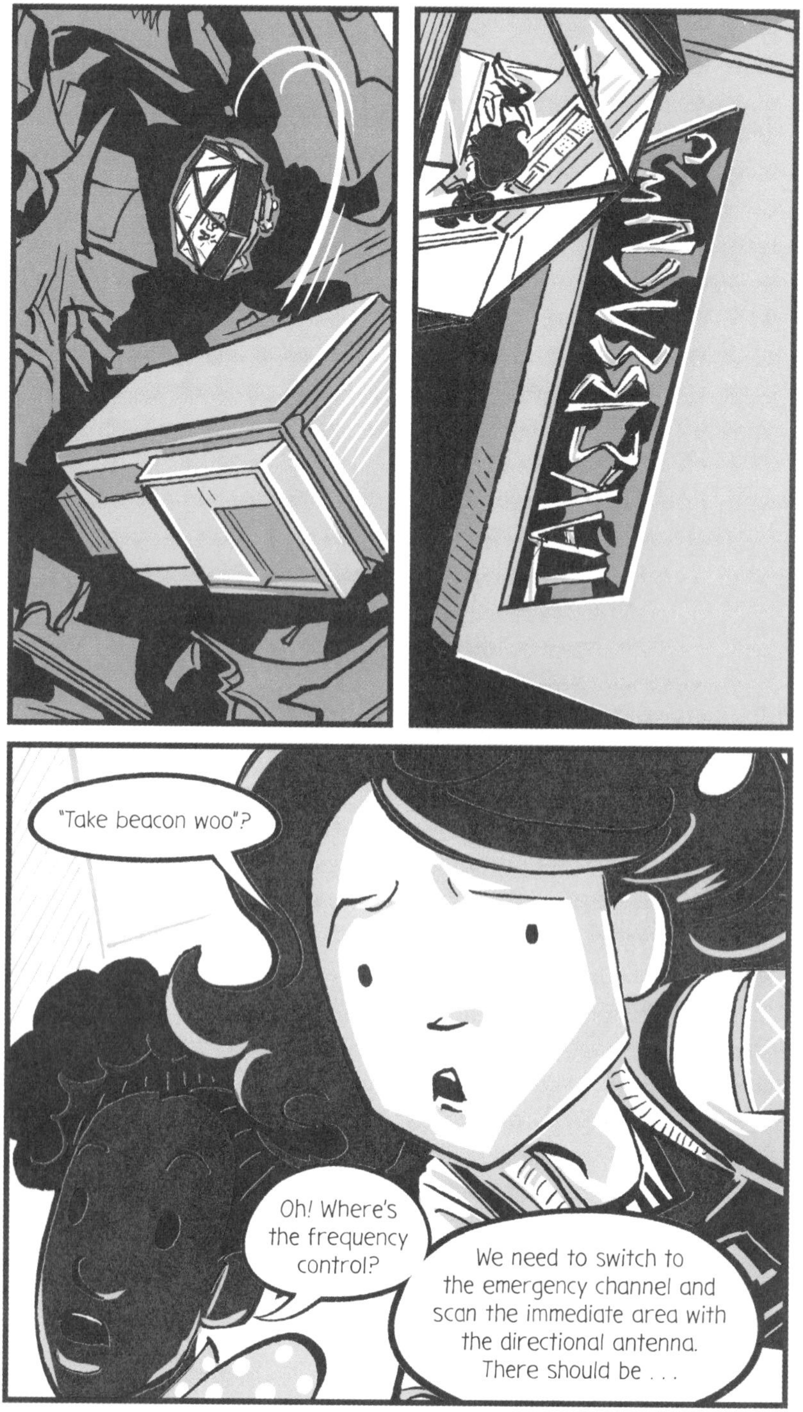
"Take beacon woo"?
Oh! Where's the frequency control?
We need to switch to the emergency channel and scan the immediate area with the directional antenna. There should be . . .

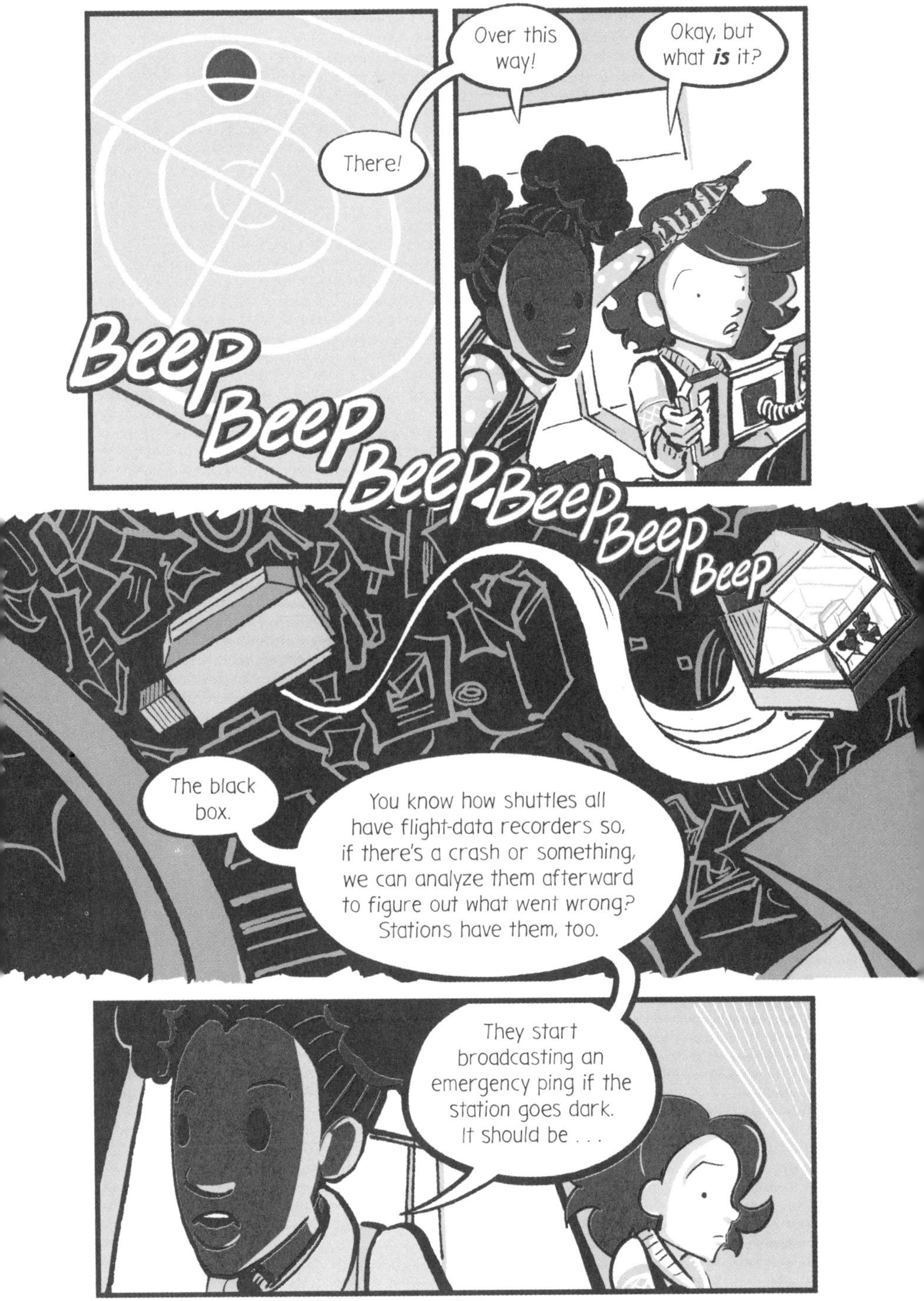
There!
Over this way!
Okay, but what **is** it?
Beep Beep Beep Beep Beep Beep
The black box.
You know how shuttles all have flight-data recorders so, if there's a crash or something, we can analyze them afterward to figure out what went wrong? Stations have them, too.
They start broadcasting an emergency ping if the station goes dark. It should be . . .

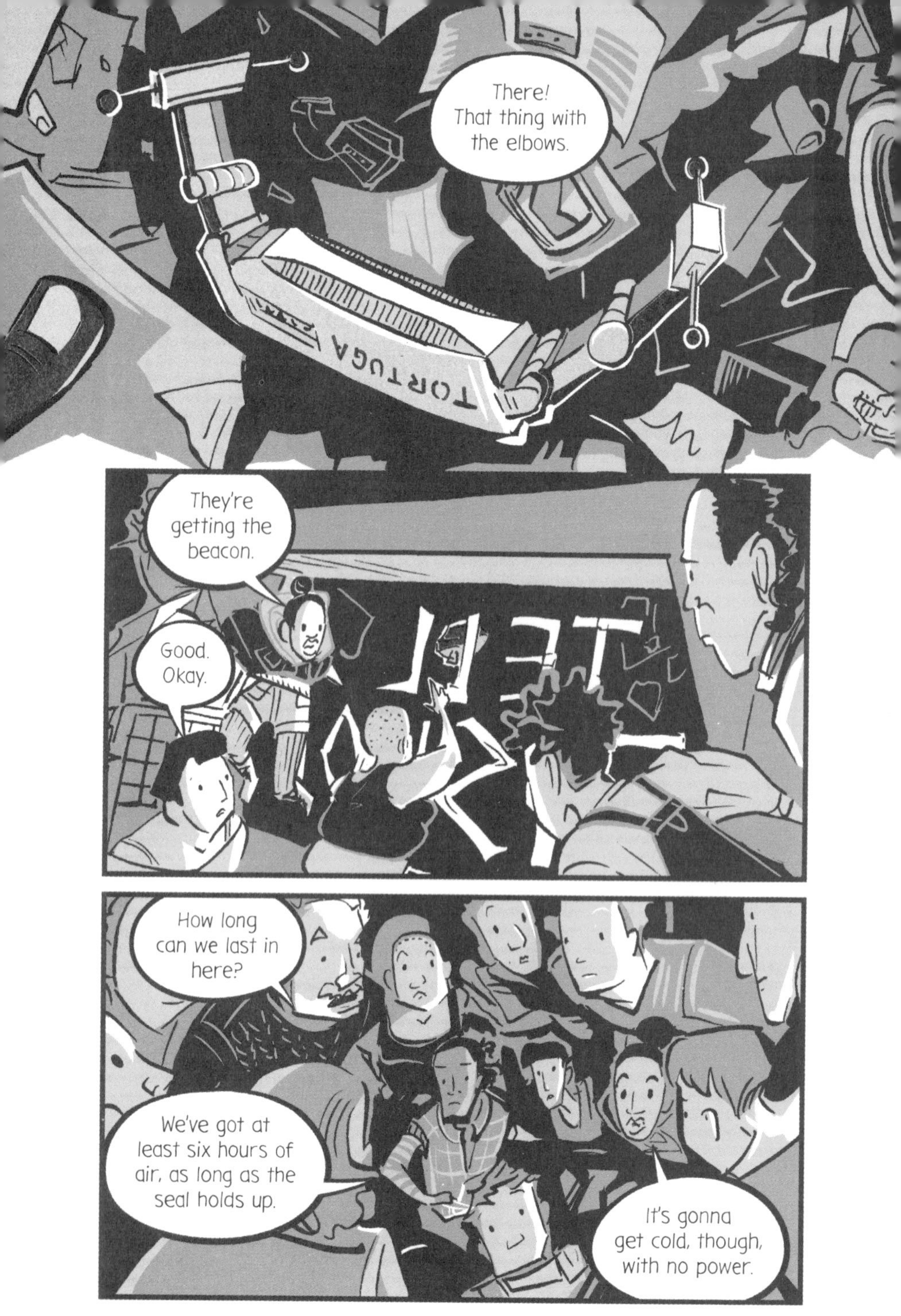
There! That thing with the elbows.
TORTUGA
They're getting the beacon.
Good. Okay.
How long can we last in here?
We've got at least six hours of air, as long as the seal holds up.
It's gonna get cold, though, with no power.

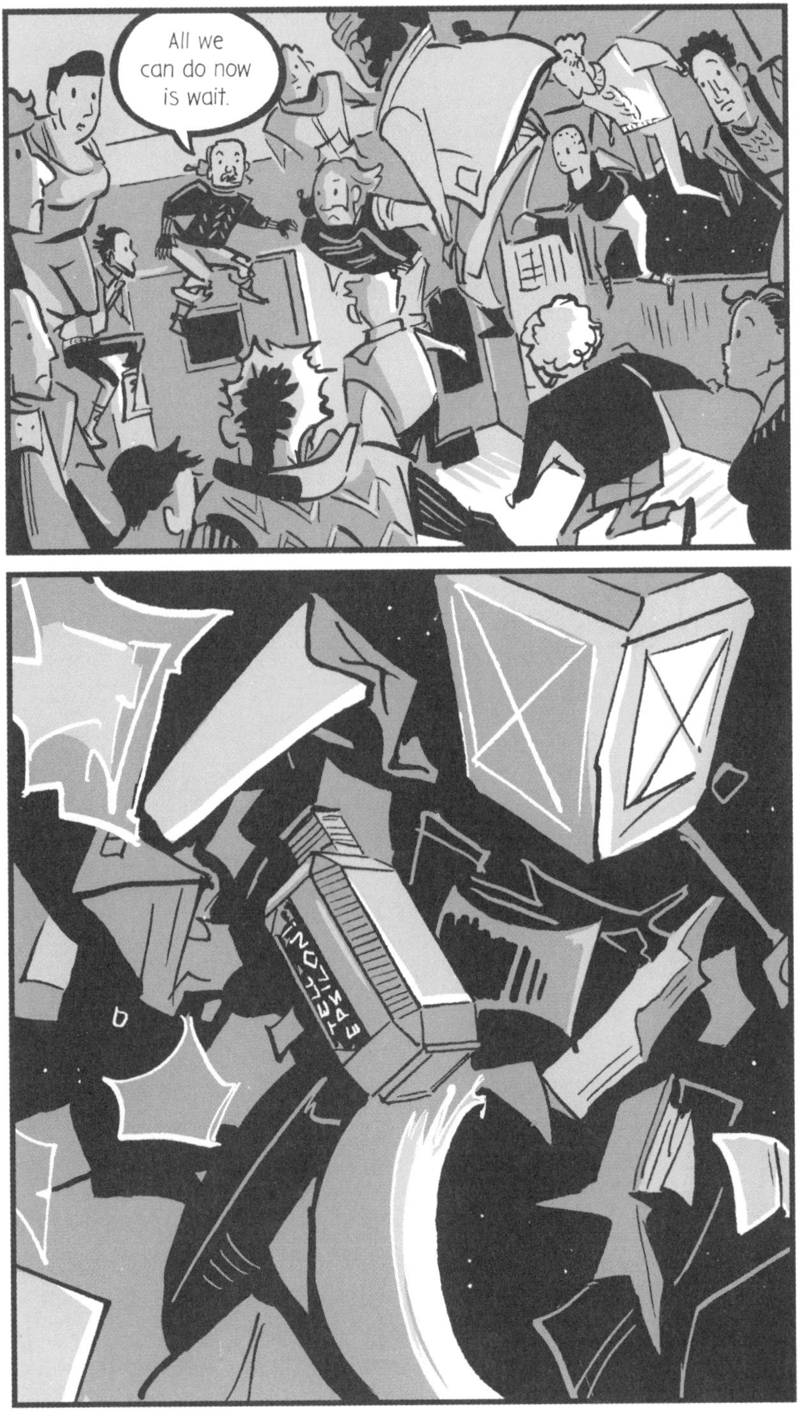
All we can do now is wait.

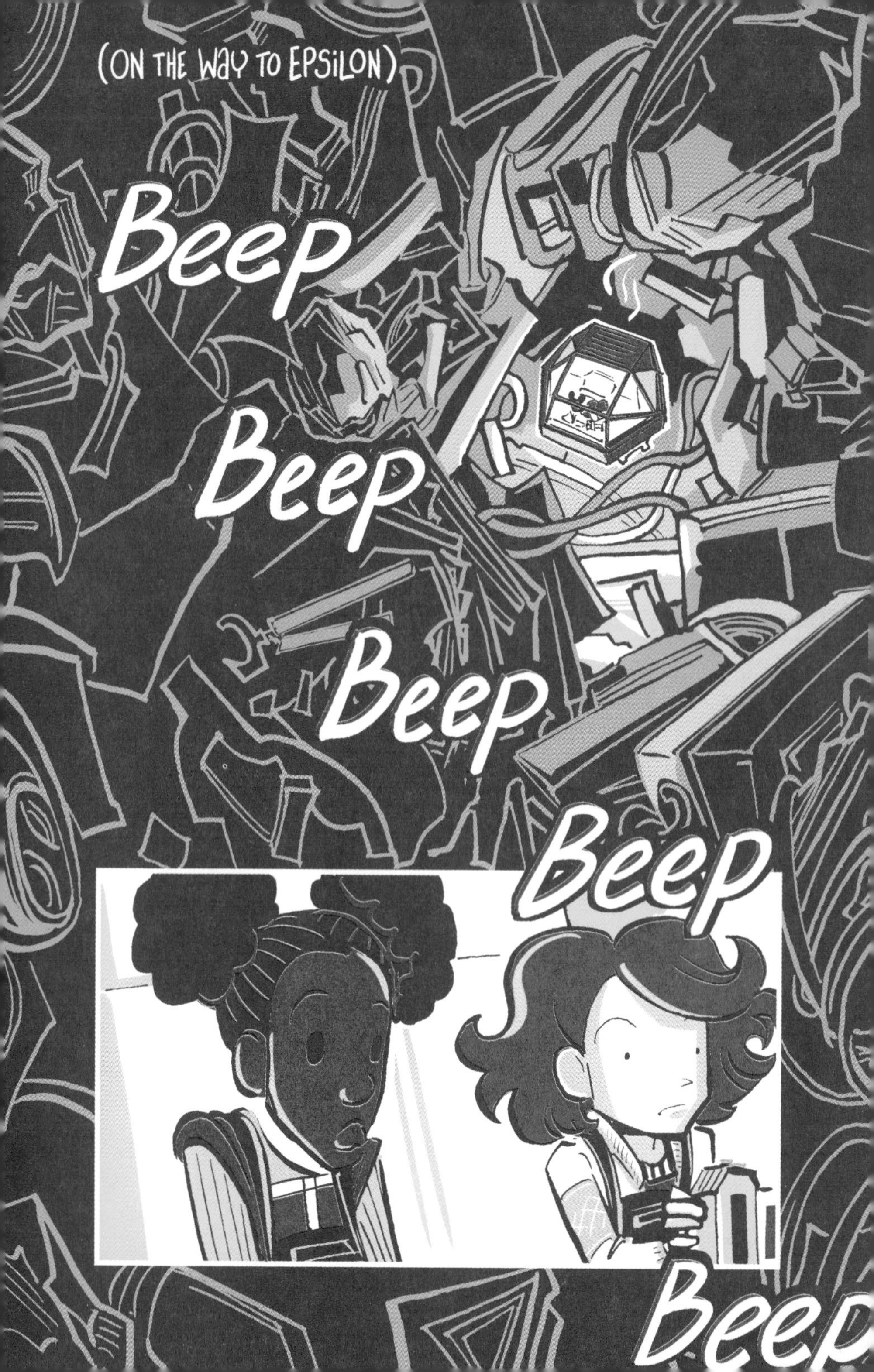
(ON THE WAY TO EPSILON)
Beep
Beep
Beep
Beep
Beep

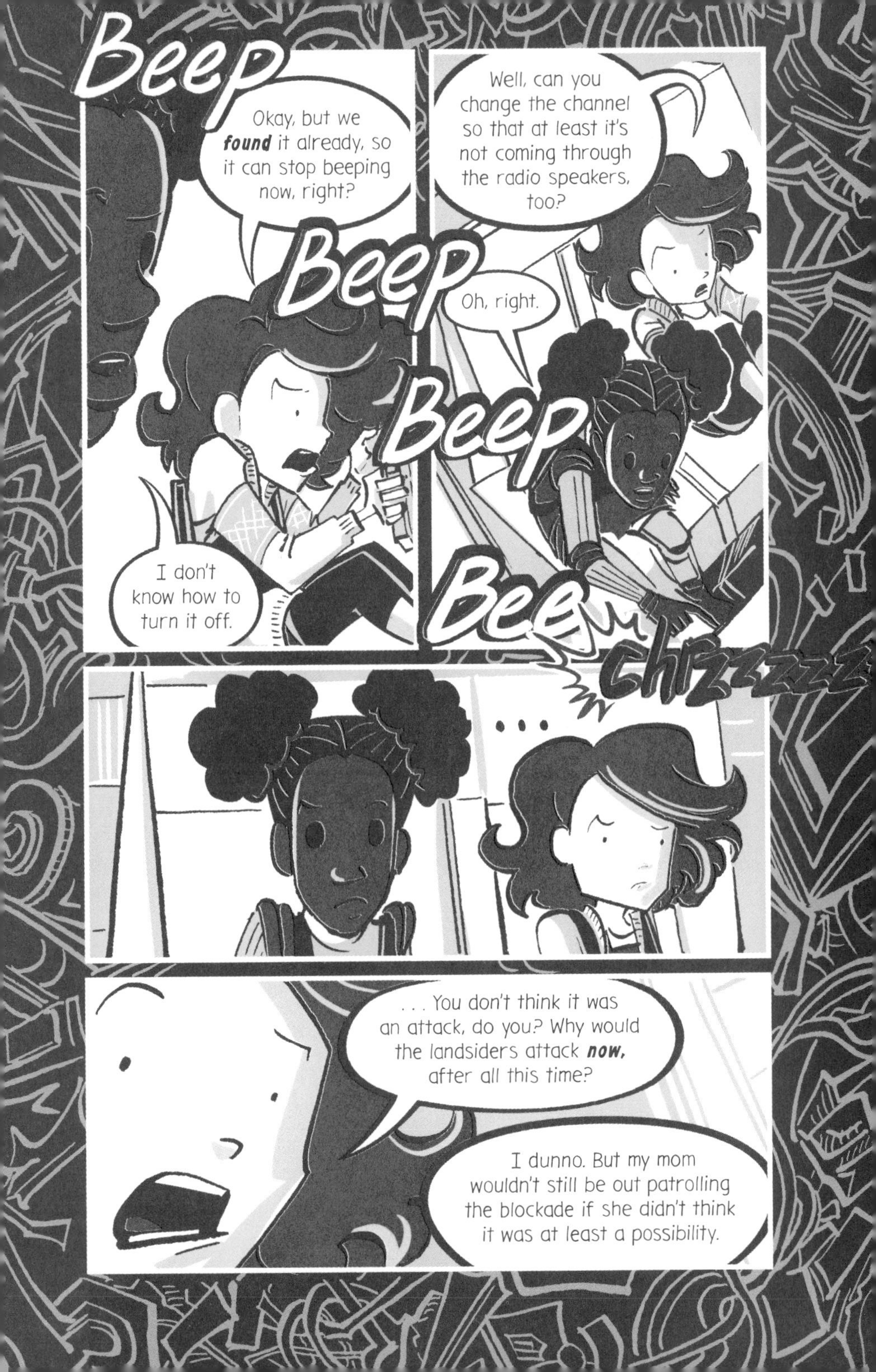
Beep
Okay, but we **found** it already, so it can stop beeping now, right?
I don't know how to turn it off.
Beep
Well, can you change the channel so that at least it's not coming through the radio speakers, too?
Oh, right.
Beep
Bee
chrzzzzzz
...
. . . You don't think it was an attack, do you? Why would the landsiders attack **now,** after all this time?
I dunno. But my mom wouldn't still be out patrolling the blockade if she didn't think it was at least a possibility.

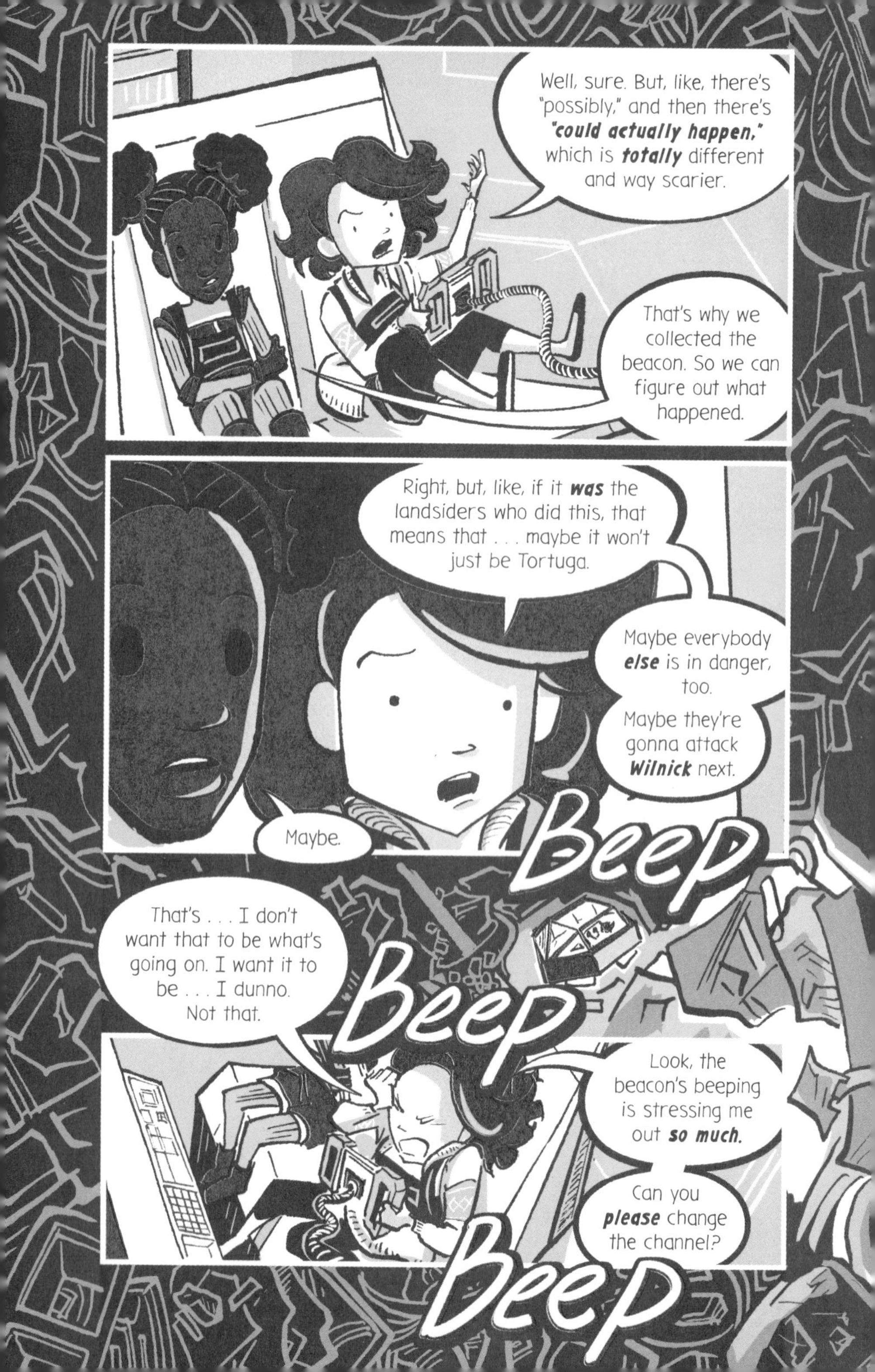
Well, sure. But, like, there's "possibly," and then there's "could actually happen," which is totally different and way scarier.
That's why we collected the beacon. So we can figure out what happened.
Right, but, like, if it was the landsiders who did this, that means that . . . maybe it won't just be Tortuga.
Maybe everybody else is in danger, too.
Maybe they're gonna attack Wilnick next.
Maybe.
Beep
That's . . . I don't want that to be what's going on. I want it to be . . . I dunno. Not that.
Beep
Look, the beacon's beeping is stressing me out so much.
Can you please change the channel?
Beep

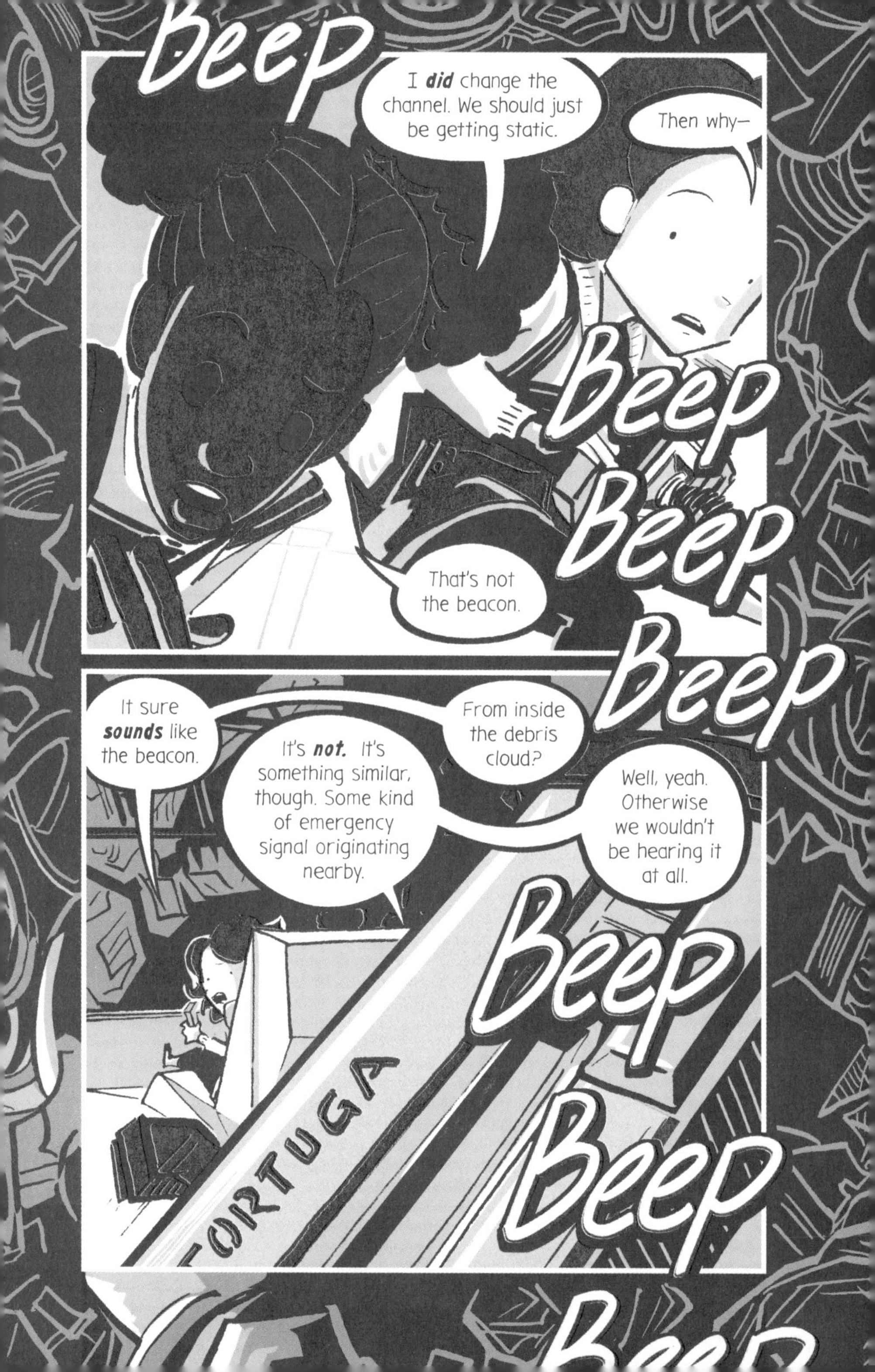
Beep
I **did** change the channel. We should just be getting static.
Then why—
Beep
Beep
That's not the beacon.
Beep
It sure **sounds** like the beacon.
From inside the debris cloud?
It's **not.** It's something similar, though. Some kind of emergency signal originating nearby.
Well, yeah. Otherwise we wouldn't be hearing it at all.
Beep
TORTUGA
Beep

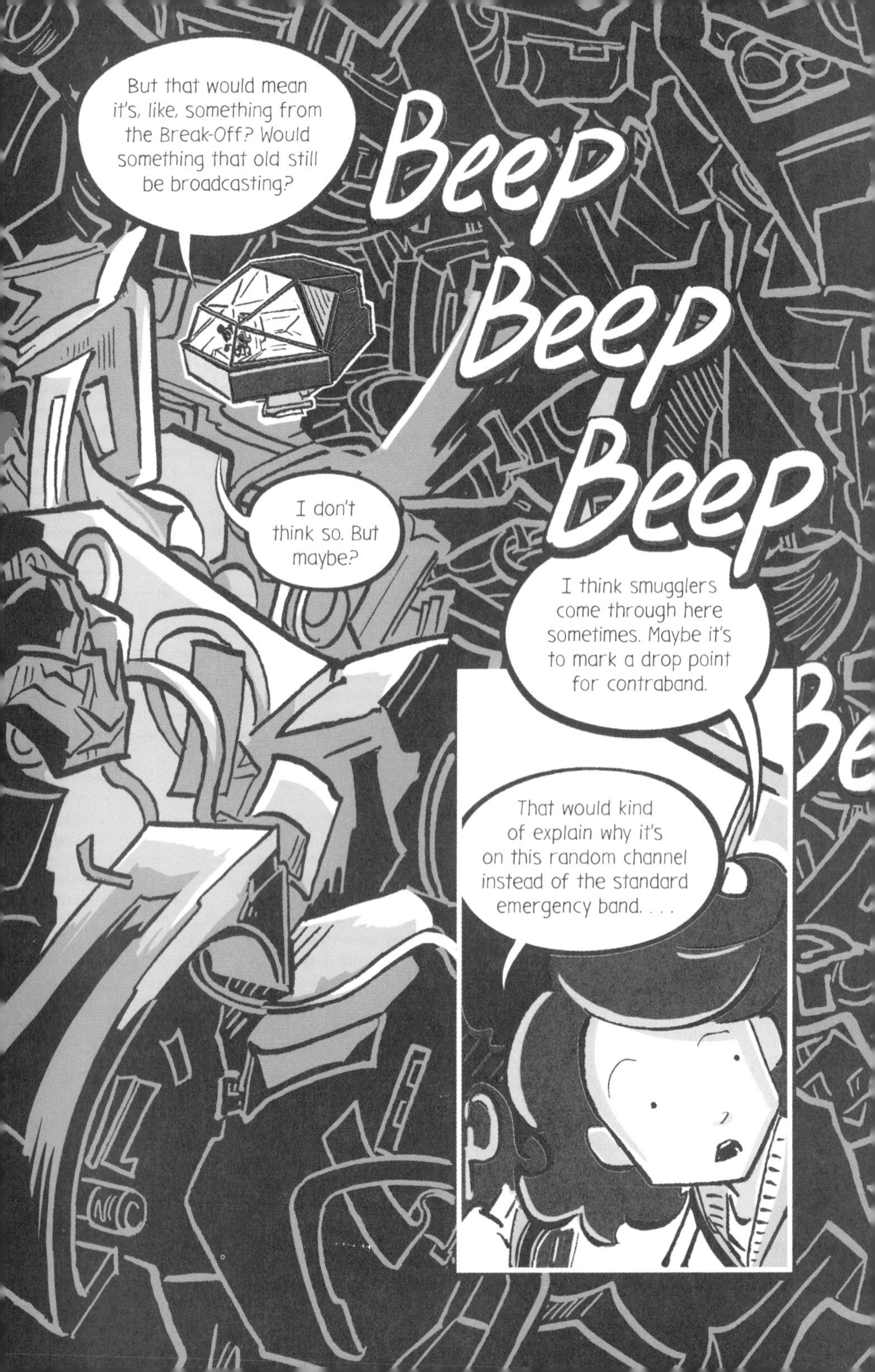
But that would mean it's, like, something from the Break-Off? Would something that old still be broadcasting?
Beep
Beep
Beep
I don't think so. But maybe?
I think smugglers come through here sometimes. Maybe it's to mark a drop point for contraband.
That would kind of explain why it's on this random channel instead of the standard emergency band. . . .

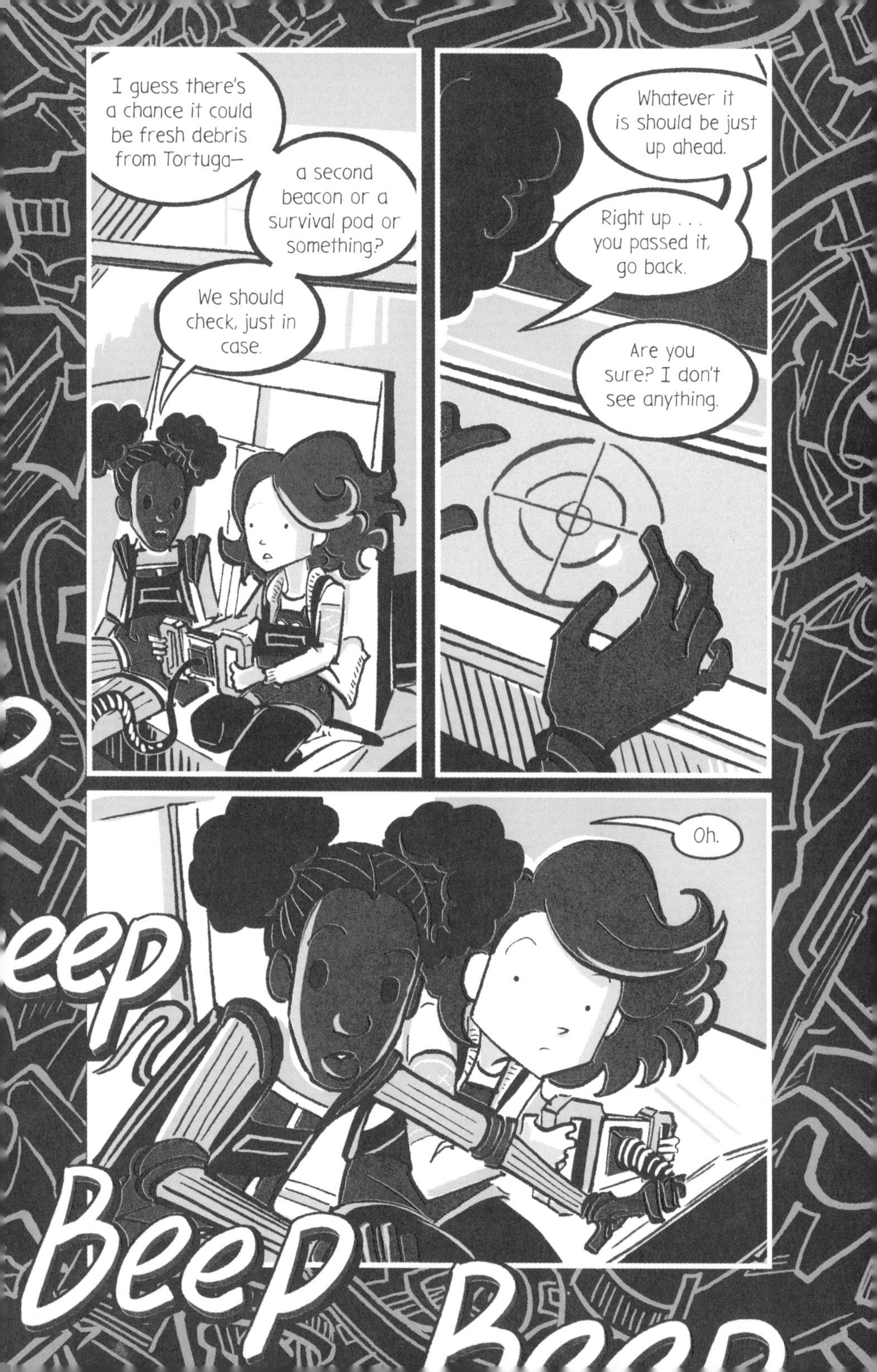
I guess there's a chance it could be fresh debris from Tortuga—
a second beacon or a survival pod or something?
We should check, just in case.
Whatever it is should be just up ahead.
Right up . . . you passed it, go back.
Are you sure? I don't see anything.
Oh.
eep
Beep

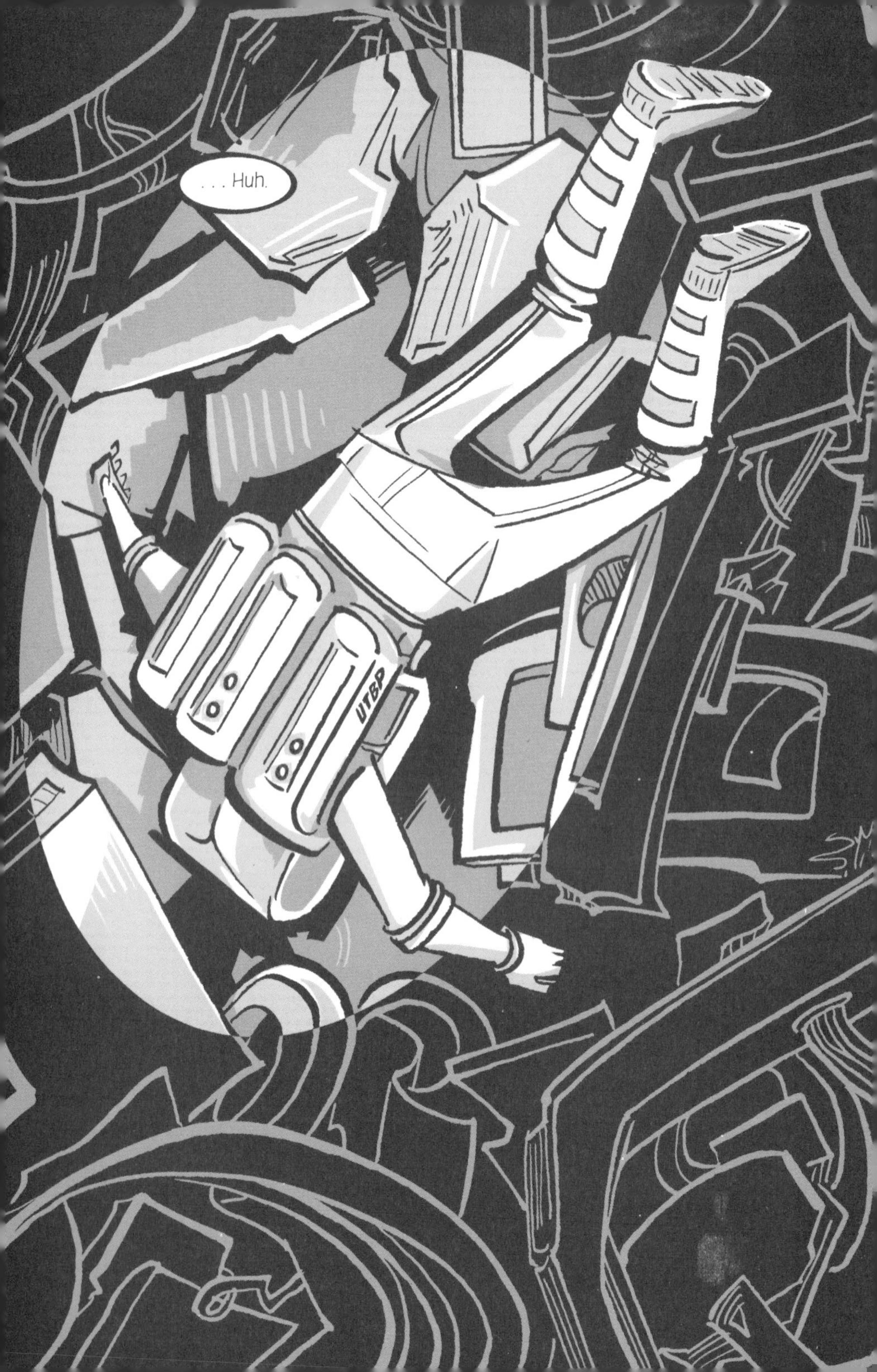
. . . Huh.
UTBP

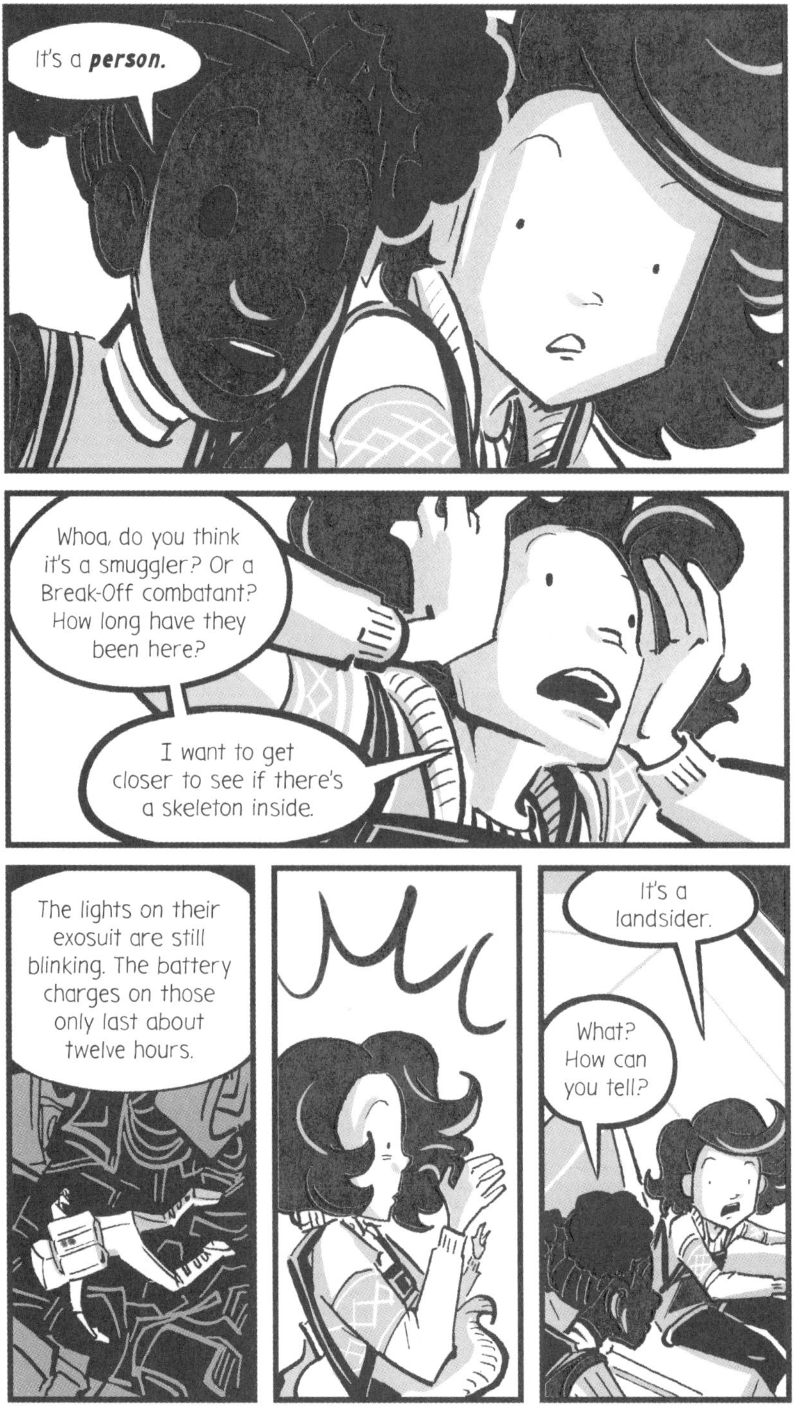

It's a **person.**
Whoa, do you think it's a smuggler? Or a Break-Off combatant? How long have they been here?
I want to get closer to see if there's a skeleton inside.
The lights on their exosuit are still blinking. The battery charges on those only last about twelve hours.
It's a landsider.
What? How can you tell?

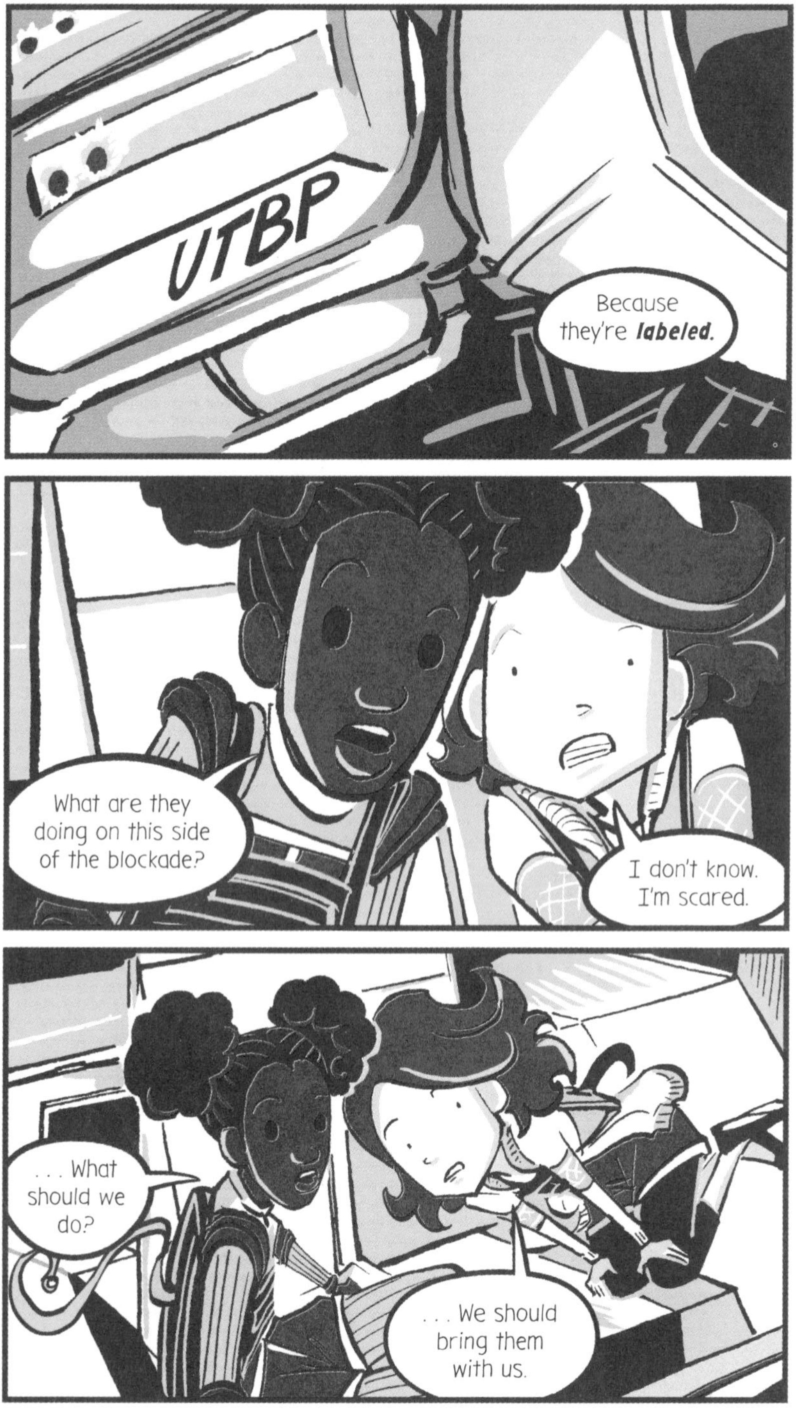
UTBP
Because they're ***labeled.***
What are they doing on this side of the blockade?
I don't know. I'm scared.
. . . What should we do?
. . . We should bring them with us.

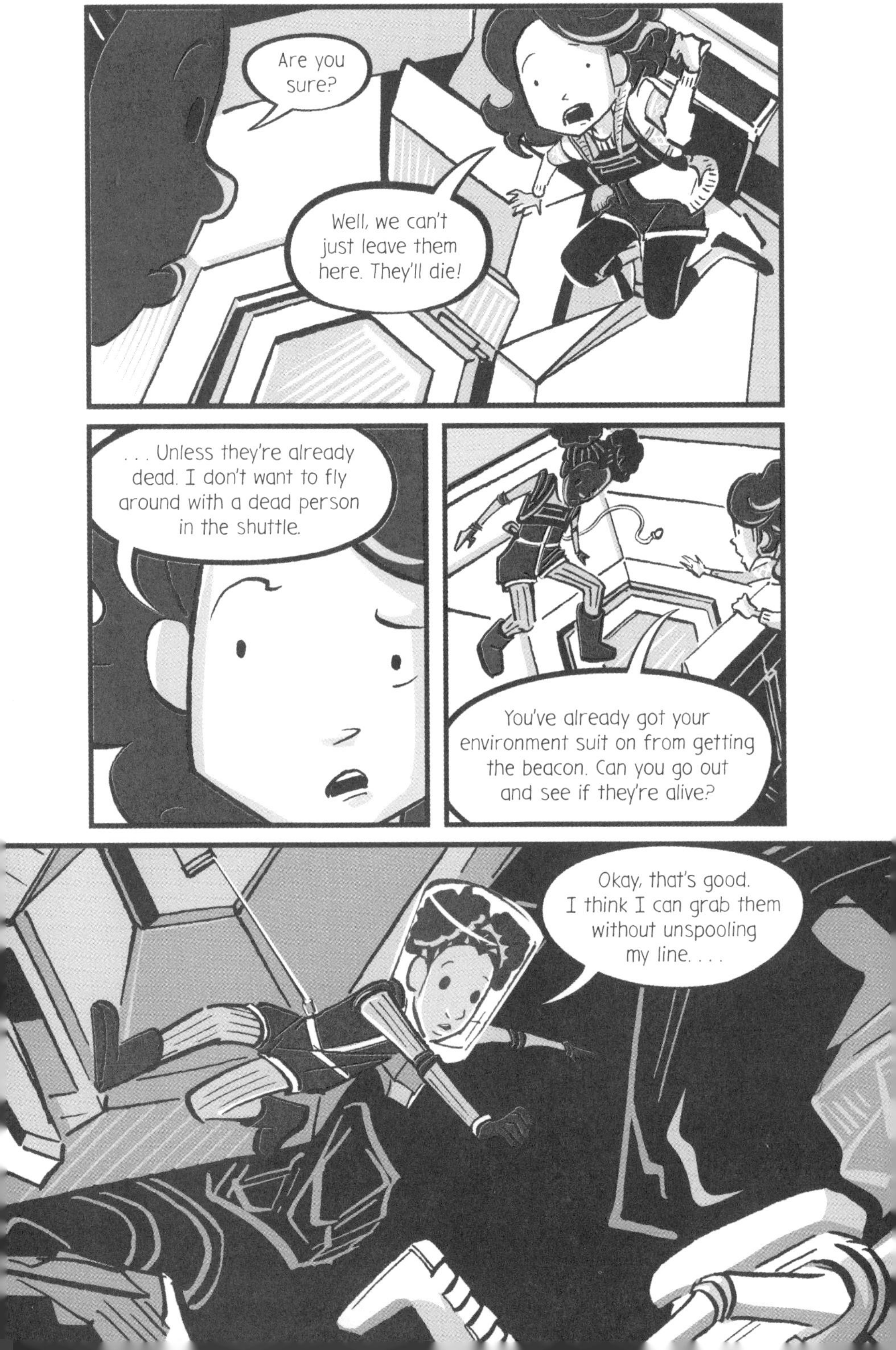
Are you sure?
Well, we can't just leave them here. They'll die!
. . . Unless they're already dead. I don't want to fly around with a dead person in the shuttle.
You've already got your environment suit on from getting the beacon. Can you go out and see if they're alive?
Okay, that's good. I think I can grab them without unspooling my line. . . .

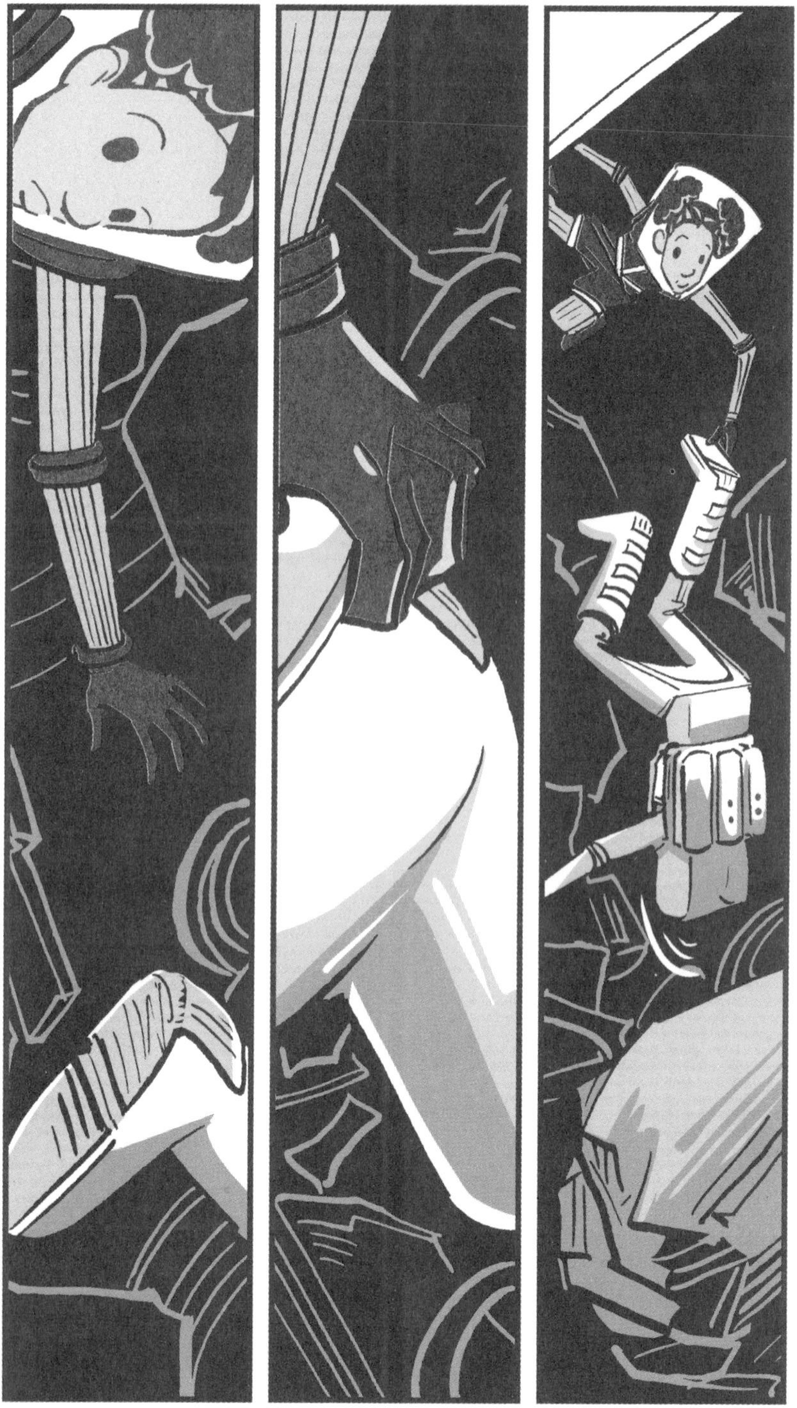

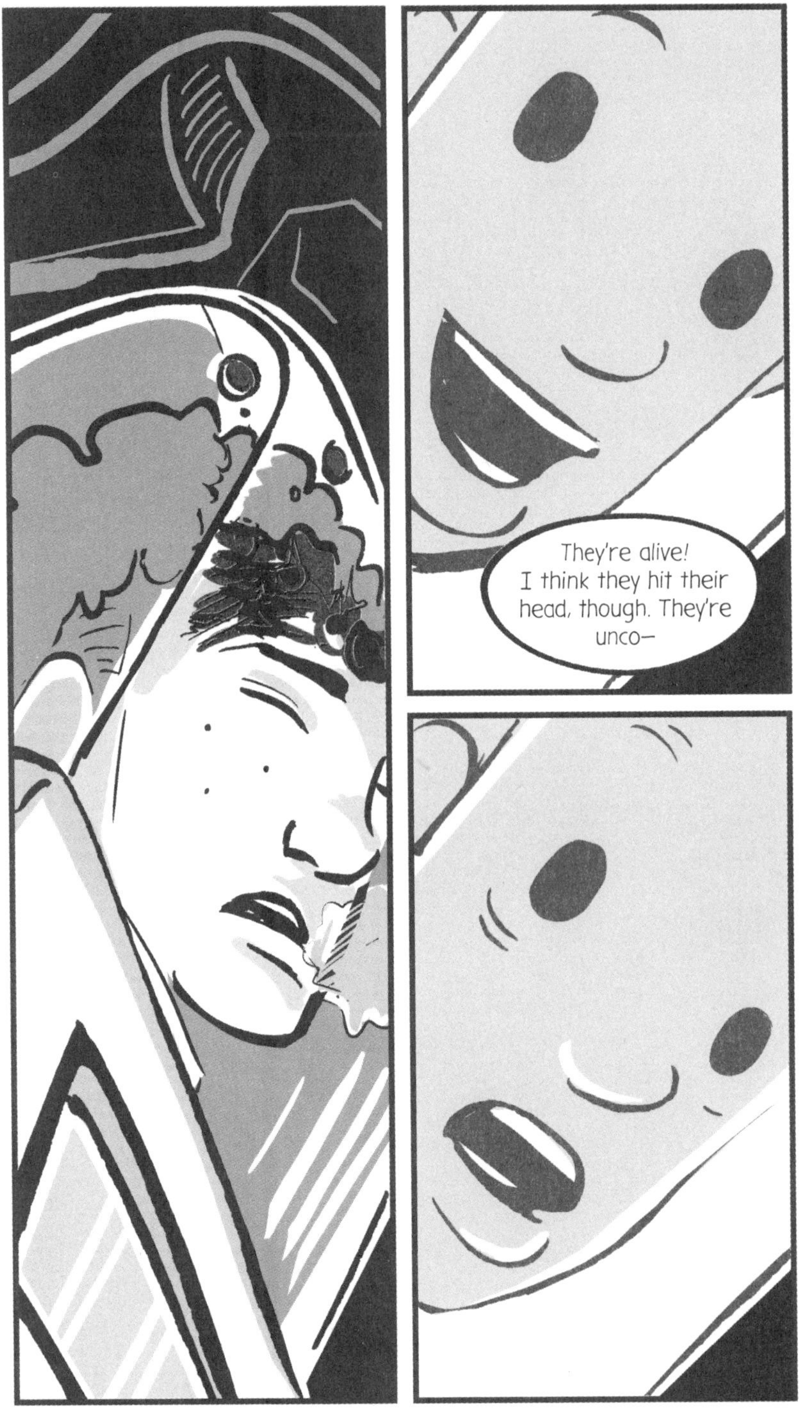
They're alive! I think they hit their head, though. They're unco—

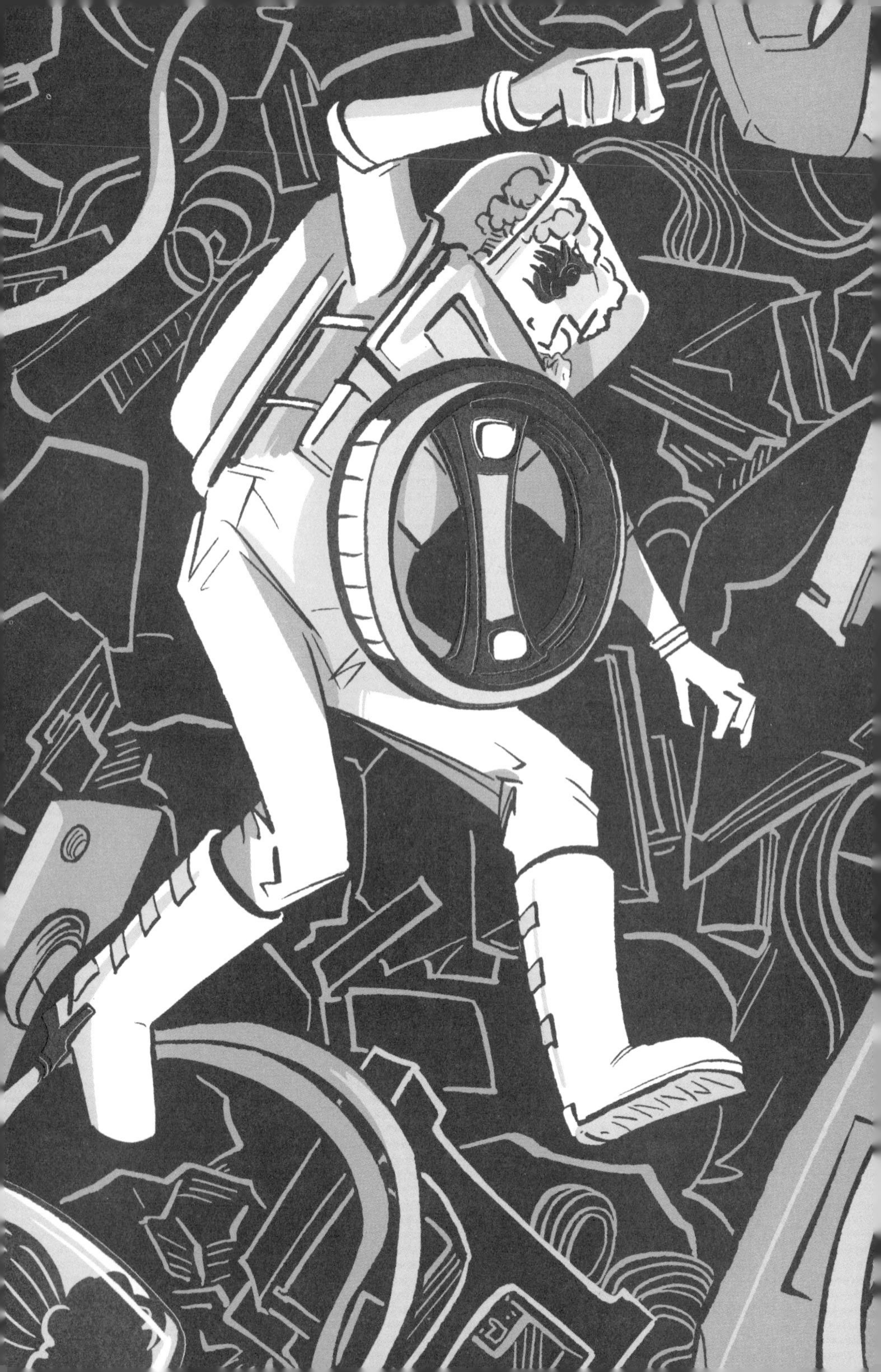

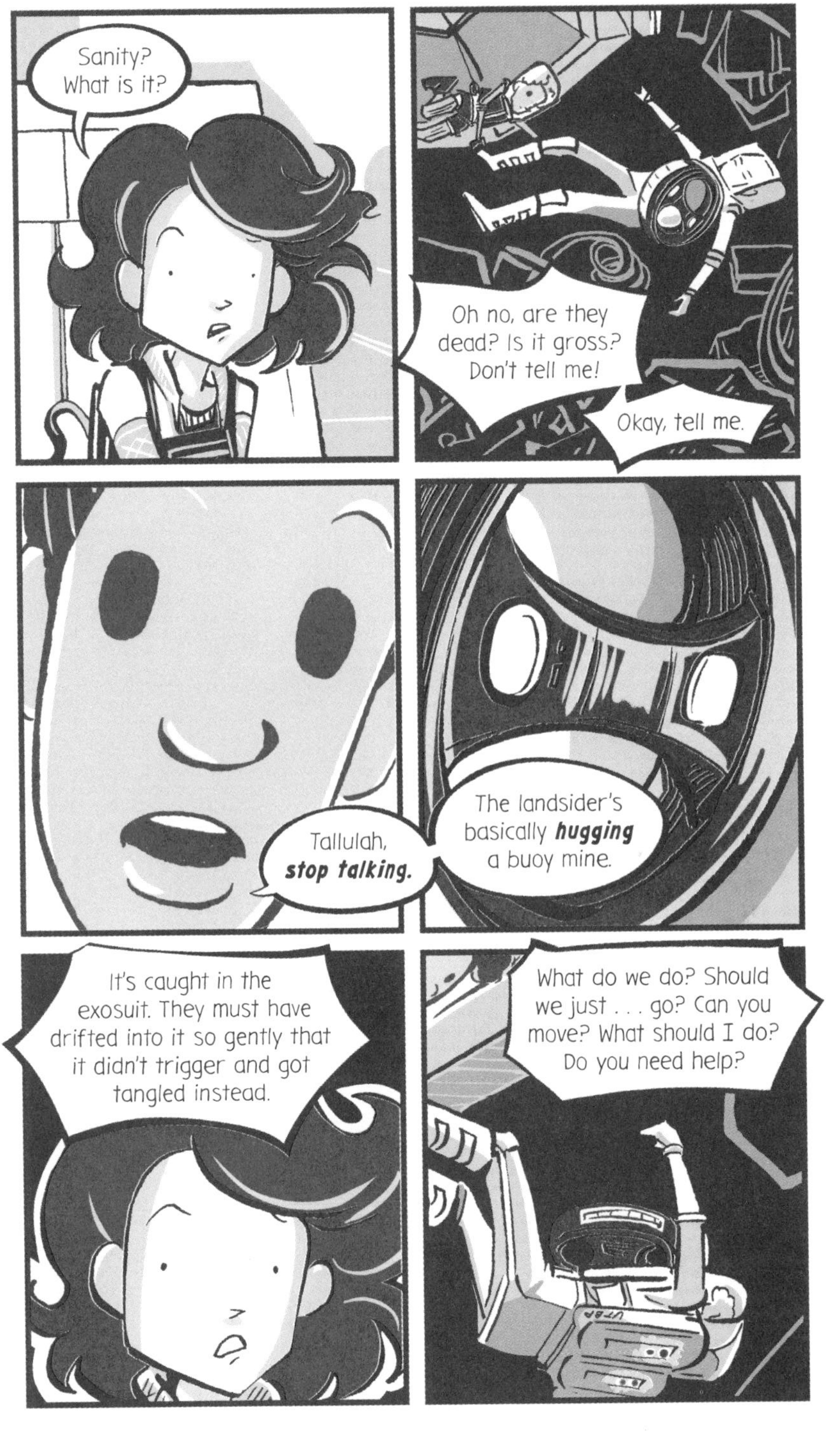
Sanity? What is it?
Oh no, are they dead? Is it gross? Don't tell me!
Okay, tell me.
Tallulah, **stop talking.**
The landsider's basically **hugging** a buoy mine.
It's caught in the exosuit. They must have drifted into it so gently that it didn't trigger and got tangled instead.
What do we do? Should we just . . . go? Can you move? What should I do? Do you need help?

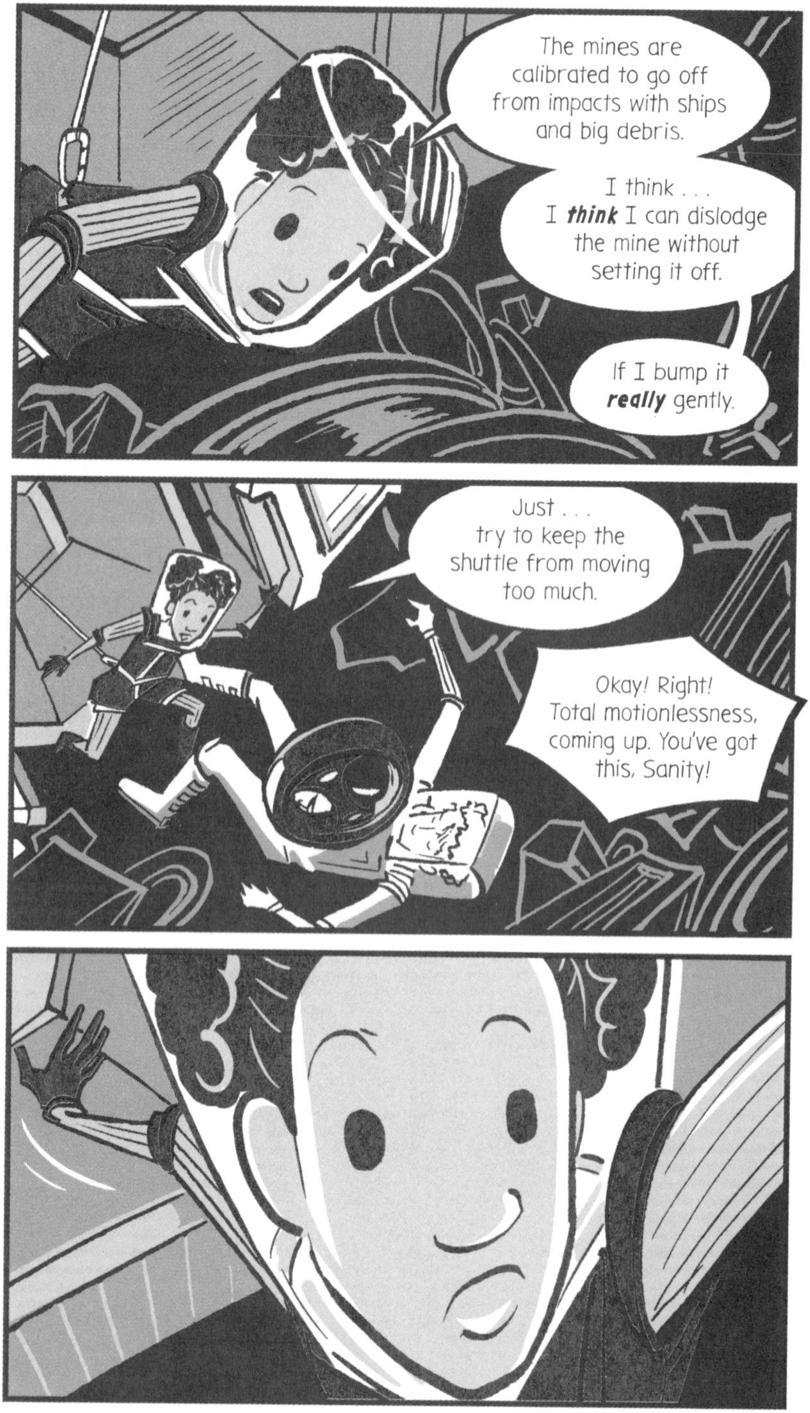
The mines are calibrated to go off from impacts with ships and big debris.
I think . . . I **think** I can dislodge the mine without setting it off.
If I bump it ***really*** gently.
Just . . . try to keep the shuttle from moving too much.
Okay! Right! Total motionlessness, coming up. You've got this, Sanity!

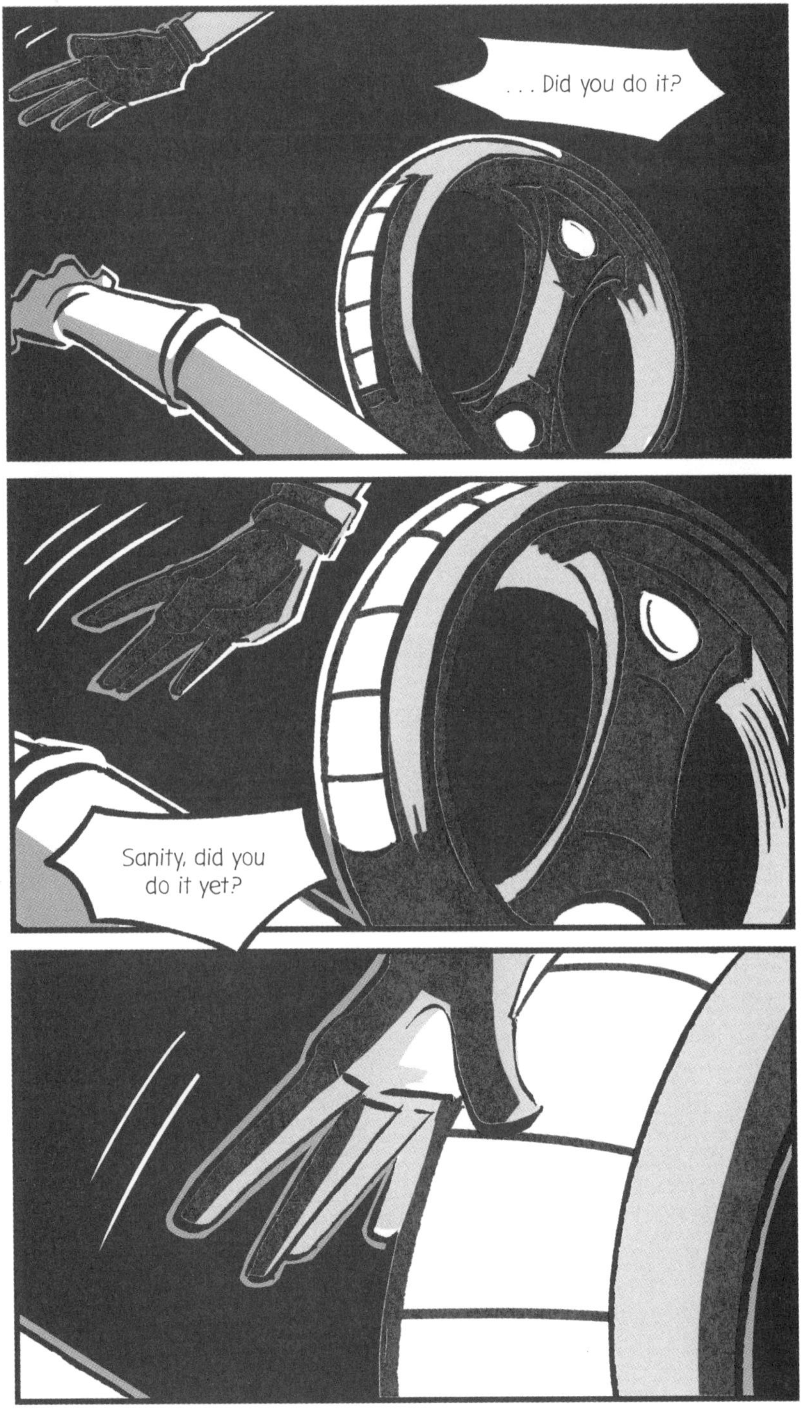

. . . Did you do it?
Sanity, did you do it yet?

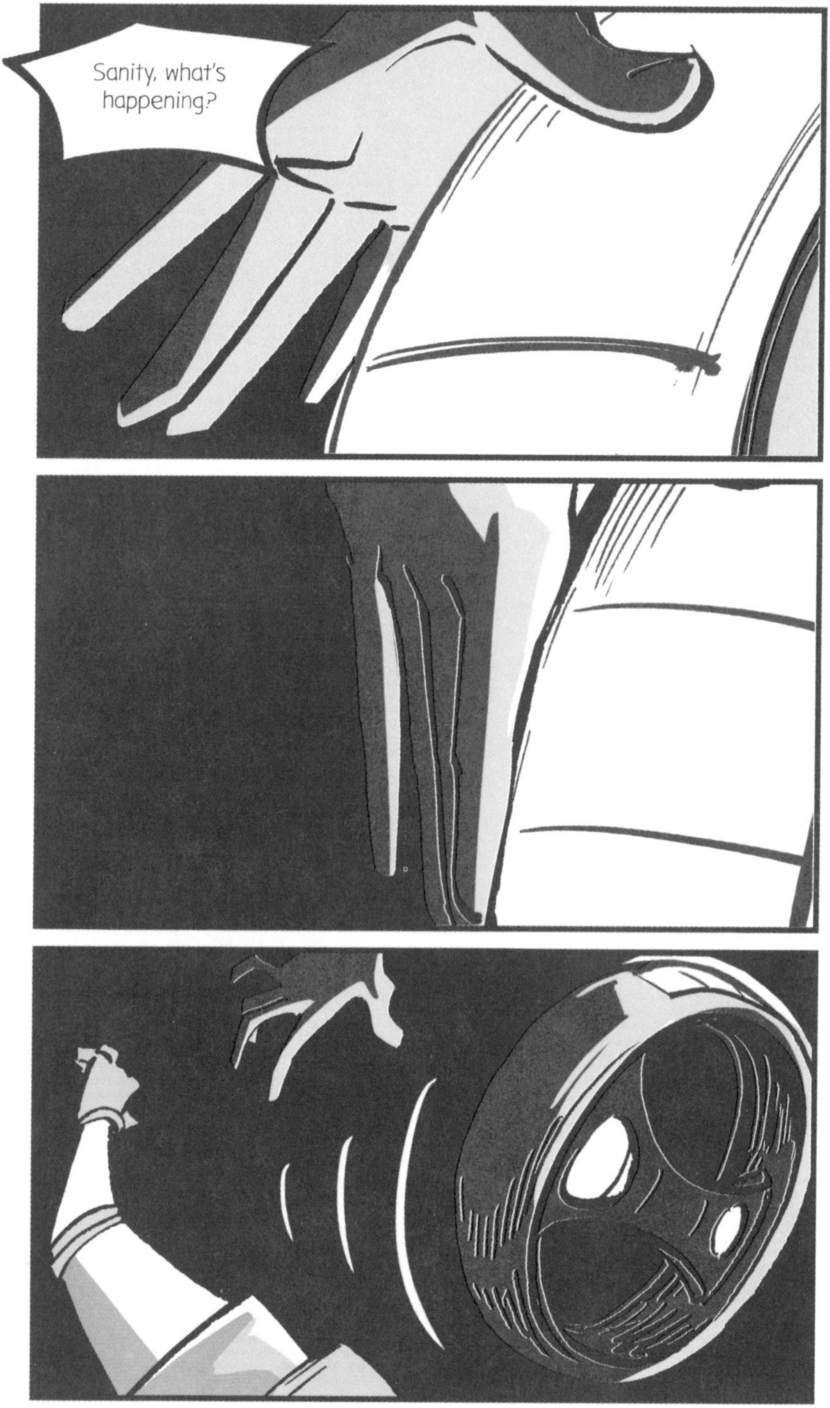
Sanity, what's happening?

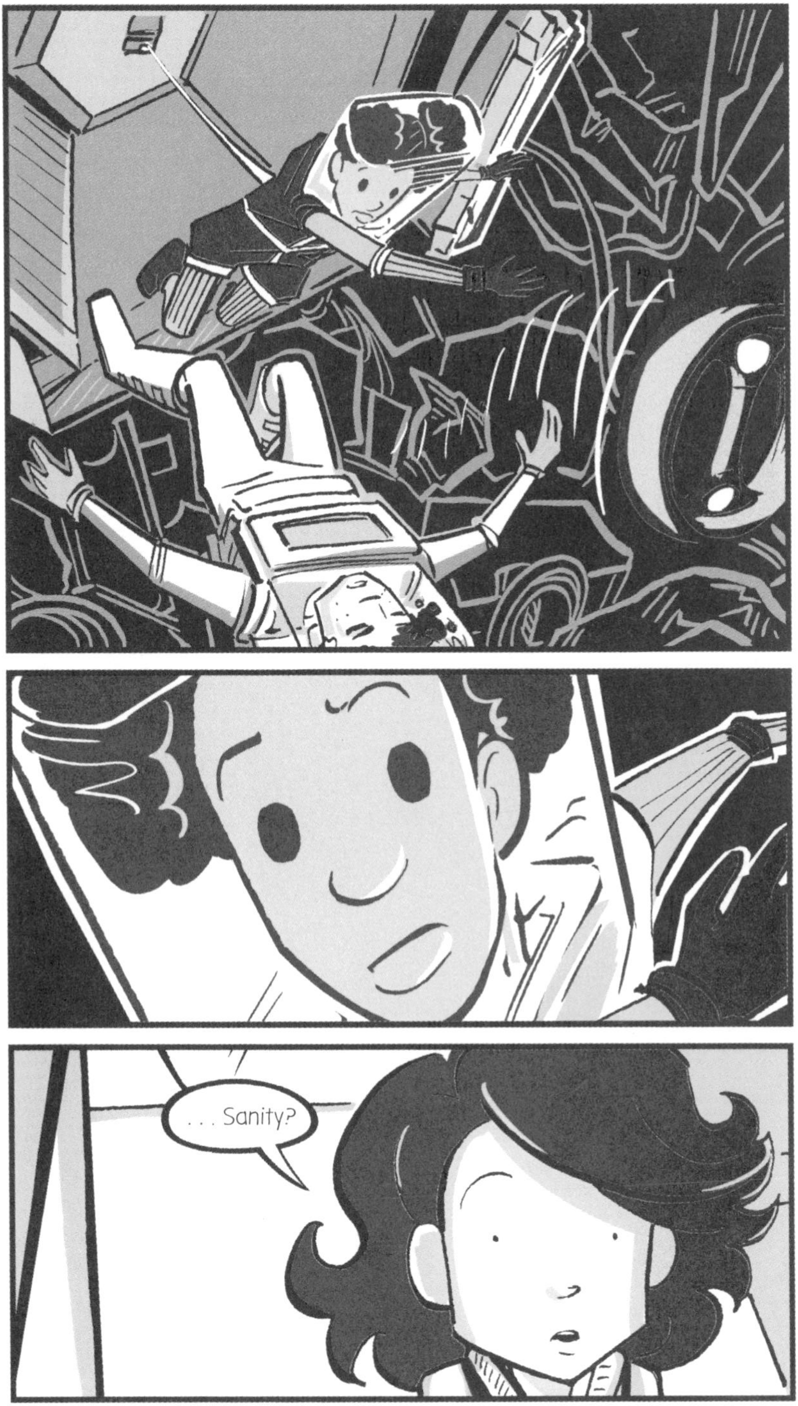
. . . Sanity?

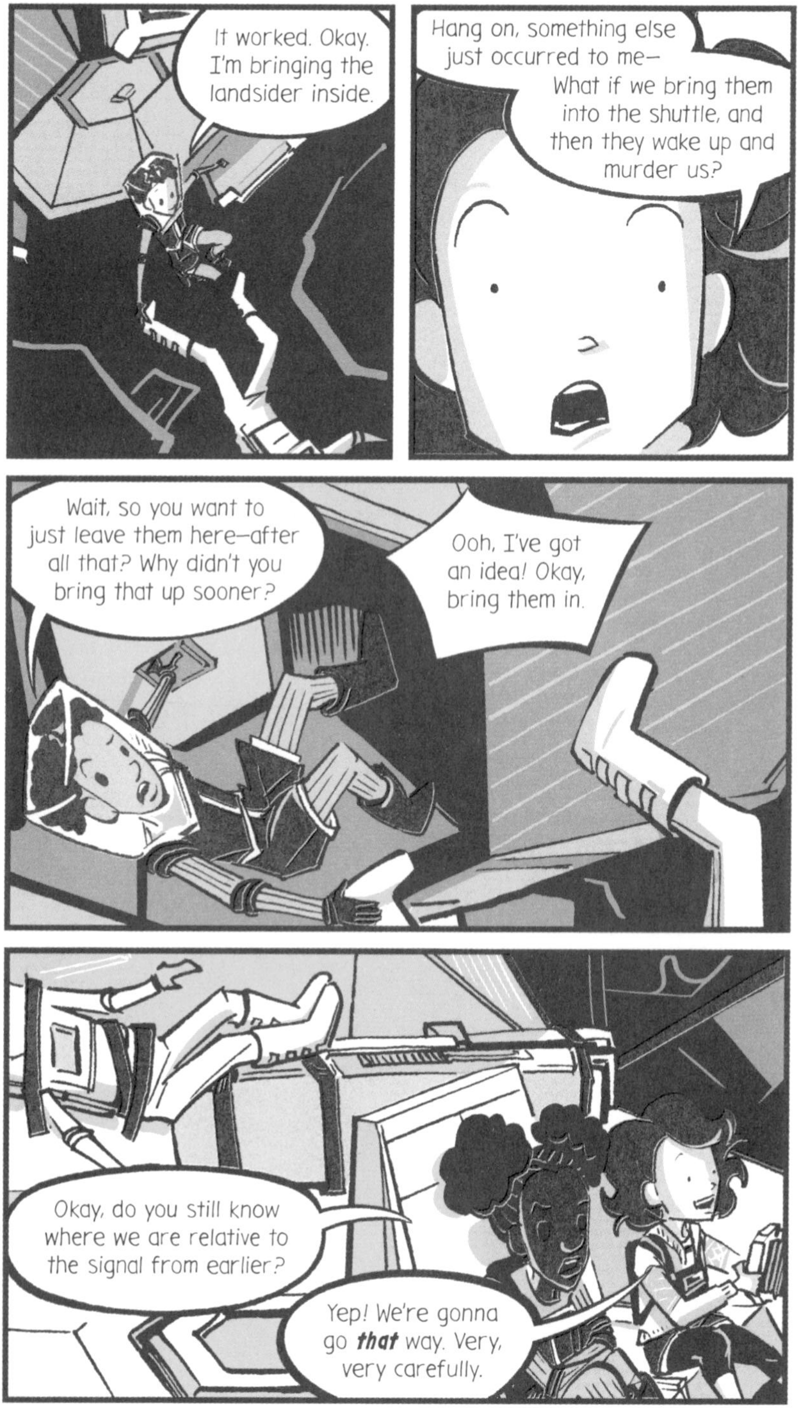
It worked. Okay. I'm bringing the landsider inside.
Hang on, something else just occurred to me—
What if we bring them into the shuttle, and then they wake up and murder us?
Wait, so you want to just leave them here—after all that? Why didn't you bring that up sooner?
Ooh, I've got an idea! Okay, bring them in.
Okay, do you still know where we are relative to the signal from earlier?
Yep! We're gonna go ***that*** way. Very, very carefully.

(Still Waiting)

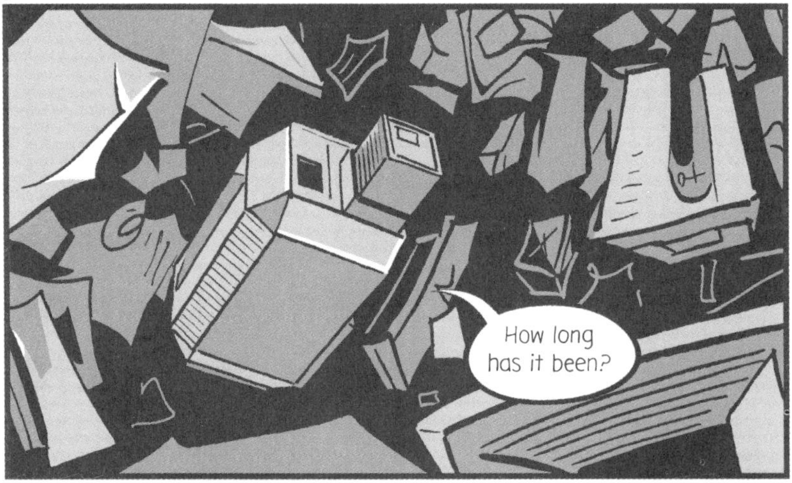
How long has it been?

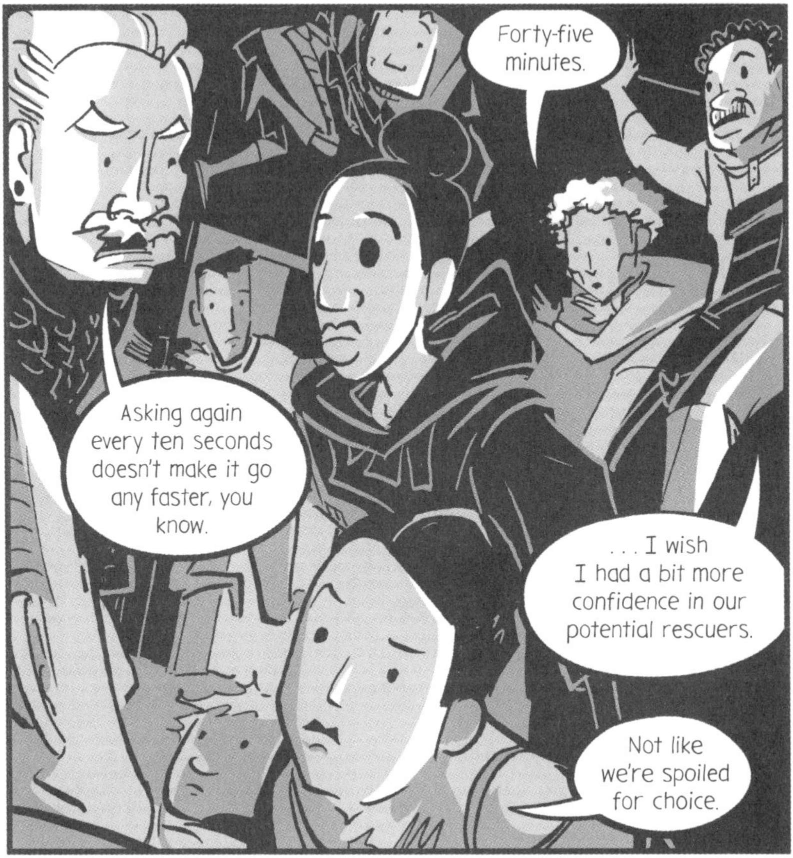
Forty-five minutes.
Asking again every ten seconds doesn't make it go any faster, you know.
. . . I wish I had a bit more confidence in our potential rescuers.
Not like we're spoiled for choice.

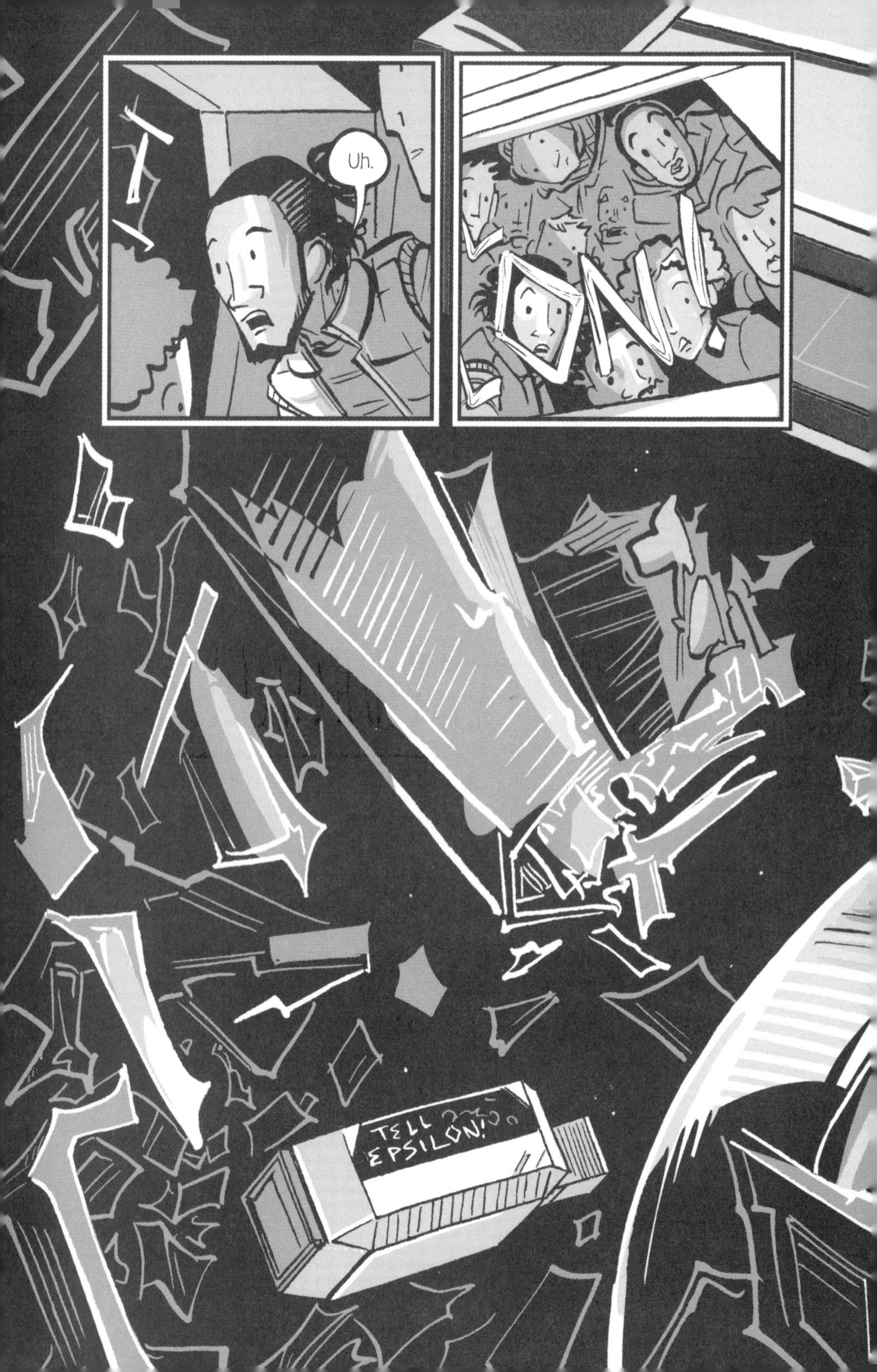
Uh.
TELL EPSILON!

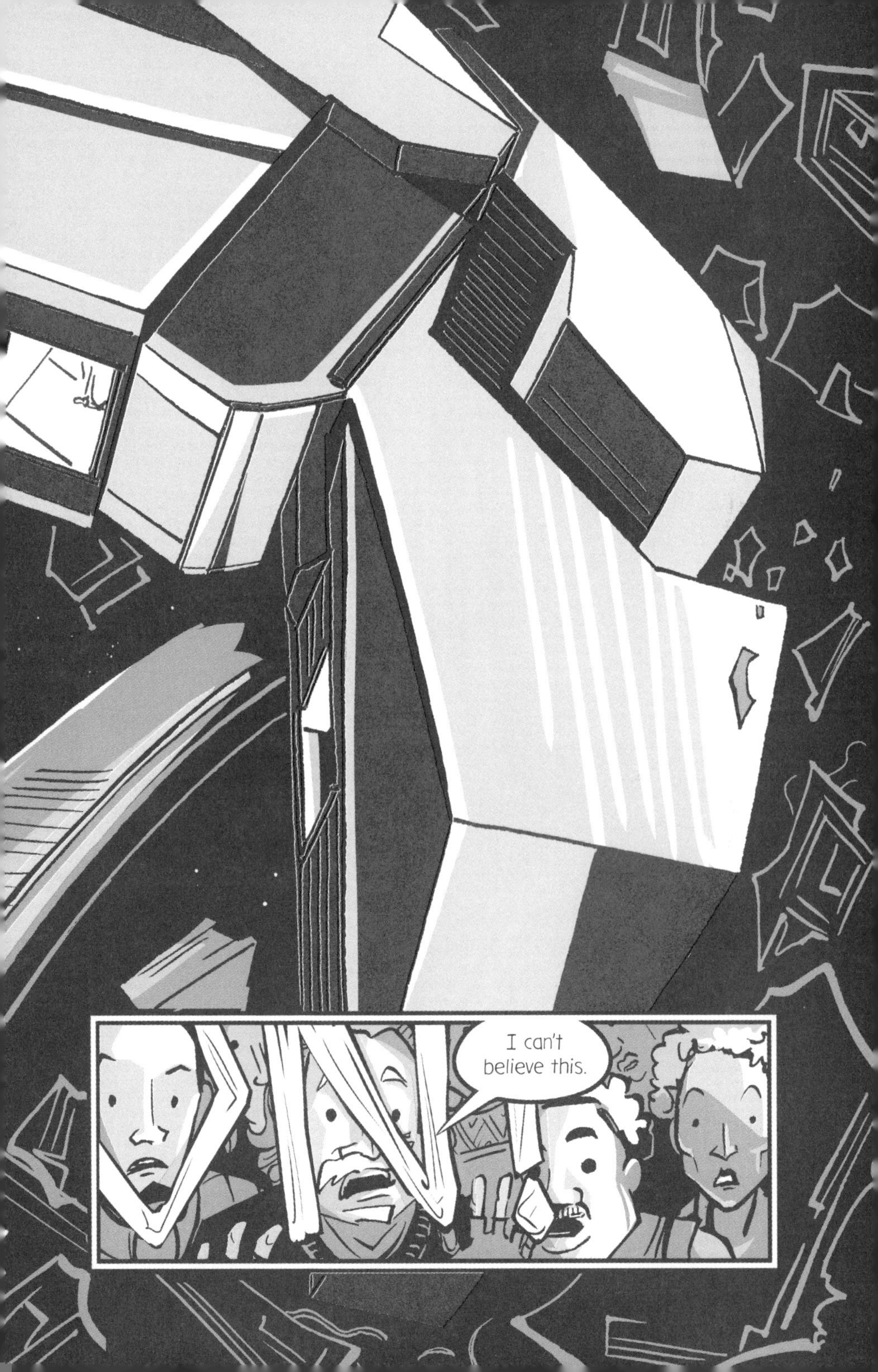
I can't believe this.

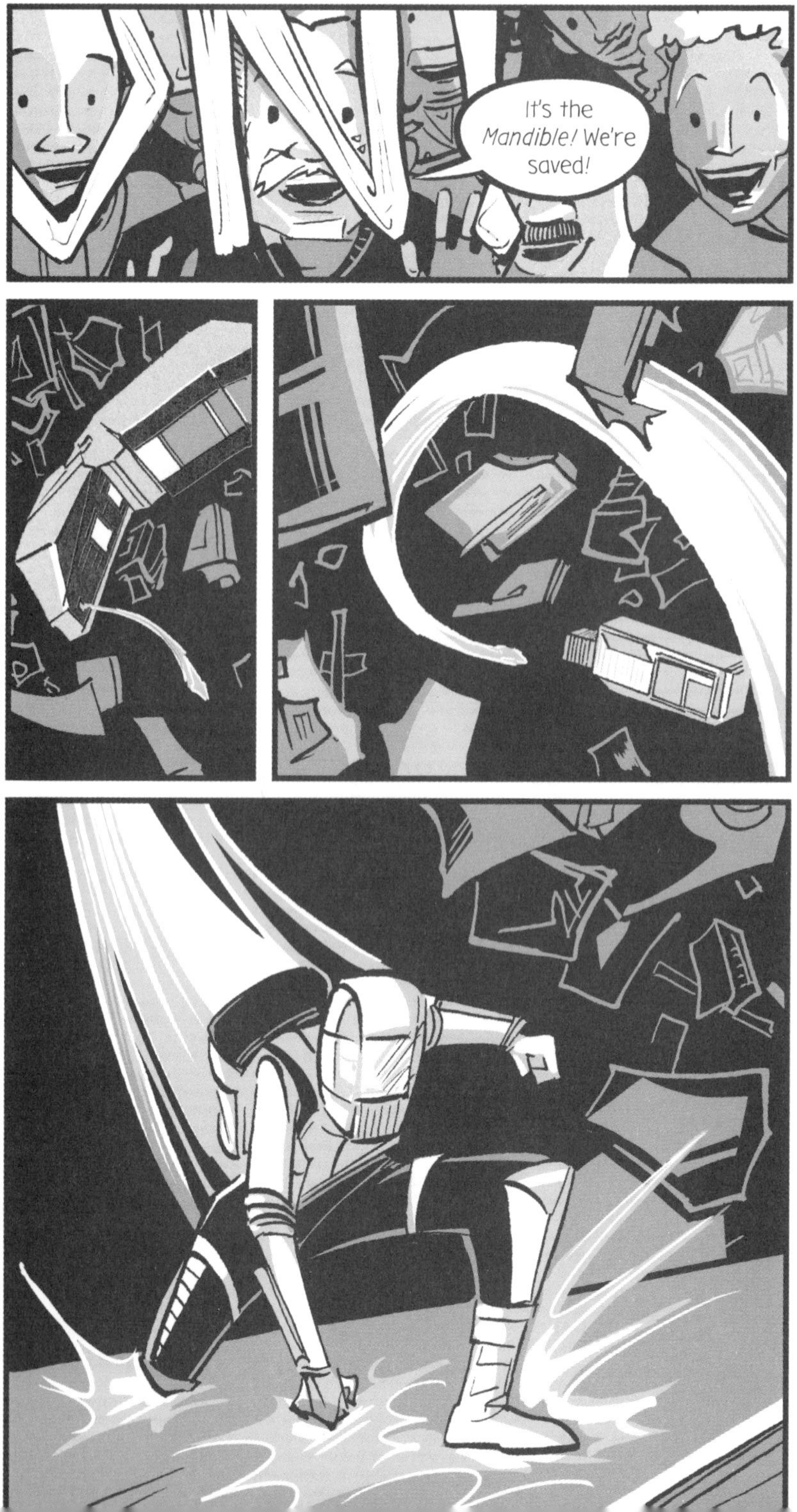
It's the *Mandible!* We're saved!

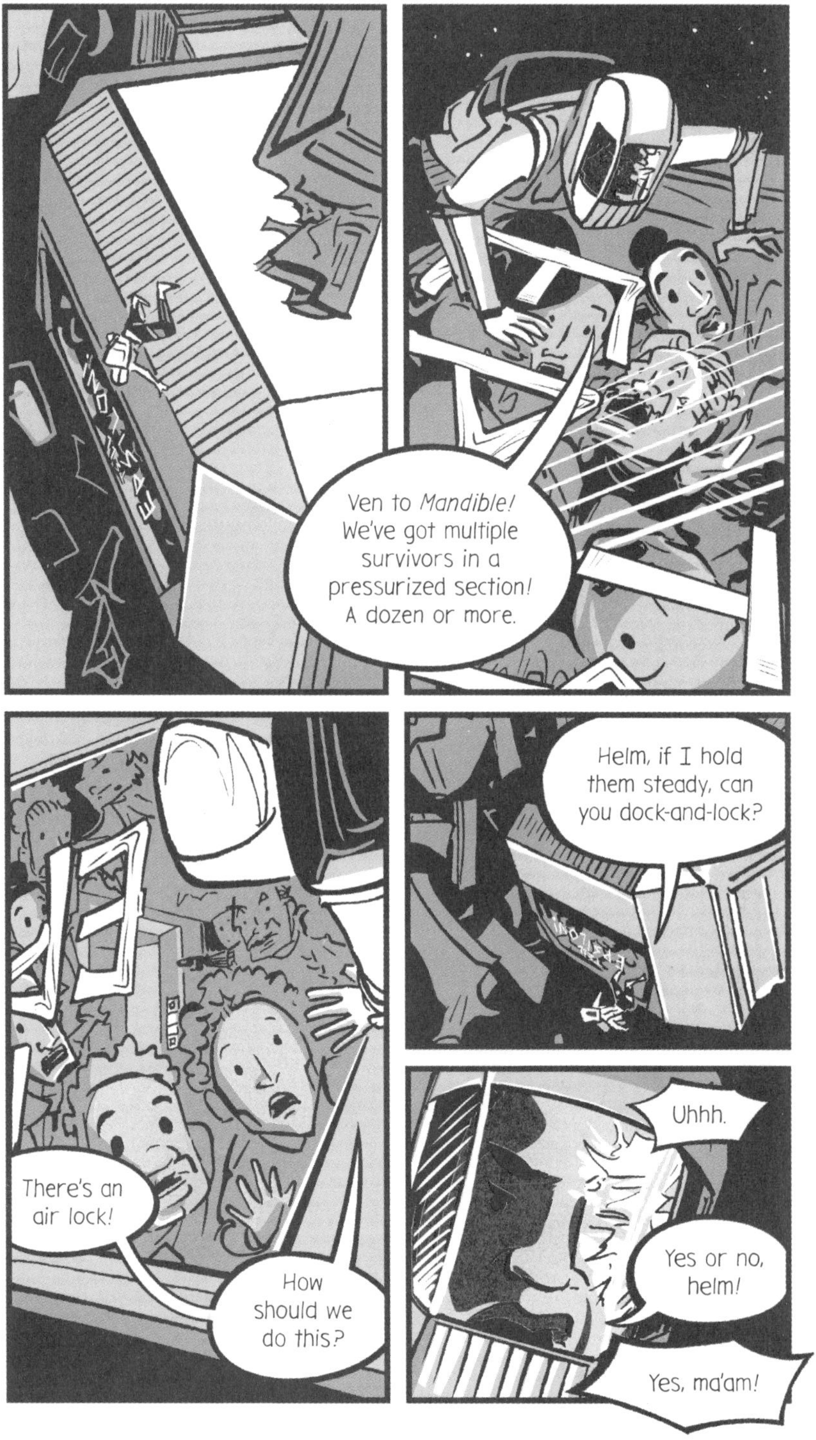
Ven to *Mandible!* We've got multiple survivors in a pressurized section! A dozen or more.
There's an air lock!
How should we do this?
Helm, if I hold them steady, can you dock-and-lock?
Uhhh.
Yes or no, helm!
Yes, ma'am!

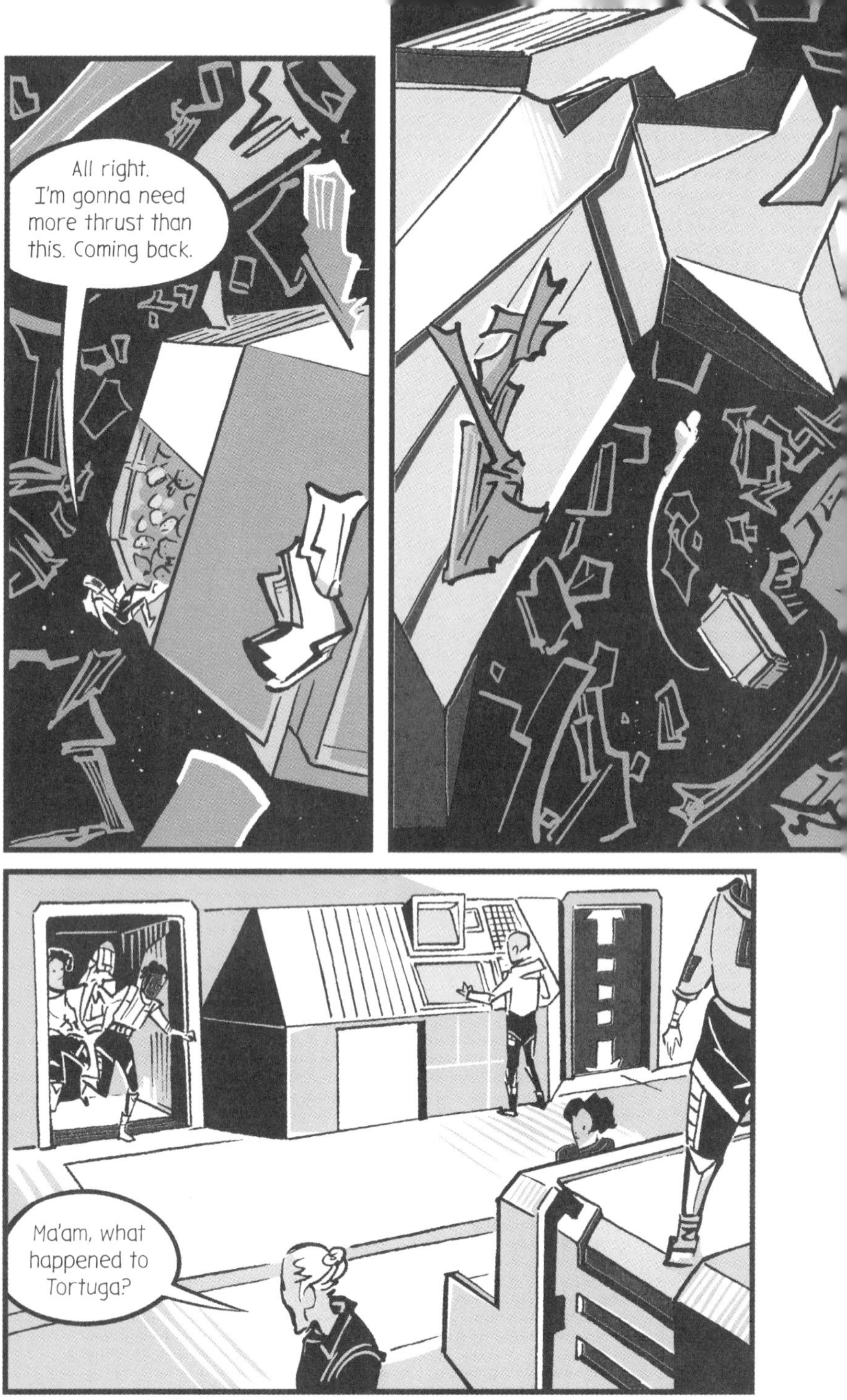
All right. I'm gonna need more thrust than this. Coming back.
Ma'am, what happened to Tortuga?

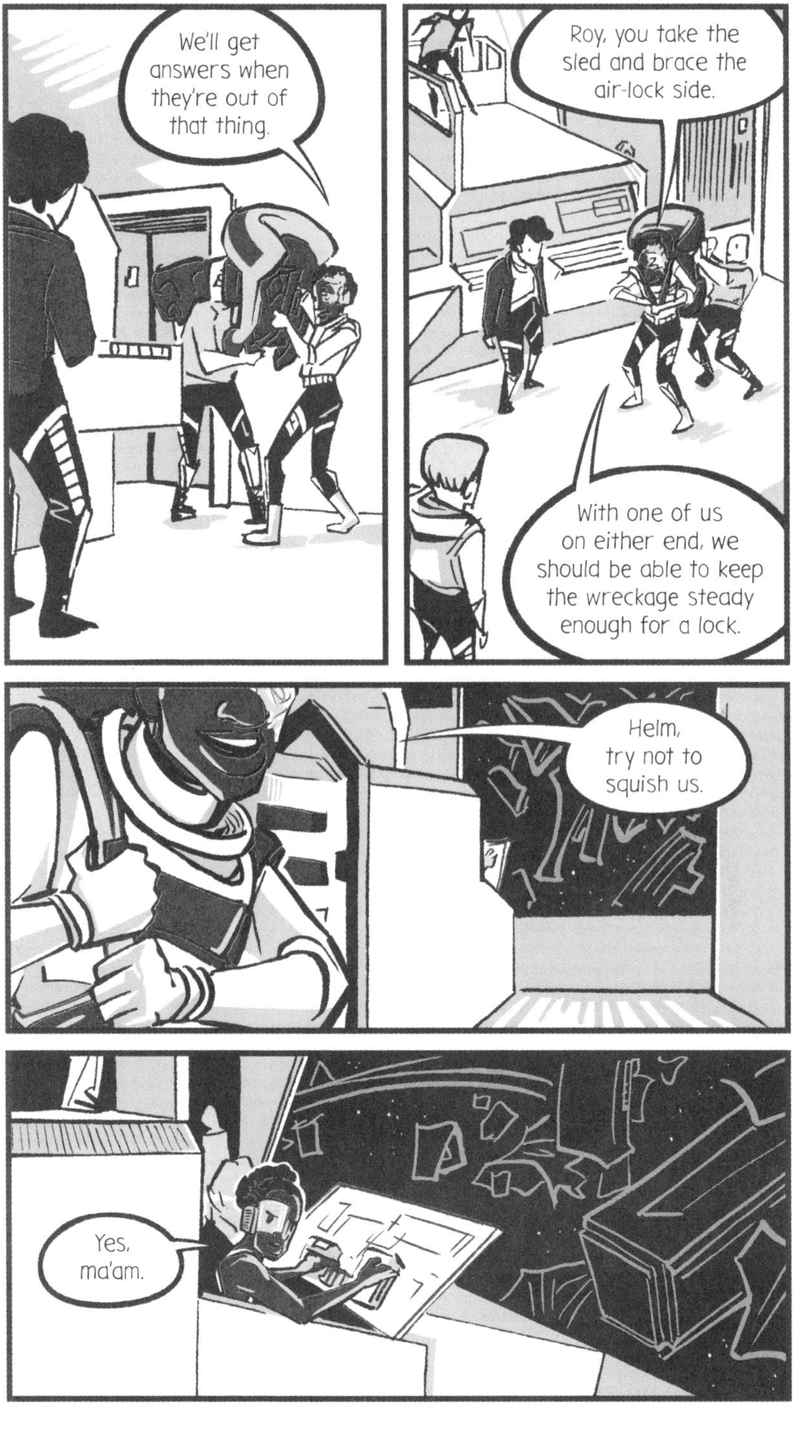
We'll get answers when they're out of that thing.
Roy, you take the sled and brace the air-lock side.
With one of us on either end, we should be able to keep the wreckage steady enough for a lock.
Helm, try not to squish us.
Yes, ma'am.

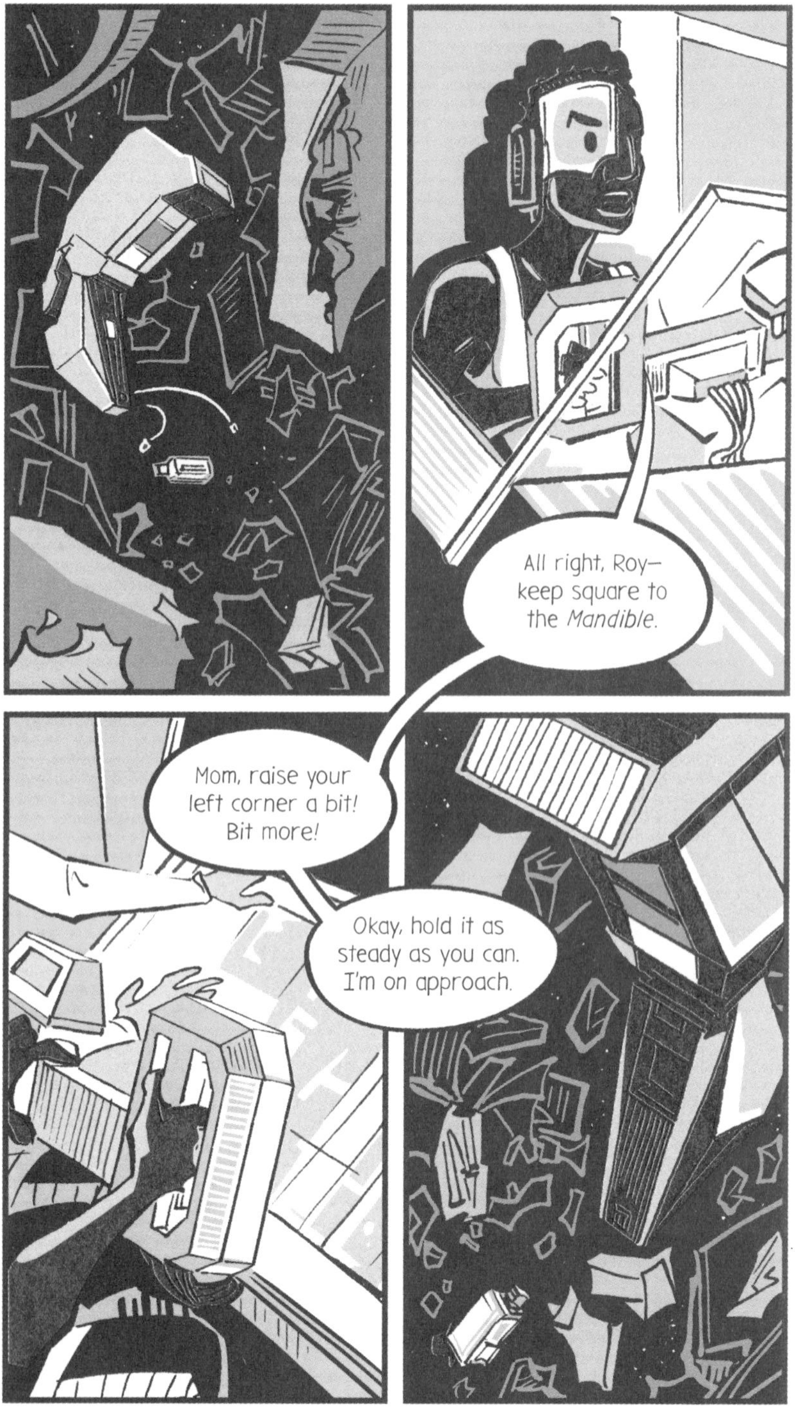
All right, Roy—
keep square to
the *Mandible*.
Mom, raise your
left corner a bit!
Bit more!
Okay, hold it as
steady as you can.
I'm on approach.

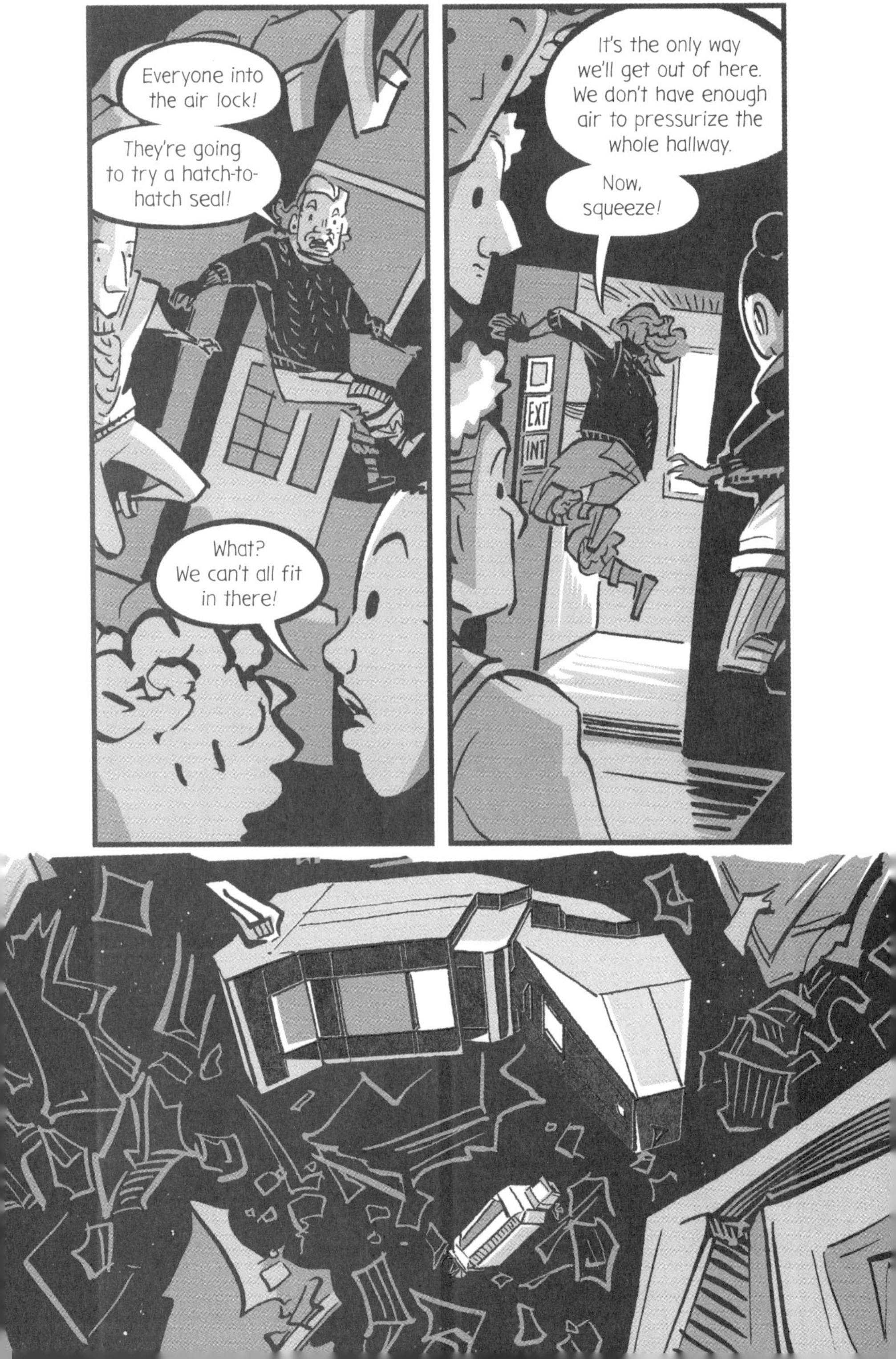
Everyone into the air lock!
They're going to try a hatch-to-hatch seal!
What? We can't all fit in there!
It's the only way we'll get out of here. We don't have enough air to pressurize the whole hallway.
Now, squeeze!
EXT
INT

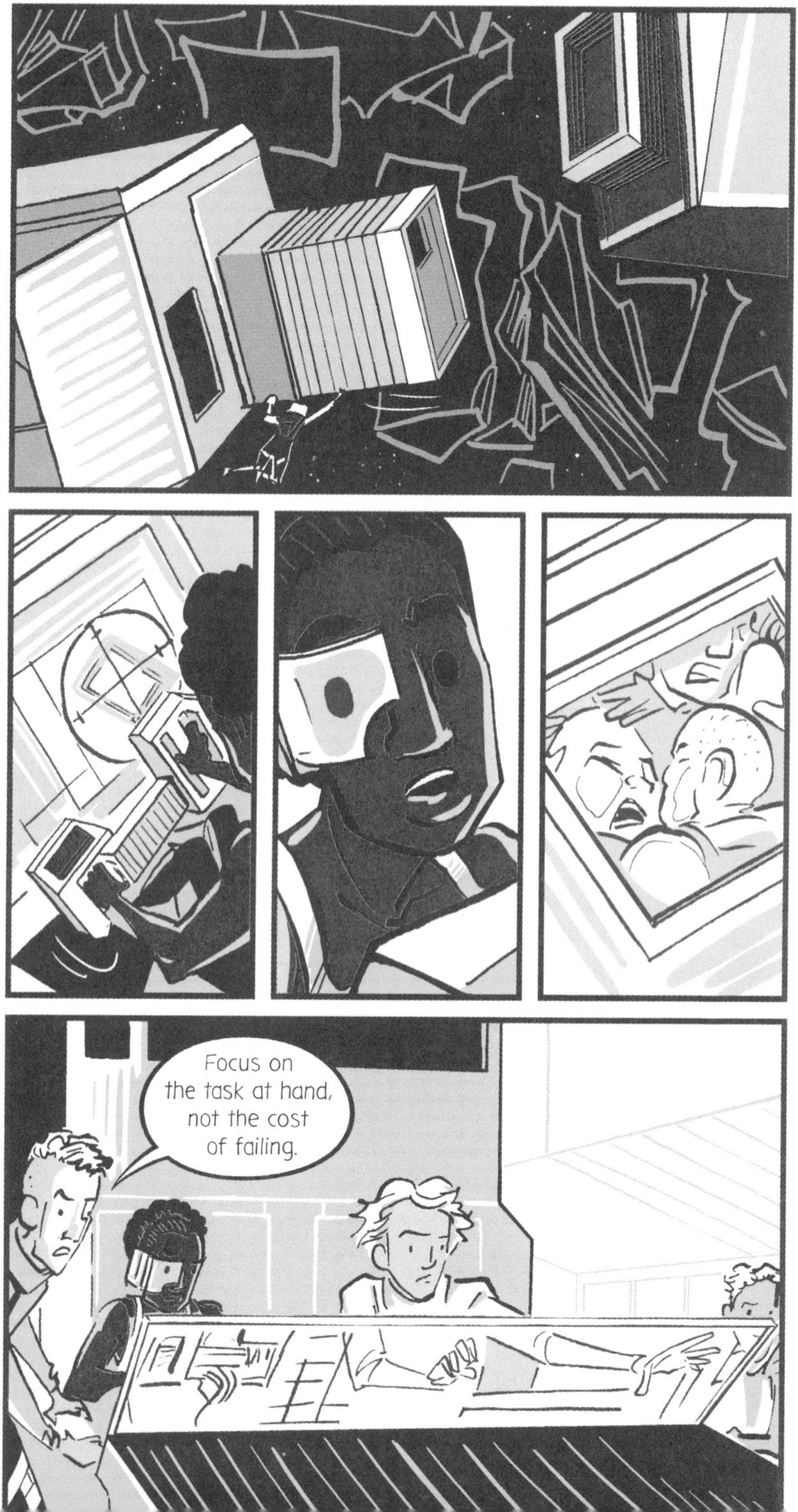
Focus on the task at hand, not the cost of failing.

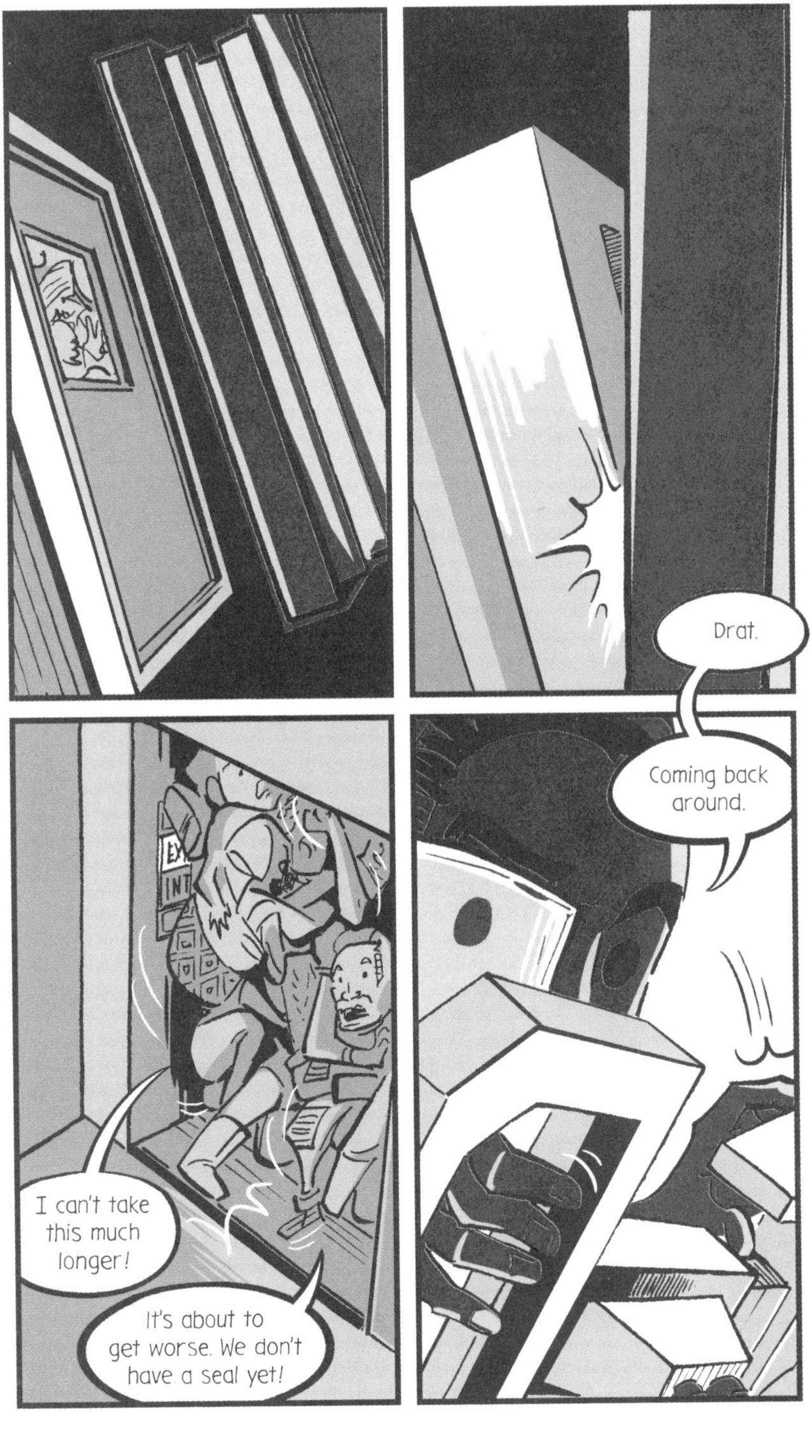
Drat.
Coming back around.
I can't take this much longer!
It's about to get worse. We don't have a seal yet!

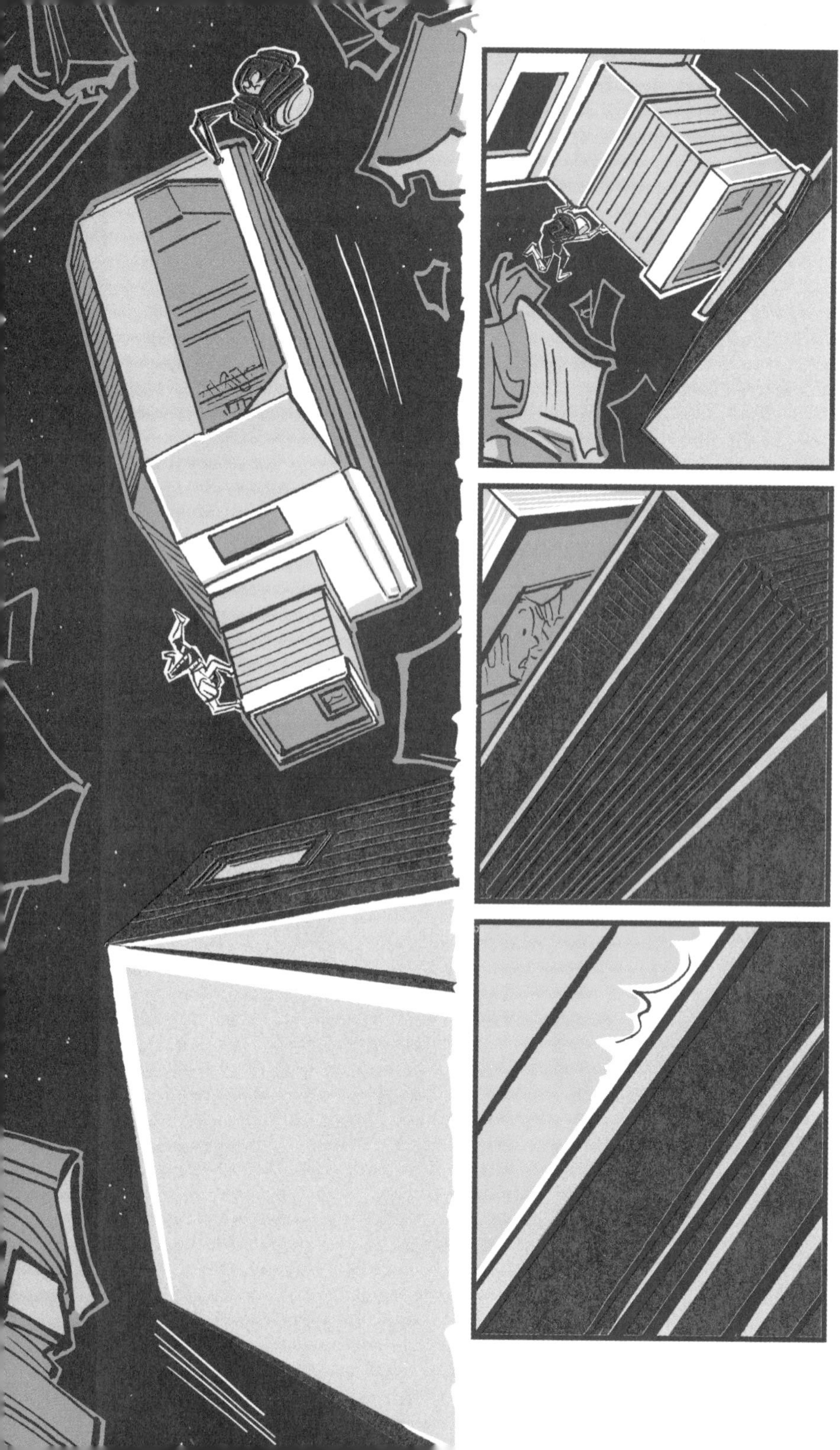

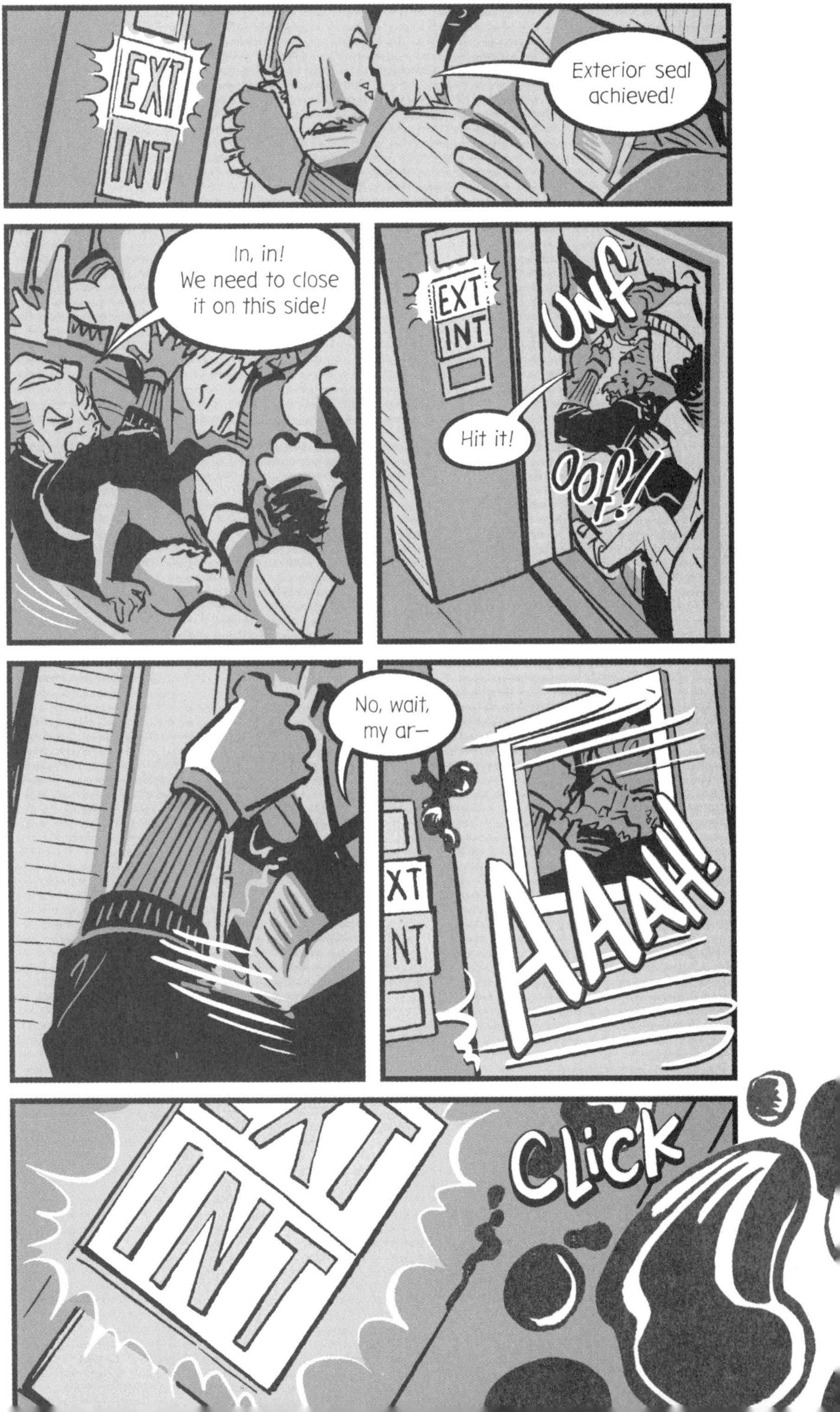
EXT
INT
Exterior seal achieved!
In, in! We need to close it on this side!
EXT
INT
UNF
Hit it!
OOF!
No, wait, my ar—
XT
NT
AAAH!
XT
INT
CLICK

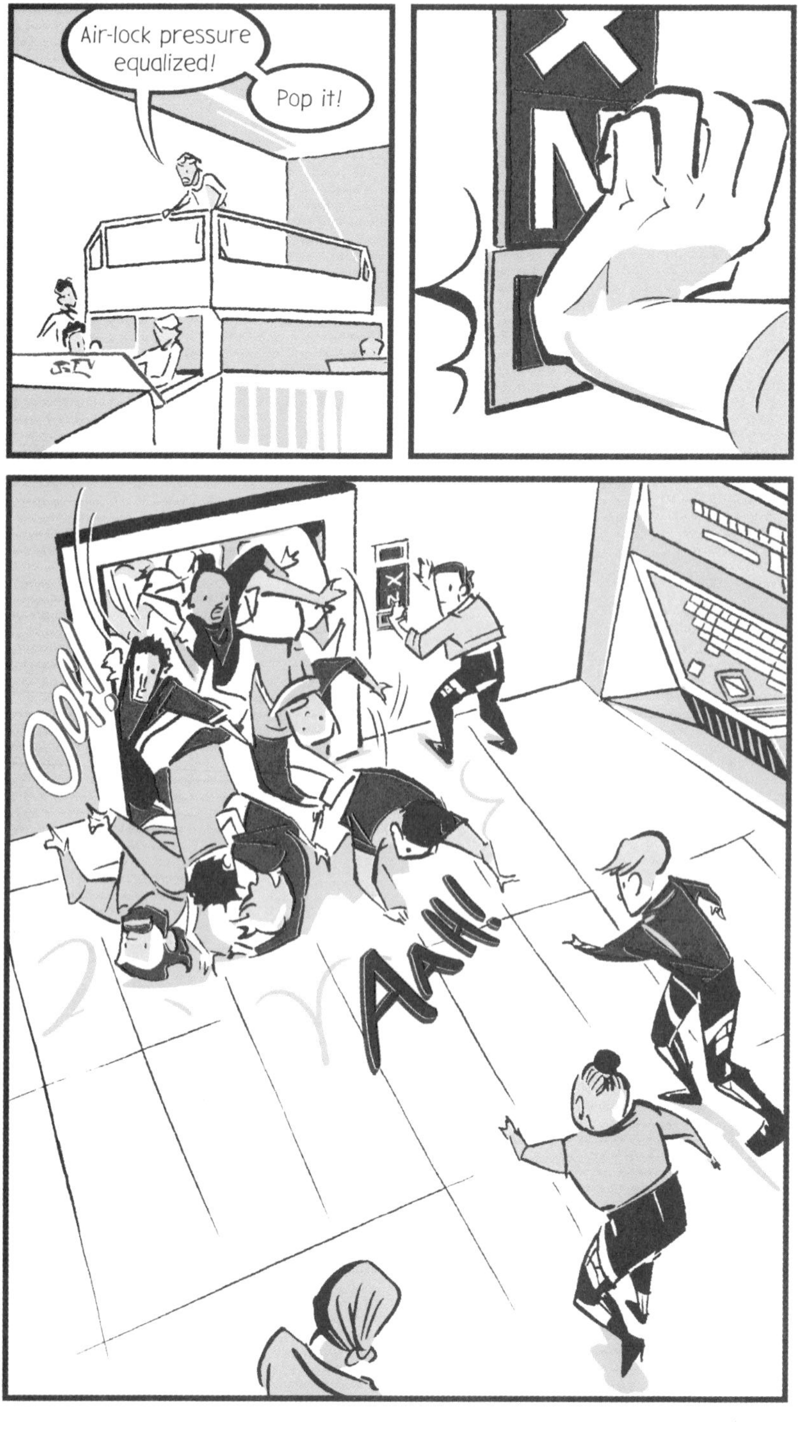
Air-lock pressure equalized!
Pop it!
OOF!
AAH!

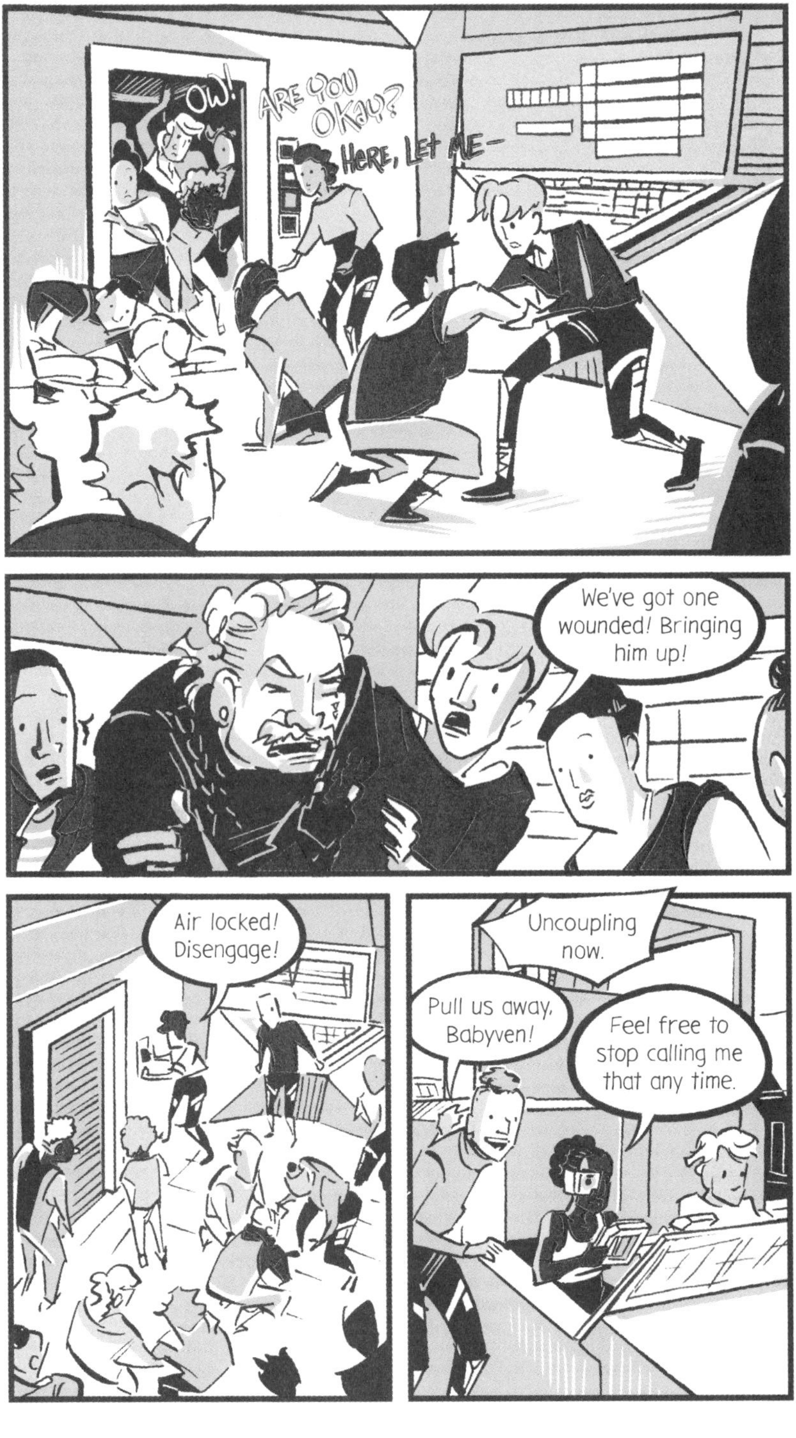
OW!
ARE YOU OKAY?
HERE, LET ME—
We've got one wounded! Bringing him up!
Air locked! Disengage!
Uncoupling now.
Pull us away, Babyven!
Feel free to stop calling me that any time.

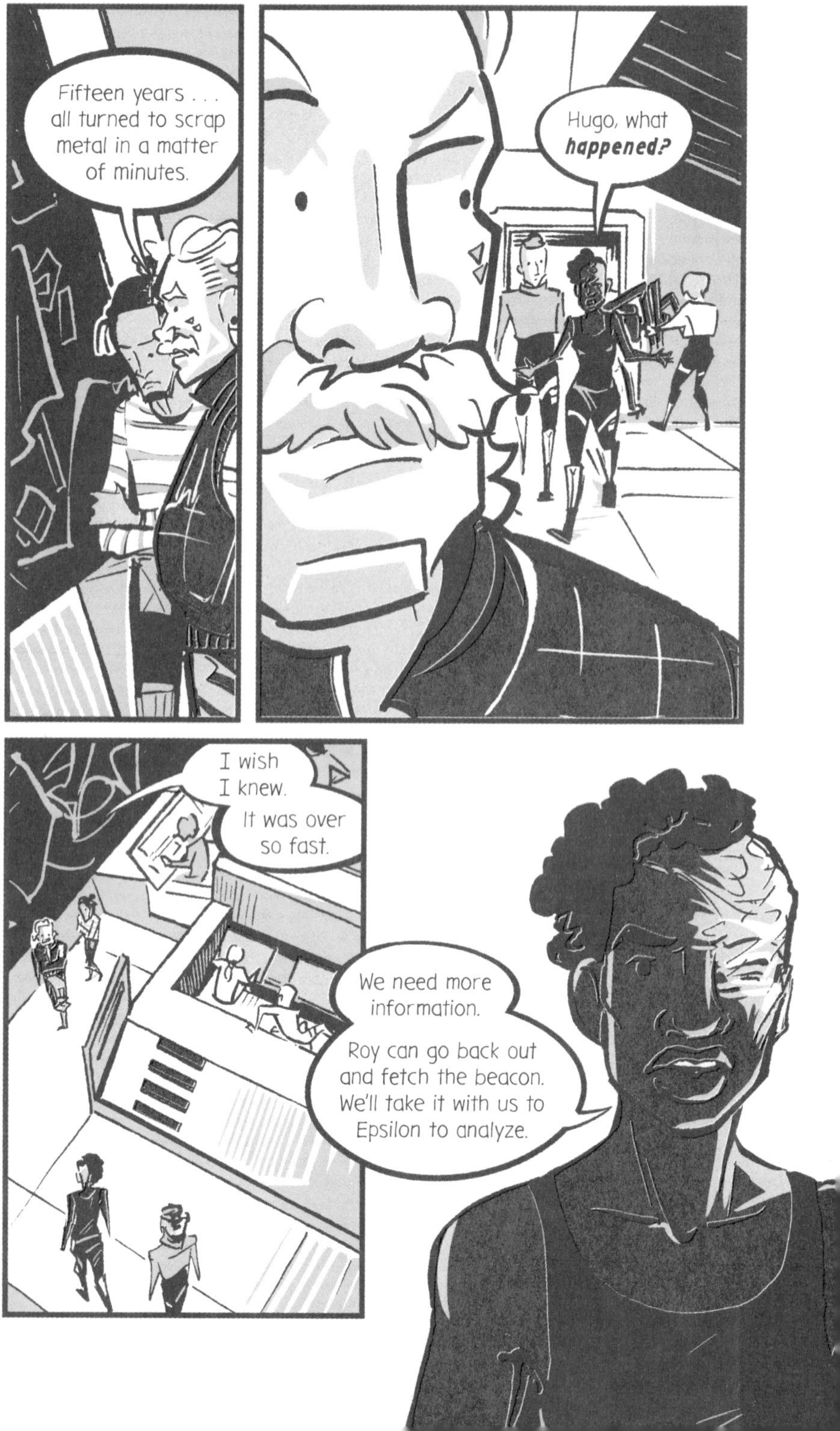
Fifteen years . . . all turned to scrap metal in a matter of minutes.
Hugo, what ***happened?***
I wish I knew.
It was over so fast.
We need more information.
Roy can go back out and fetch the beacon. We'll take it with us to Epsilon to analyze.

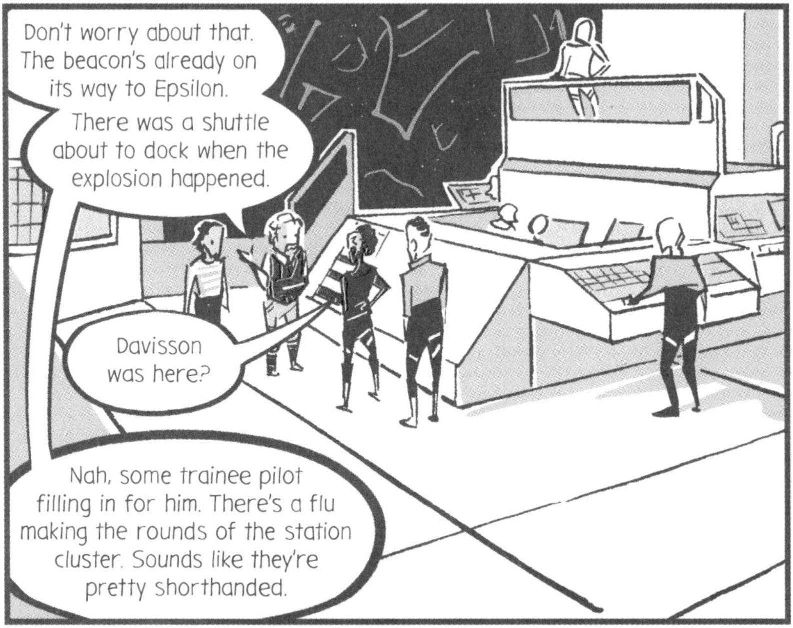
Don't worry about that. The beacon's already on its way to Epsilon.
There was a shuttle about to dock when the explosion happened.
Davisson was here?
Nah, some trainee pilot filling in for him. There's a flu making the rounds of the station cluster. Sounds like they're pretty shorthanded.
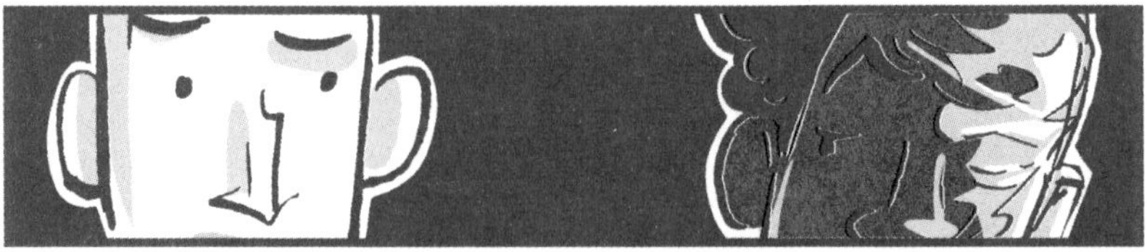
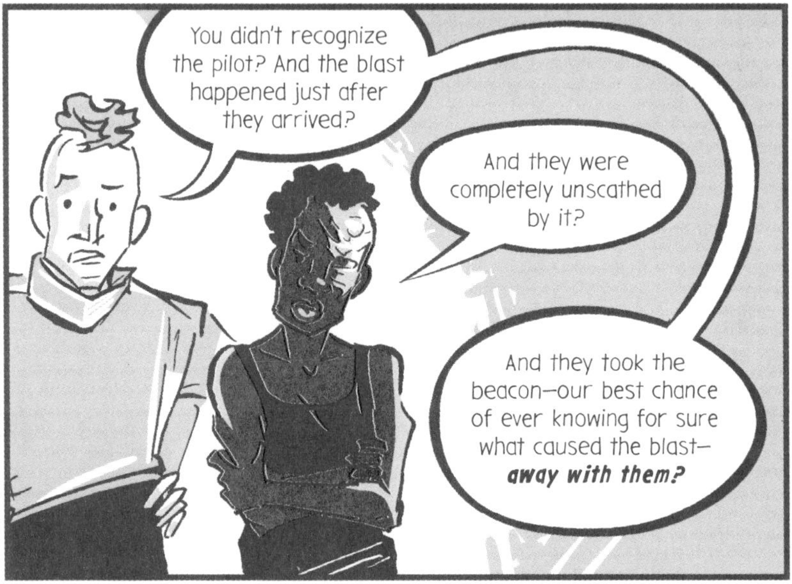
You didn't recognize the pilot? And the blast happened just after they arrived?
And they were completely unscathed by it?
And they took the beacon—our best chance of ever knowing for sure what caused the blast—***away with them?***

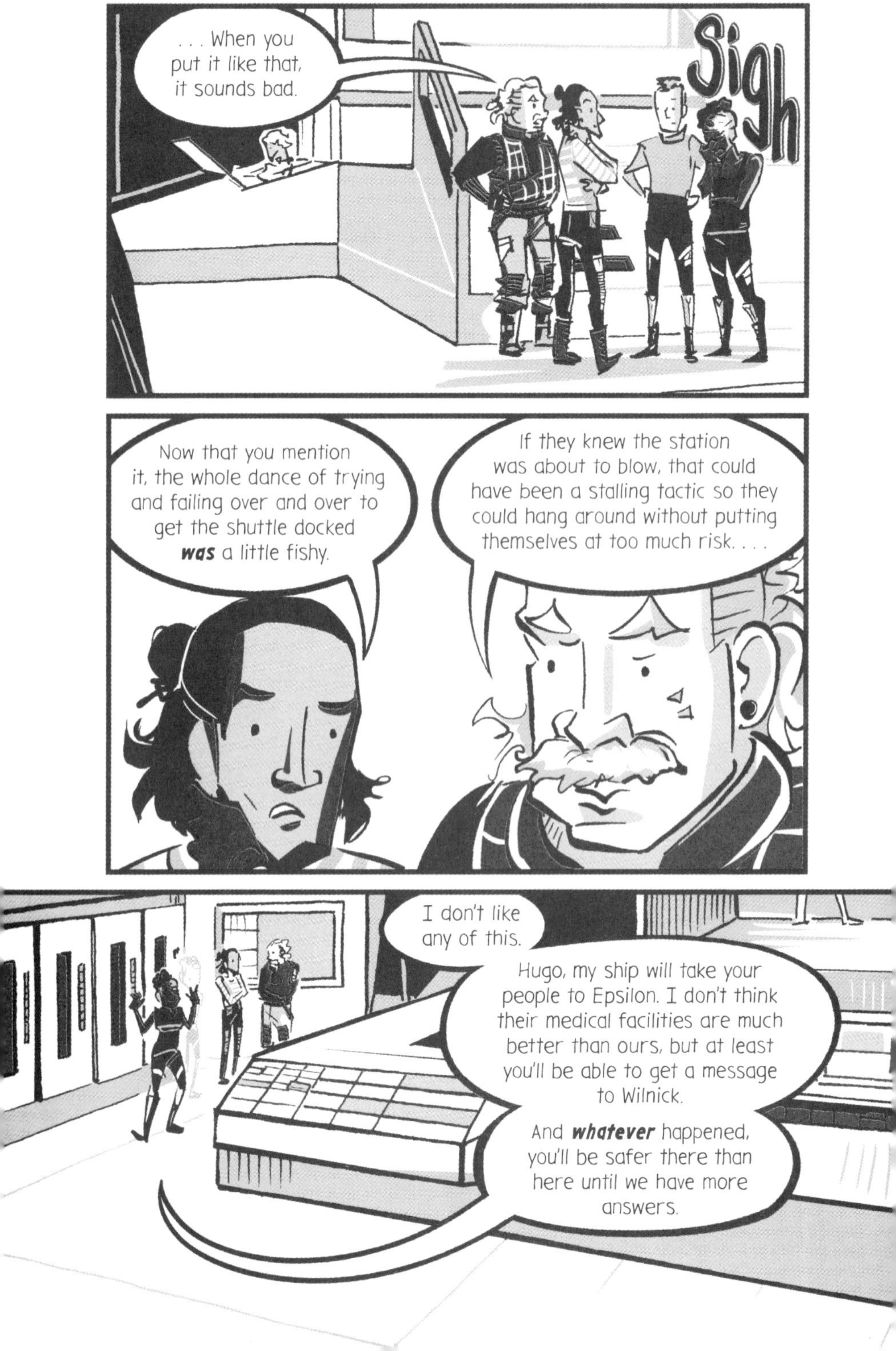
. . . When you put it like that, it sounds bad.
Sigh
Now that you mention it, the whole dance of trying and failing over and over to get the shuttle docked **was** a little fishy.
If they knew the station was about to blow, that could have been a stalling tactic so they could hang around without putting themselves at too much risk. . . .
I don't like any of this.
Hugo, my ship will take your people to Epsilon. I don't think their medical facilities are much better than ours, but at least you'll be able to get a message to Wilnick.
And **whatever** happened, you'll be safer there than here until we have more answers.

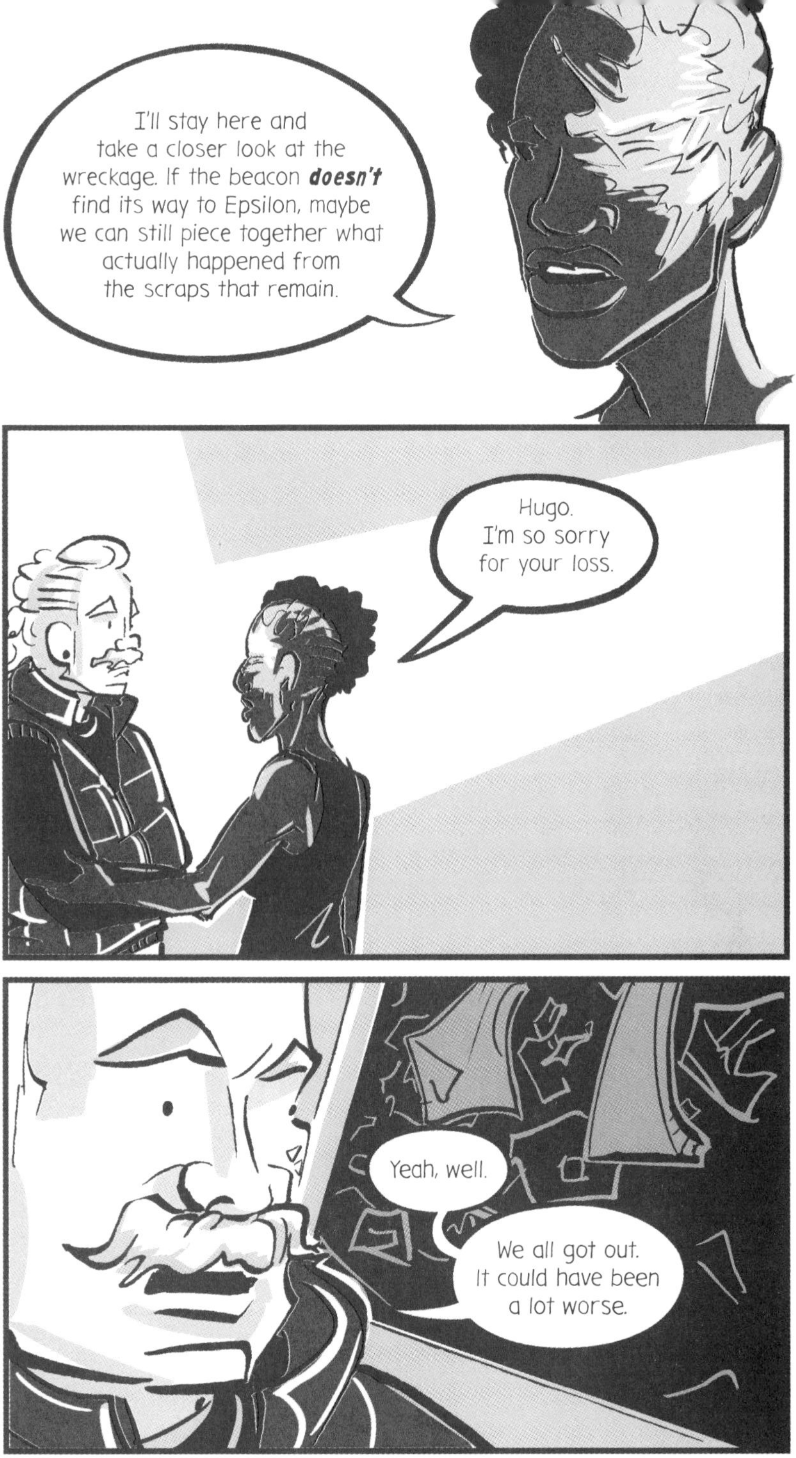
I'll stay here and take a closer look at the wreckage. If the beacon **doesn't** find its way to Epsilon, maybe we can still piece together what actually happened from the scraps that remain.
Hugo. I'm so sorry for your loss.
Yeah, well.
We all got out. It could have been a lot worse.

(COMMS CENTER ON EPSILON STATION)

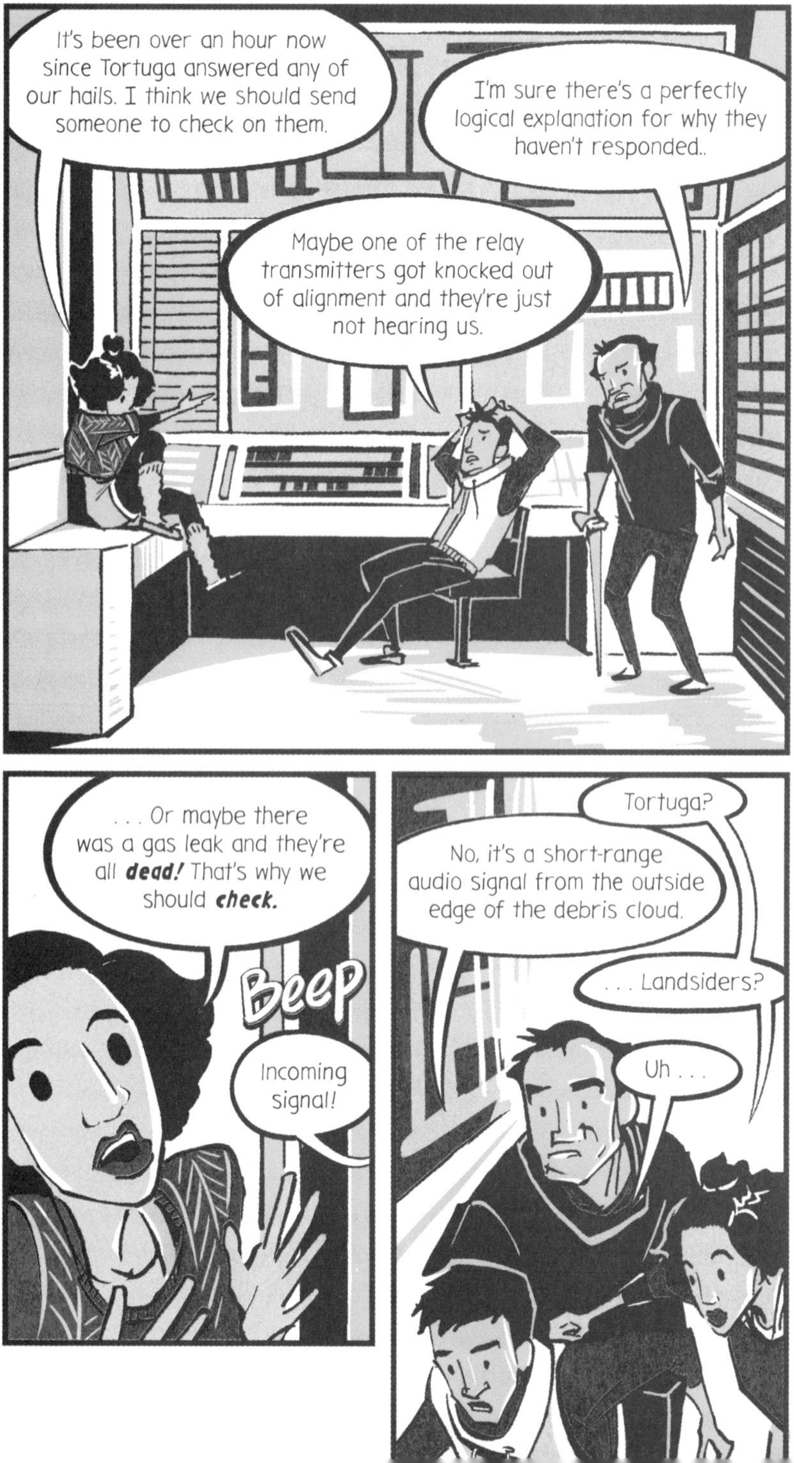

It's been over an hour now since Tortuga answered any of our hails. I think we should send someone to check on them.
I'm sure there's a perfectly logical explanation for why they haven't responded..
Maybe one of the relay transmitters got knocked out of alignment and they're just not hearing us.
. . . Or maybe there was a gas leak and they're all **dead!** That's why we should **check.**
Beep
Incoming signal!
Tortuga?
No, it's a short-range audio signal from the outside edge of the debris cloud.
. . . Landsiders?
Uh . . .

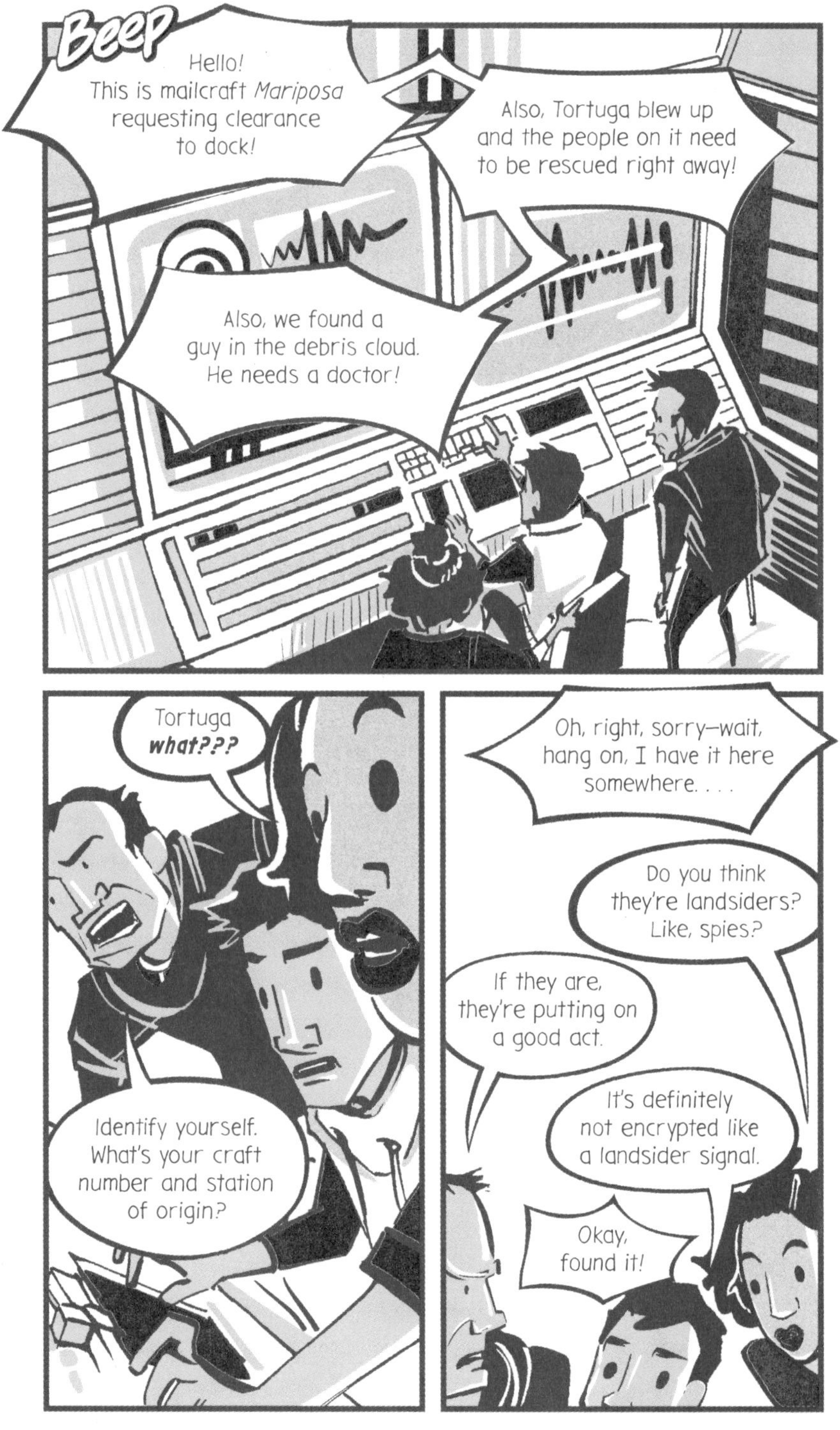
Beep
Hello! This is mailcraft *Mariposa* requesting clearance to dock!
Also, Tortuga blew up and the people on it need to be rescued right away!
Also, we found a guy in the debris cloud. He needs a doctor!
Tortuga ***what???***
Identify yourself. What's your craft number and station of origin?
Oh, right, sorry—wait, hang on, I have it here somewhere. . . .
Do you think they're landsiders? Like, spies?
If they are, they're putting on a good act.
It's definitely not encrypted like a landsider signal.
Okay, found it!

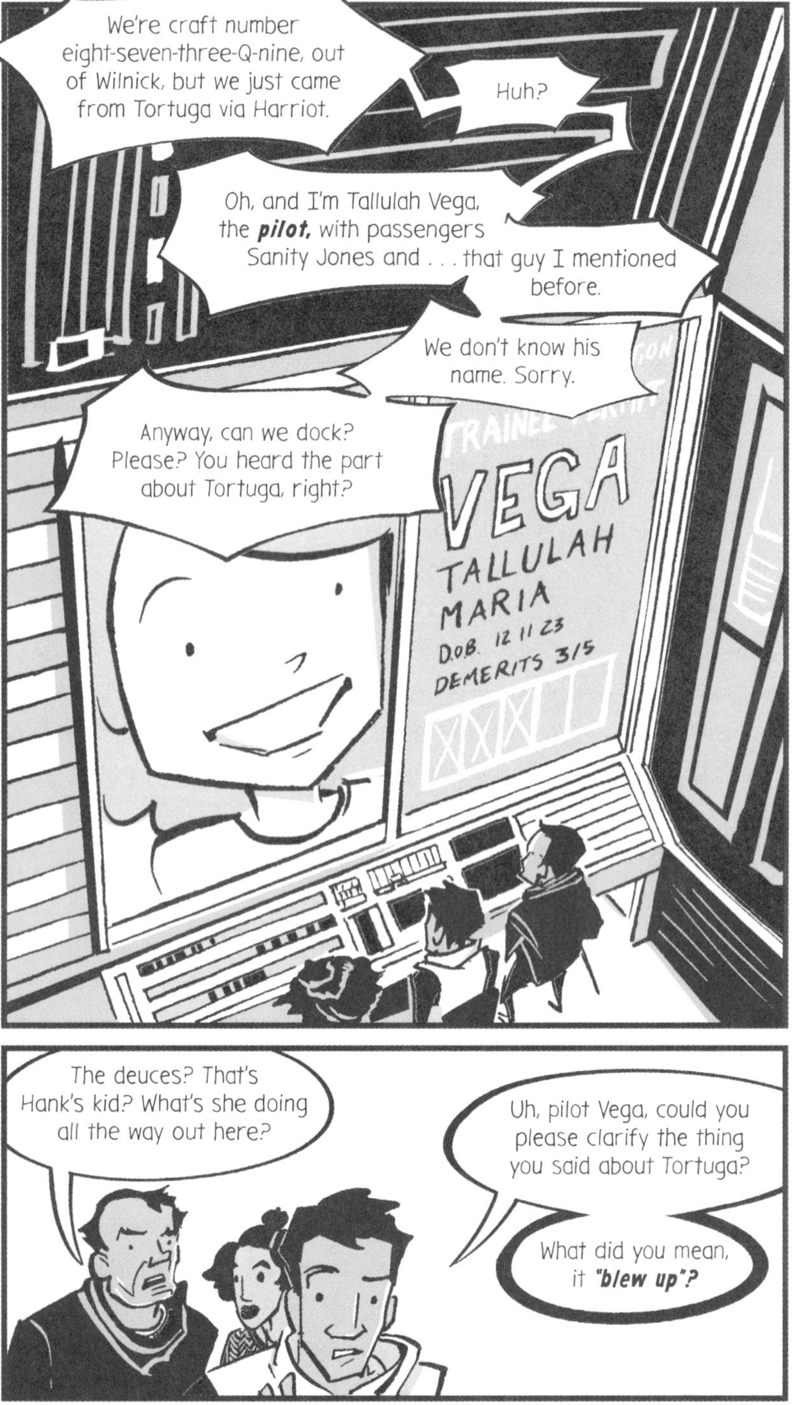
We're craft number eight-seven-three-Q-nine, out of Wilnick, but we just came from Tortuga via Harriot.
Huh?
Oh, and I'm Tallulah Vega, the **pilot,** with passengers Sanity Jones and . . . that guy I mentioned before.
We don't know his name. Sorry.
Anyway, can we dock? Please? You heard the part about Tortuga, right?
VEGA
TALLULAH
MARIA
D.O.B. 12 11 23
DEMERITS 3/5
The deuces? That's Hank's kid? What's she doing all the way out here?
Uh, pilot Vega, could you please clarify the thing you said about Tortuga?
What did you mean, it ***"blew up"?***

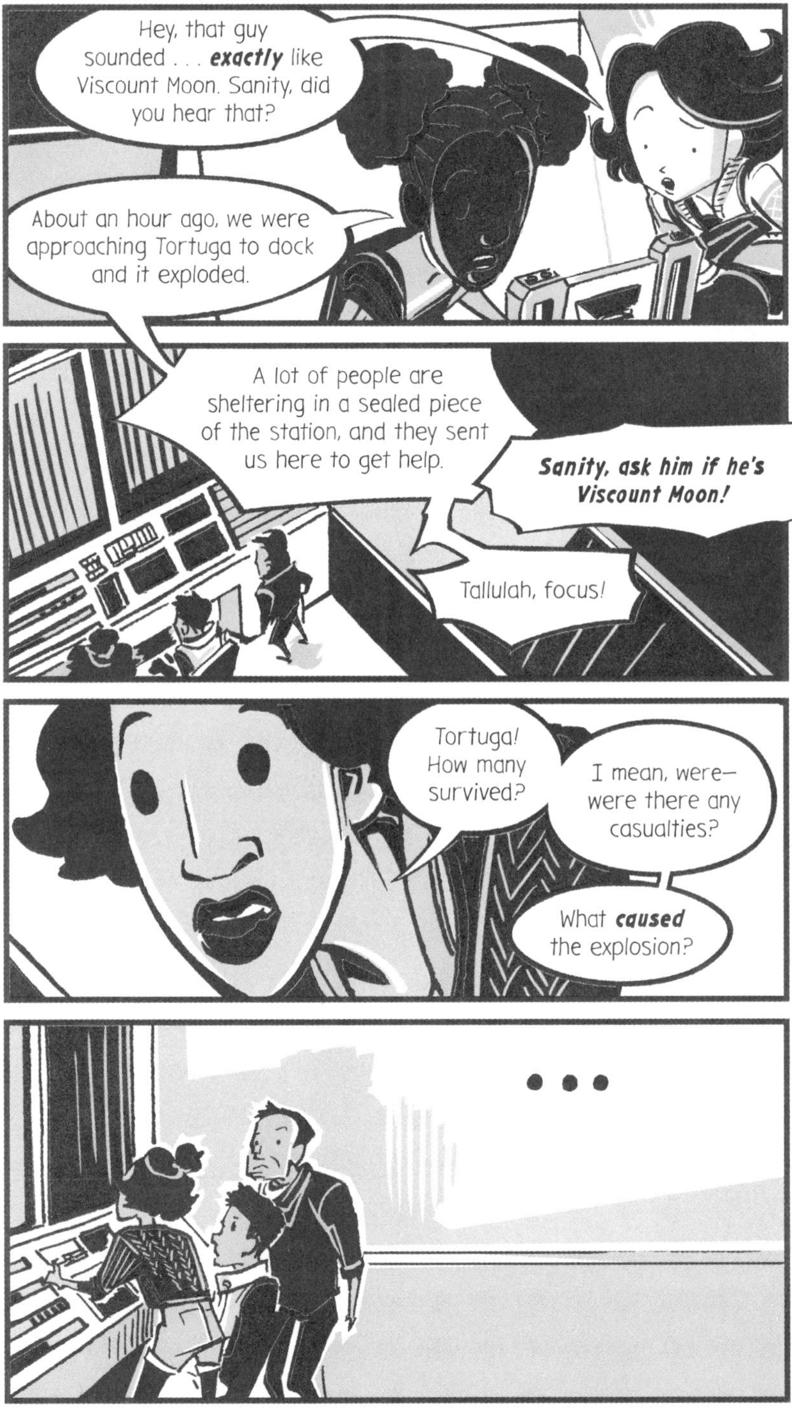
Hey, that guy sounded . . . **exactly** like Viscount Moon. Sanity, did you hear that?
About an hour ago, we were approaching Tortuga to dock and it exploded.
A lot of people are sheltering in a sealed piece of the station, and they sent us here to get help.
Sanity, ask him if he's Viscount Moon!
Tallulah, focus!
Tortuga! How many survived?
I mean, were— were there any casualties?
What **caused** the explosion?
• • •

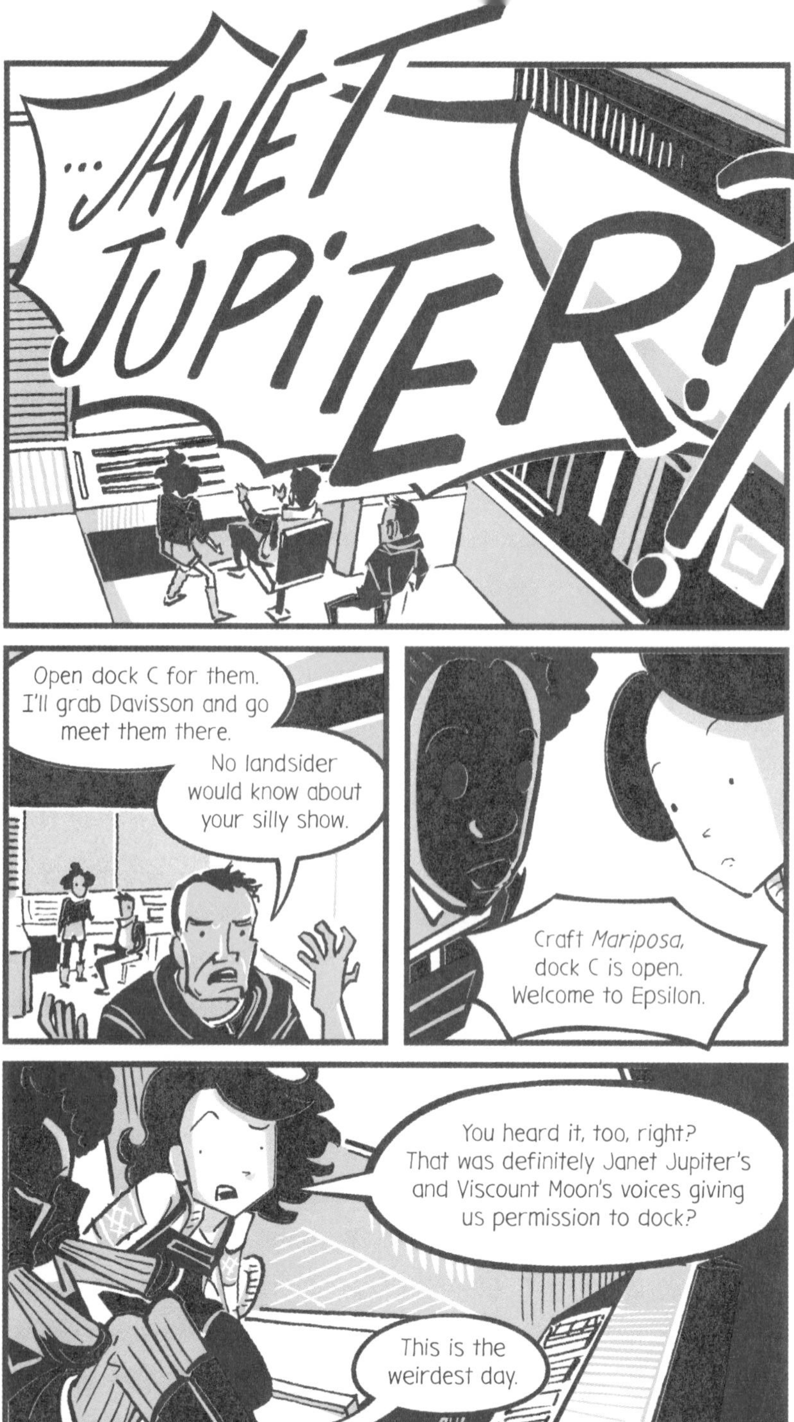
...JANET JUPITER?!
Open dock C for them. I'll grab Davisson and go meet them there.
No landsider would know about your silly show.
Craft *Mariposa,* dock C is open. Welcome to Epsilon.
You heard it, too, right? That was definitely Janet Jupiter's and Viscount Moon's voices giving us permission to dock?
This is the weirdest day.

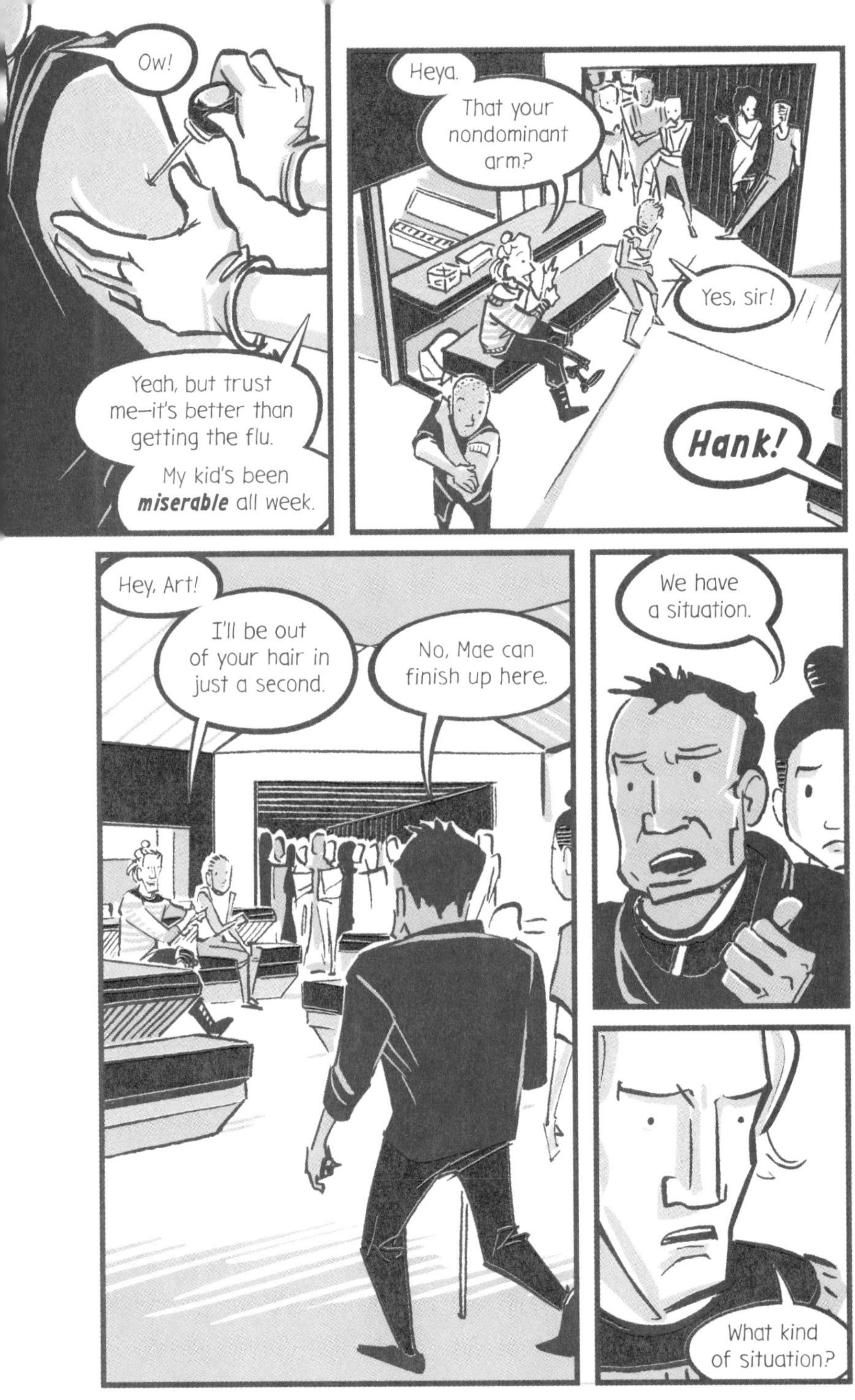

Ow!
Yeah, but trust me—it's better than getting the flu.
My kid's been **miserable** all week.
Heya.
That your nondominant arm?
Yes, sir!
Hank!
Hey, Art!
I'll be out of your hair in just a second.
No, Mae can finish up here.
We have a situation.
What kind of situation?

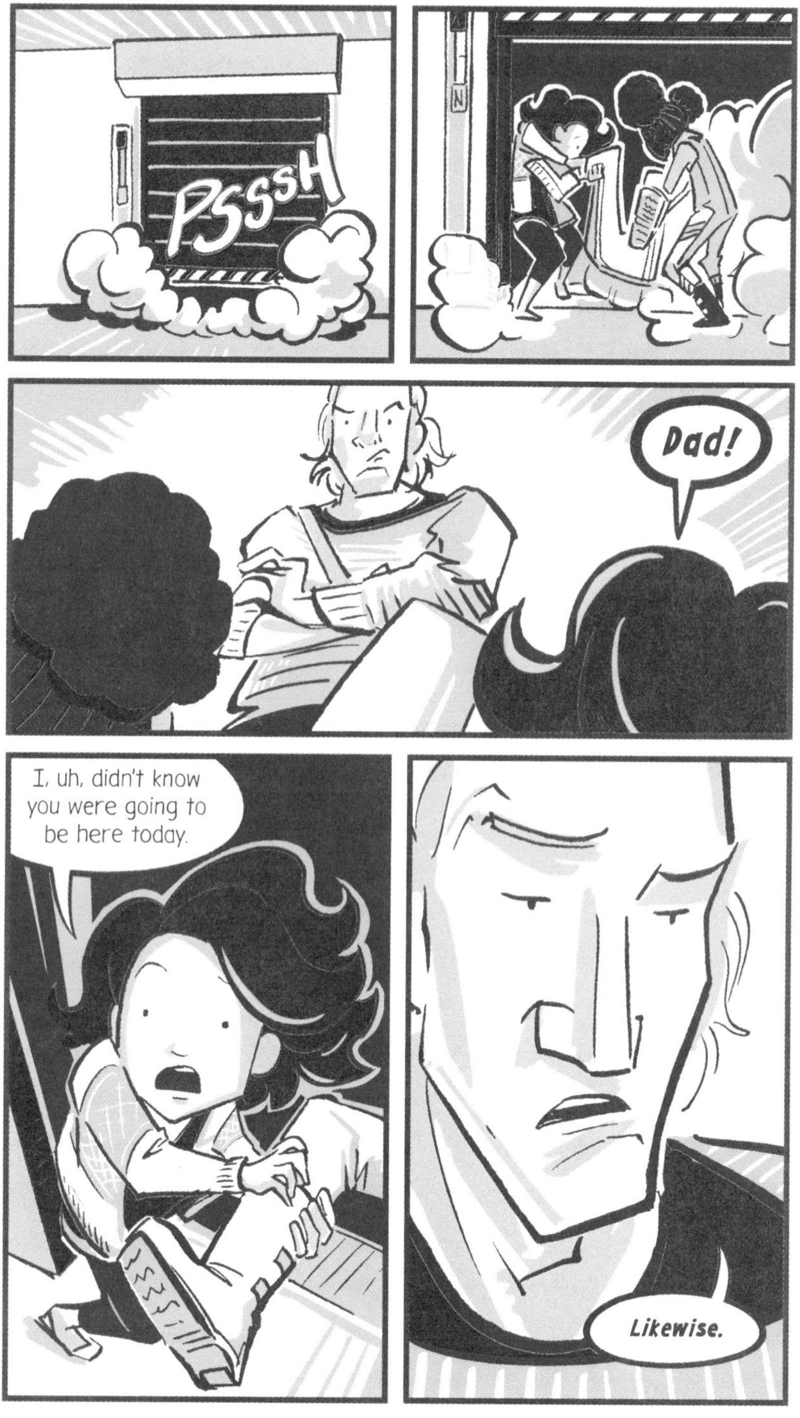
PSSSH
Dad!
I, uh, didn't know you were going to be here today.
Likewise.

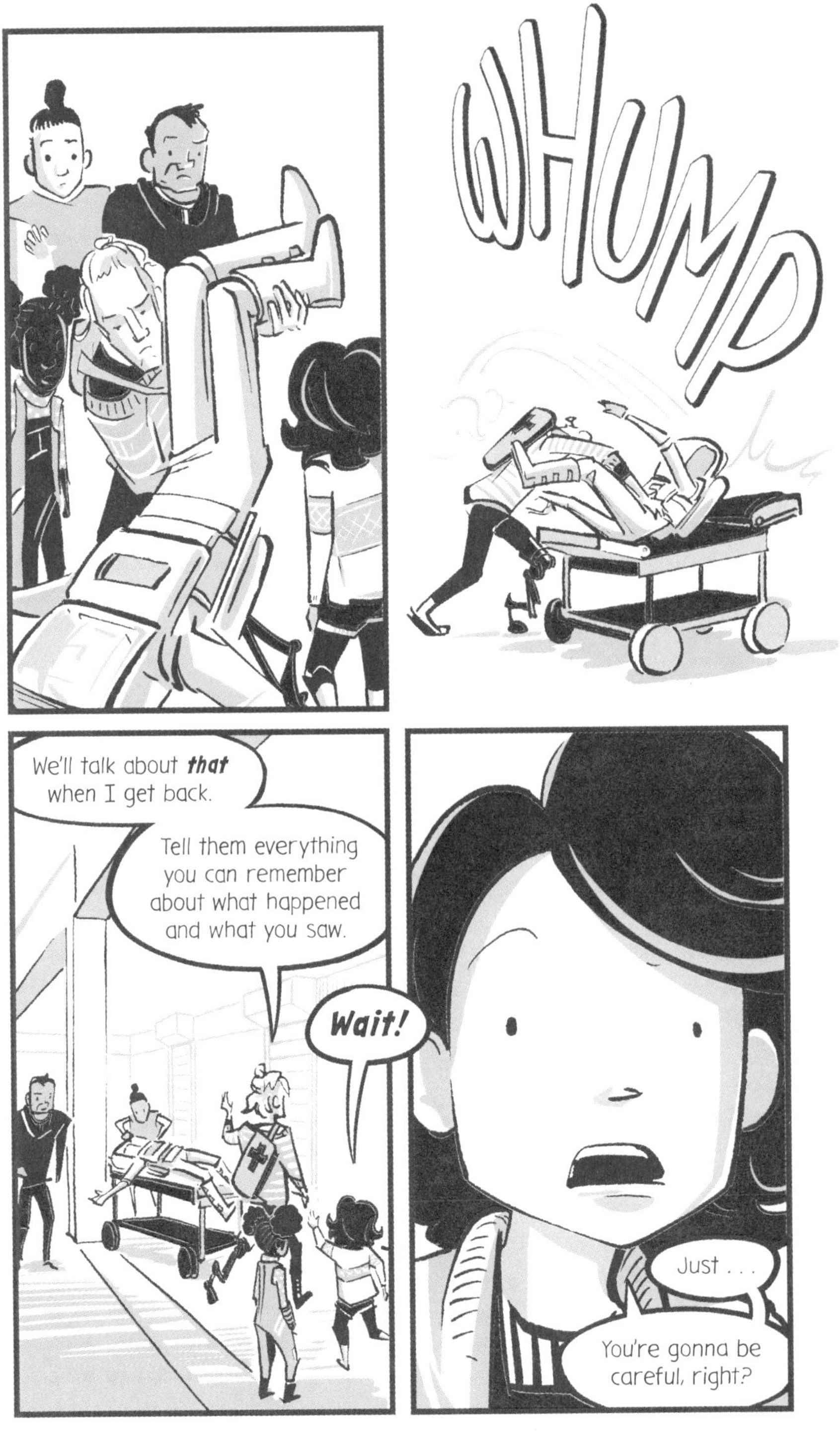
WHUMP
We'll talk about **that** when I get back.
Tell them everything you can remember about what happened and what you saw.
Wait!
Just . . .
You're gonna be careful, right?

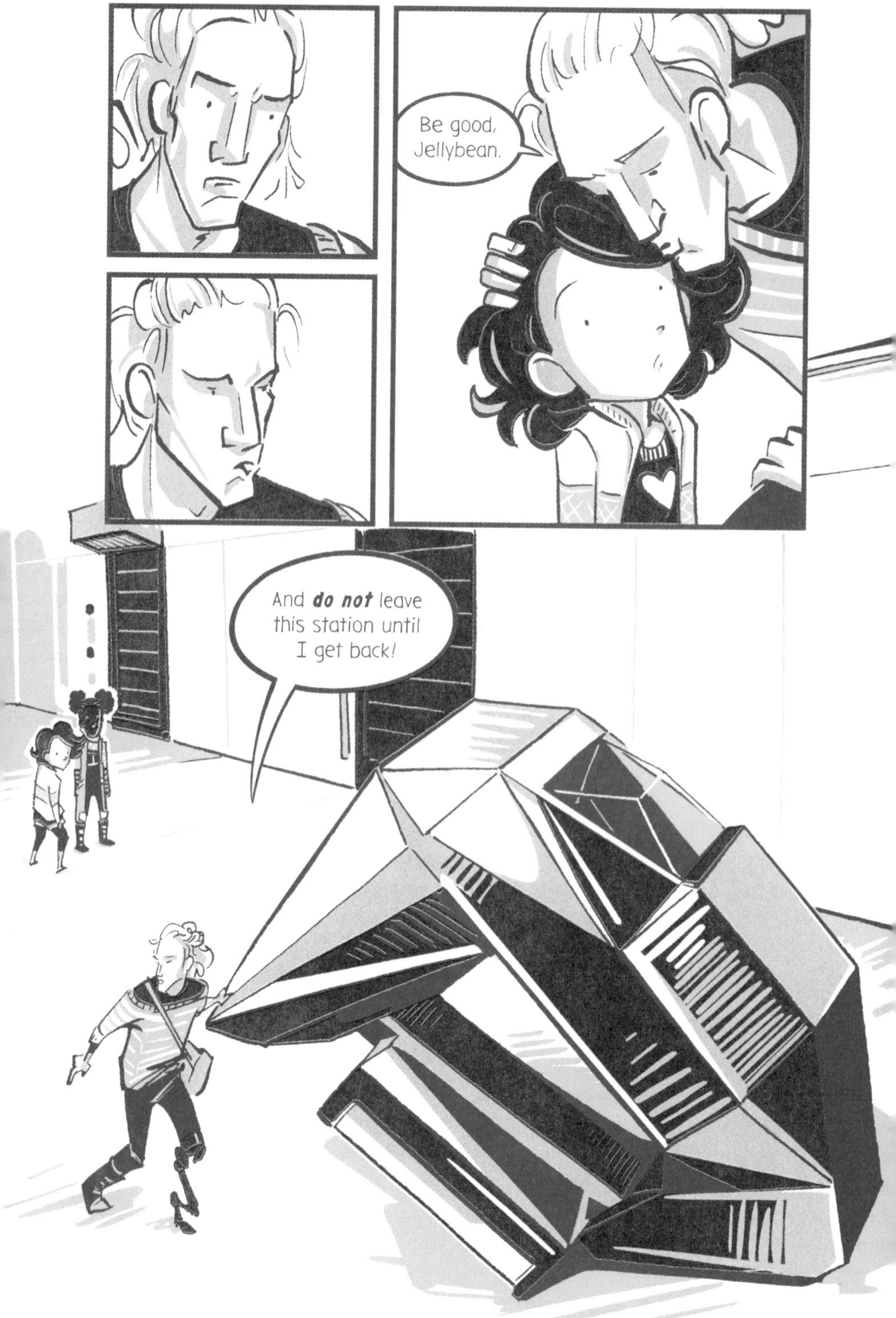

Be good, Jellybean.
And **do not** leave this station until I get back!

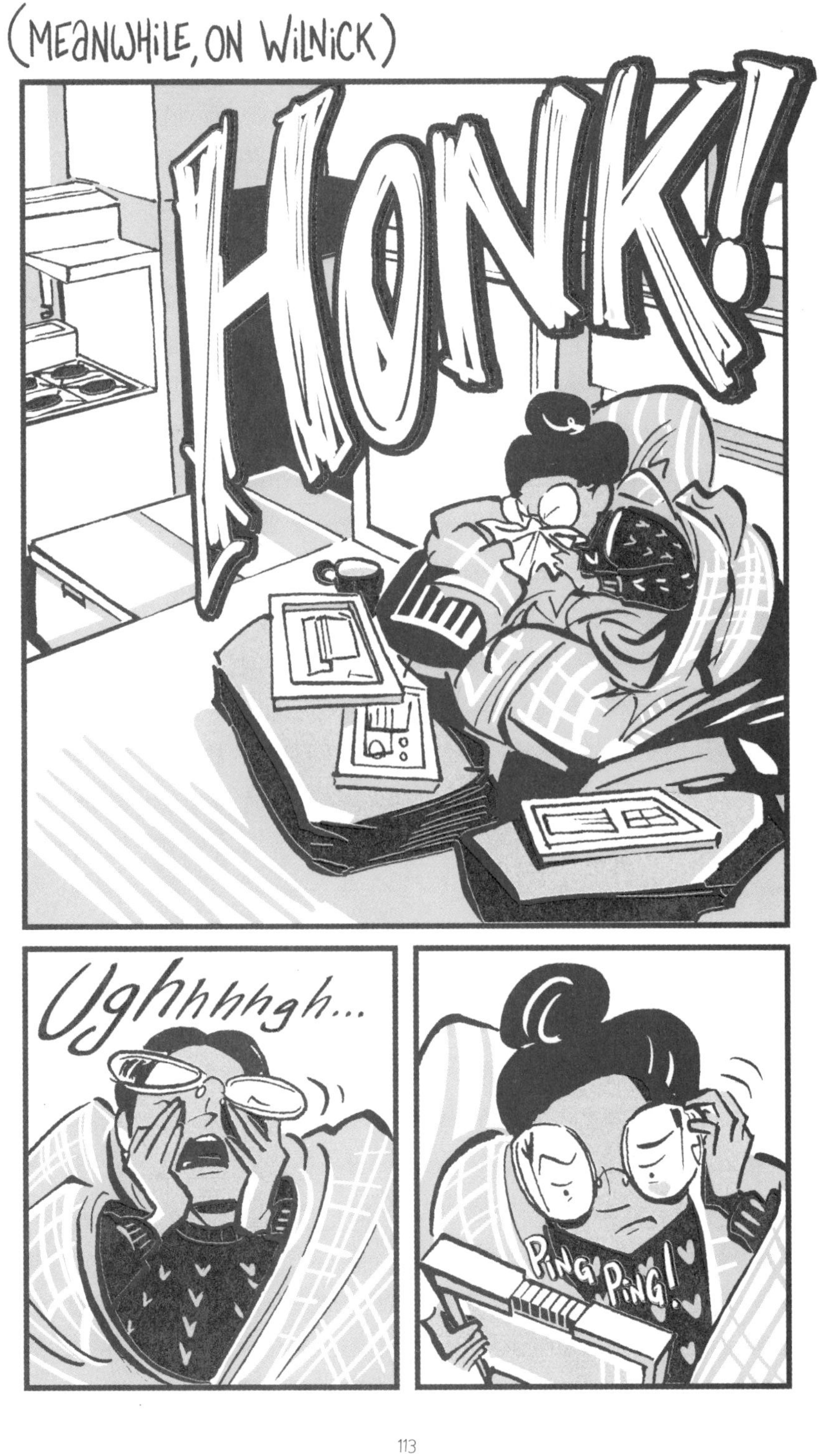
(MEANWHILE, ON WILNICK)
HONK!
Ughhhhgh...
PING PING!

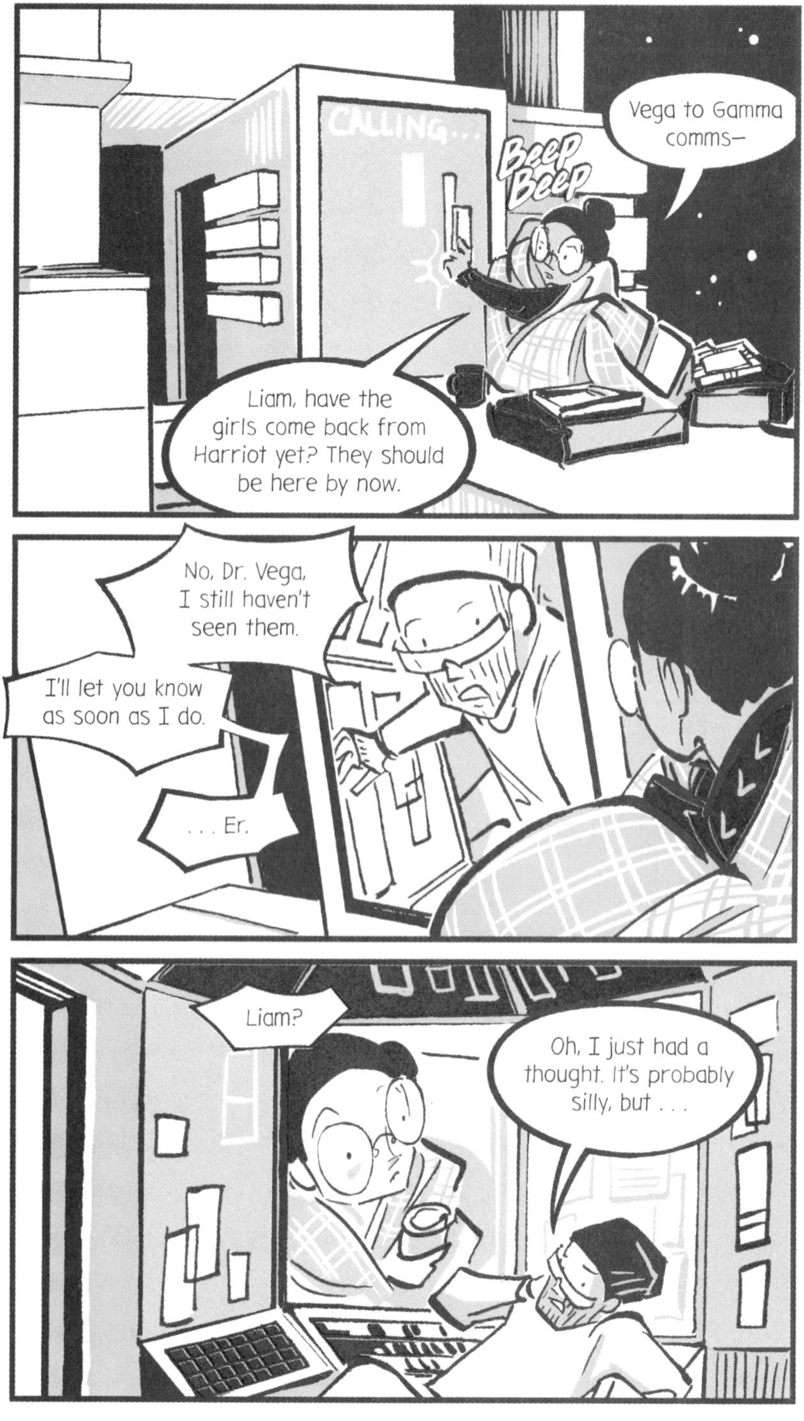
CALLING...
Beep Beep
Vega to Gamma comms—
Liam, have the girls come back from Harriot yet? They should be here by now.
No, Dr. Vega, I still haven't seen them.
I'll let you know as soon as I do.
. . . Er.
Liam?
Oh, I just had a thought. It's probably silly, but . . .

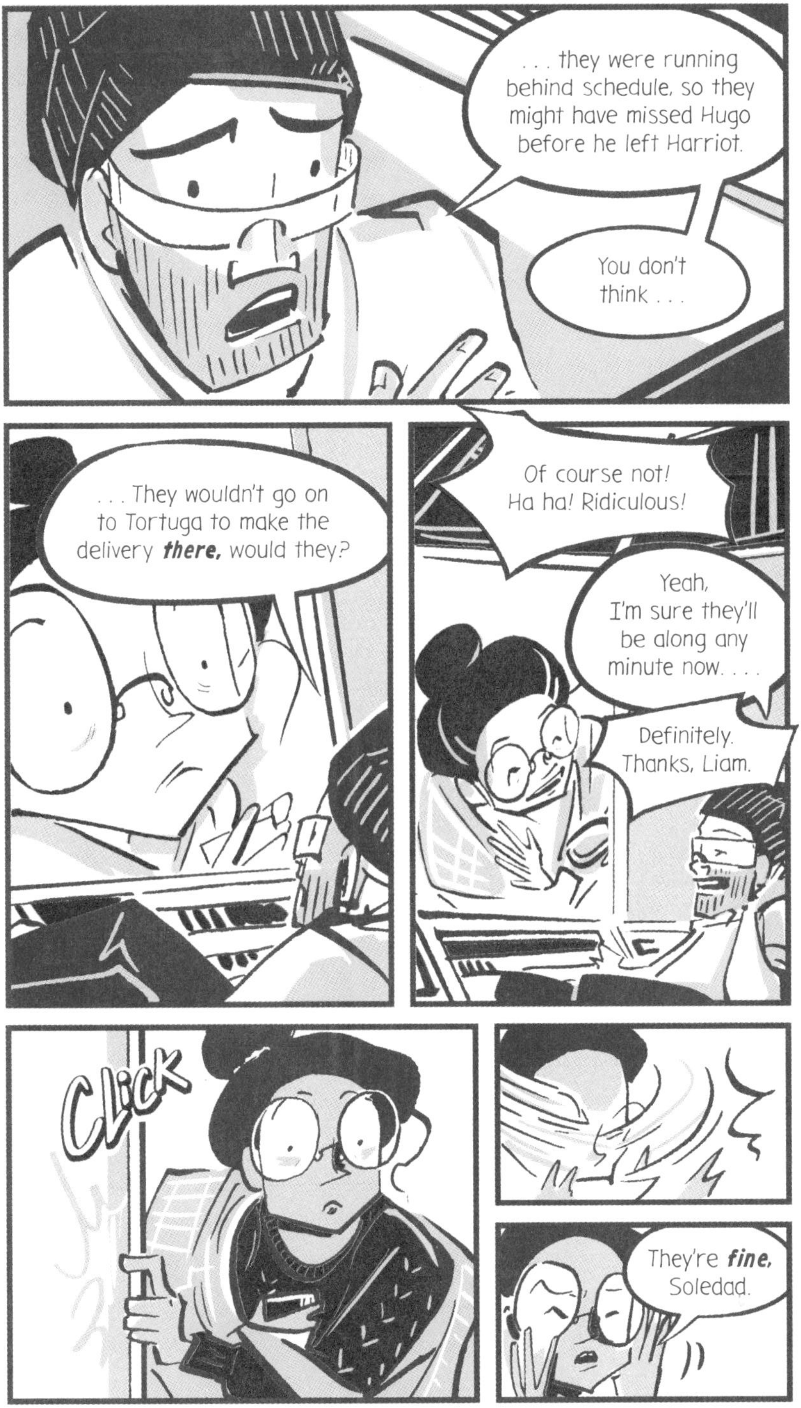

. . . they were running behind schedule, so they might have missed Hugo before he left Harriot.
You don't think . . .
. . . They wouldn't go on to Tortuga to make the delivery ***there,*** would they?
Of course not! Ha ha! Ridiculous!
Yeah, I'm sure they'll be along any minute now. . . .
Definitely. Thanks, Liam.
CLICK
They're ***fine,*** Soledad.

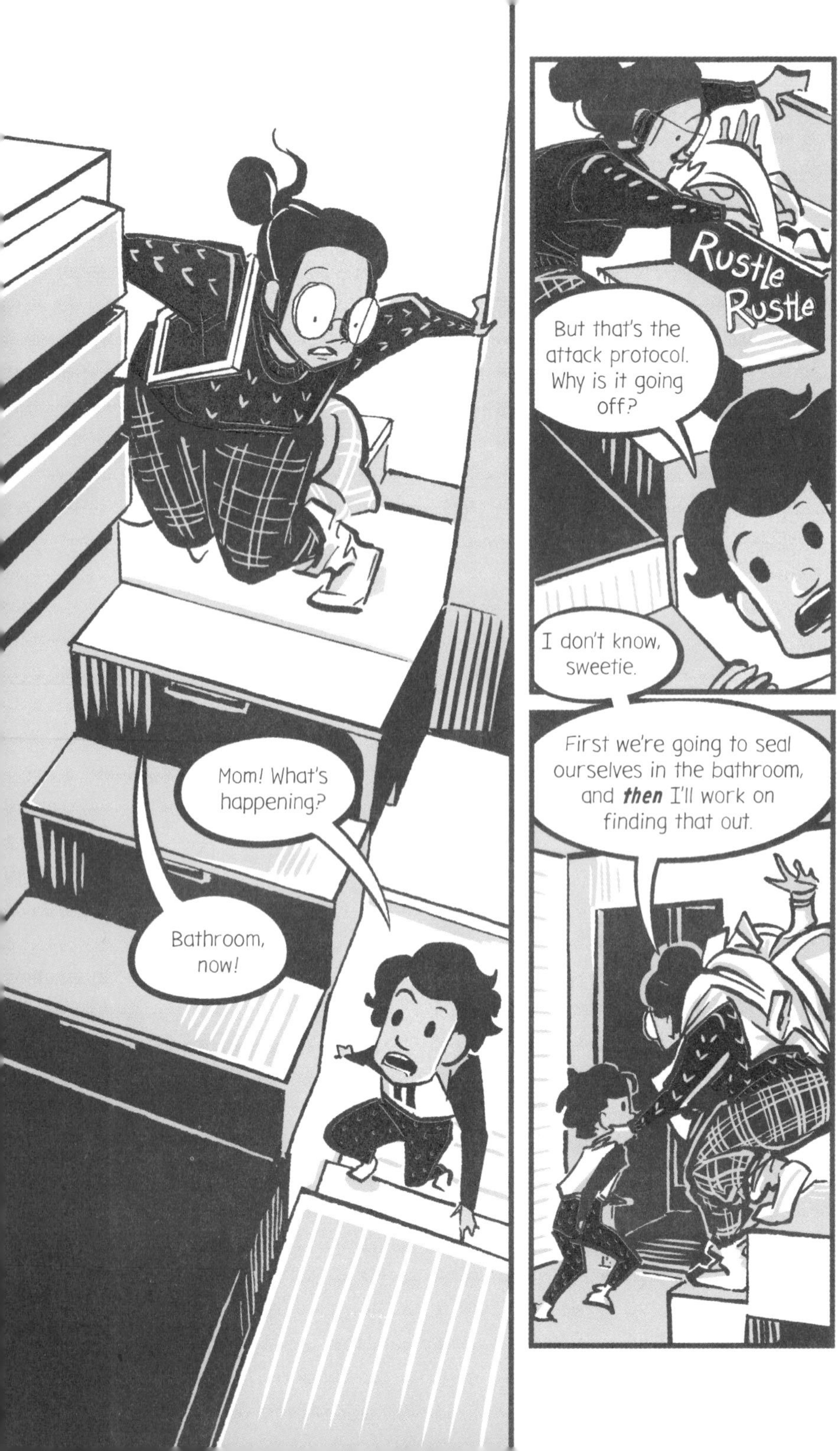
Mom! What's happening?
Bathroom, now!
Rustle Rustle
But that's the attack protocol. Why is it going off?
I don't know, sweetie.
First we're going to seal ourselves in the bathroom, and **then** I'll work on finding that out.

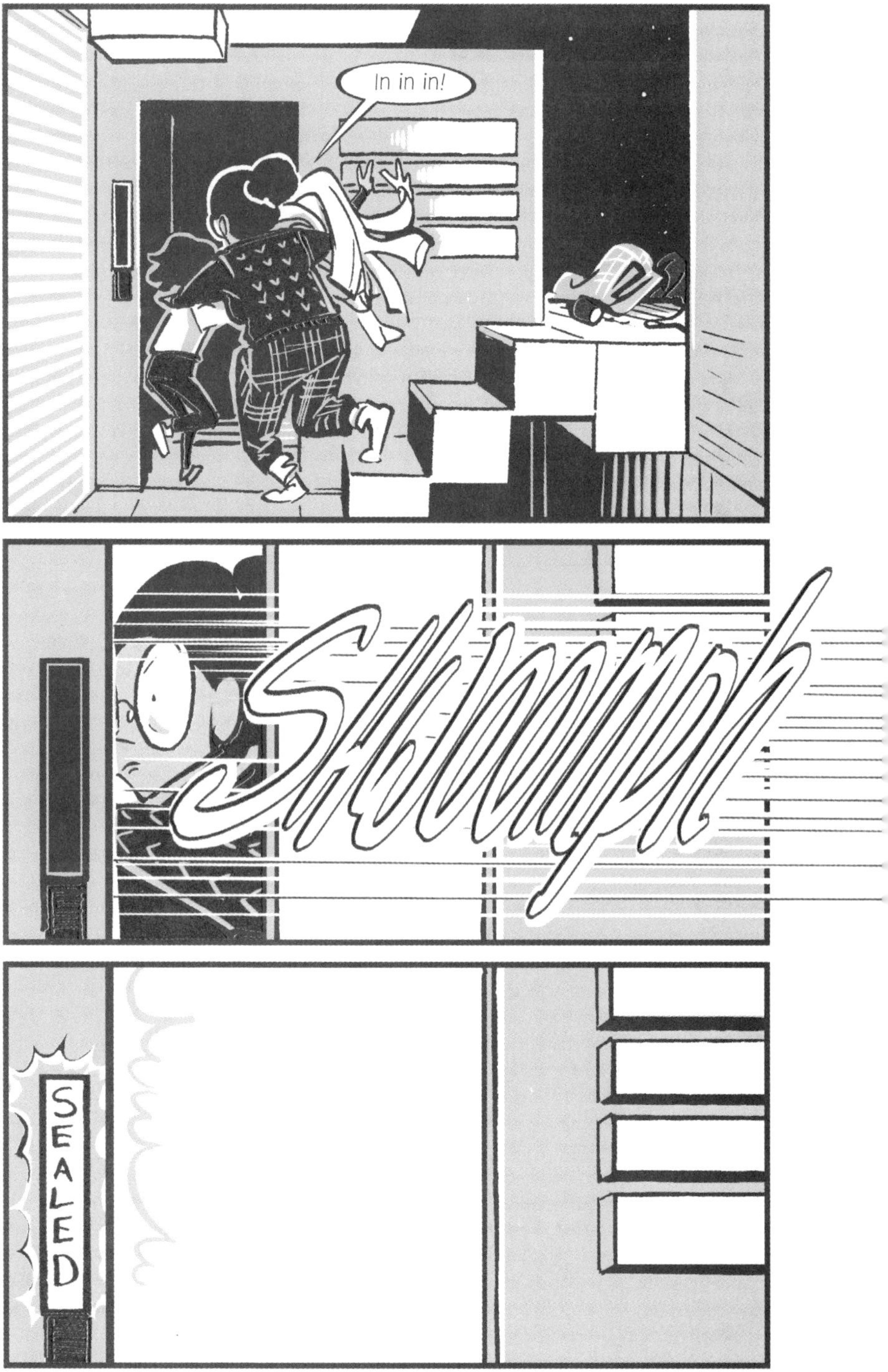
In in in!
SHUMPH
SEALED

(COMMS CENTER ON GAMMA STATION)

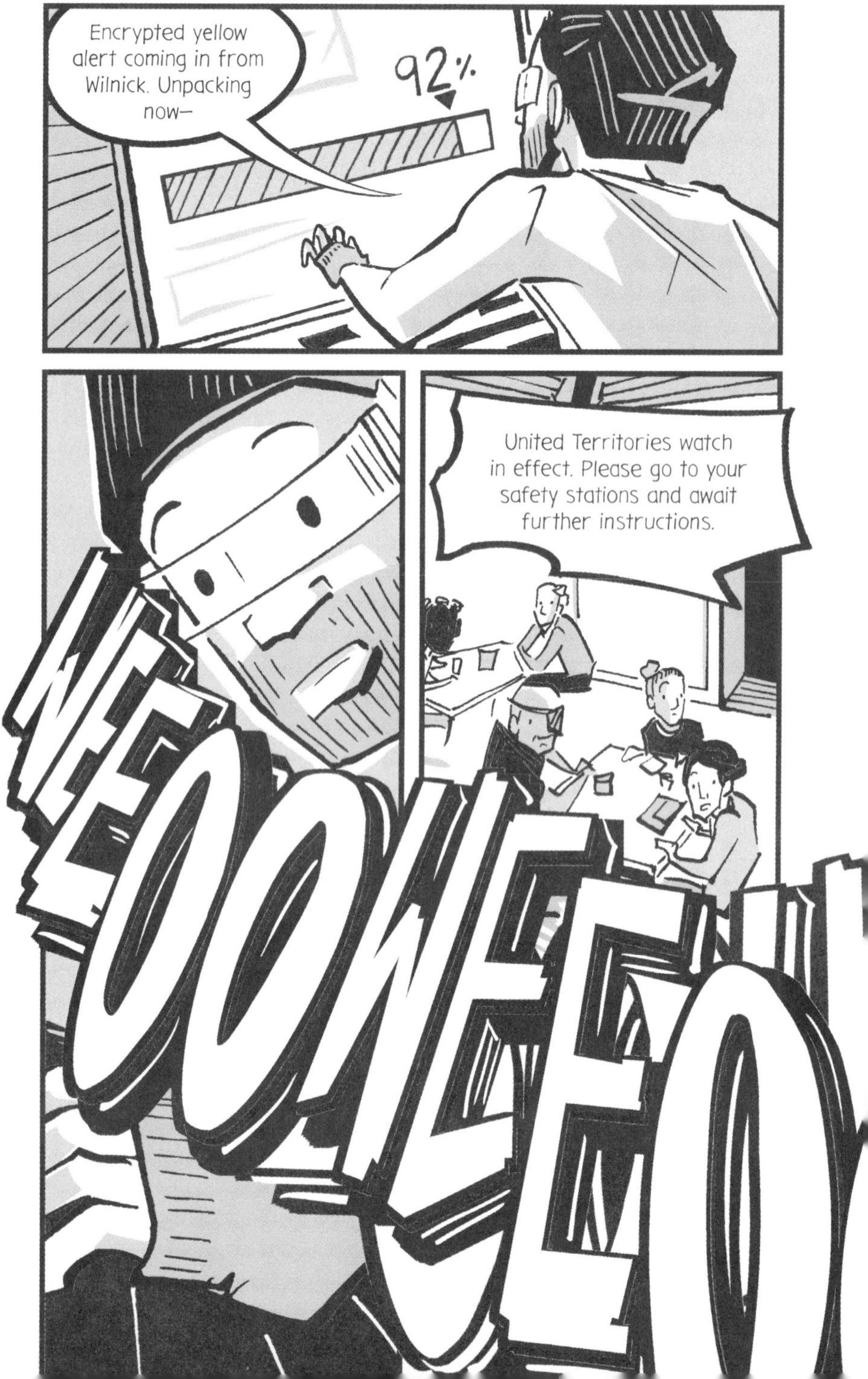
Encrypted yellow alert coming in from Wilnick. Unpacking now—
92%
United Territories watch in effect. Please go to your safety stations and await further instructions.

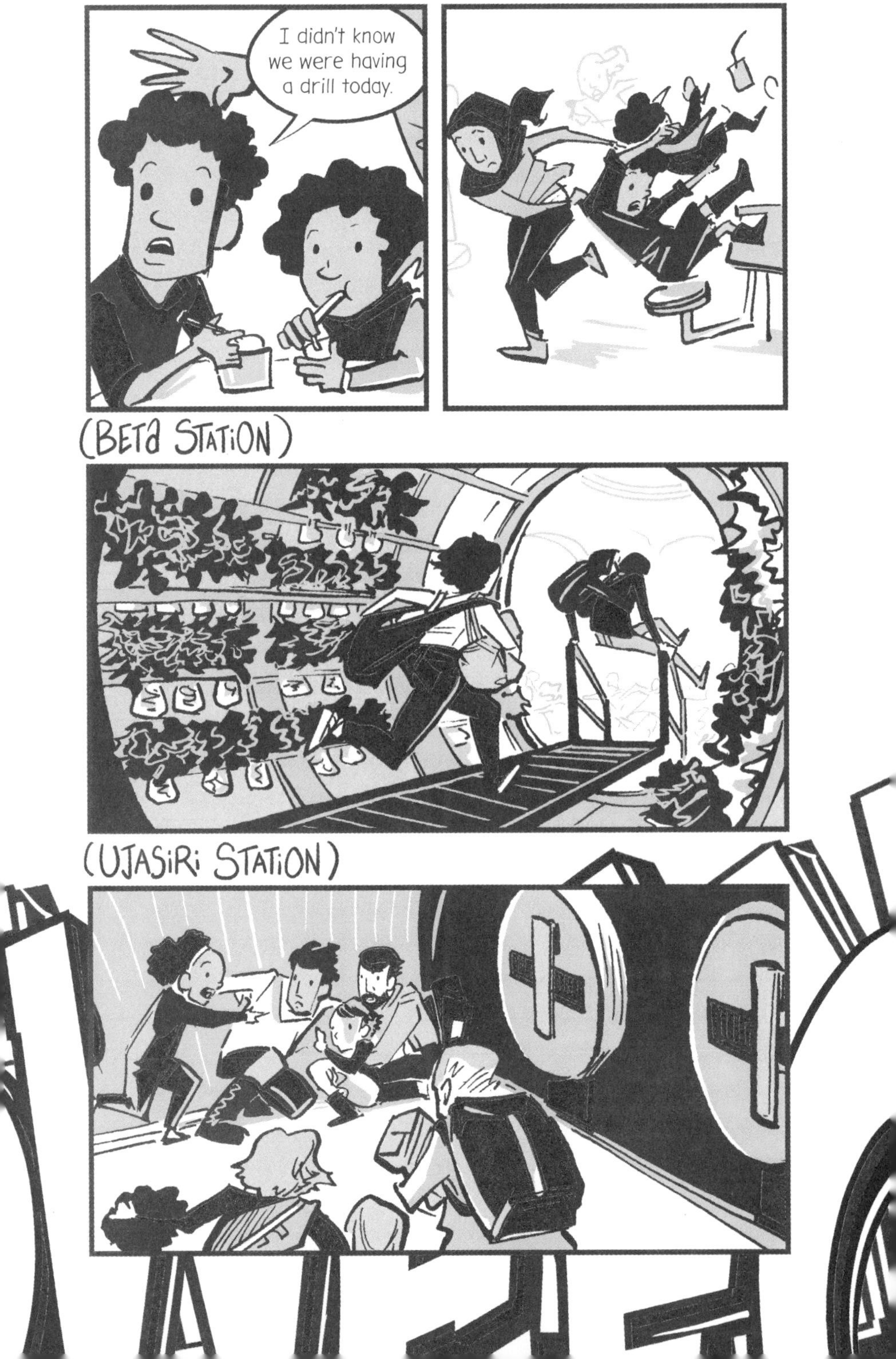

I didn't know we were having a drill today.
(BETA STATION)
(UJASIRI STATION)

(SAMRDDHi STATiON)

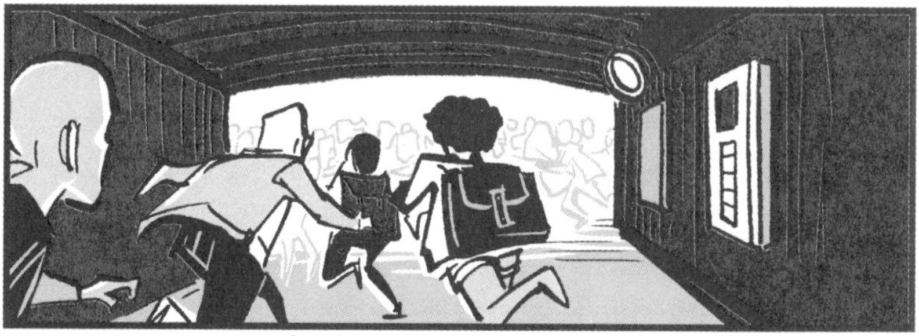

(La PAZ STATiON)

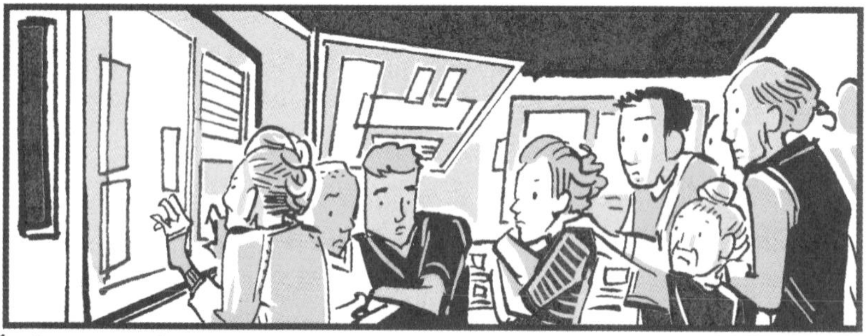

(TARNa STATiON)

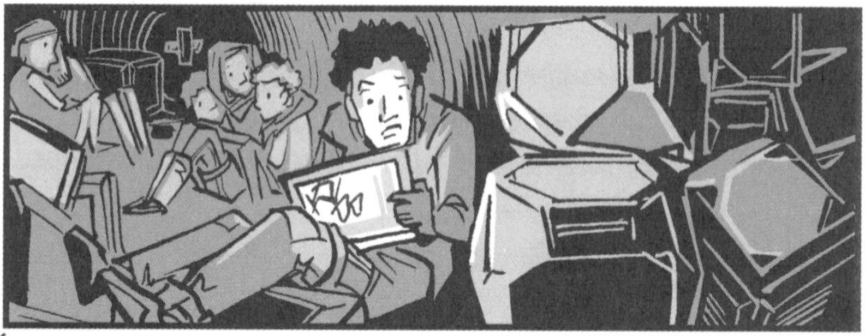

(WiLNiCK STATiON)

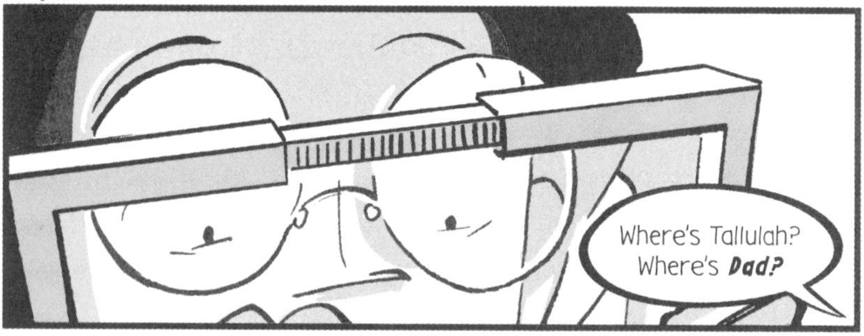
Where's Tallulah? Where's **Dad?**

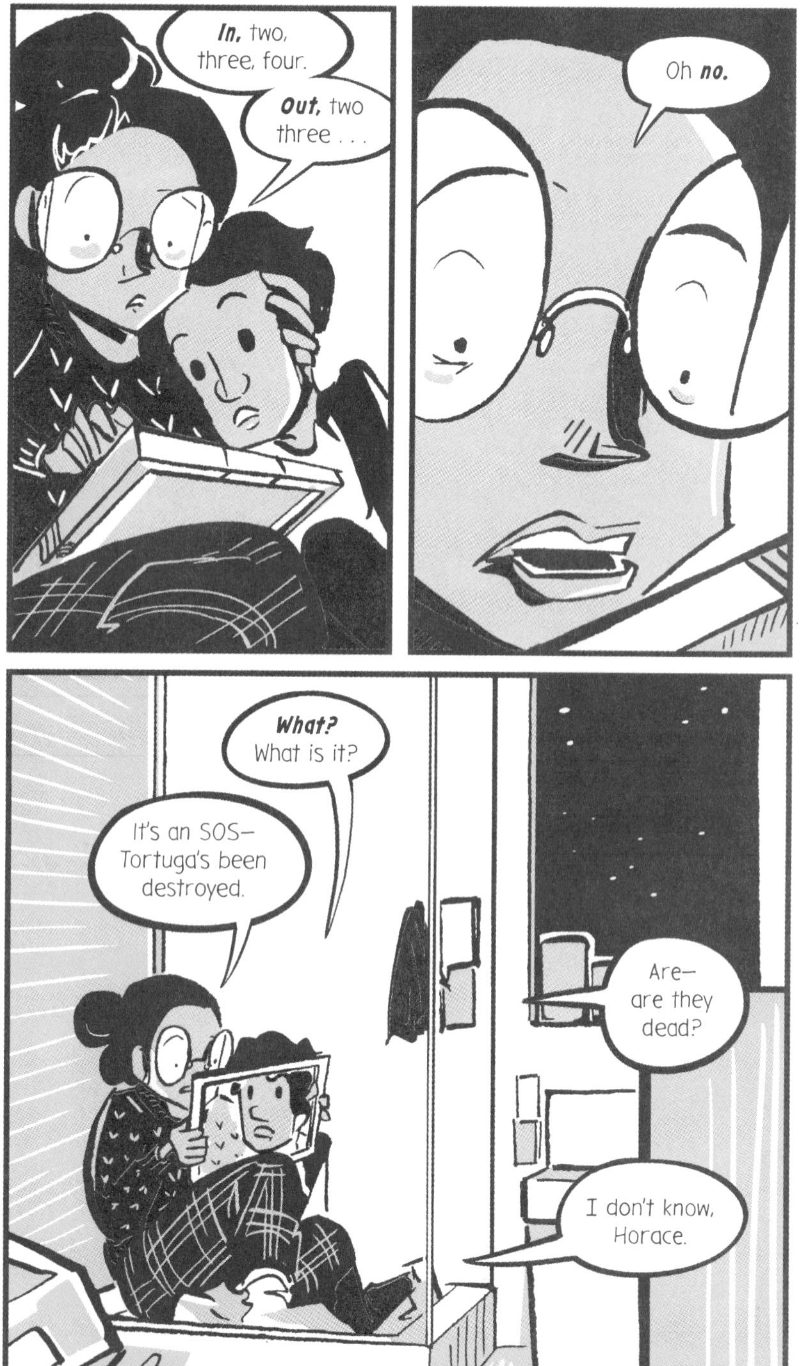
In, two, three, four.
Out, two three . . .
Oh **no.**
What? What is it?
It's an SOS— Tortuga's been destroyed.
Are— are they dead?
I don't know, Horace.

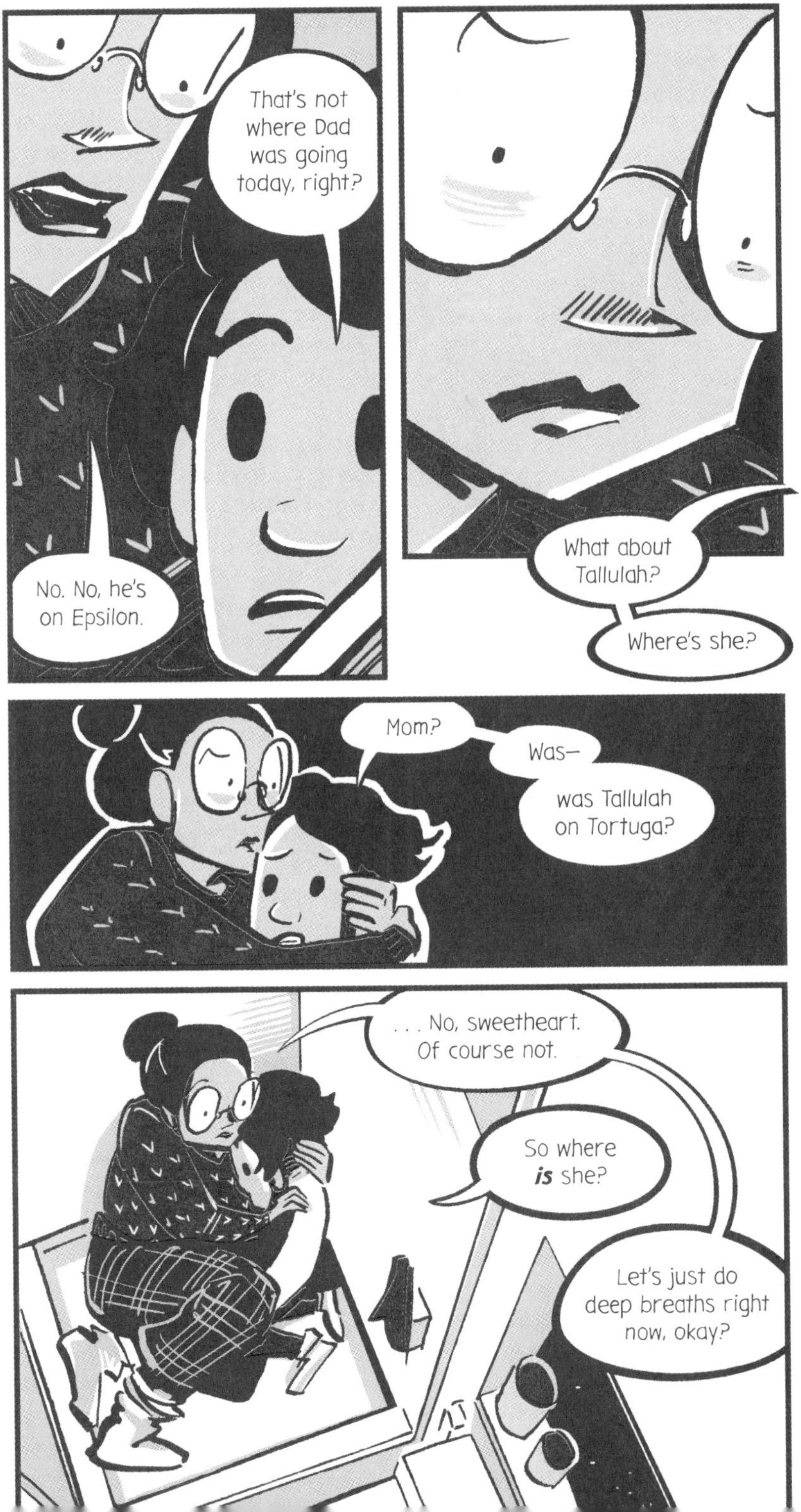
That's not where Dad was going today, right?
No. No, he's on Epsilon.
What about Tallulah?
Where's she?
Mom?
Was—
was Tallulah on Tortuga?
. . . No, sweetheart. Of course not.
So where *is* she?
Let's just do deep breaths right now, okay?

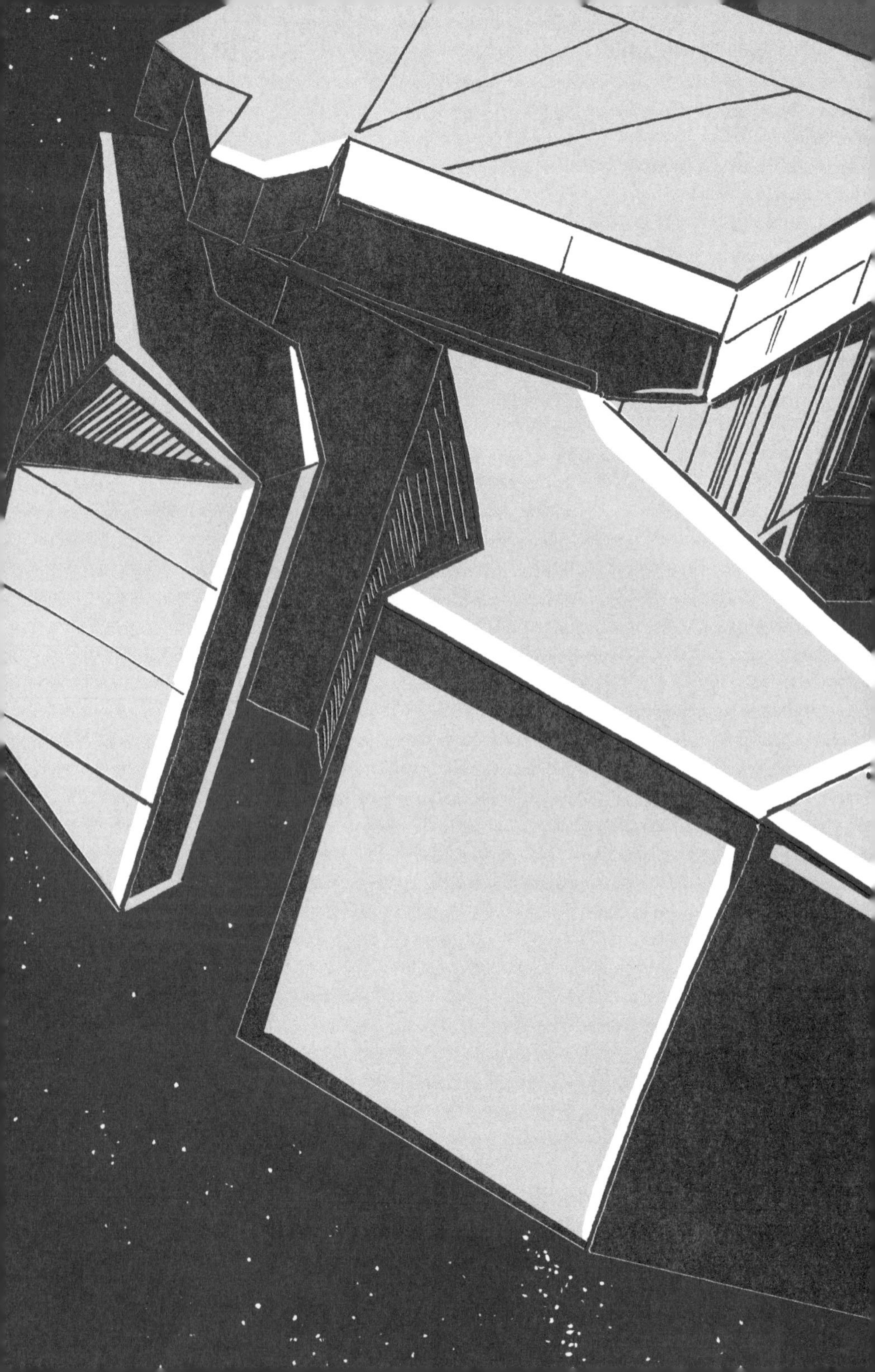

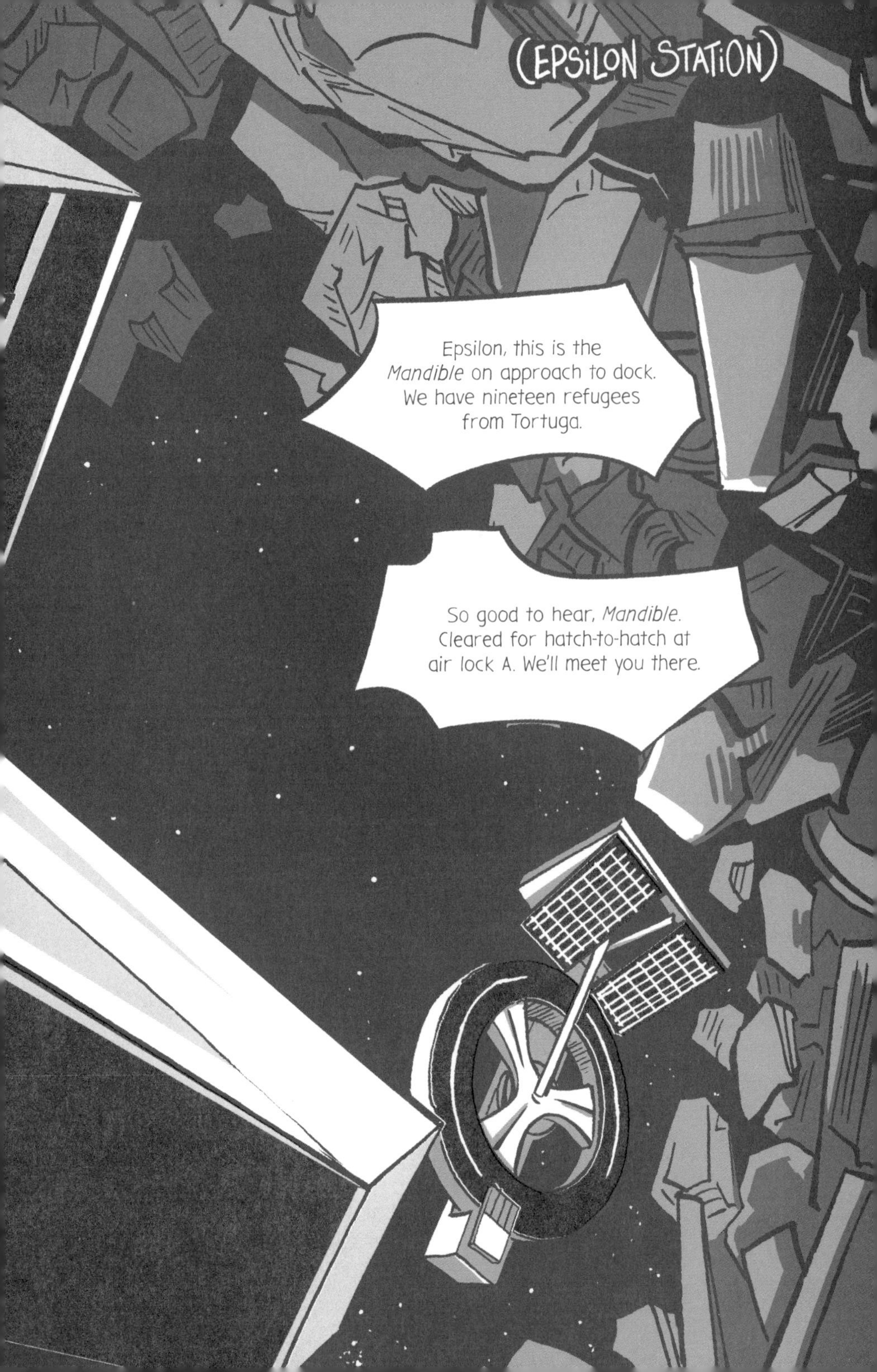
(EPSILON STATION)
Epsilon, this is the *Mandible* on approach to dock. We have nineteen refugees from Tortuga.
So good to hear, *Mandible*. Cleared for hatch-to-hatch at air lock A. We'll meet you there.

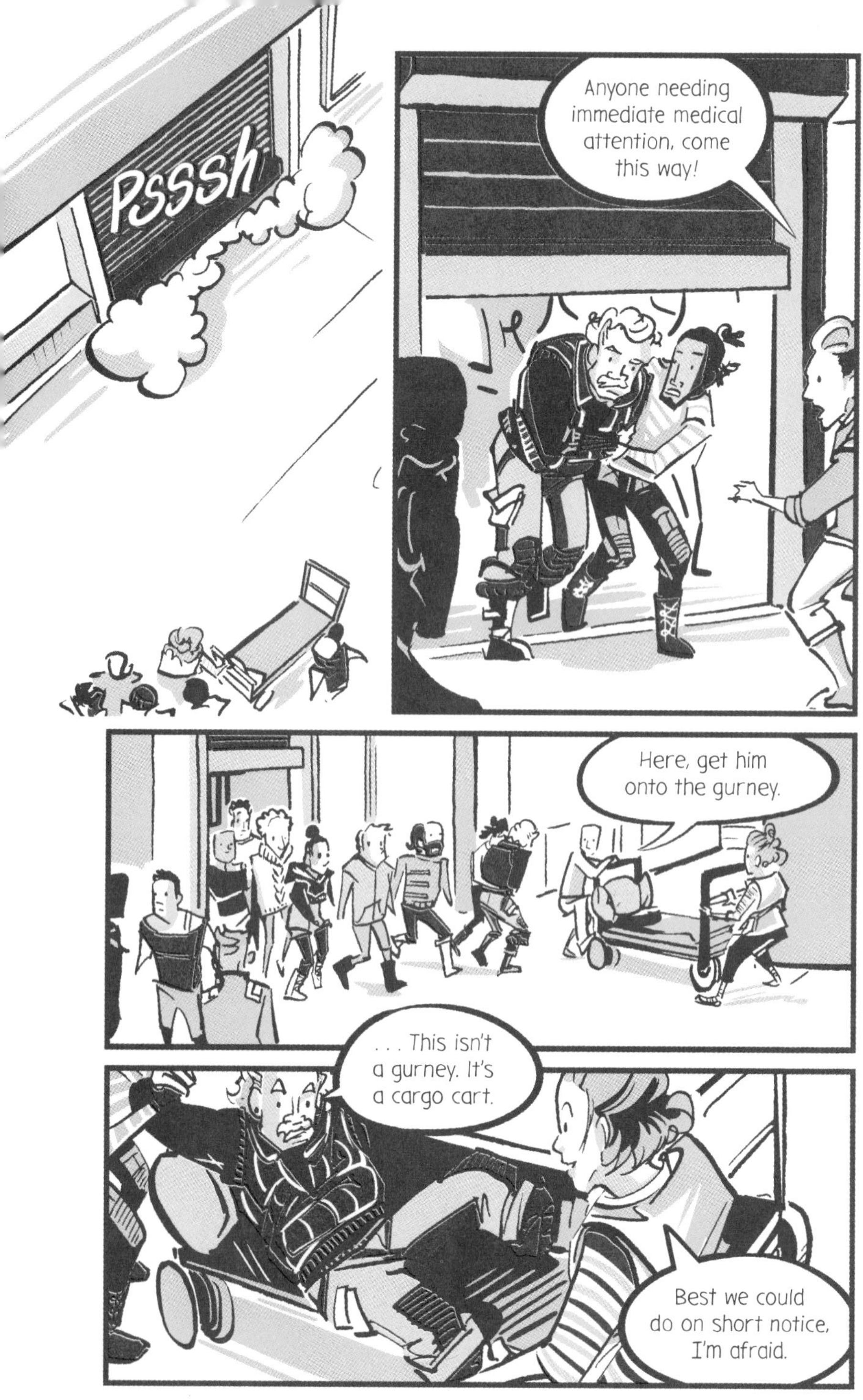
Psssh
Anyone needing immediate medical attention, come this way!
Here, get him onto the gurney.
. . . This isn't a gurney. It's a cargo cart.
Best we could do on short notice, I'm afraid.

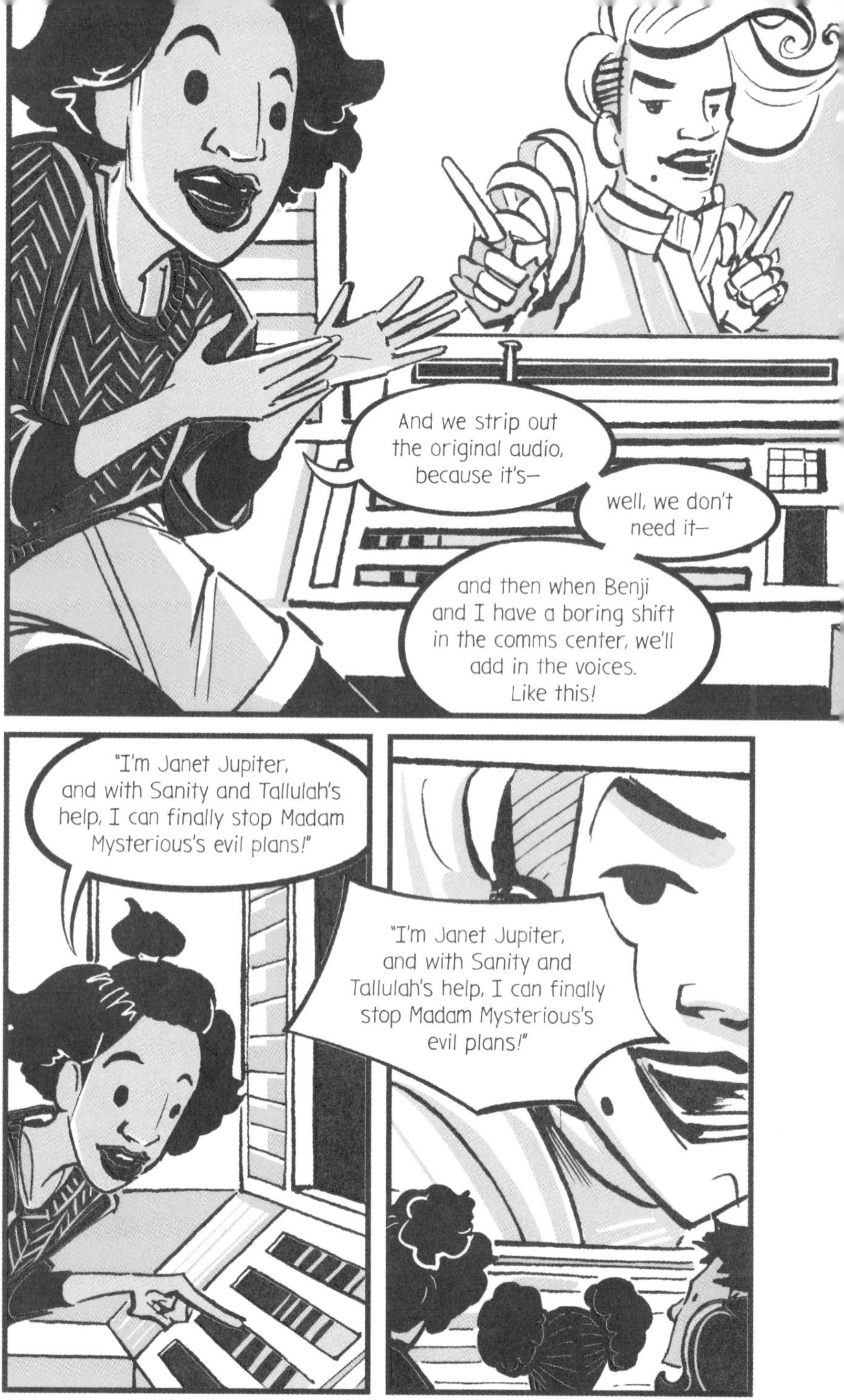
And we strip out the original audio, because it's—
well, we don't need it—
and then when Benji and I have a boring shift in the comms center, we'll add in the voices. Like this!
"I'm Janet Jupiter, and with Sanity and Tallulah's help, I can finally stop Madam Mysterious's evil plans!"
"I'm Janet Jupiter, and with Sanity and Tallulah's help, I can finally stop Madam Mysterious's evil plans!"

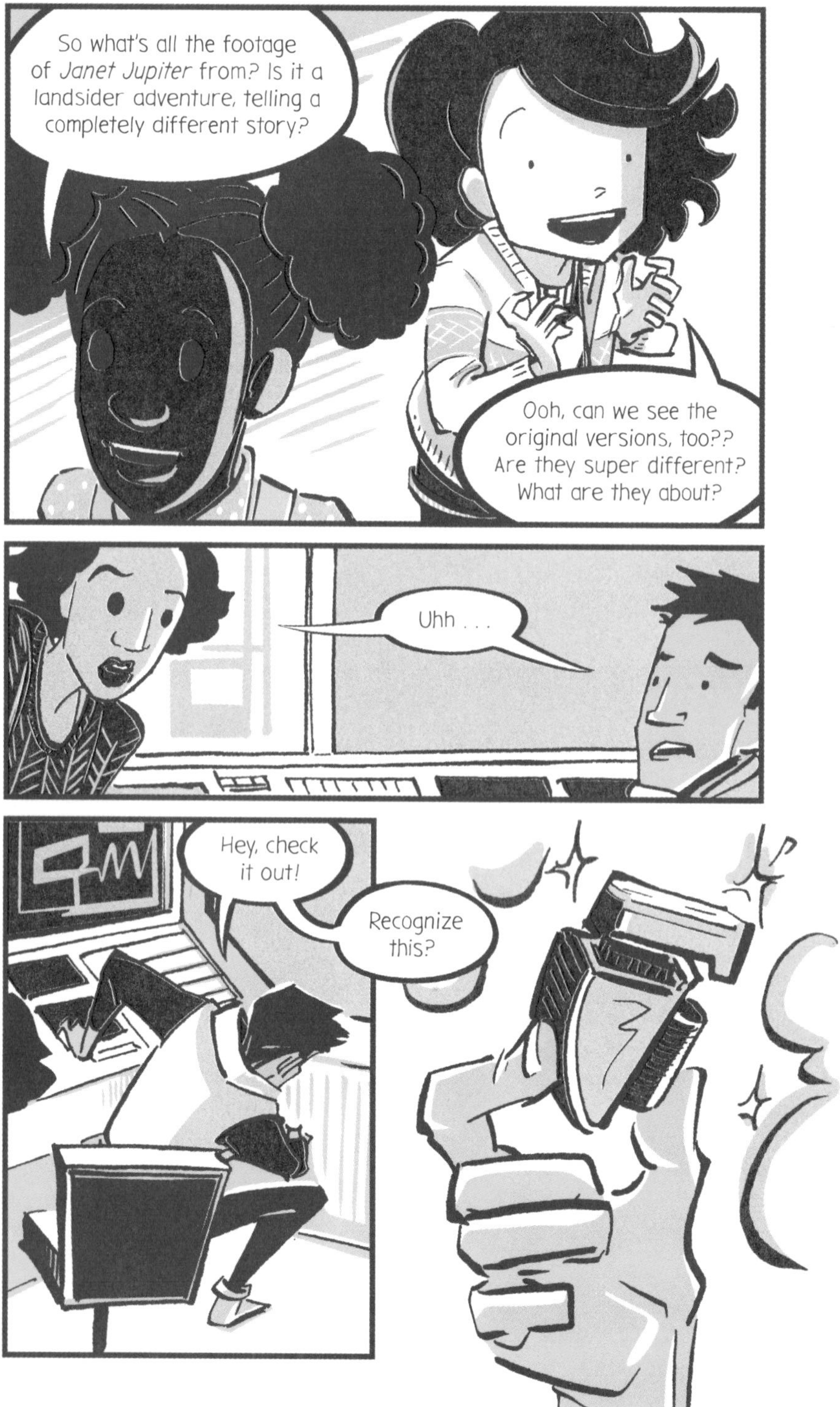

So what's all the footage of *Janet Jupiter* from? Is it a landsider adventure, telling a completely different story?
Ooh, can we see the original versions, too?? Are they super different? What are they about?
Uhh . . .
Hey, check it out!
Recognize this?

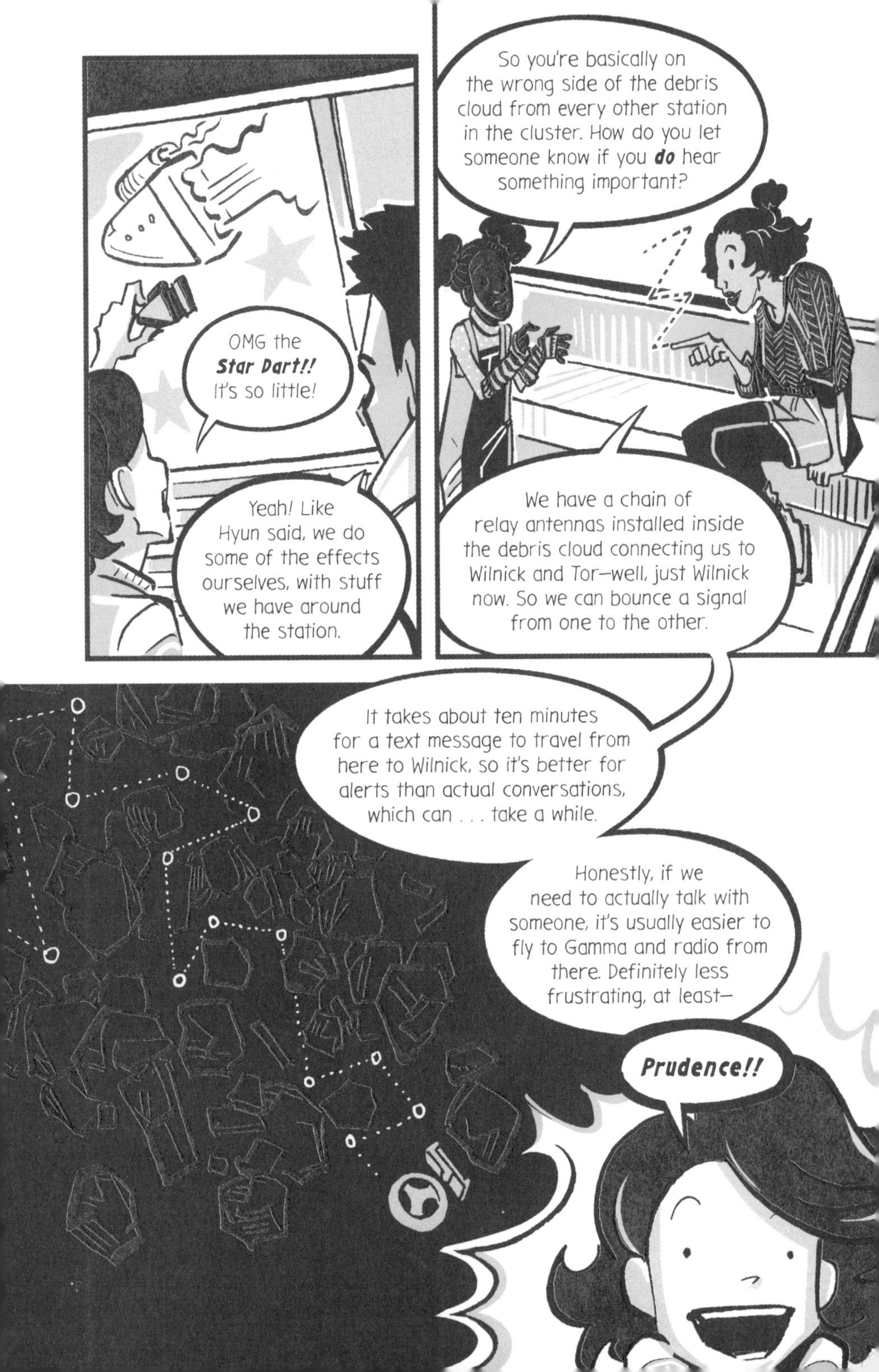
OMG the **Star Dart!!** It's so little!
Yeah! Like Hyun said, we do some of the effects ourselves, with stuff we have around the station.
So you're basically on the wrong side of the debris cloud from every other station in the cluster. How do you let someone know if you ***do*** hear something important?
We have a chain of relay antennas installed inside the debris cloud connecting us to Wilnick and Tor—well, just Wilnick now. So we can bounce a signal from one to the other.
It takes about ten minutes for a text message to travel from here to Wilnick, so it's better for alerts than actual conversations, which can . . . take a while.
Honestly, if we need to actually talk with someone, it's usually easier to fly to Gamma and radio from there. Definitely less frustrating, at least—
Prudence!!

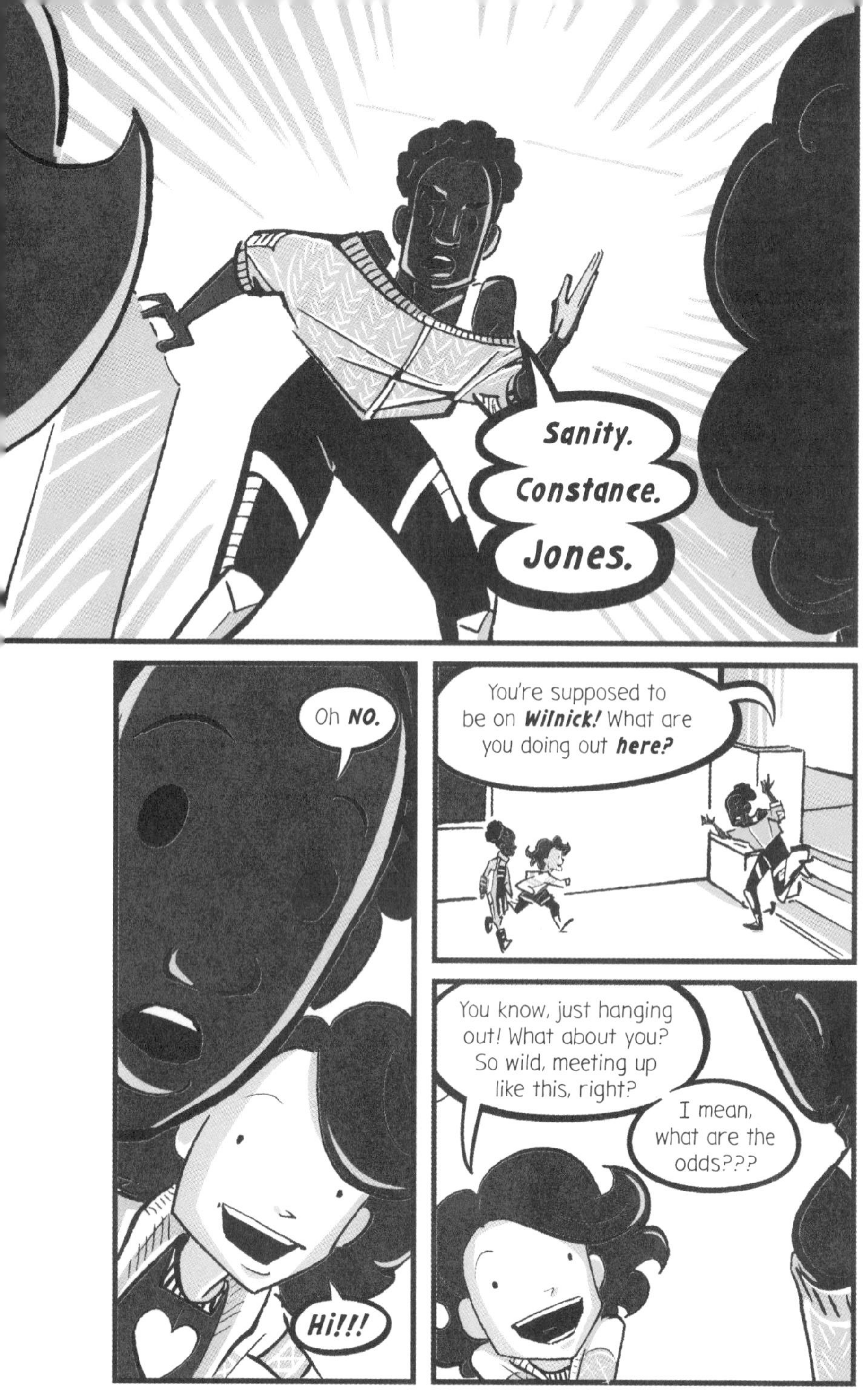

Sanity. Constance. Jones.
Oh **NO.**
You're supposed to be on ***Wilnick!*** What are you doing out ***here?***
Hi!!!
You know, just hanging out! What about you? So wild, meeting up like this, right?
I mean, what are the odds???

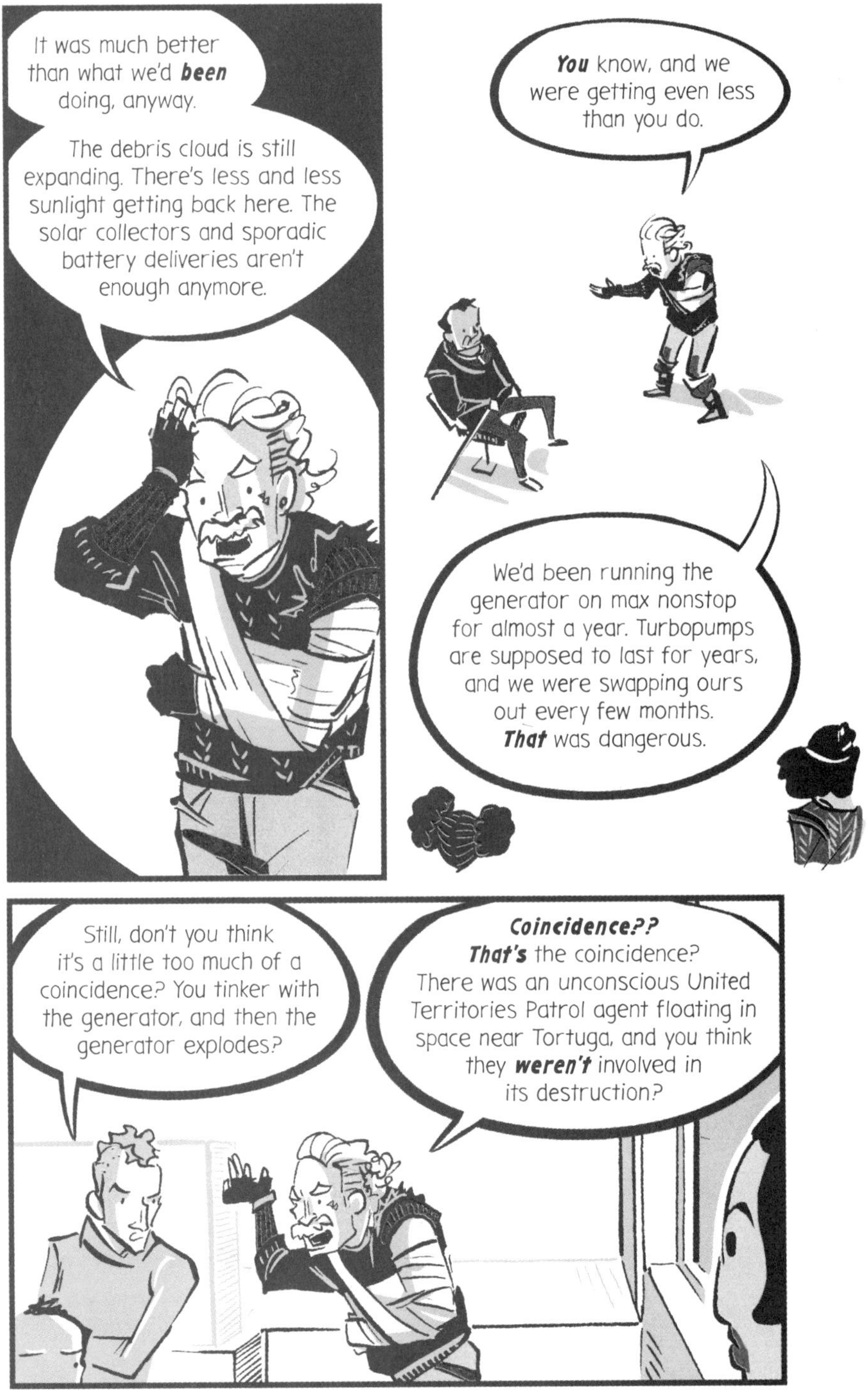

It was much better than what we'd **been** doing, anyway.
The debris cloud is still expanding. There's less and less sunlight getting back here. The solar collectors and sporadic battery deliveries aren't enough anymore.
You know, and we were getting even less than you do.
We'd been running the generator on max nonstop for almost a year. Turbopumps are supposed to last for years, and we were swapping ours out every few months. **That** was dangerous.
Still, don't you think it's a little too much of a coincidence? You tinker with the generator, and then the generator explodes?
Coincidence?? **That's** the coincidence? There was an unconscious United Territories Patrol agent floating in space near Tortuga, and you think they **weren't** involved in its destruction?

(MEANWHILE, ELSEWHERE ON EPSILON)

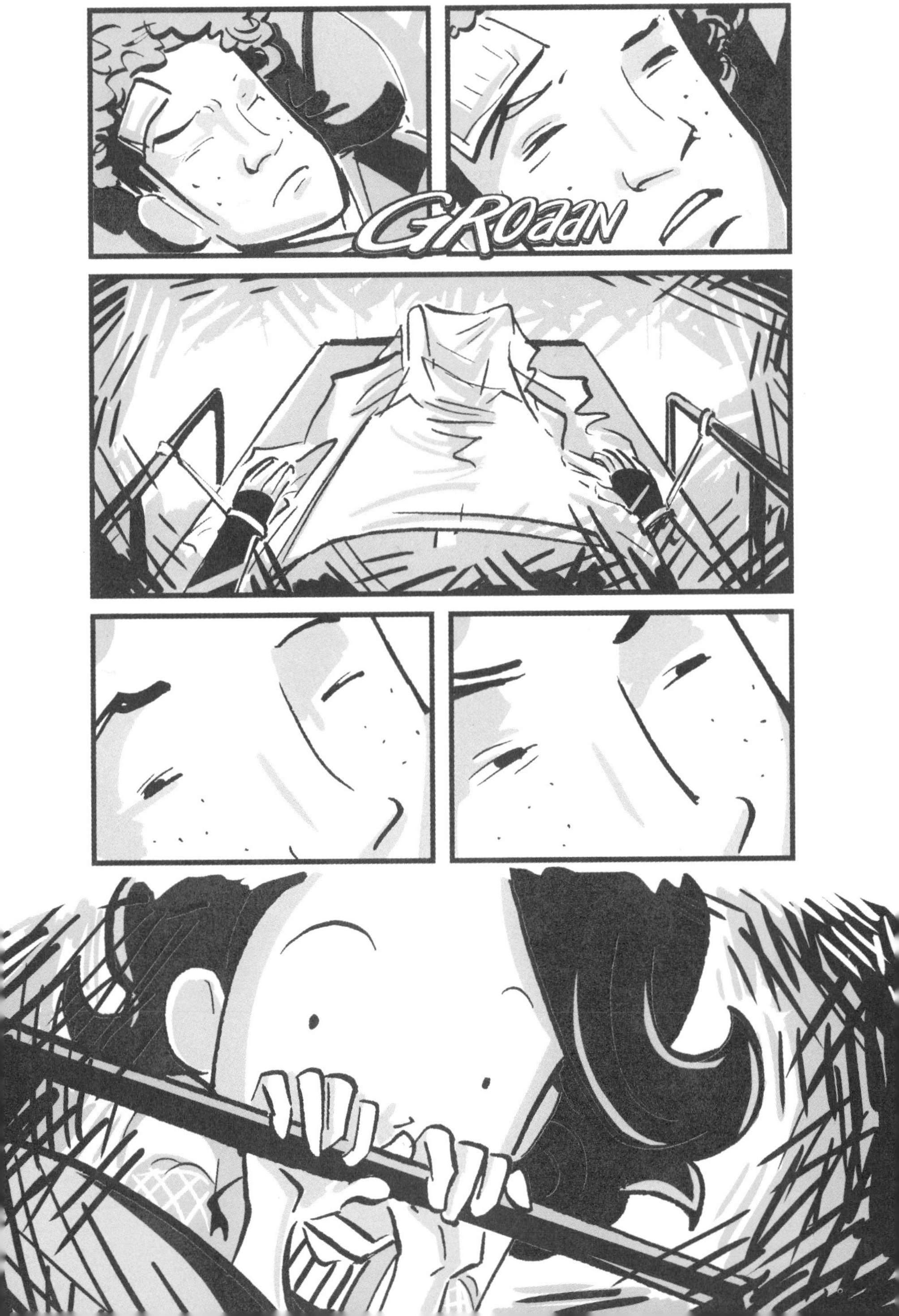
GROAAN

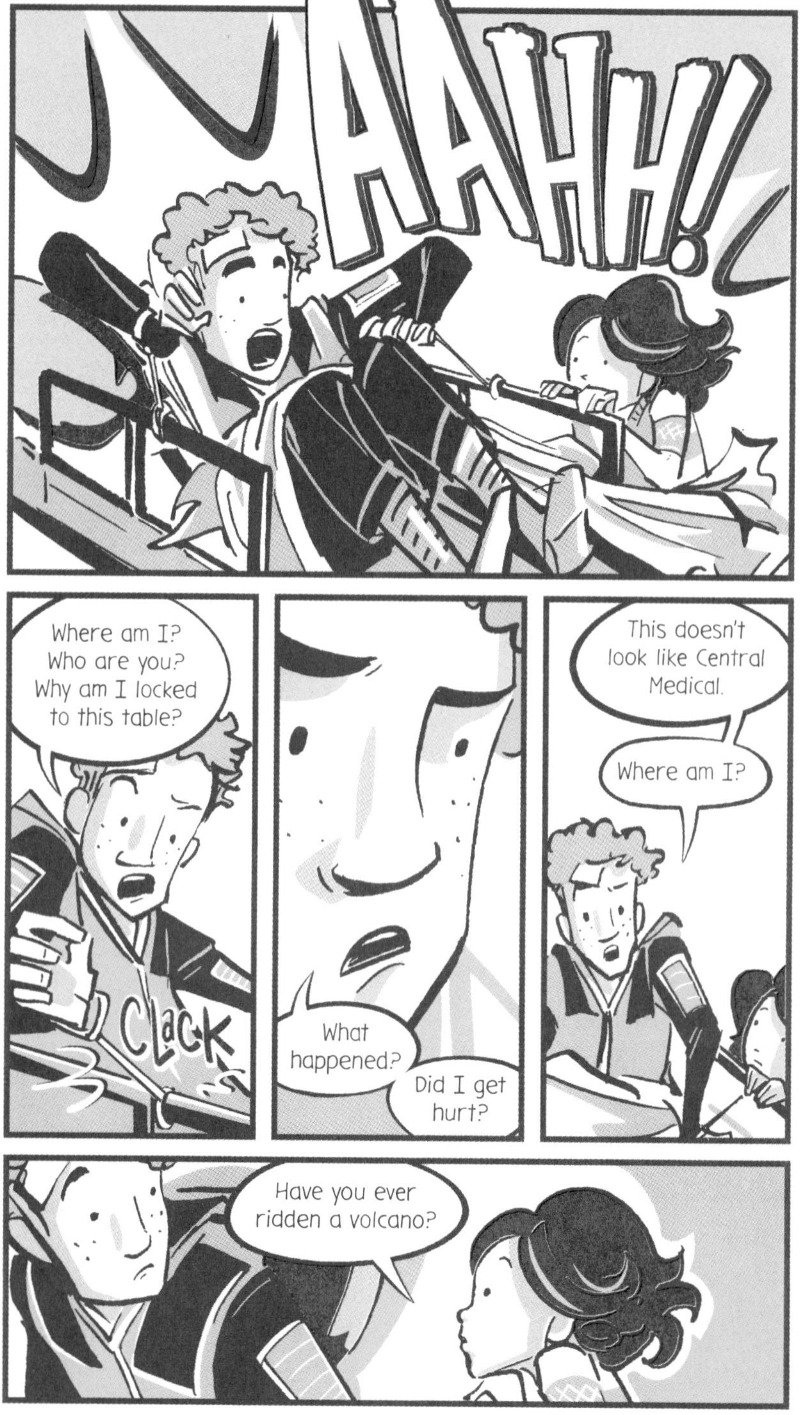
AAHH!!
Where am I? Who are you? Why am I locked to this table?
CLACK
What happened?
Did I get hurt?
This doesn't look like Central Medical.
Where am I?
Have you ever ridden a volcano?

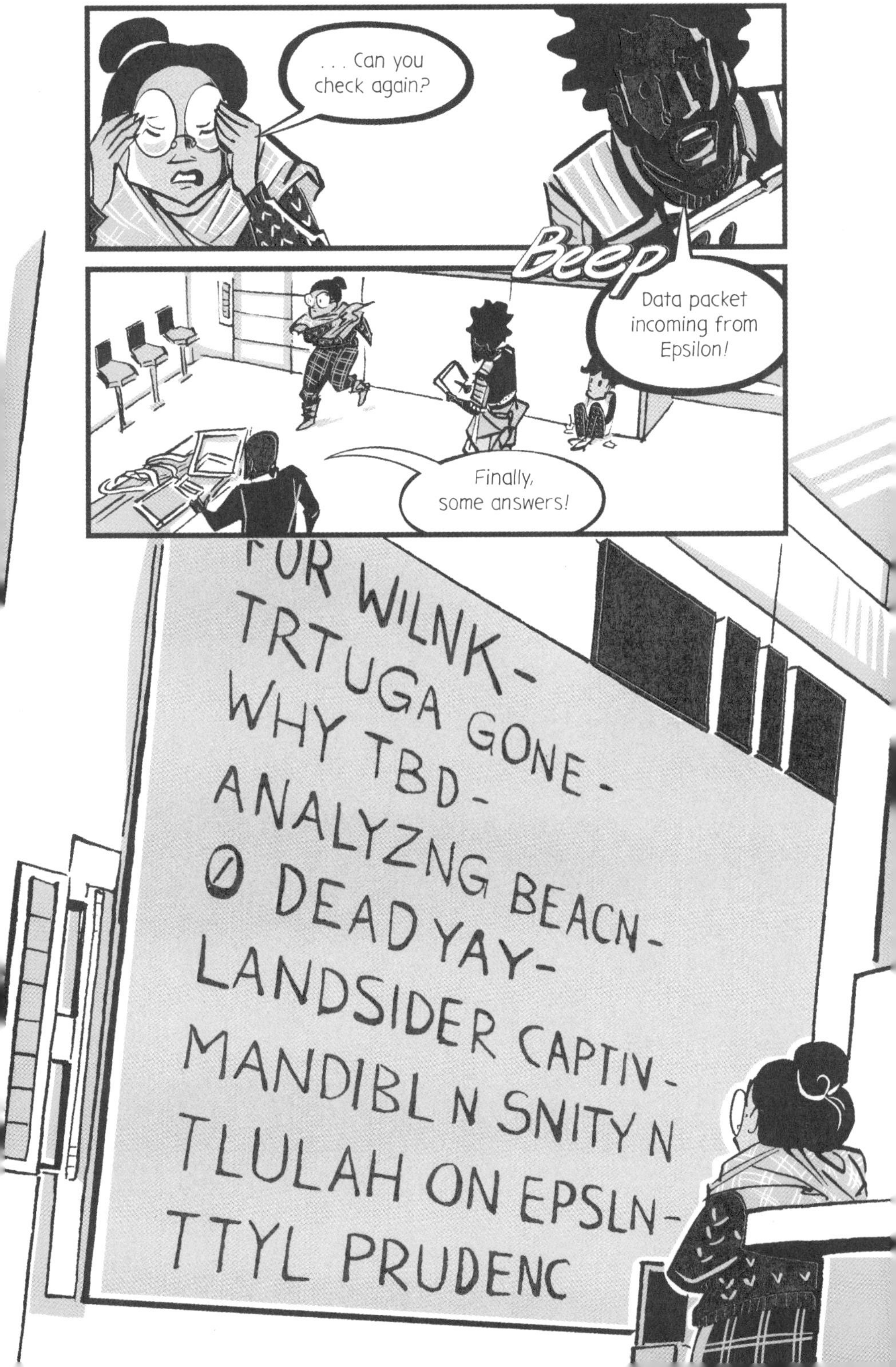
. . . Can you check again?
Beep
Data packet incoming from Epsilon!
Finally, some answers!
FOR WILNK-
TRTUGA GONE-
WHY TBD-
ANALYZNG BEACN-
Ø DEAD YAY-
LANDSIDER CAPTIV-
MANDIBL N SNITY N
TLULAH ON EPSLN-
TTYL PRUDENC

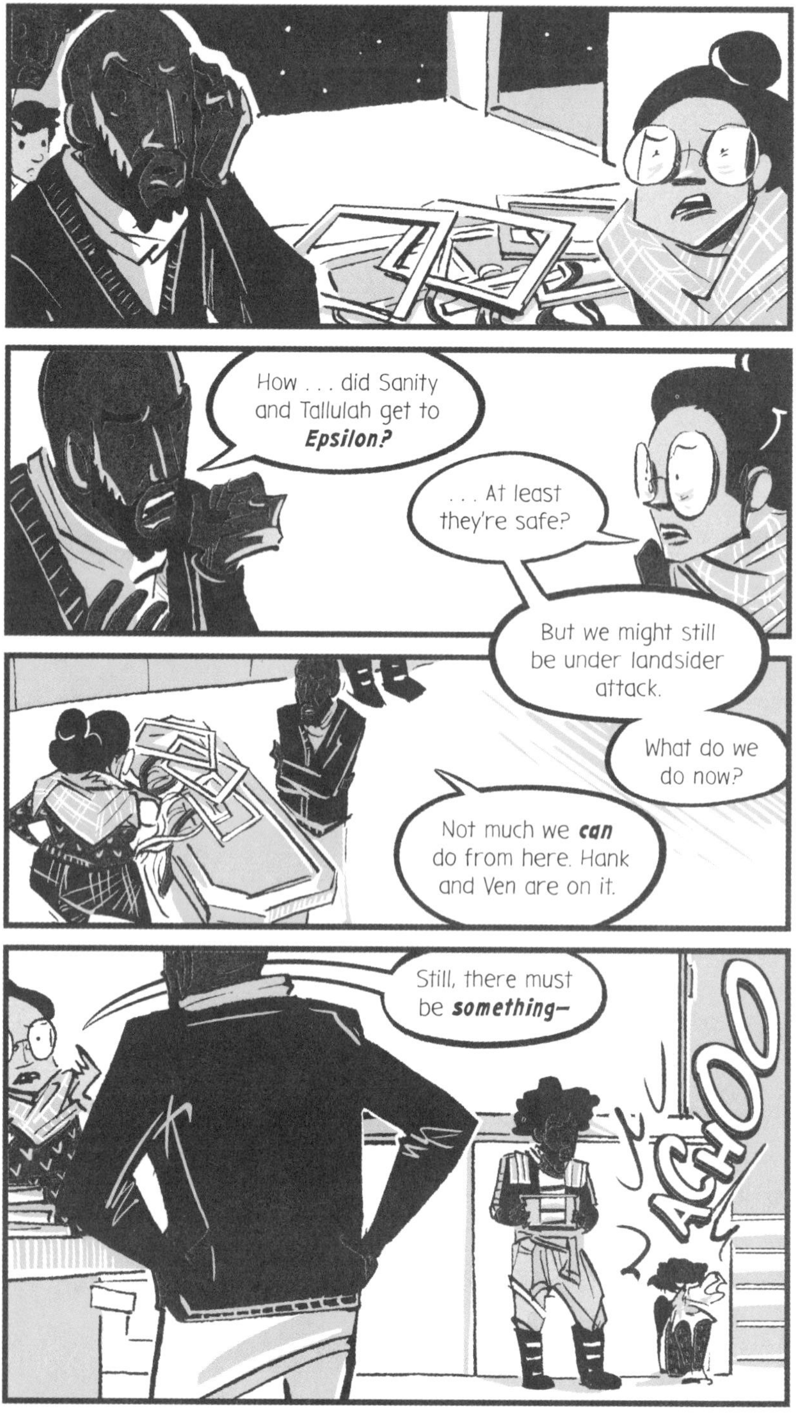
How . . . did Sanity and Tallulah get to **Epsilon?**
. . . At least they're safe?
But we might still be under landsider attack.
What do we do now?
Not much we **can** do from here. Hank and Ven are on it.
Still, there must be **something—**
ACHOO

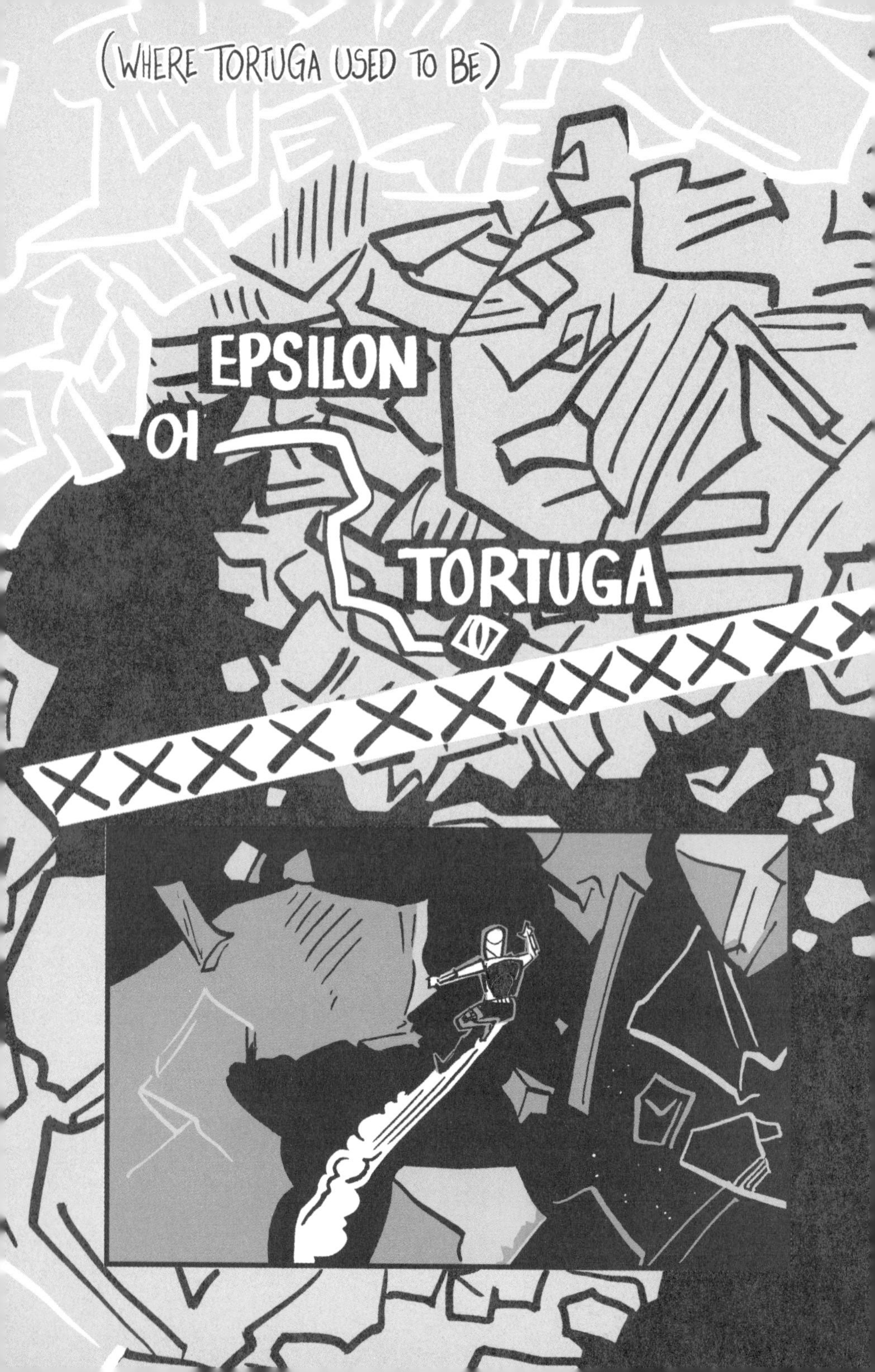

(WHERE TORTUGA USED TO BE)
EPSILON
01
TORTUGA

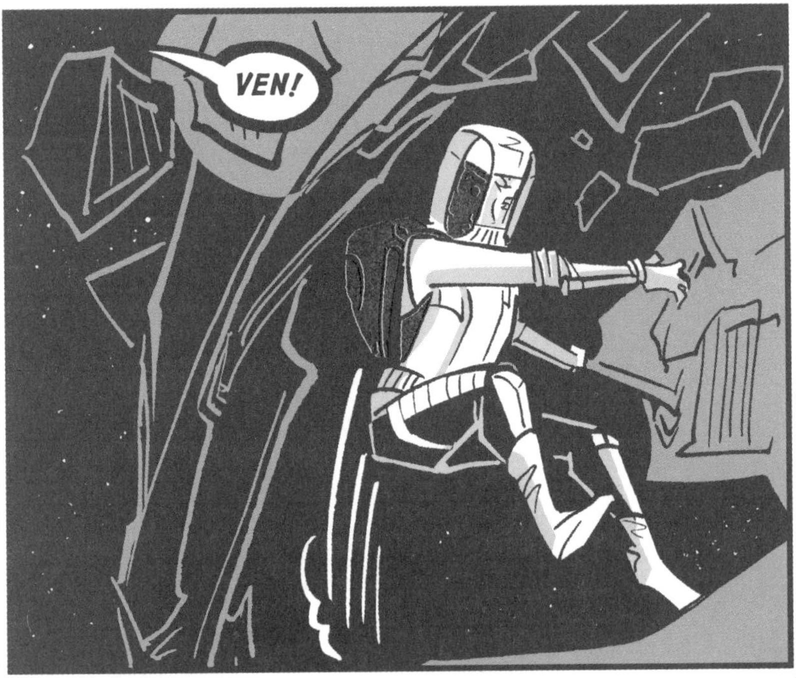
VEN!

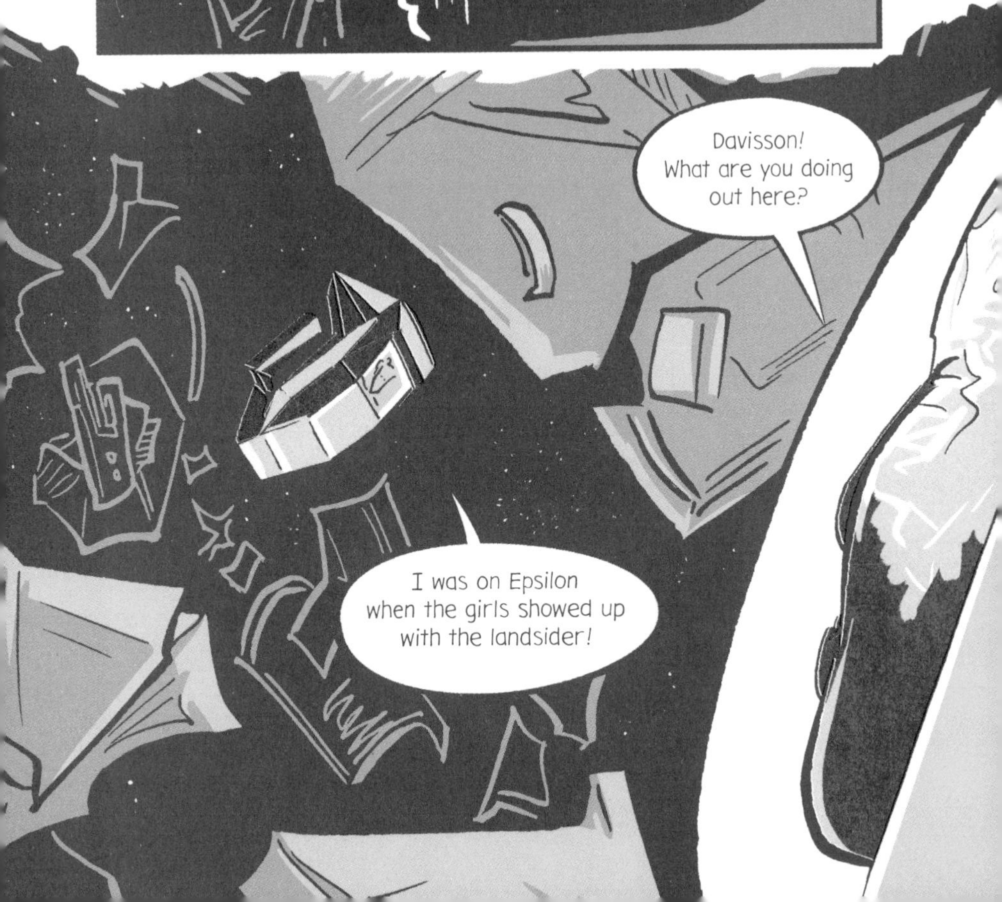
Davisson!
What are you doing
out here?
I was on Epsilon
when the girls showed up
with the landsider!

(UNITED TERRITORIES BLOCKADE POST)

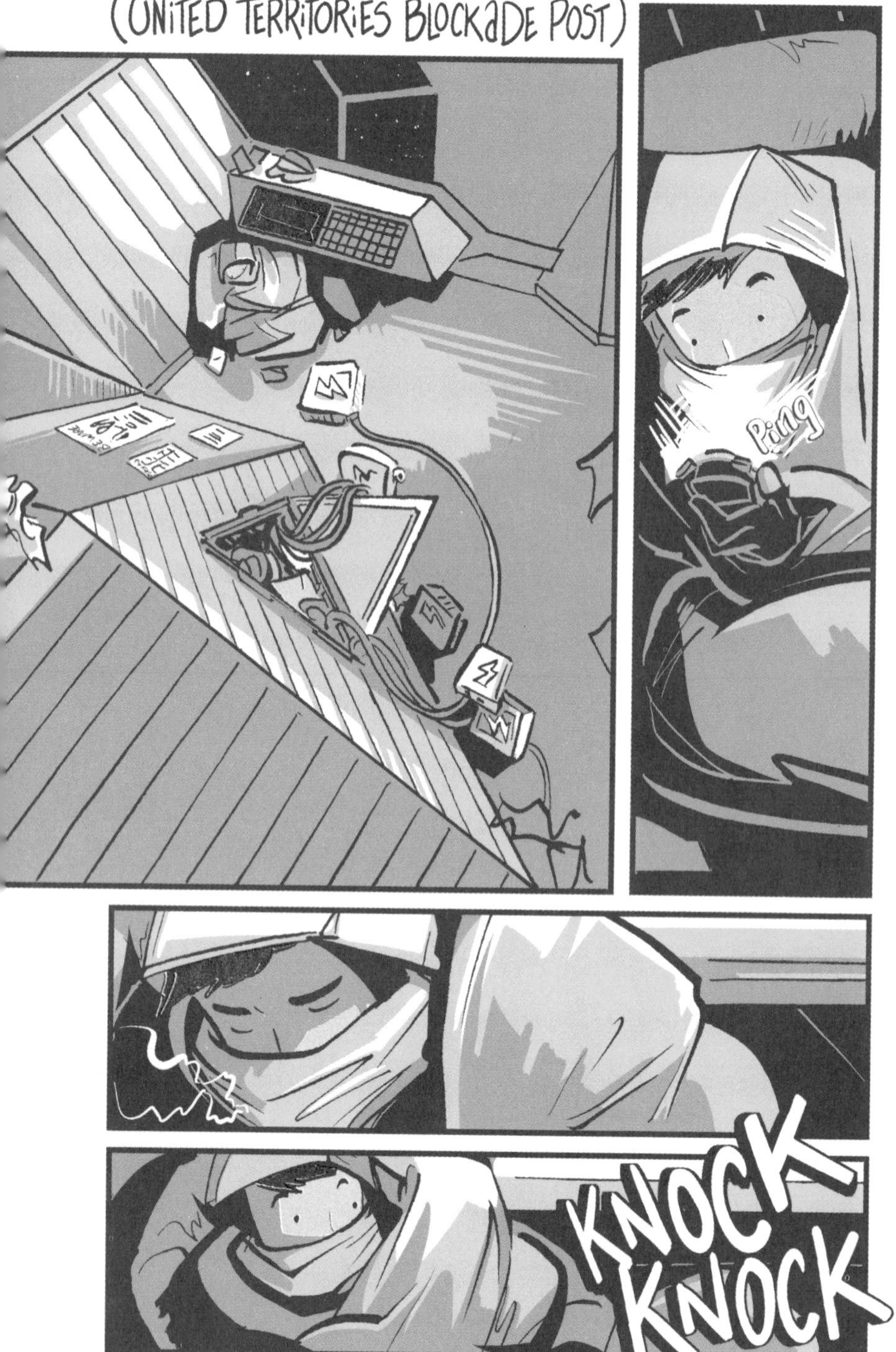
Ping
KNOCK KNOCK

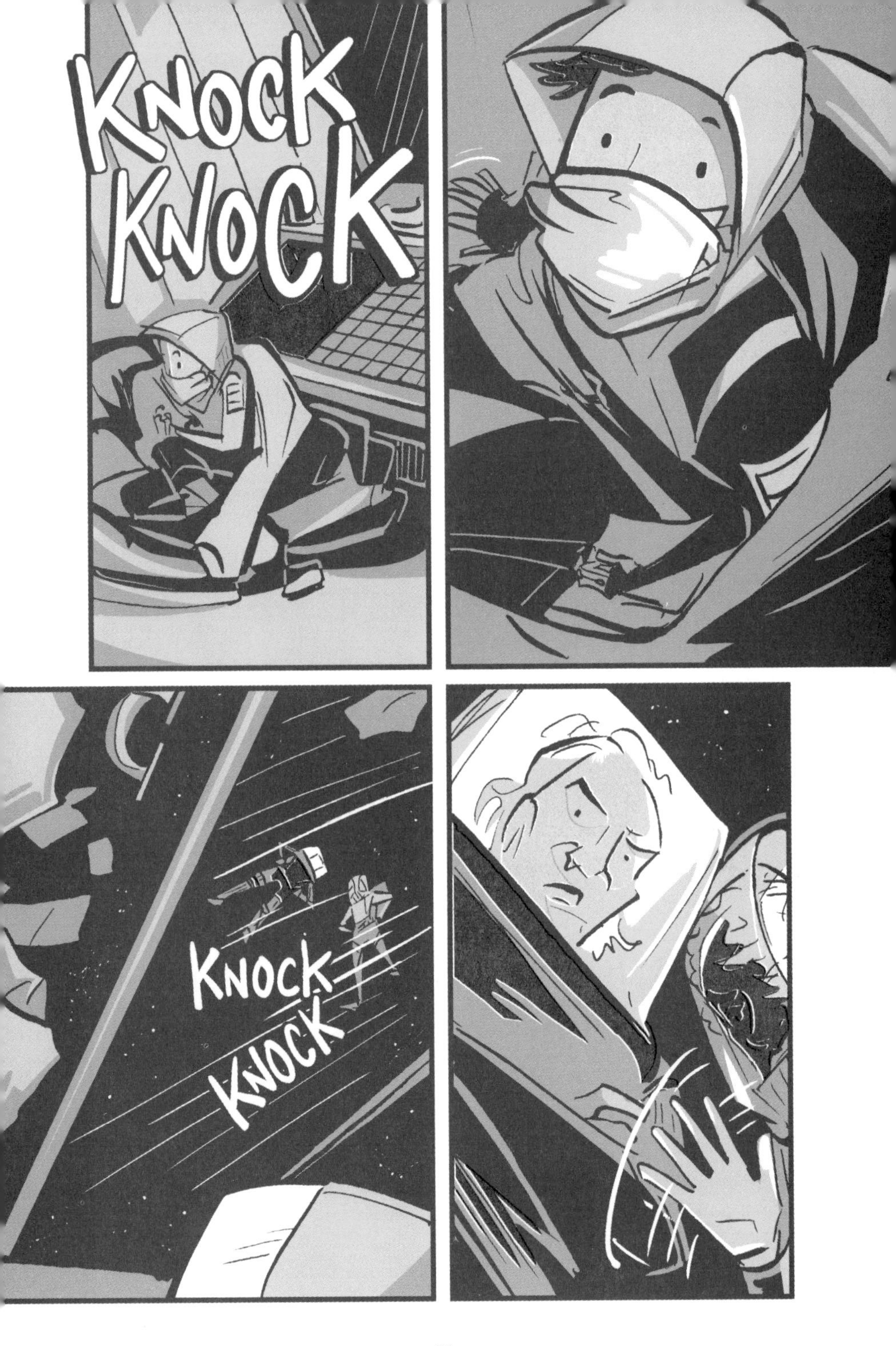
KNOCK KNOCK
KNOCK KNOCK

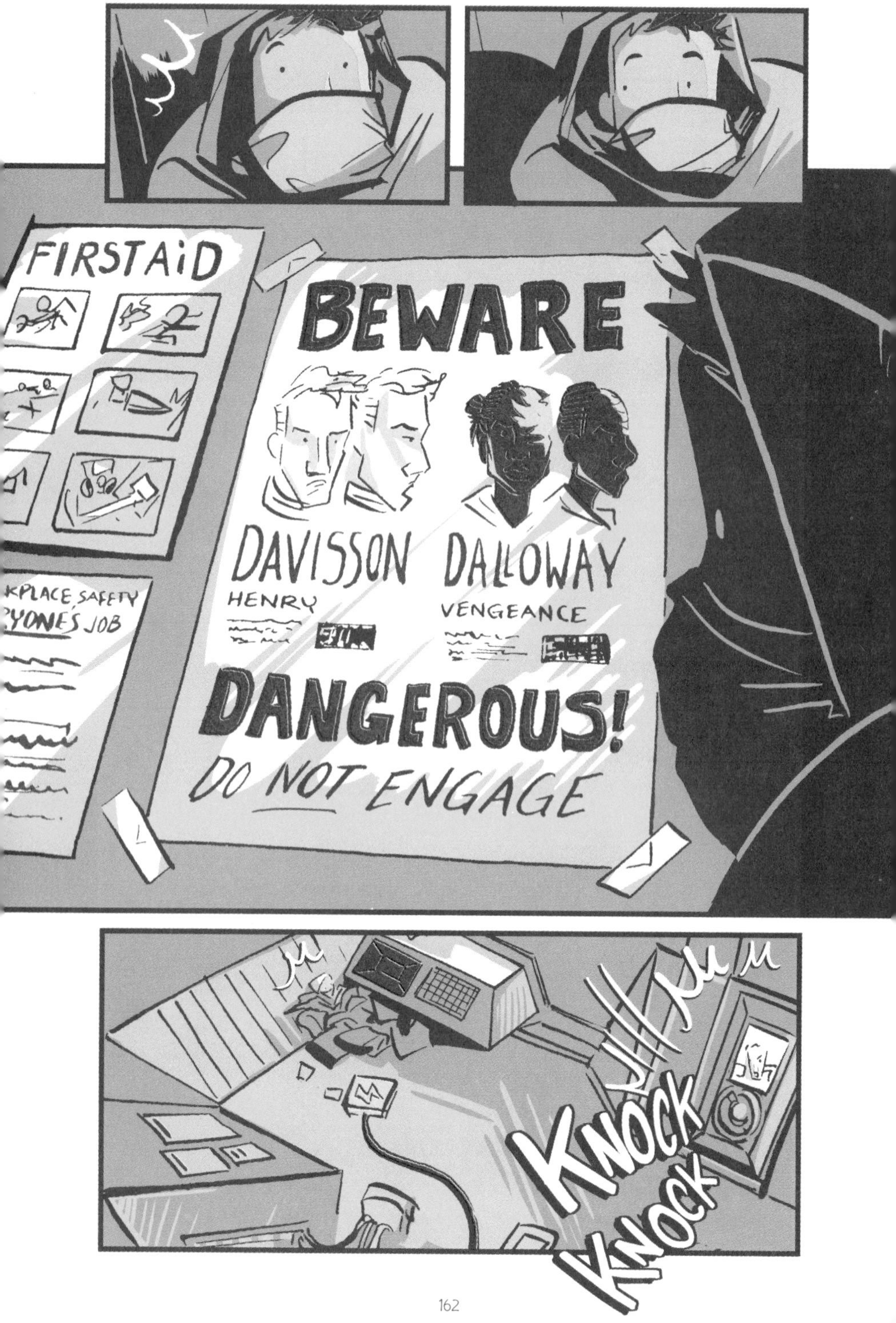
FIRSTAID
KPLACE SAFETY
YONE'S JOB
BEWARE
DAVISSON
HENRY
DALLOWAY
VENGEANCE
DANGEROUS!
DO NOT ENGAGE
KNOCK
KNOCK

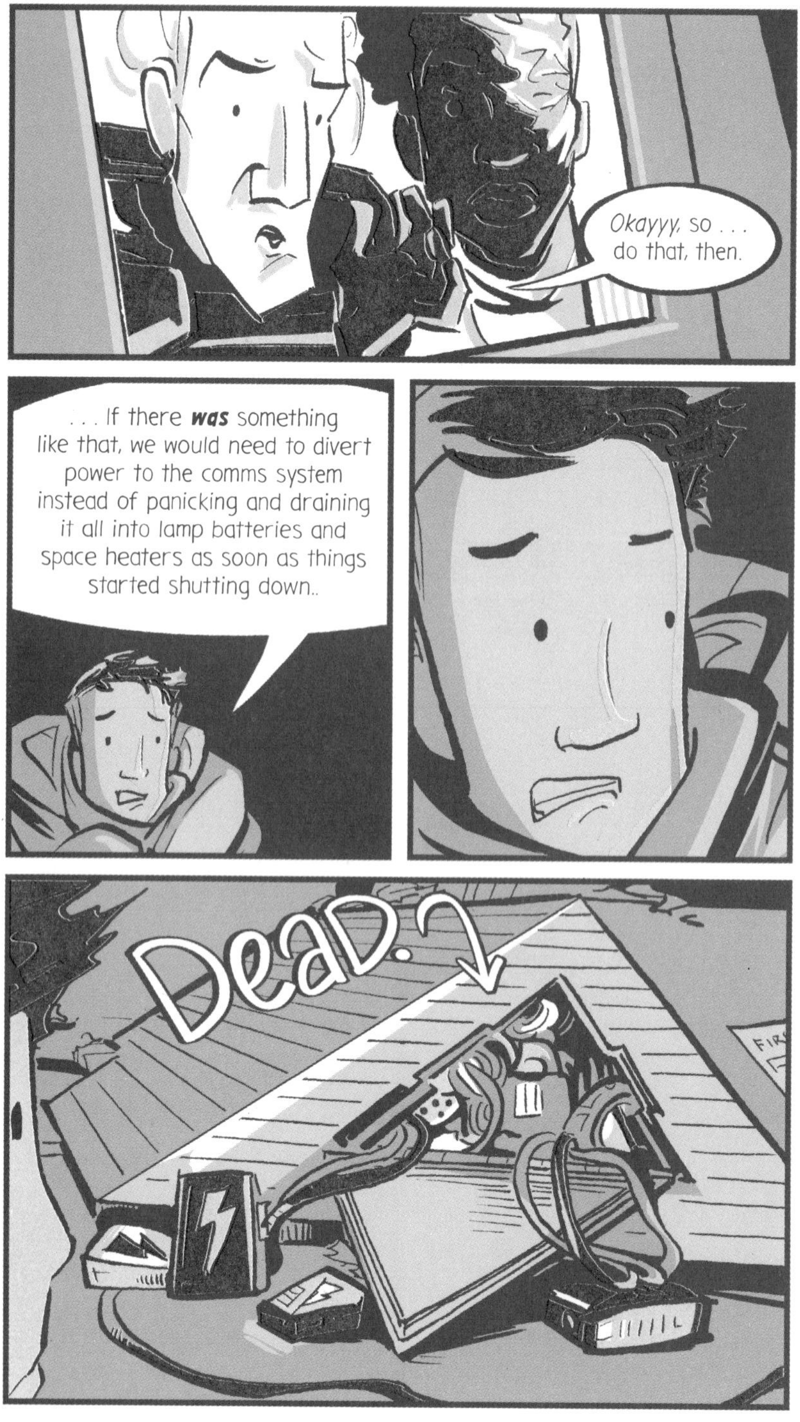
Okayyy, so . . . do that, then.
. . . If there *was* something like that, we would need to divert power to the comms system instead of panicking and draining it all into lamp batteries and space heaters as soon as things started shutting down..
DEAD.

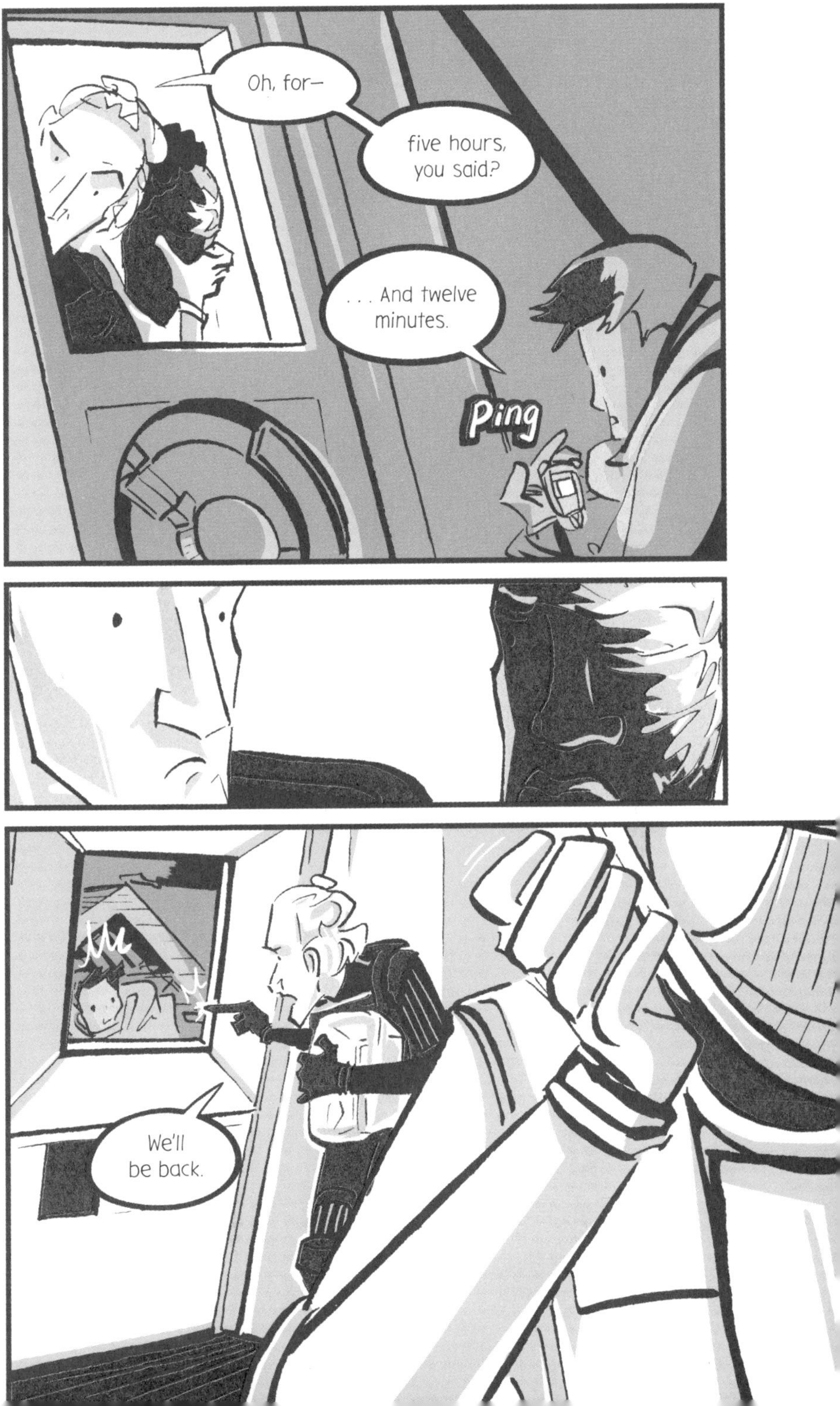
Oh, for–
five hours, you said?
. . . And twelve minutes.
Ping
We'll be back.

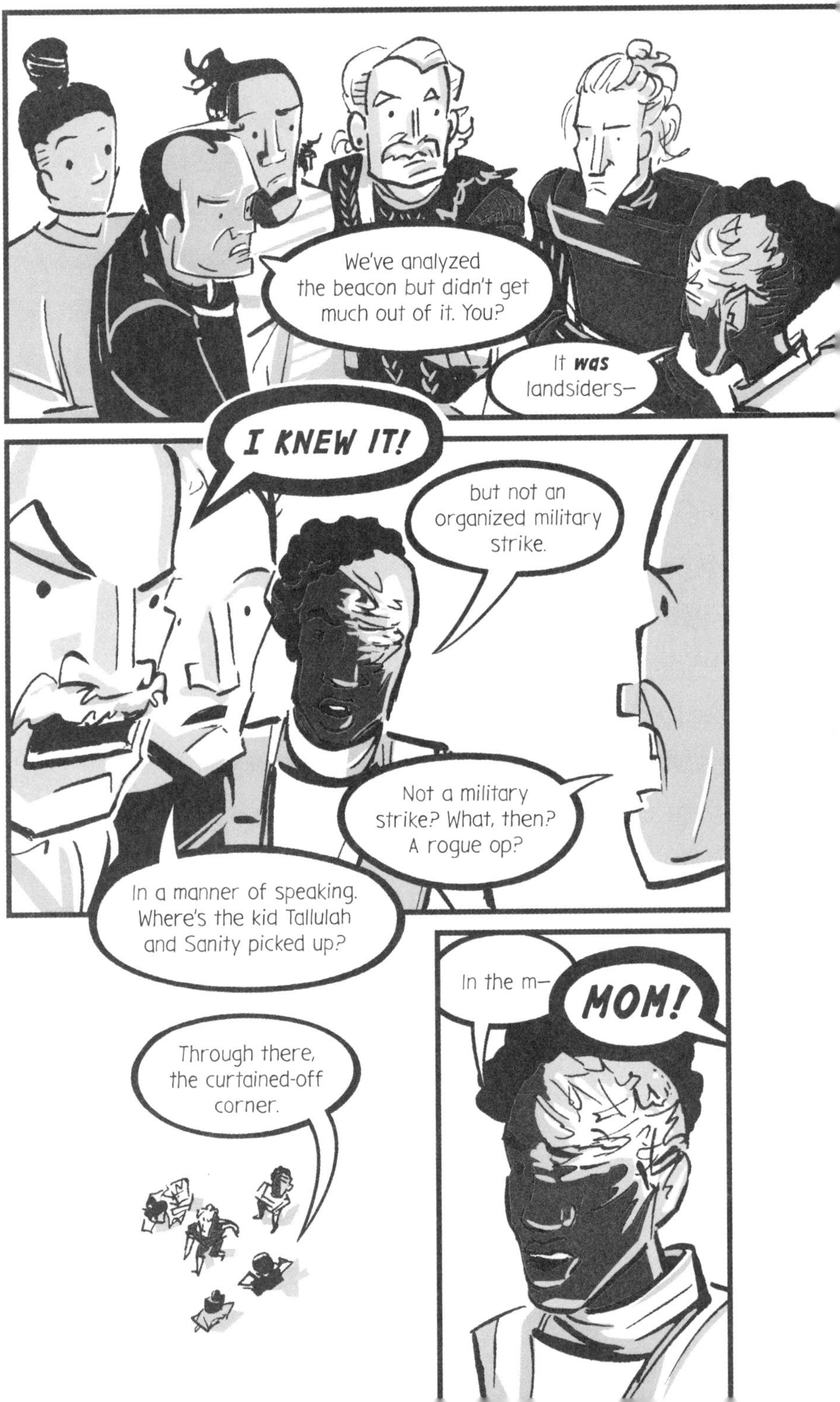
We've analyzed the beacon but didn't get much out of it. You?
It **was** landsiders—
I KNEW IT!
but not an organized military strike.
Not a military strike? What, then? A rogue op?
In a manner of speaking. Where's the kid Tallulah and Sanity picked up?
Through there, the curtained-off corner.
In the m—
MOM!

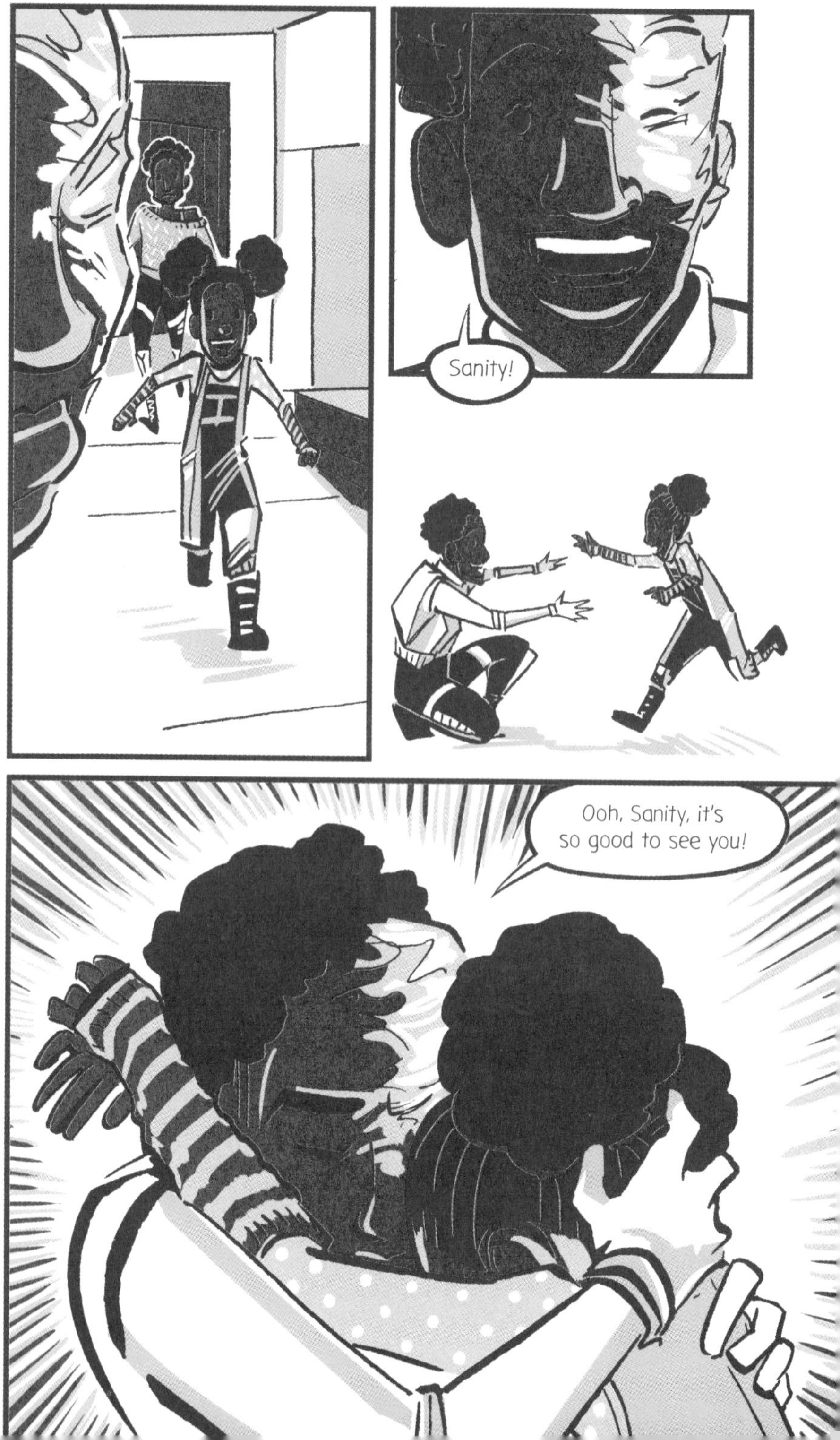
Sanity!
Ooh, Sanity, it's so good to see you!

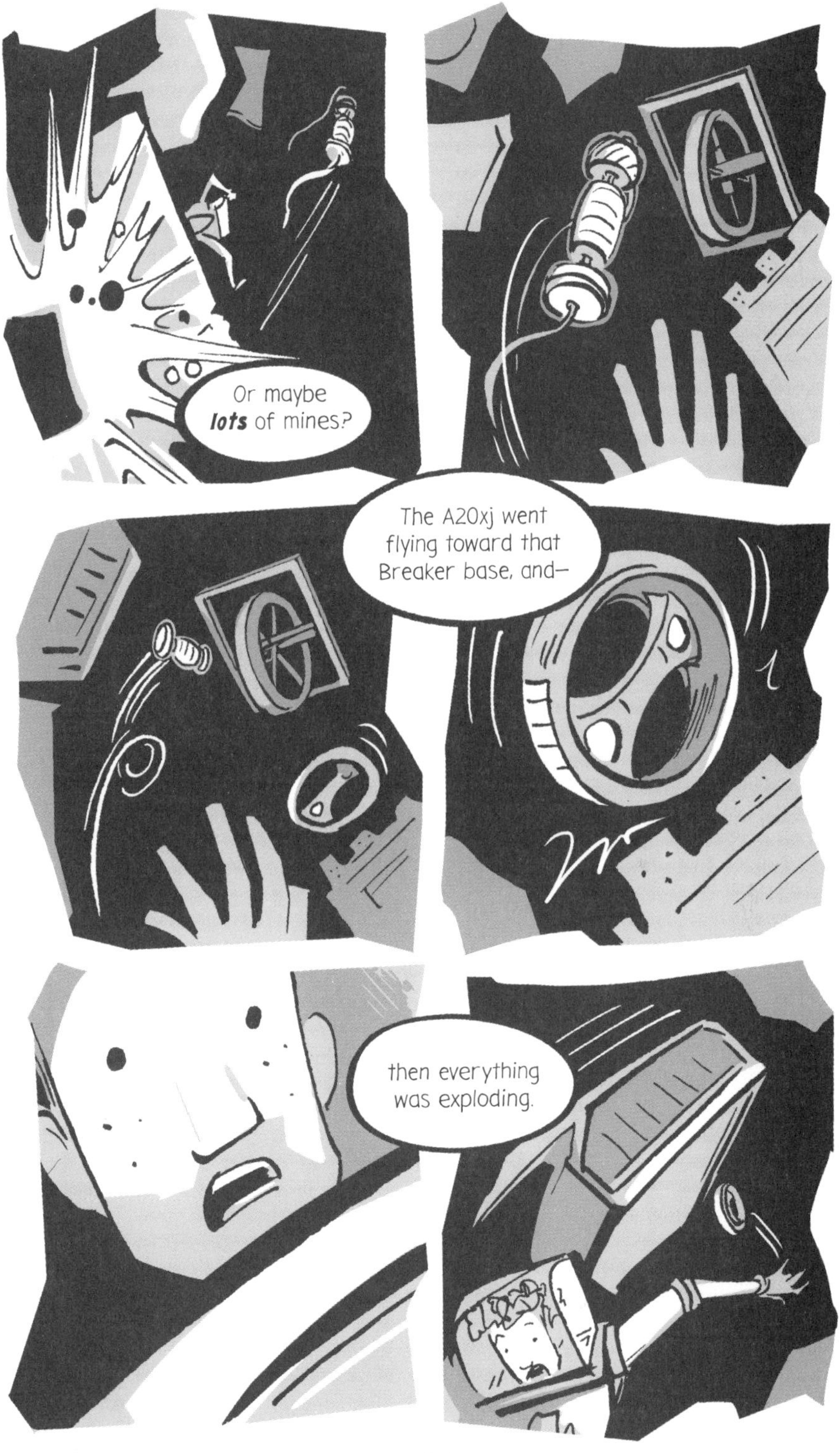
Or maybe **lots** of mines?
The A20xj went flying toward that Breaker base, and—
then everything was exploding.

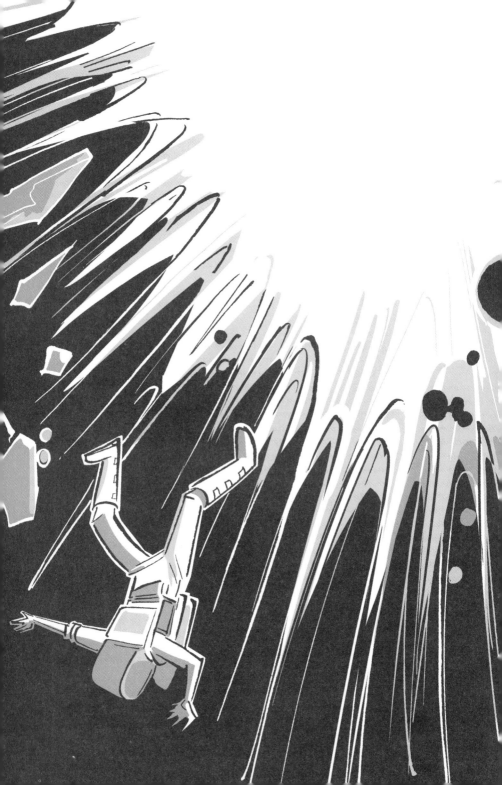

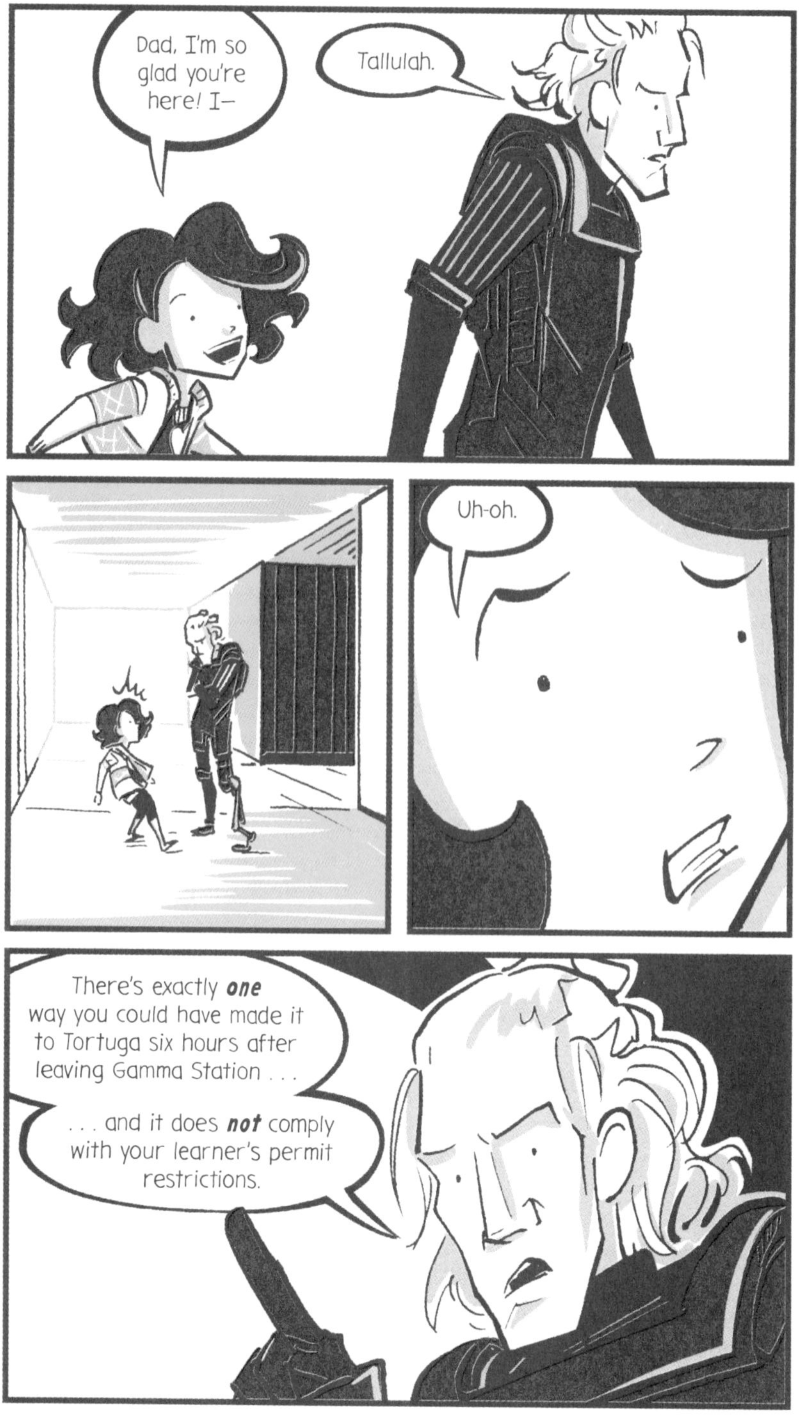
Dad, I'm so glad you're here! I–
Tallulah.
Uh-oh.
There's exactly **one** way you could have made it to Tortuga six hours after leaving Gamma Station . . .
. . . and it does **not** comply with your learner's permit restrictions.

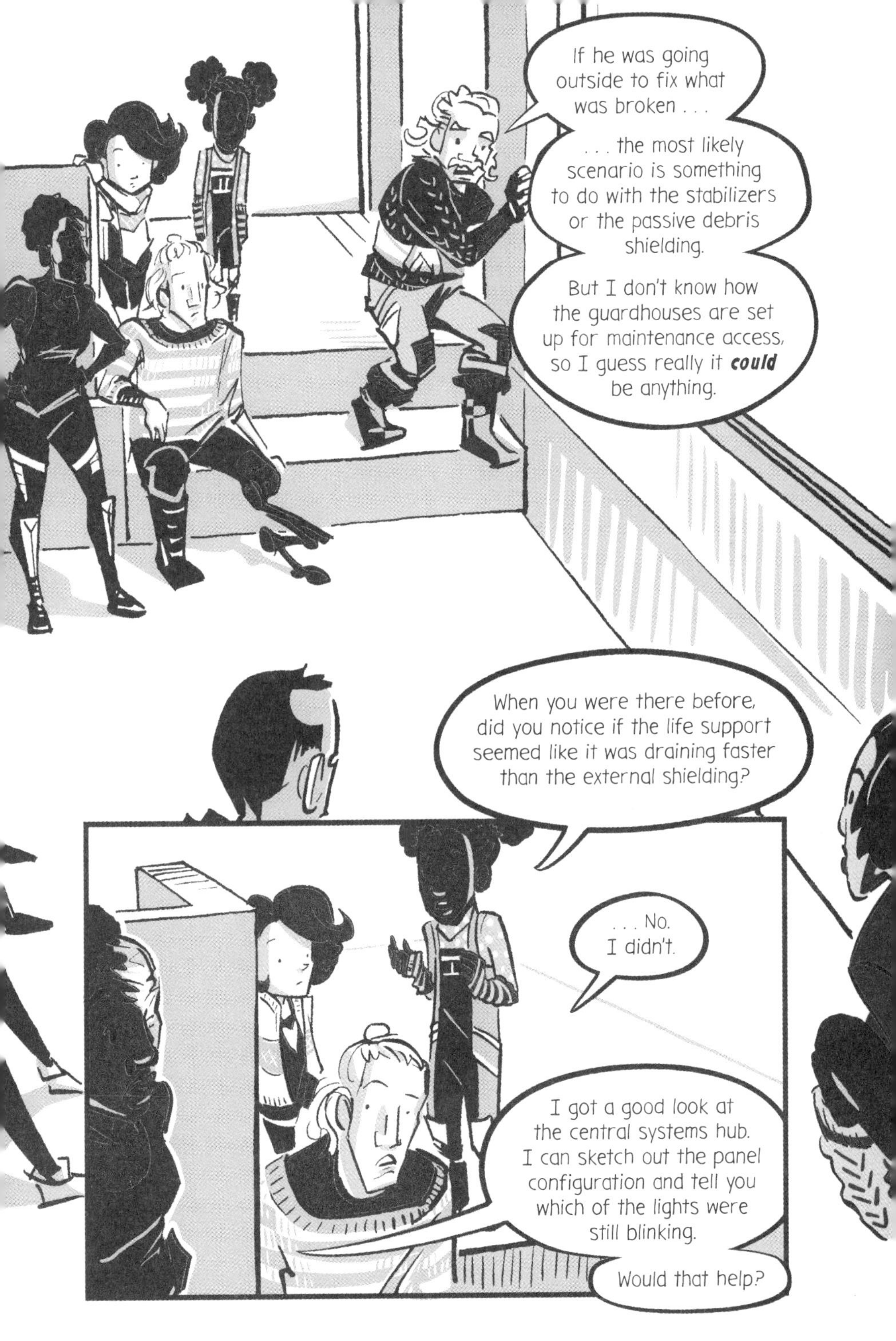
If he was going outside to fix what was broken . . .
. . . the most likely scenario is something to do with the stabilizers or the passive debris shielding.
But I don't know how the guardhouses are set up for maintenance access, so I guess really it **could** be anything.
When you were there before, did you notice if the life support seemed like it was draining faster than the external shielding?
. . . No. I didn't.
I got a good look at the central systems hub. I can sketch out the panel configuration and tell you which of the lights were still blinking.
Would that help?

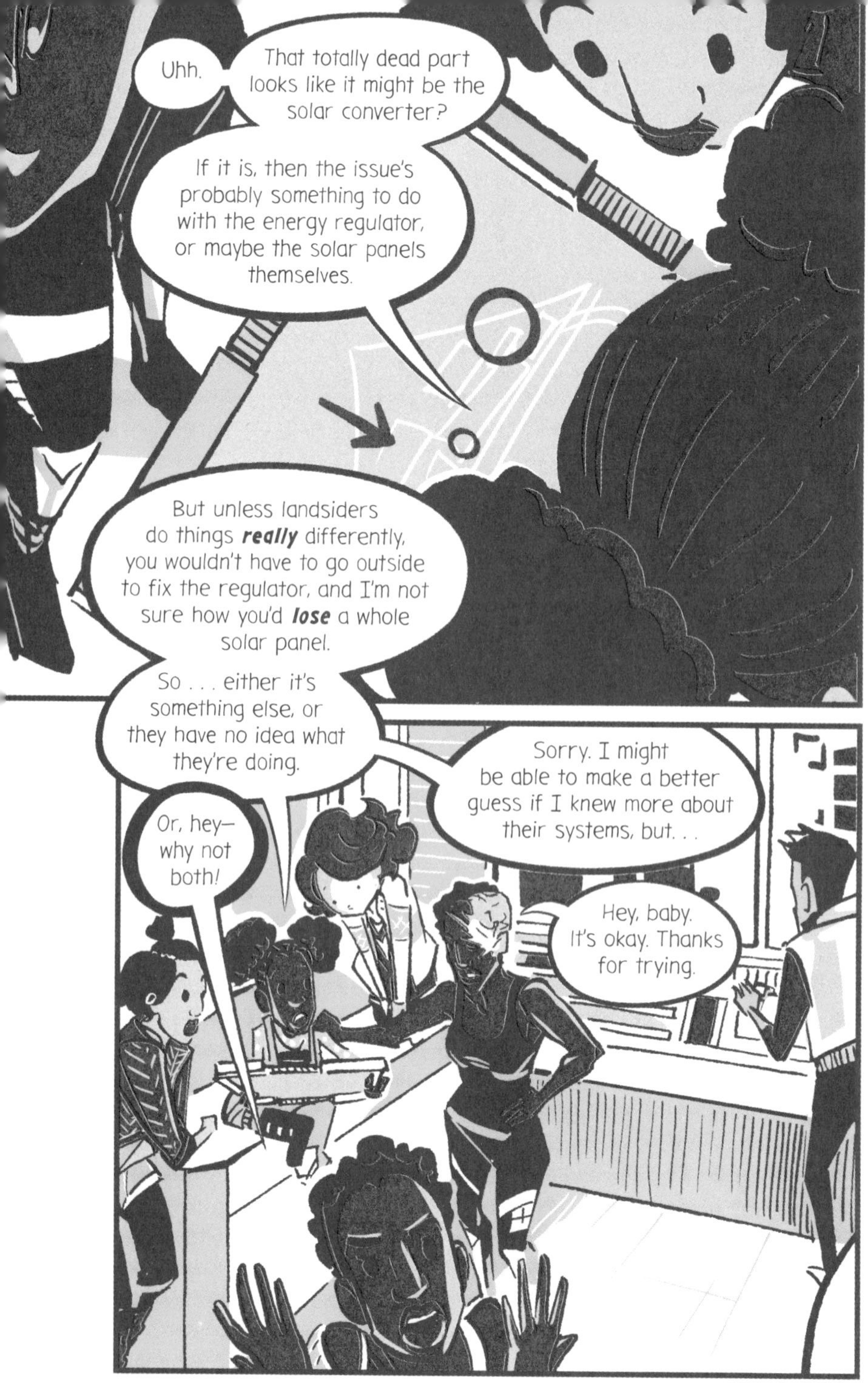
Uhh.
That totally dead part looks like it might be the solar converter?
If it is, then the issue's probably something to do with the energy regulator, or maybe the solar panels themselves.
But unless landsiders do things ***really*** differently, you wouldn't have to go outside to fix the regulator, and I'm not sure how you'd ***lose*** a whole solar panel.
So . . . either it's something else, or they have no idea what they're doing.
Sorry. I might be able to make a better guess if I knew more about their systems, but. . .
Or, hey— why not both!
Hey, baby. It's okay. Thanks for trying.

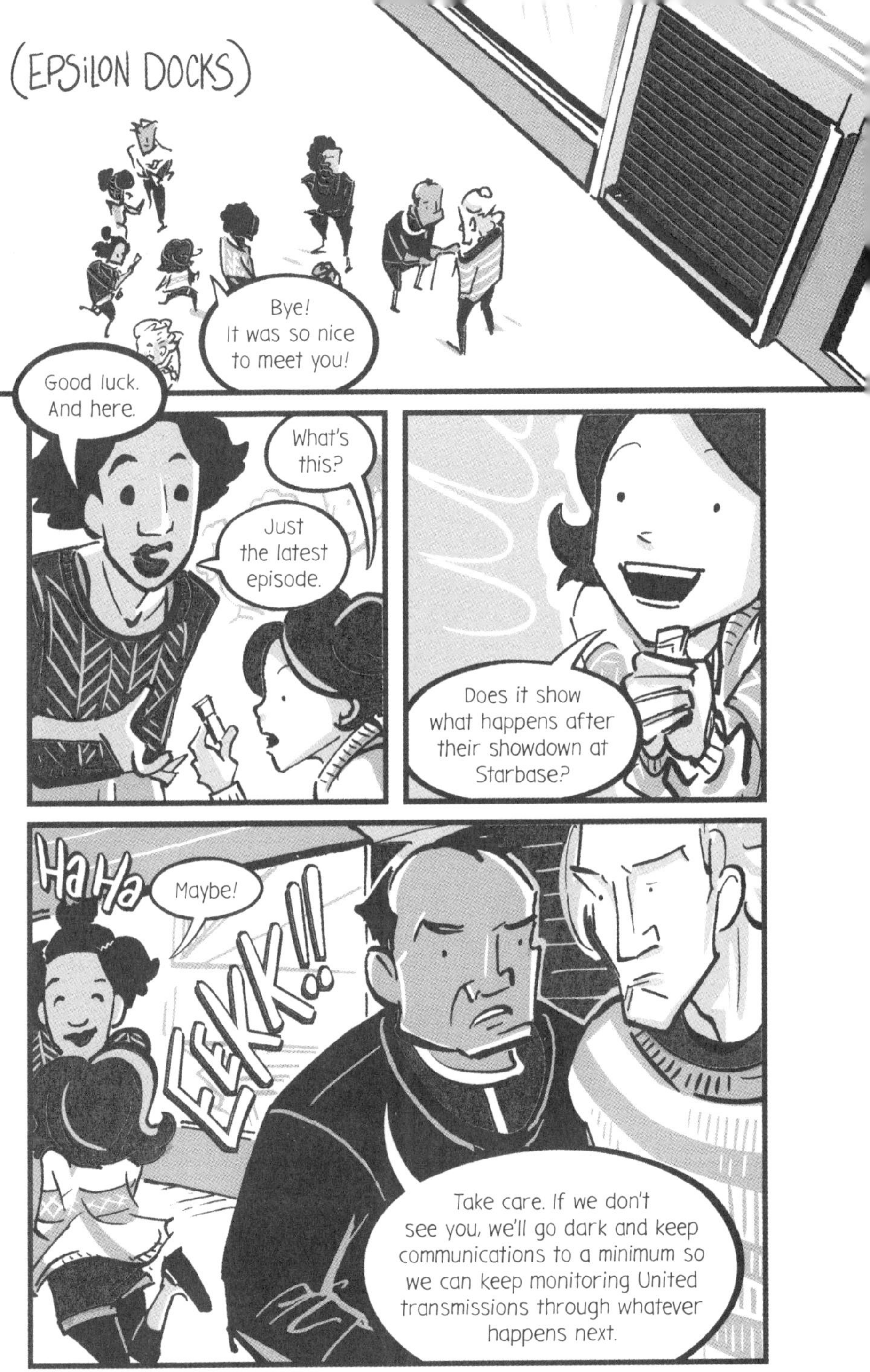
(EPSILON DOCKS)
Bye! It was so nice to meet you!
Good luck. And here.
What's this?
Just the latest episode.
Does it show what happens after their showdown at Starbase?
HaHa
Maybe!
EEKK!!
Take care. If we don't see you, we'll go dark and keep communications to a minimum so we can keep monitoring United transmissions through whatever happens next.

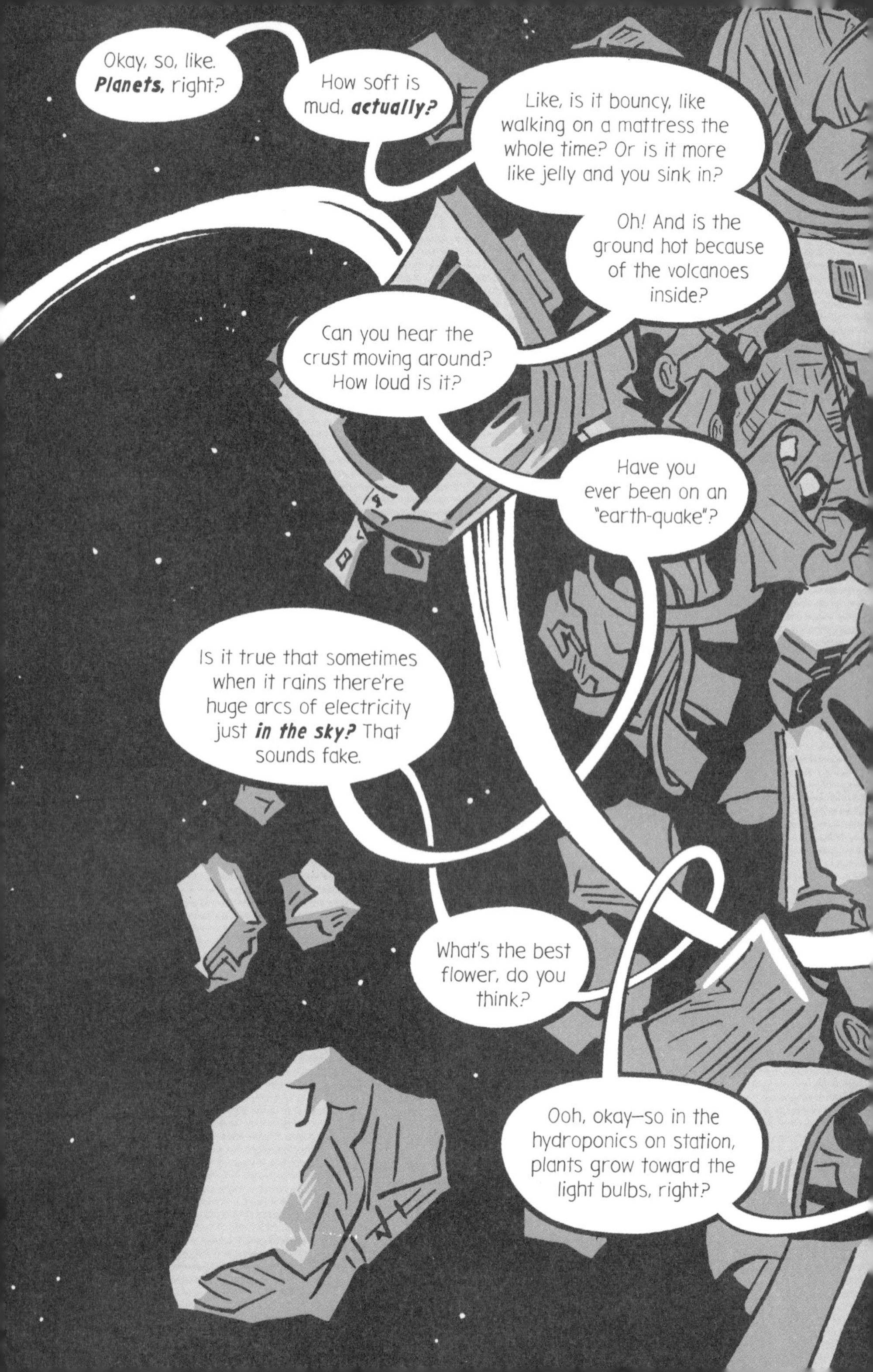
Okay, so, like. **Planets,** right?
How soft is mud, ***actually?***
Like, is it bouncy, like walking on a mattress the whole time? Or is it more like jelly and you sink in?
Oh! And is the ground hot because of the volcanoes inside?
Can you hear the crust moving around? How loud is it?
Have you ever been on an "earth-quake"?
Is it true that sometimes when it rains there're huge arcs of electricity just ***in the sky?*** That sounds fake.
What's the best flower, do you think?
Ooh, okay—so in the hydroponics on station, plants grow toward the light bulbs, right?

200

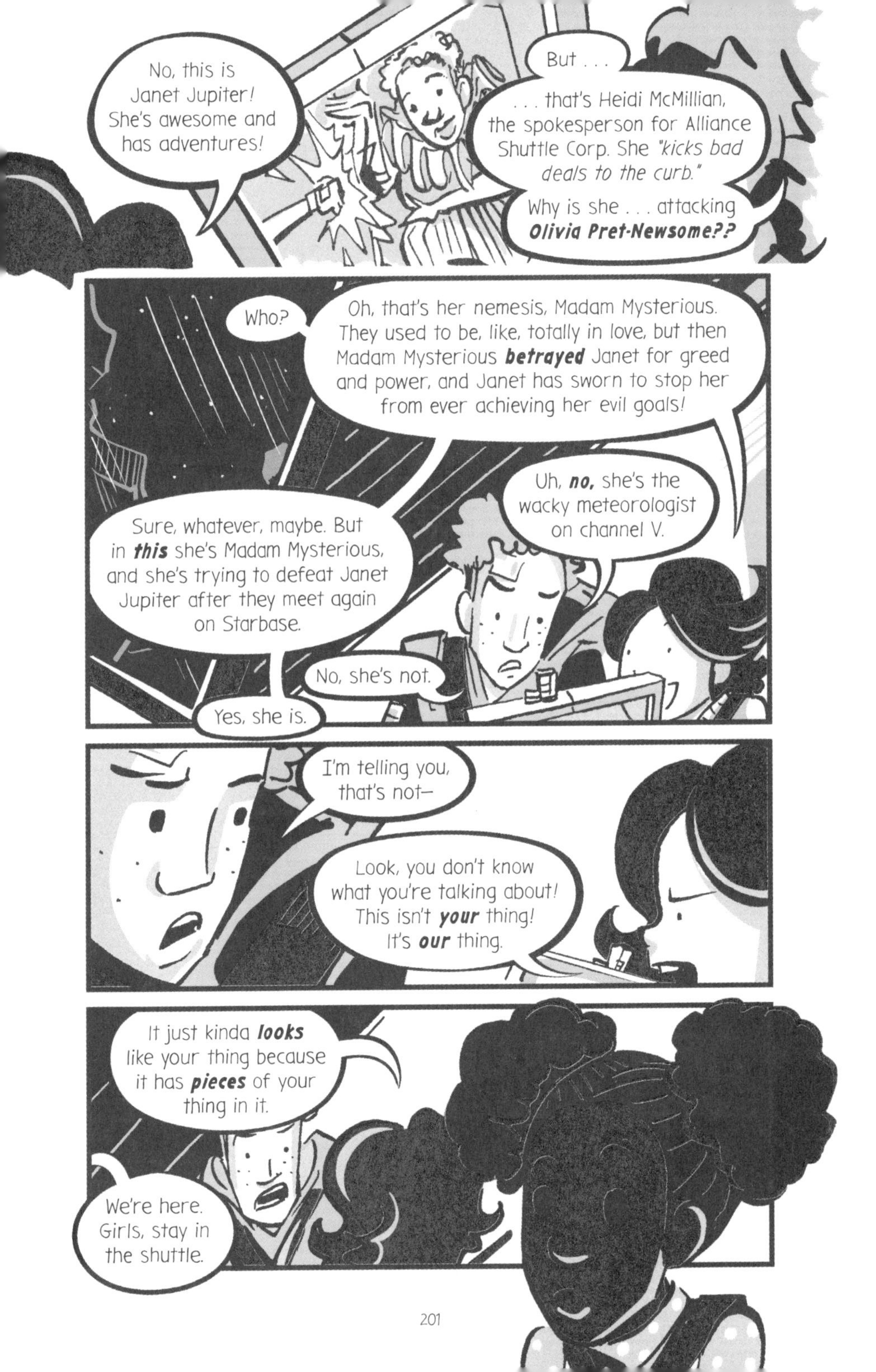

No, this is Janet Jupiter! She's awesome and has adventures!
But . . .
. . . that's Heidi McMillian, the spokesperson for Alliance Shuttle Corp. She *"kicks bad deals to the curb."*
Why is she . . . attacking ***Olivia Pret-Newsome??***
Who?
Oh, that's her nemesis, Madam Mysterious. They used to be, like, totally in love, but then Madam Mysterious ***betrayed*** Janet for greed and power, and Janet has sworn to stop her from ever achieving her evil goals!
Uh, ***no,*** she's the wacky meteorologist on channel V.
Sure, whatever, maybe. But in ***this*** she's Madam Mysterious, and she's trying to defeat Janet Jupiter after they meet again on Starbase.
No, she's not.
Yes, she is.
I'm telling you, that's not—
Look, you don't know what you're talking about! This isn't ***your*** thing! It's ***our*** thing.
It just kinda ***looks*** like your thing because it has ***pieces*** of your thing in it.
We're here. Girls, stay in the shuttle.

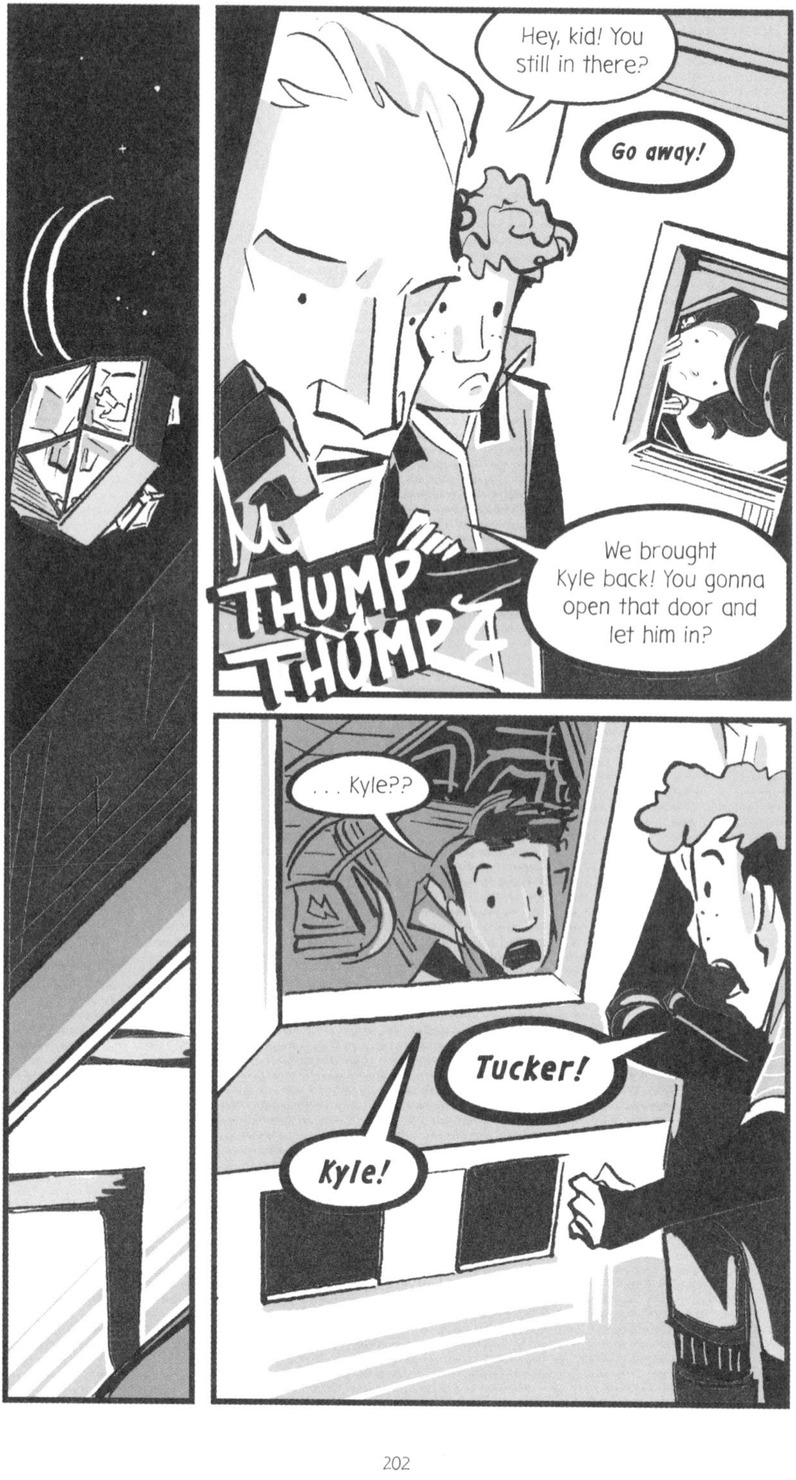
Hey, kid! You still in there?
Go away!
THUMP THUMP
We brought Kyle back! You gonna open that door and let him in?
. . . Kyle??
Tucker!
Kyle!

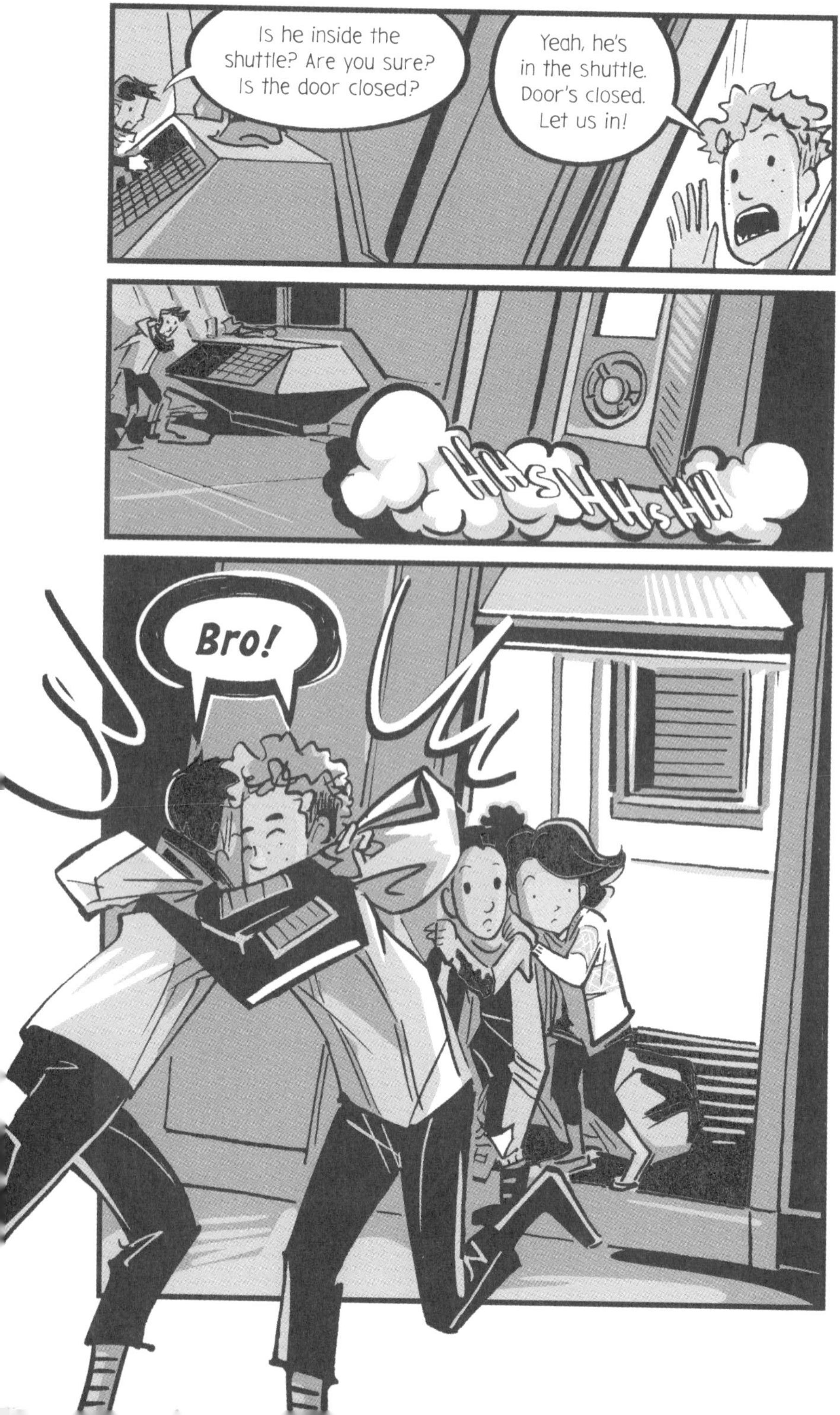
Is he inside the shuttle? Are you sure? Is the door closed?
Yeah, he's in the shuttle. Door's closed. Let us in!
HHSHHHSHH
Bro!

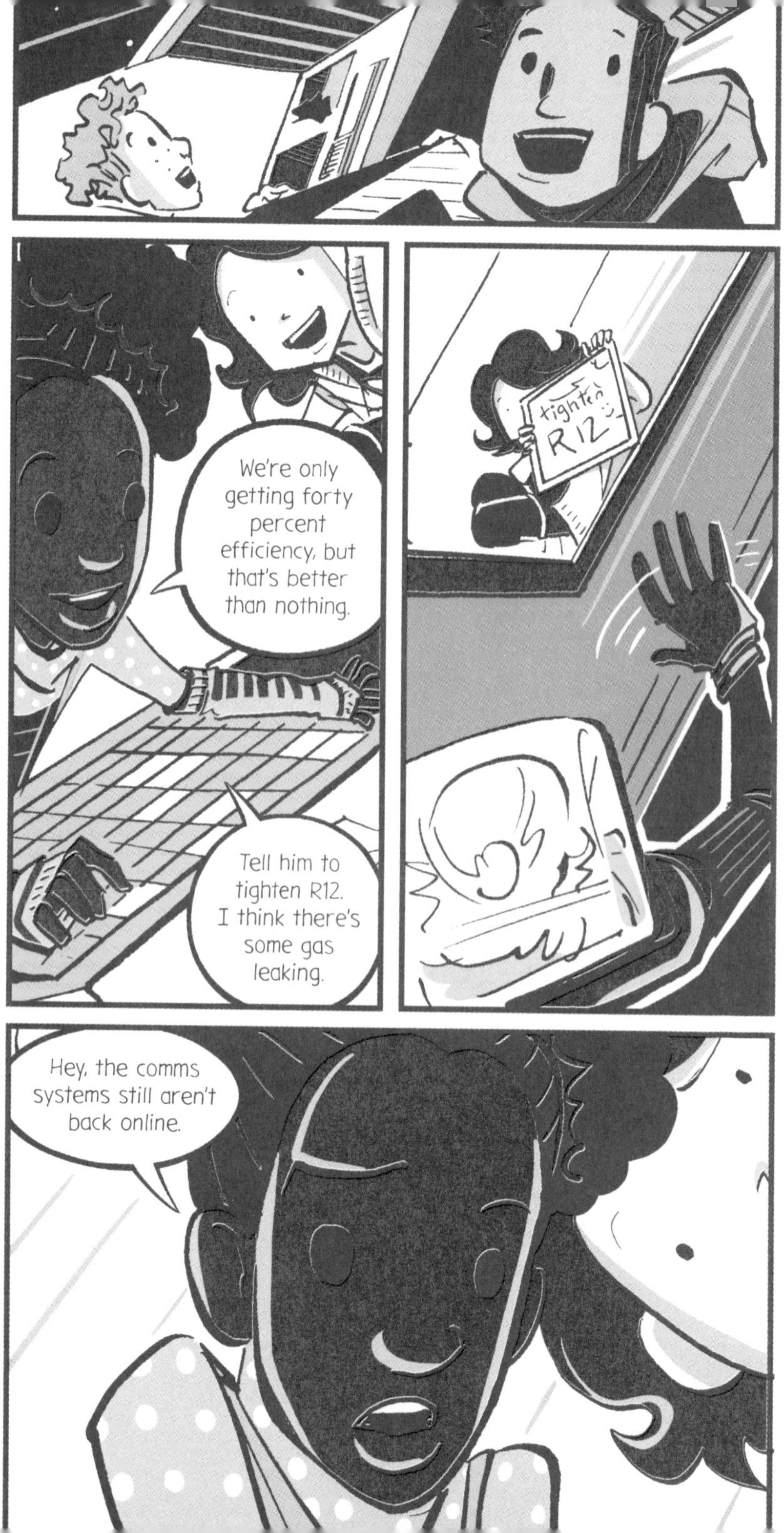
We're only getting forty percent efficiency, but that's better than nothing.
Tell him to tighten R12. I think there's some gas leaking.
tighten R12
Hey, the comms systems still aren't back online.

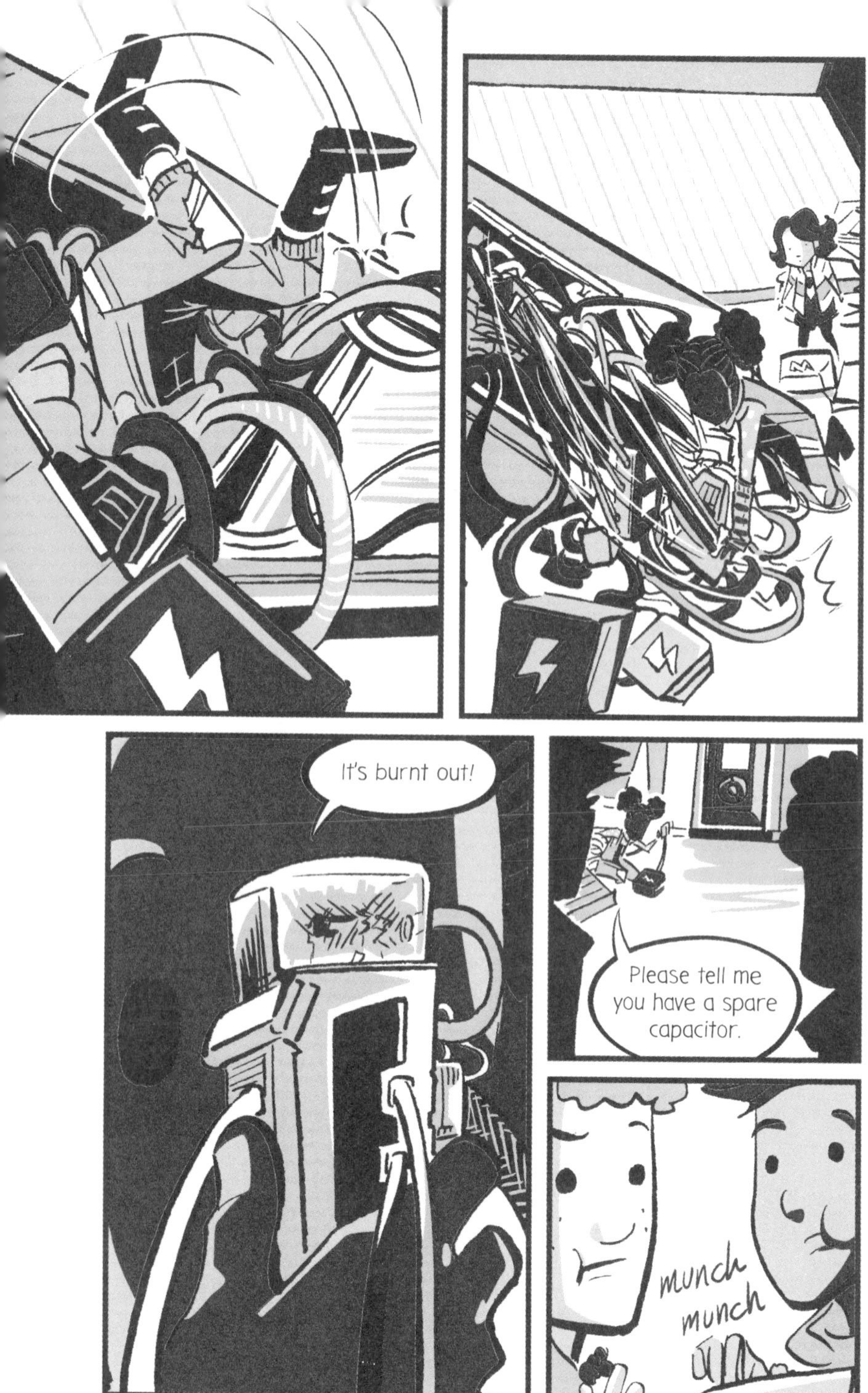
It's burnt out!
Please tell me you have a spare capacitor.
munch munch

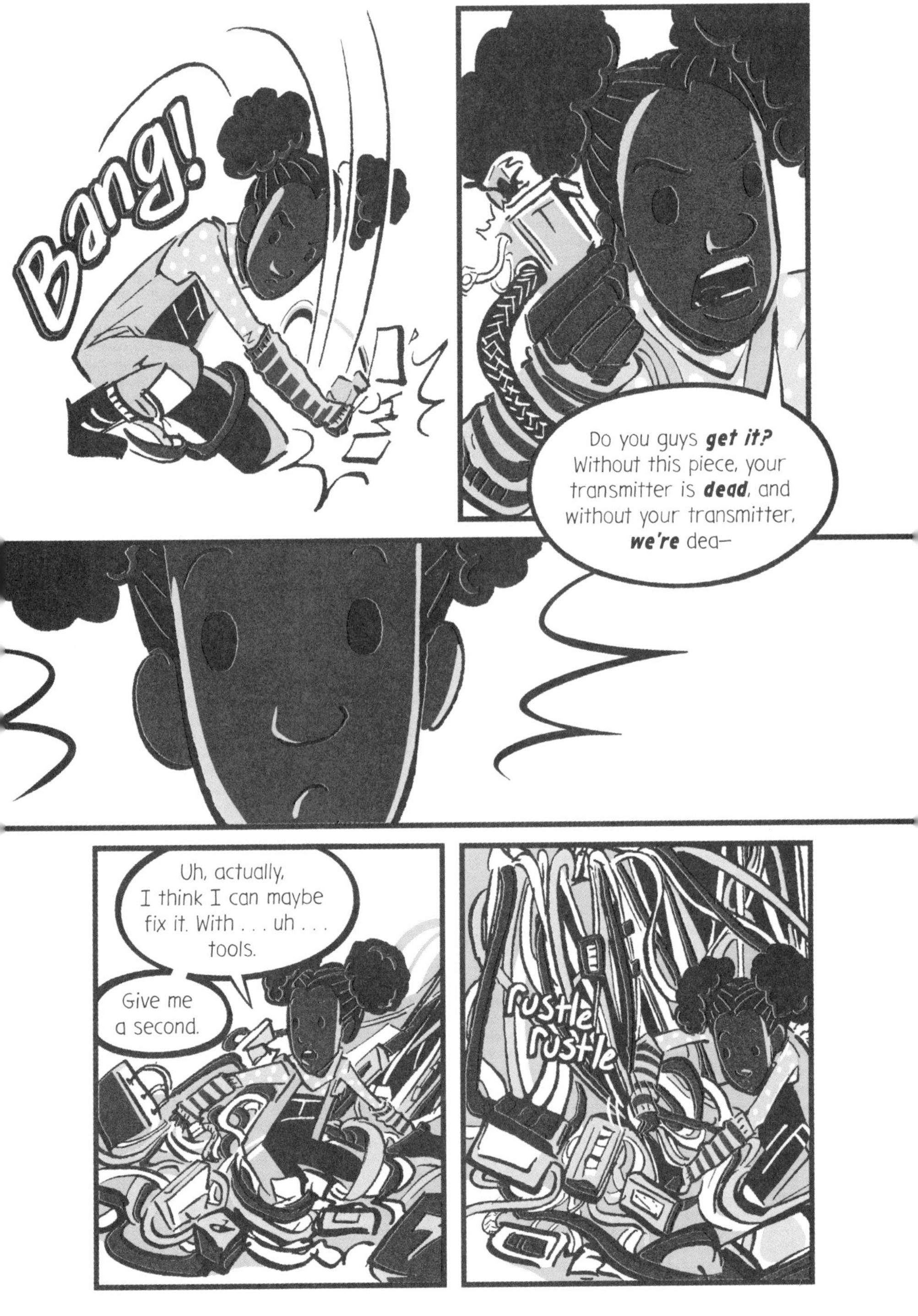
Bang!
Do you guys get it? Without this piece, your transmitter is dead, and without your transmitter, we're dea—
Uh, actually, I think I can maybe fix it. With . . . uh . . . tools.
Give me a second.
rustle rustle

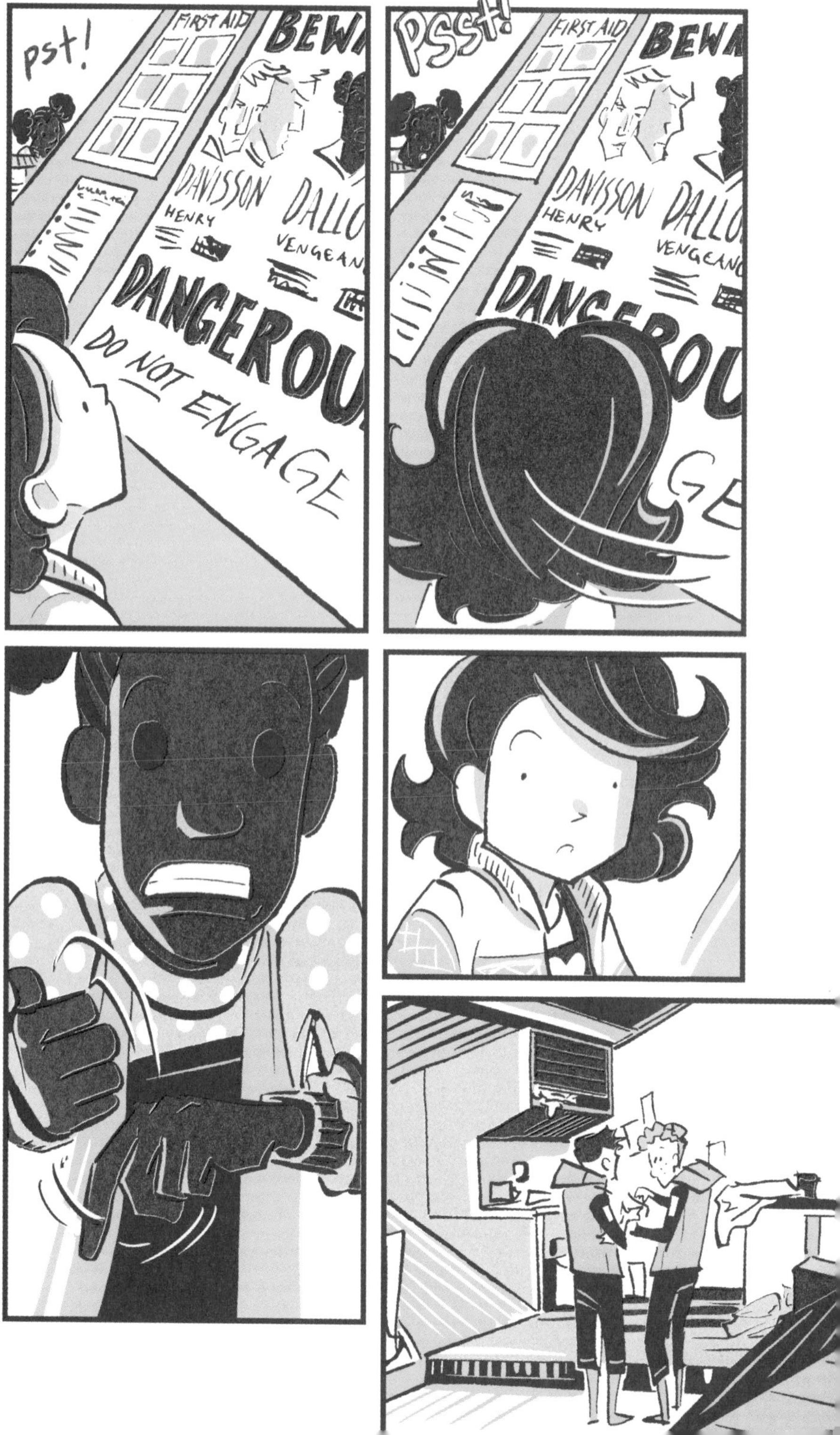
pst!
FIRST AID
BEWA
DAVISSON
HENRY
DALLO
VENGEAN
DANGEROU
DO NOT ENGAGE
PSSt!

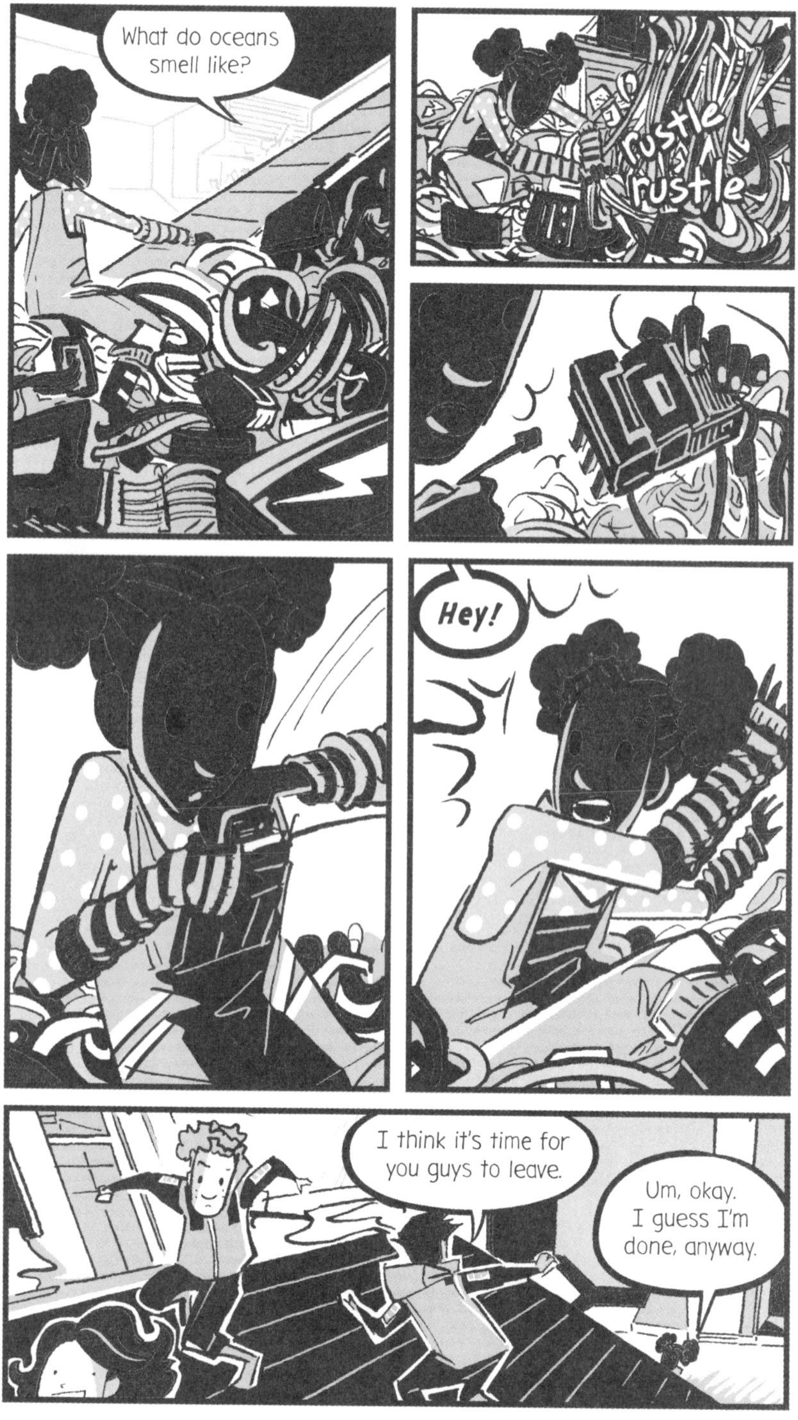
What do oceans smell like?
rustle rustle
Hey!
I think it's time for you guys to leave.
Um, okay. I guess I'm done, anyway.

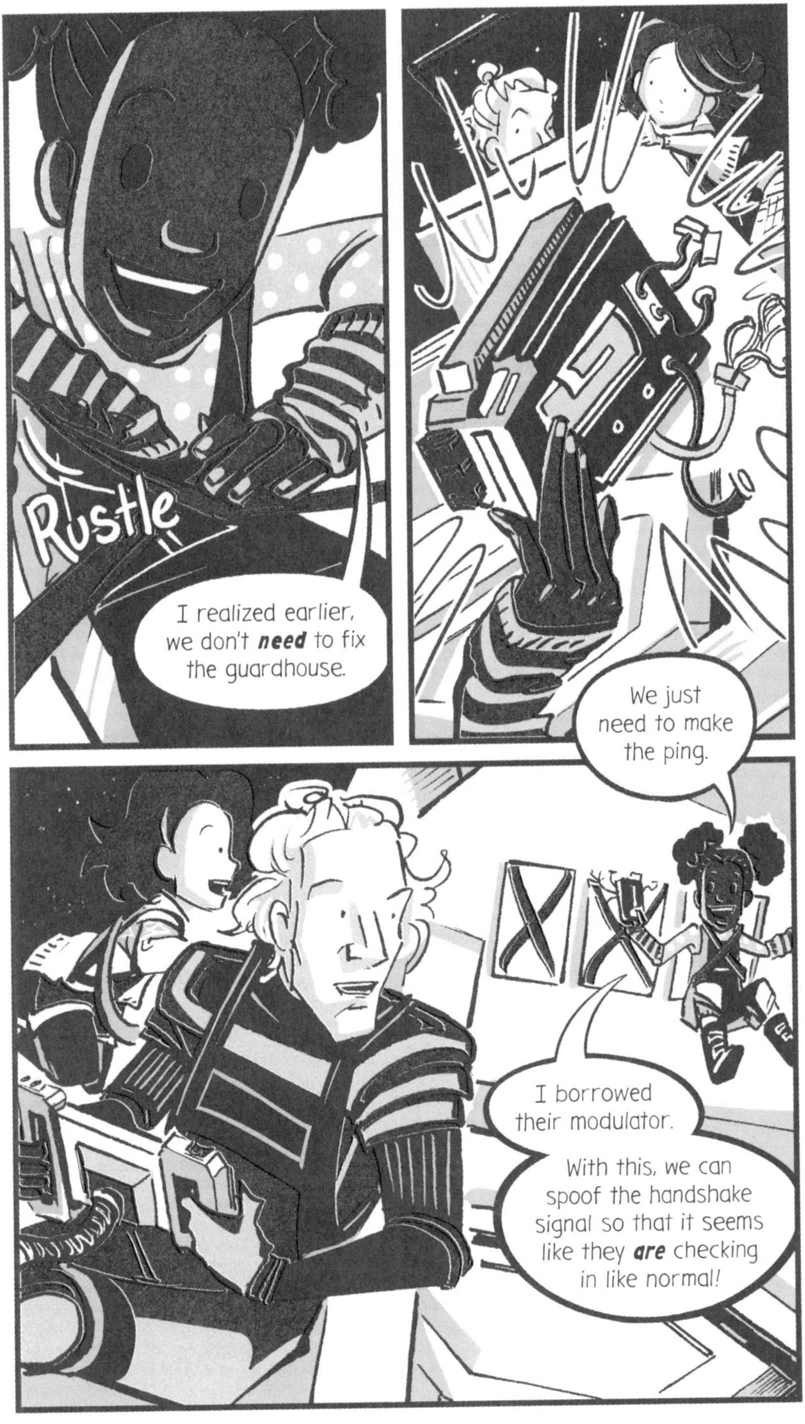
Rustle
I realized earlier, we don't **need** to fix the guardhouse.
We just need to make the ping.
I borrowed their modulator.
With this, we can spoof the handshake signal so that it seems like they **are** checking in like normal!

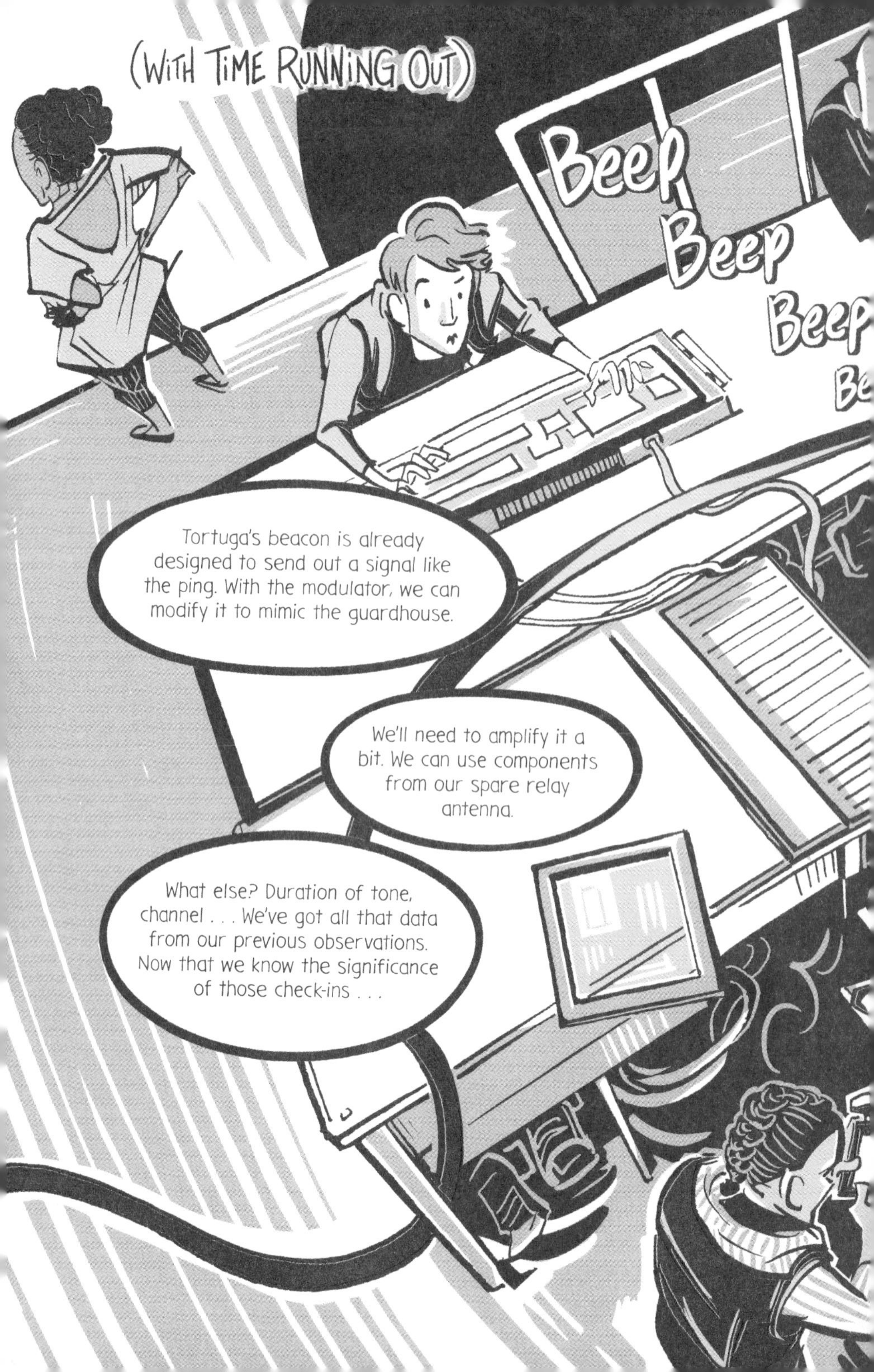
(WITH TIME RUNNING OUT)
Beep
Beep
Beep
Tortuga's beacon is already designed to send out a signal like the ping. With the modulator, we can modify it to mimic the guardhouse.
We'll need to amplify it a bit. We can use components from our spare relay antenna.
What else? Duration of tone, channel . . . We've got all that data from our previous observations. Now that we know the significance of those check-ins . . .

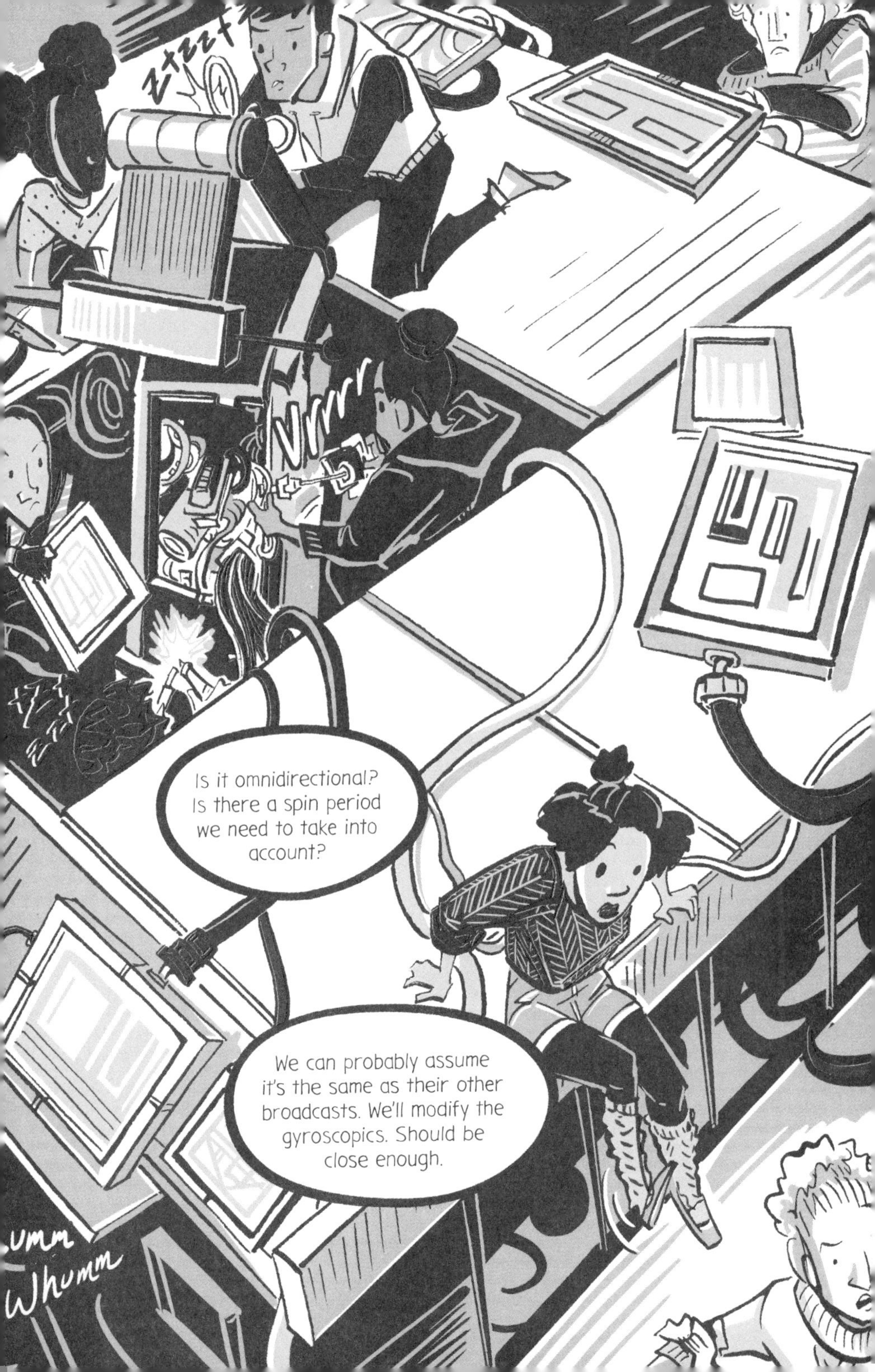

Zzzzzz
Vrrrr
Is it omnidirectional? Is there a spin period we need to take into account?
We can probably assume it's the same as their other broadcasts. We'll modify the gyroscopics. Should be close enough.
umm Whumm

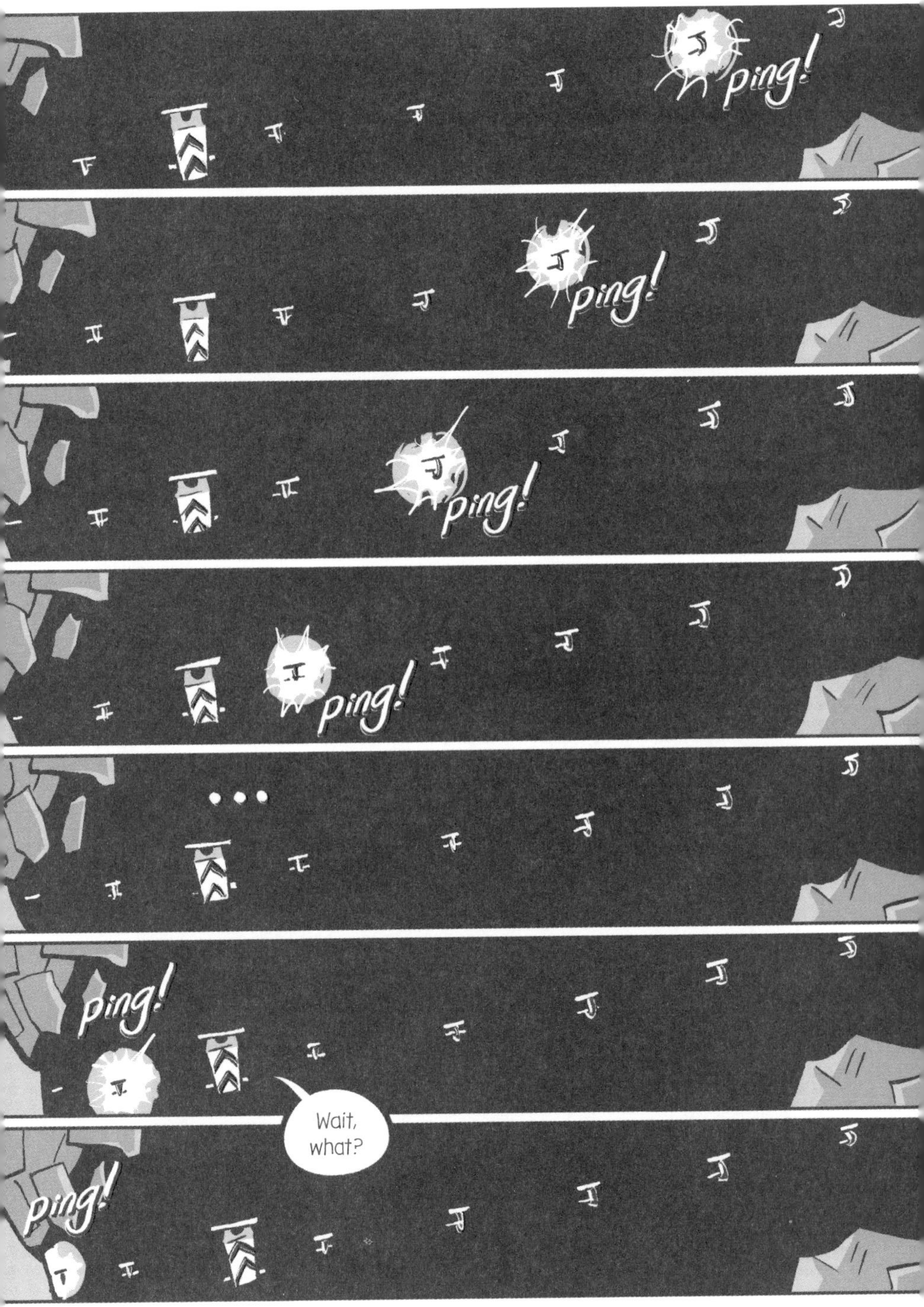
ping!
ping!
ping!
ping!
...
ping!
Wait, what?
ping!

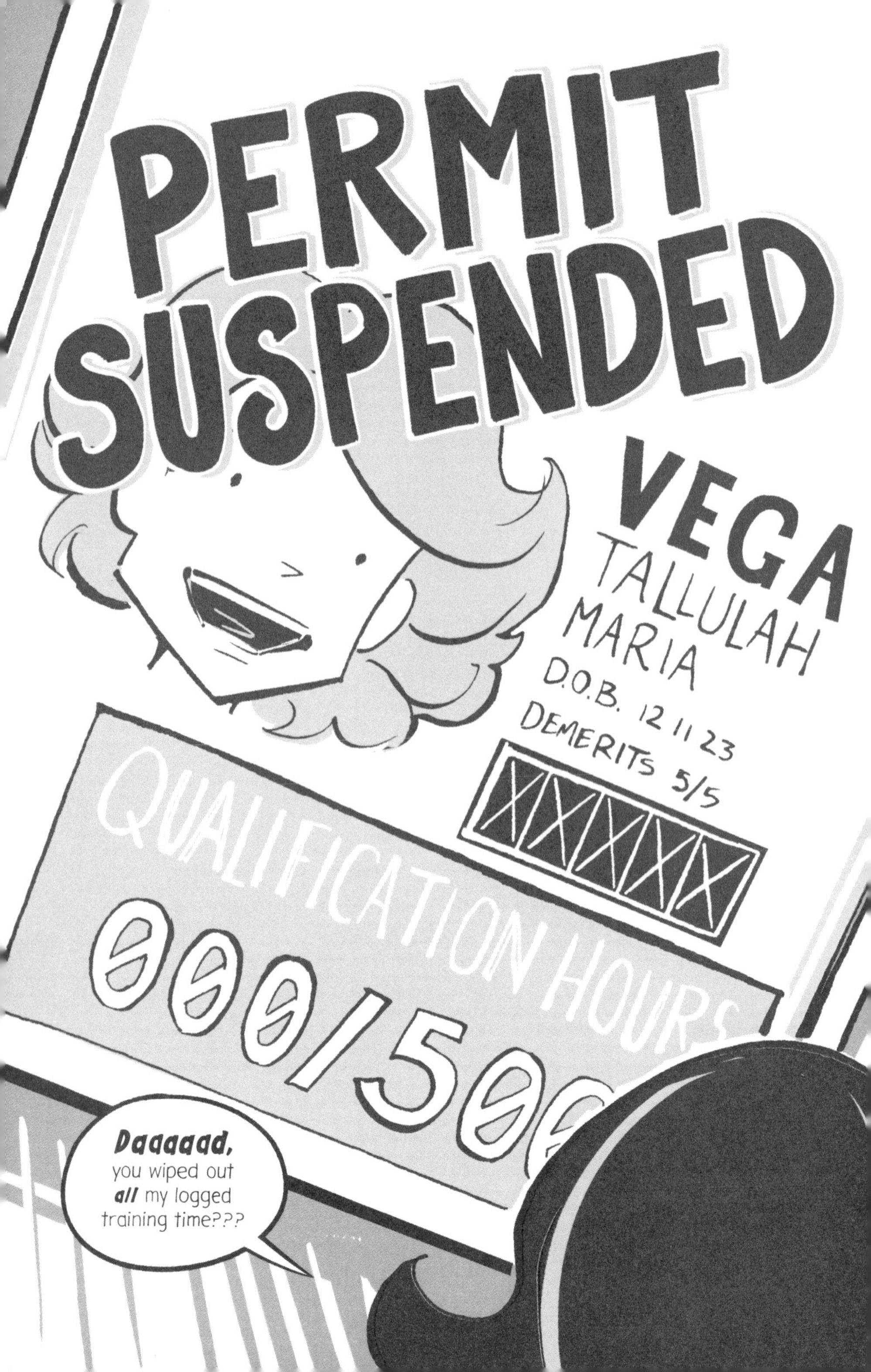
PERMIT SUSPENDED
VEGA
TALLULAH
MARIA
D.O.B. 12 11 23
DEMERITS 5/5
QUALIFICATION HOURS
000/500
Daaaaad, you wiped out ***all*** my logged training time???

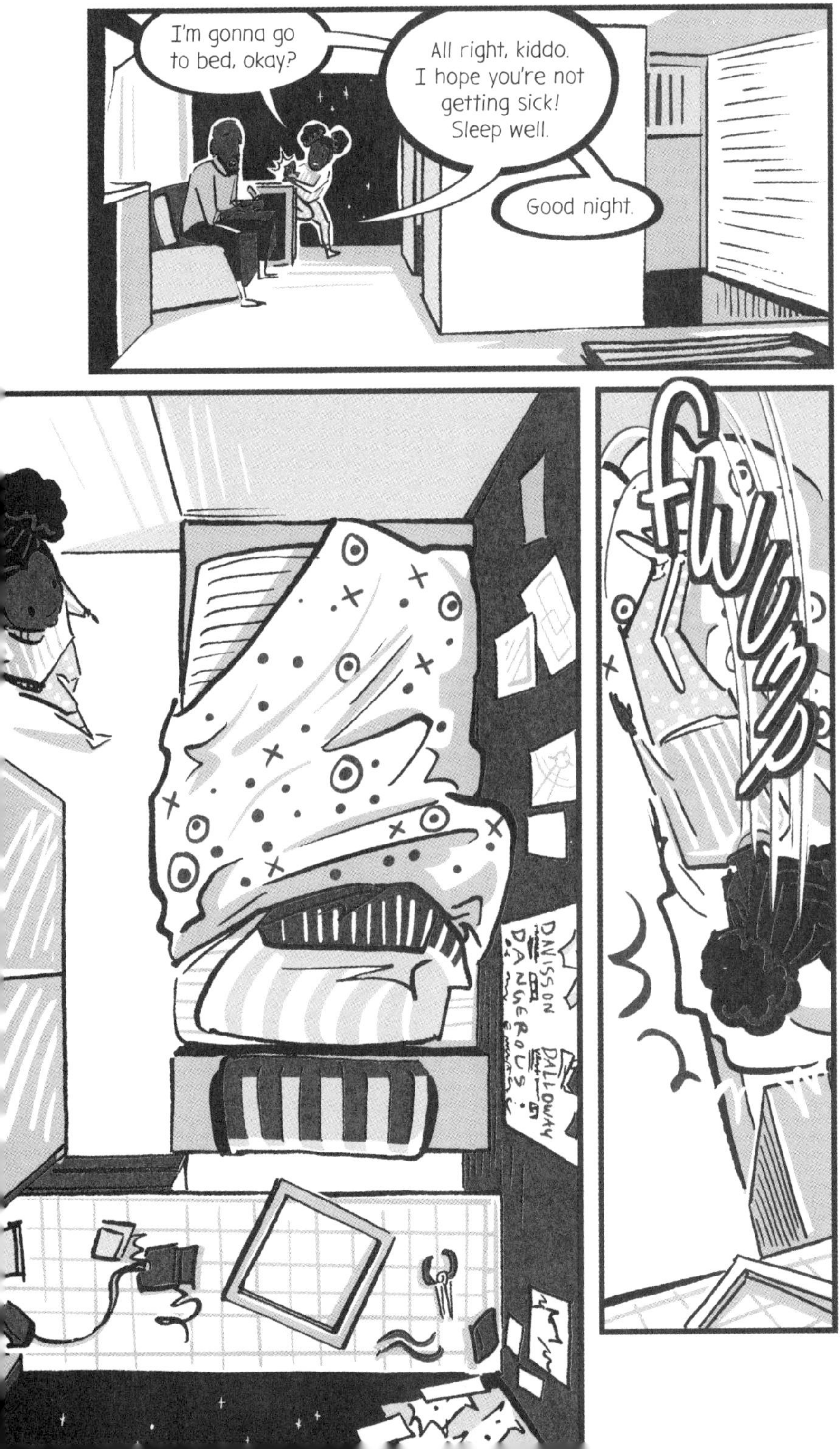
I'm gonna go to bed, okay?
All right, kiddo. I hope you're not getting sick! Sleep well.
Good night.
DAVISSON DALLOWAY
DANGEROUS
FWUMP

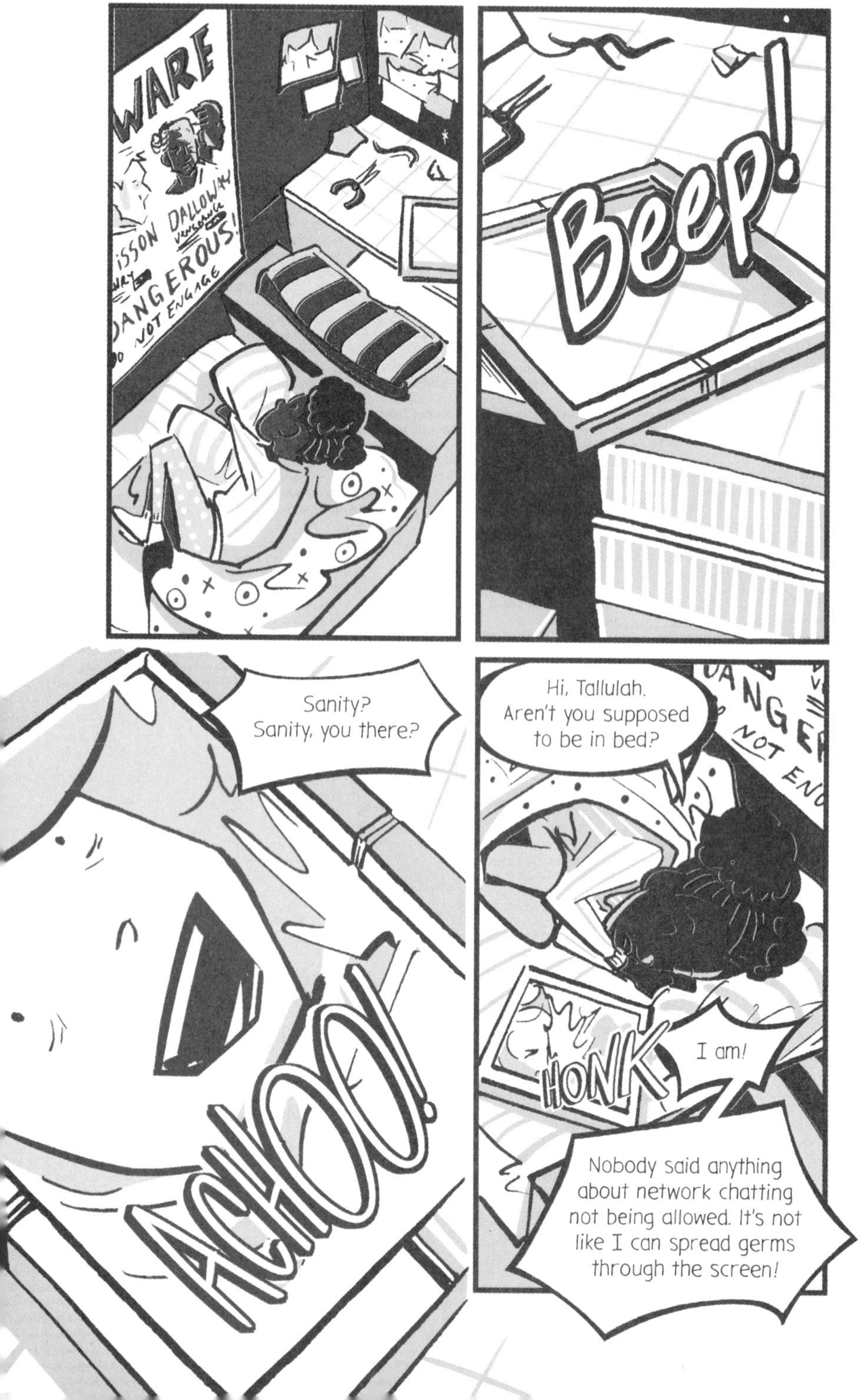
WARE
ISSON DALLOWAY
DANGEROUS!
NOT ENGAGE
Beep!
Sanity? Sanity, you there?
ACHOO!
Hi, Tallulah. Aren't you supposed to be in bed?
HONK
I am!
Nobody said anything about network chatting not being allowed. It's not like I can spread germs through the screen!

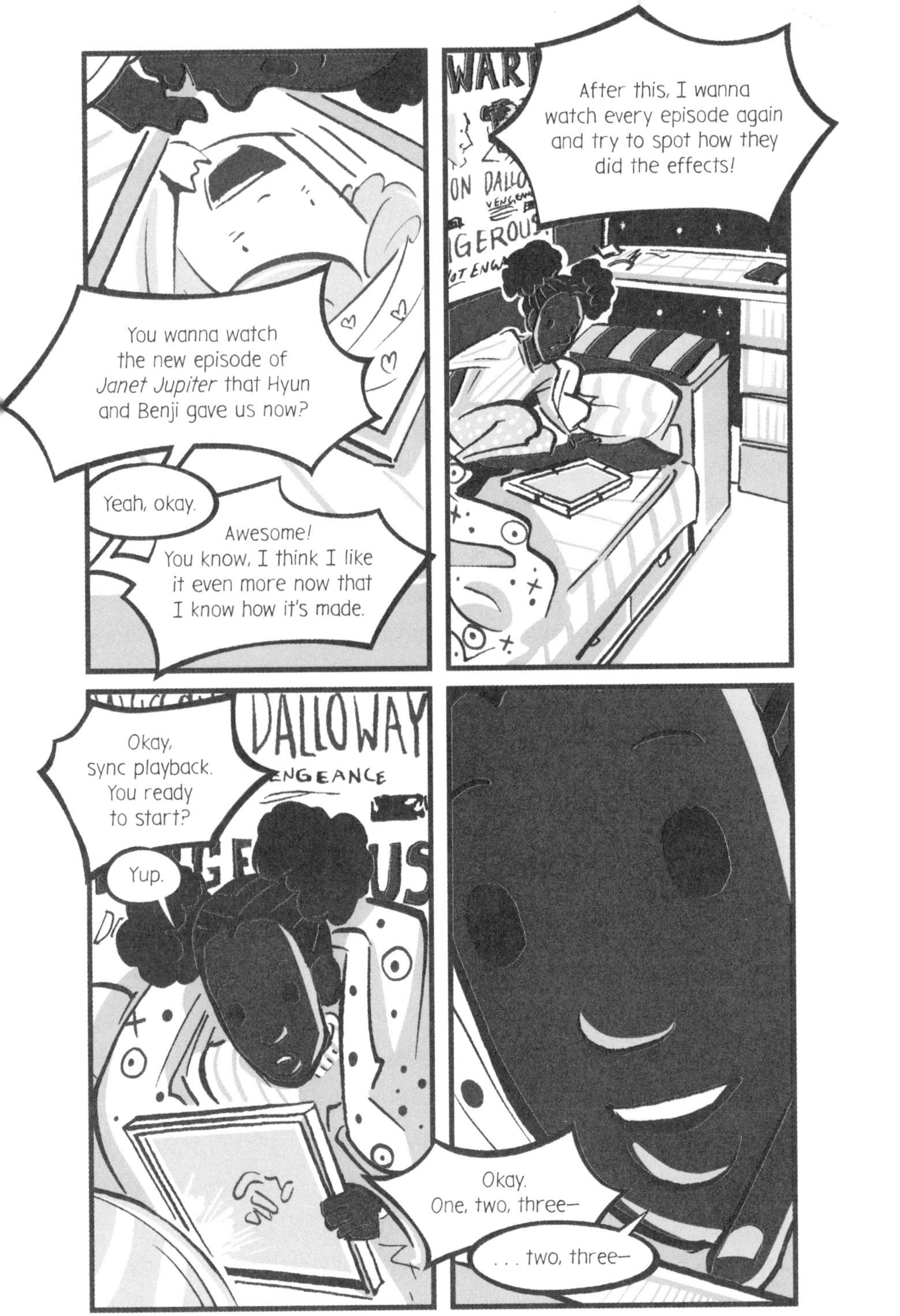
You wanna watch the new episode of *Janet Jupiter* that Hyun and Benji gave us now?
Yeah, okay.
Awesome! You know, I think I like it even more now that I know how it's made.
After this, I wanna watch every episode again and try to spot how they did the effects!
Okay, sync playback. You ready to start?
Yup.
DALLOWAY
ENGEANCE
Okay. One, two, three—
. . . two, three—

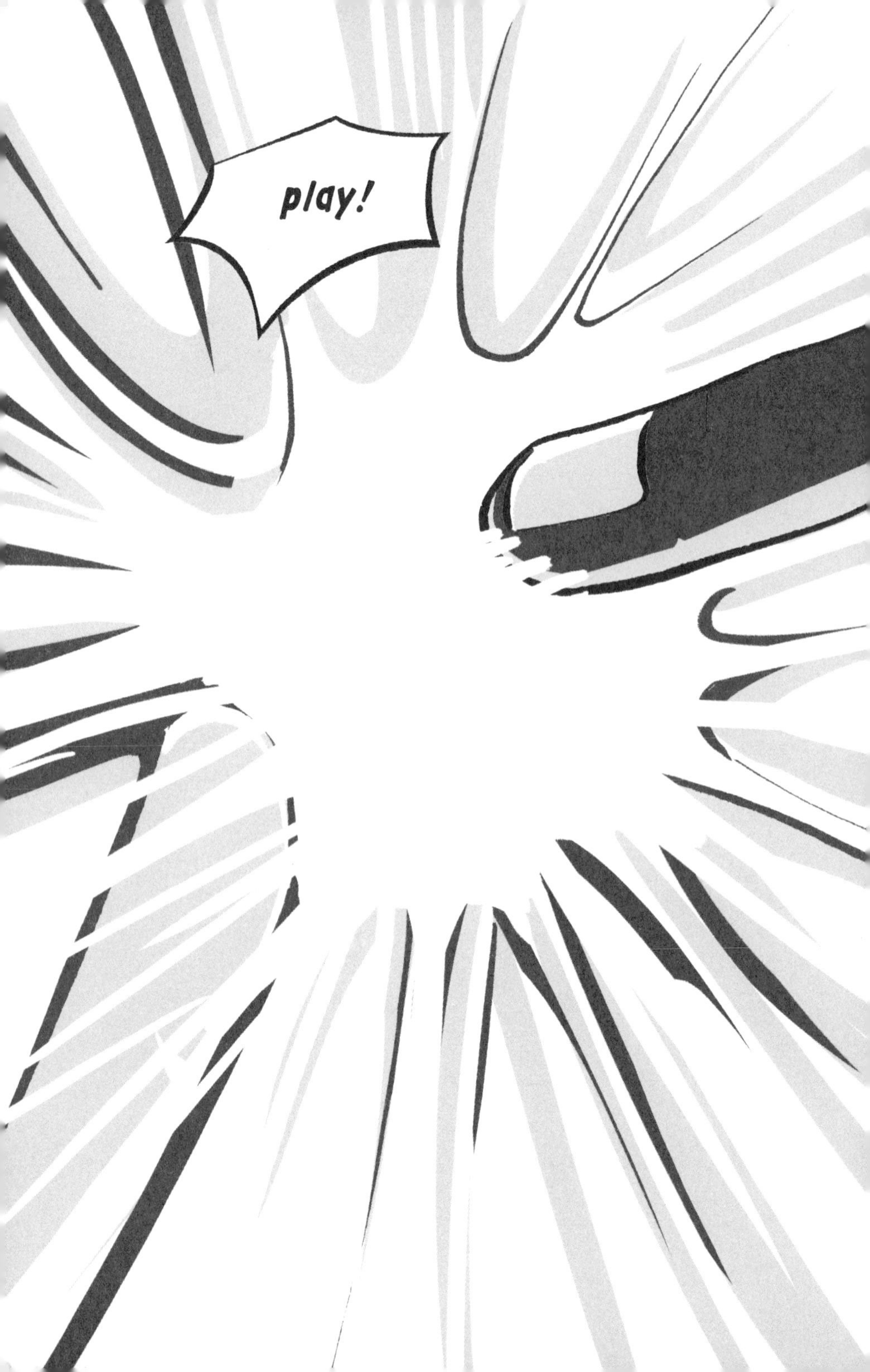
play!

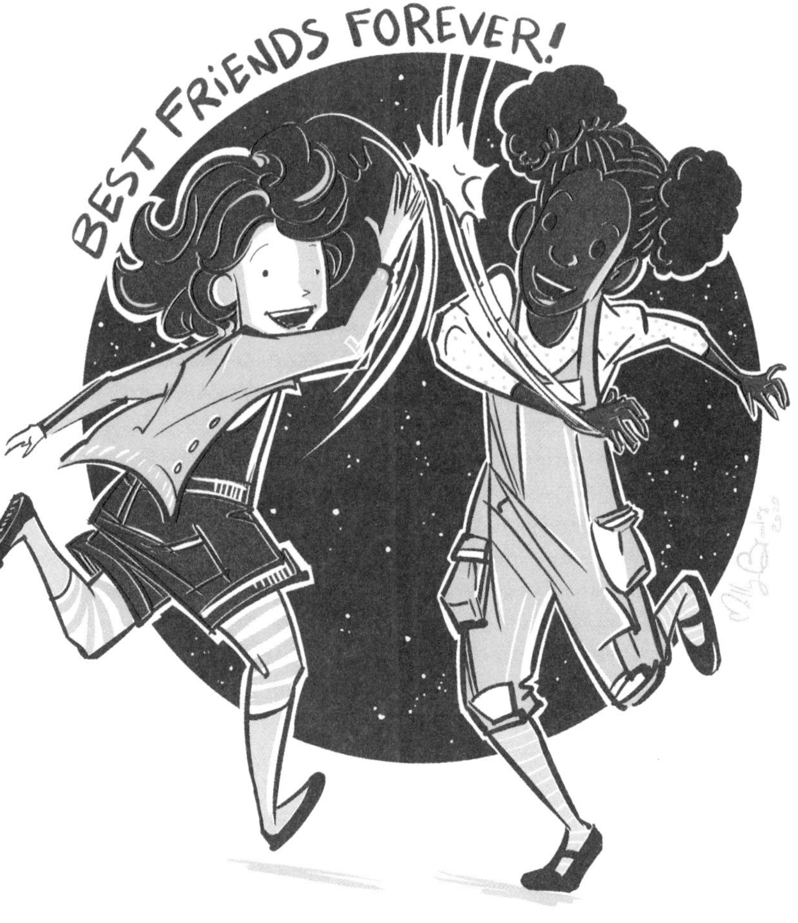
BEST FRIENDS FOREVER!

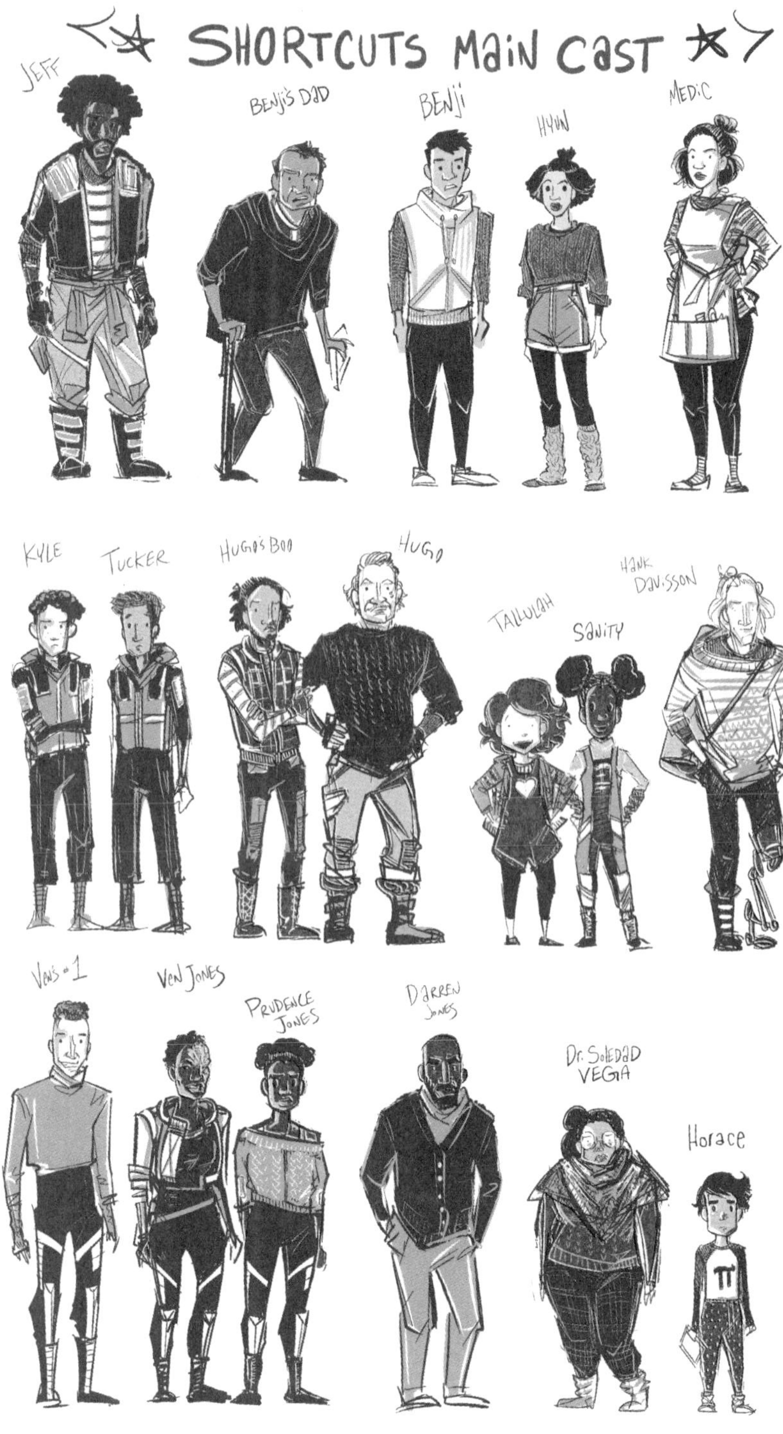
SHORTCUTS Main Cast
JEFF
BENJI'S DAD
BENJI
HYUN
MEDIC
KYLE
TUCKER
HUGO'S BOO
HUGO
TALLULAH
SANITY
HANK DAVISSON
Ven's #1
VEN JONES
PRUDENCE JONES
DARREN JONES
Dr. SOLEDAD VEGA
Horace

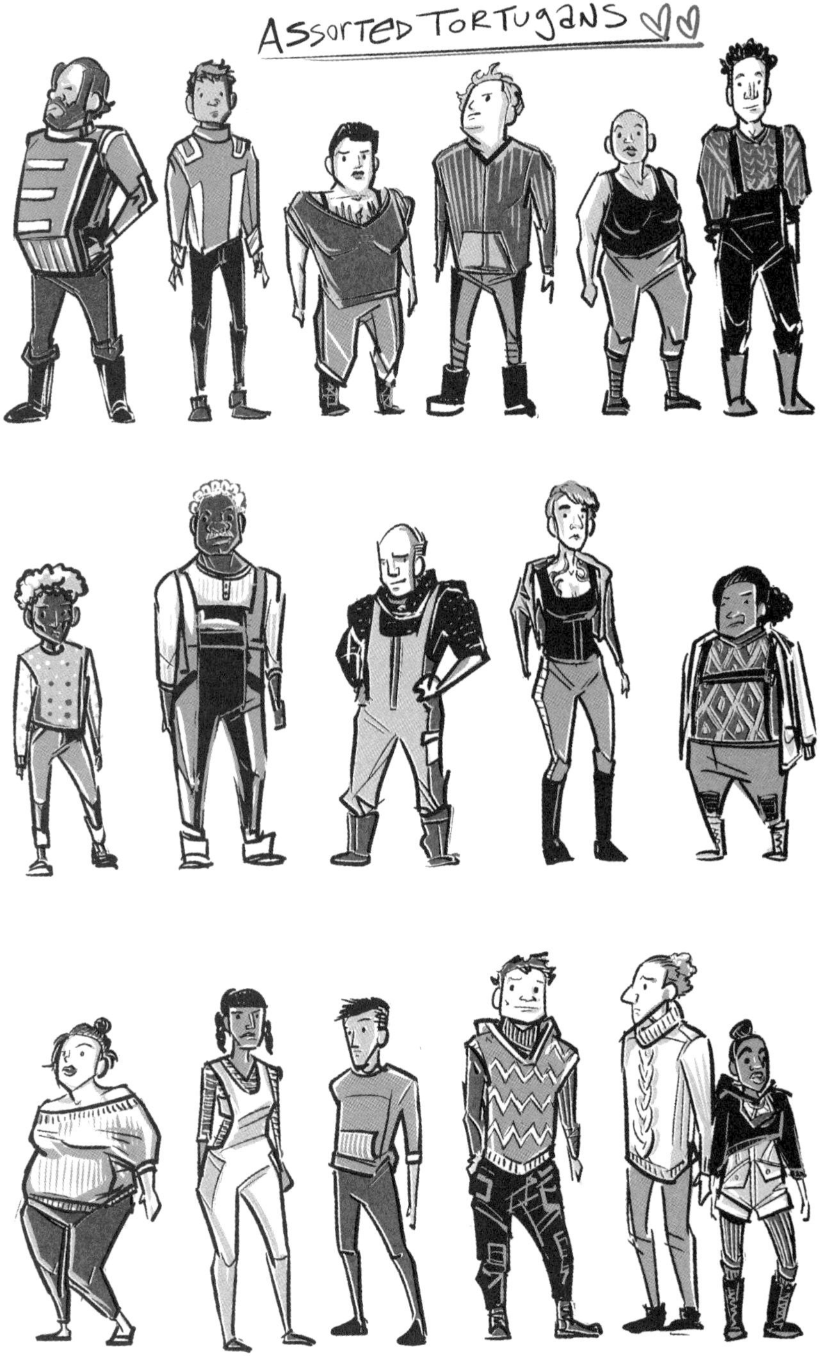
ASSORTED TORTUGANS

Sanity & Tallulah Main Cast ♡♡♡

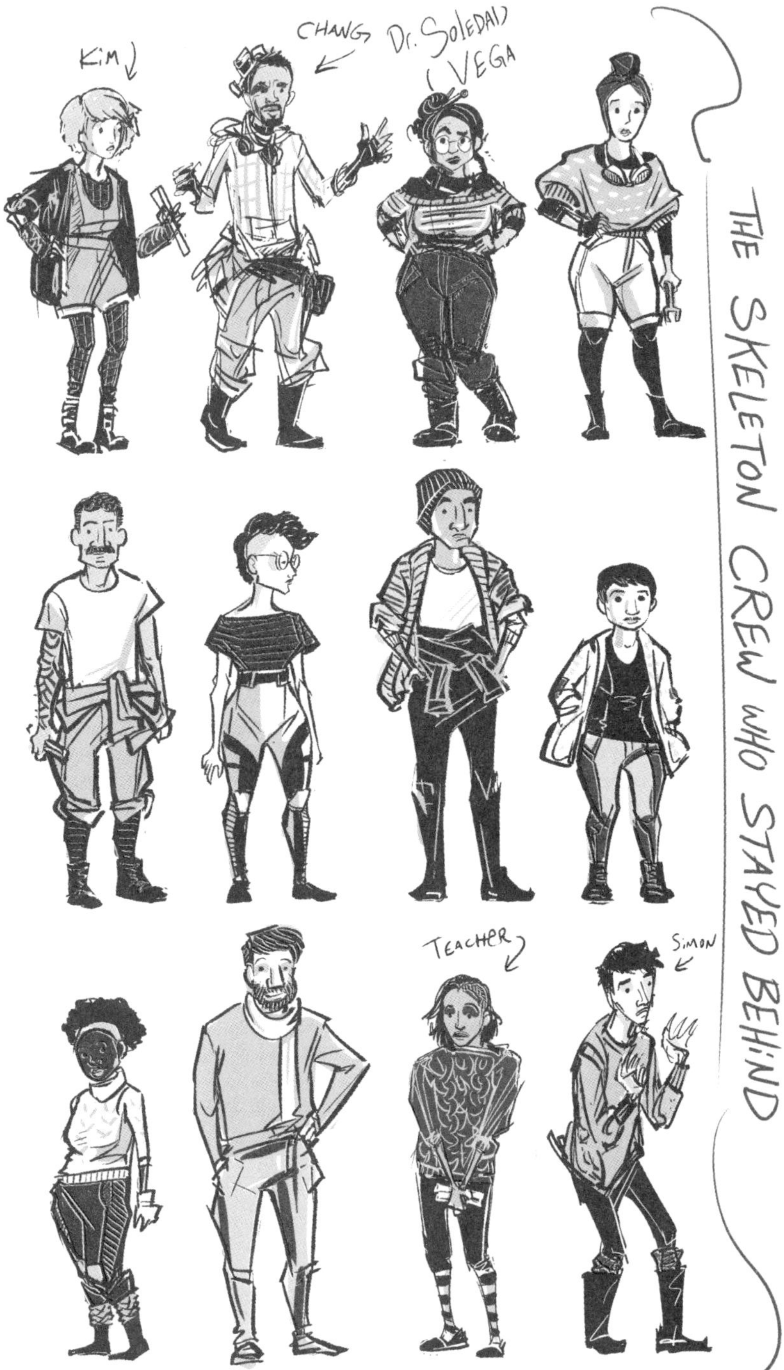
Kim
Chang
Dr. Soledad Vega
THE SKELETON CREW WHO STAYED BEHIND
Teacher
Simon

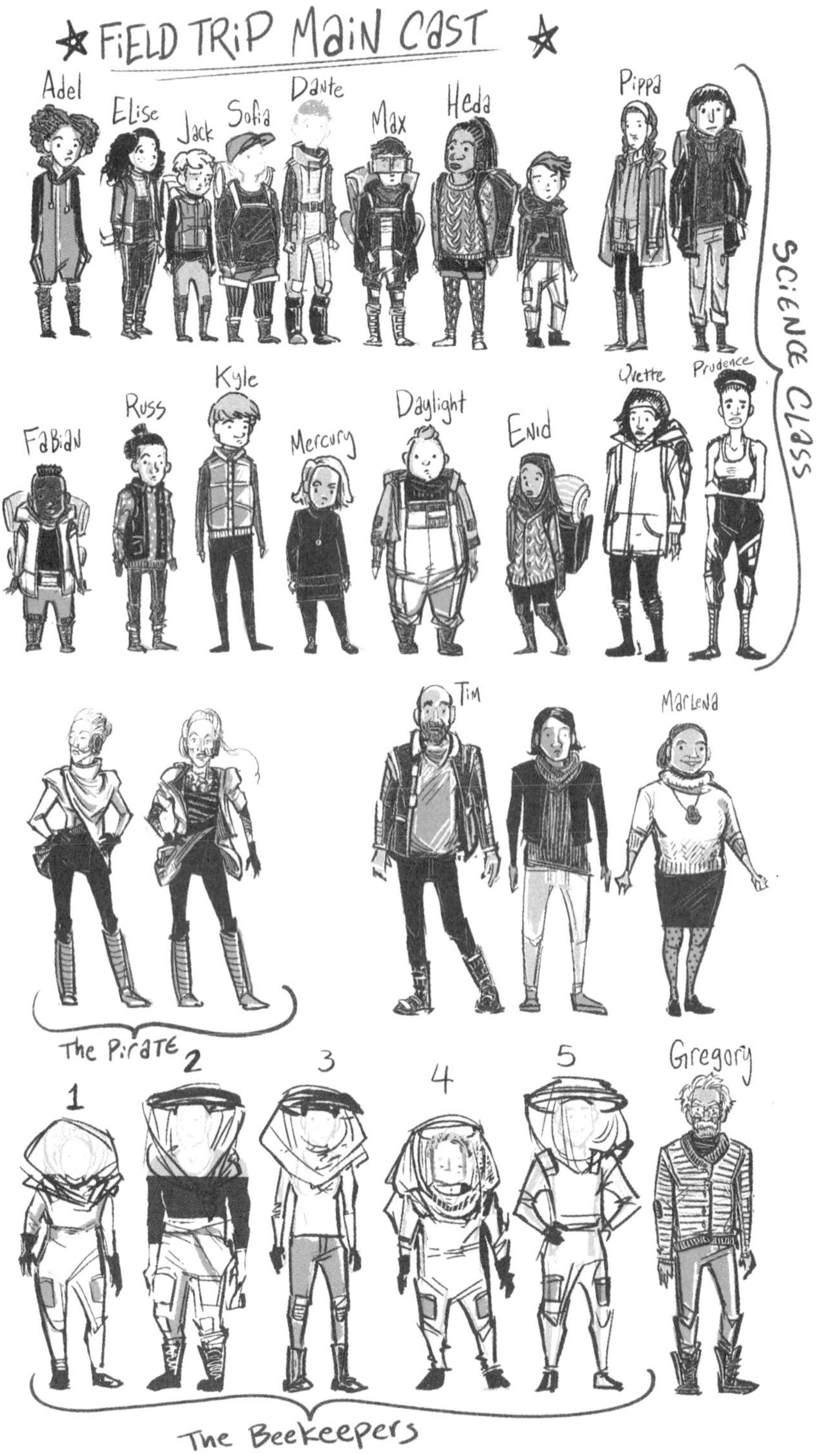

FIELD TRIP MAIN CAST
Adel
Elise
Jack
Sofia
Dante
Max
Heda
Pippa
SCIENCE CLASS
Fabian
Russ
Kyle
Mercury
Daylight
Enid
Yvette
Prudence
Tim
Marlena
The Pirate
1
2
3
4
5
Gregory
The Beekeepers

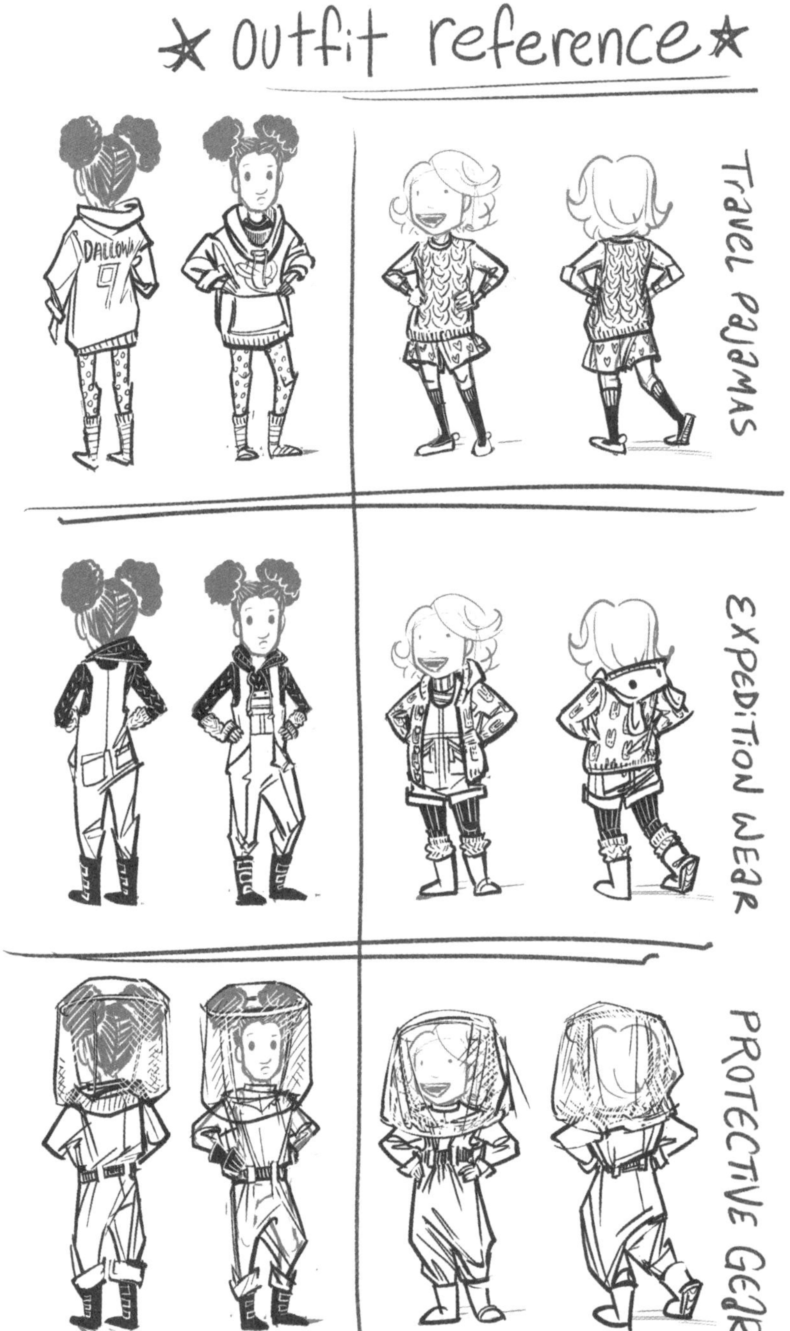
★ outfit reference ★
TRAVEL PAJAMAS
DALLOWA
9
EXPEDITION WEAR
PROTECTIVE GEAR

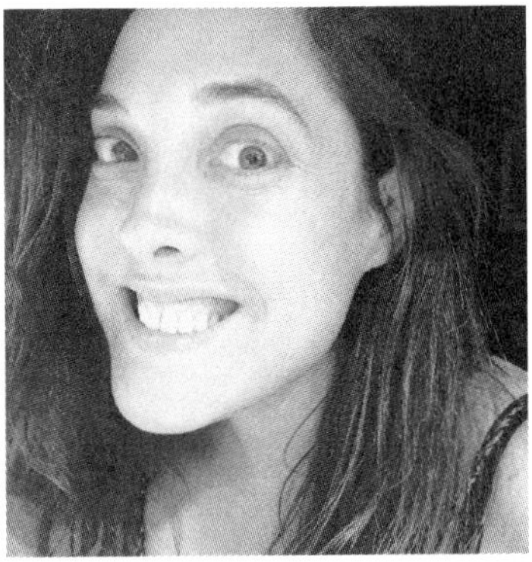

Molly Brooks

MOLLY BROOKS is the illustrator of *Growing Pangs* by Kathryn Ormsbee, out in 2022, and *Flying Machines: How the Wright Brothers Soared* by Alison Wilgus. Her work has appeared in the *Guardian*, the *Boston Globe*, *Nashville Scene*, *BUST* magazine, *Gravy*, *Kazoo* magazine, ESPN social, *Sports Illustrated* online, and others. You can find more of her art, including numerous short comics, at mollybrooks.com.

Molly lives and works in Brooklyn, where she spends her spare time watching vintage buddy-cop shows and documenting her cats.